Also by Philip Kerr

Bernie Gunther:
March Violets
The Pale Criminal
A German Requiem
The One from the Other
A Quiet Flame
If the Dead Rise Not
Field Grey
Prague Fatale
A Man Without Breath

Standalone novels:
A Philosophical Investigation
Dead Meat
Gridiron
Esau
A Five Year Plan
The Second Angel
The Shot
Dark Matter: The Private Life of Sir Isaac Newton
Hitler's Peace
Prayer
Research

For Children:
One Small Step

Children of the Lamp:
The Akhenaten Adventure
The Blue Djinn of Babylon
The Cobra King of Kathmandu
The Day of the Djinn Warriors
The Eye of the Forest
The Five Fakirs of Faizabad
The Grave Robbers of Genghis Khan

PHILIP KERR

JANUARY WINDOW

HEAD of ZEUS

Printed

This book is presented as a work of fiction and the mistakes it contains cannot be blamed on my secret manager (please don't ask). To him I feel obliged to add, you have my total confidence, and I promise not to sack you even if this novel doesn't win anything.

Philip Kerr

For Paul Sidey

CHAPTER 1
January 2014

I hate Christmas. I'm almost forty years old and it seems that I've hated it for more than half my life. I used to play professional football and I now coach others to do the same, so Christmas is a time of year I associate with a fixture list that's as crowded as Hamleys toy shop. It means early-morning training on frostbitten pitches, niggling hamstrings that don't have time to be properly rested, boozed-up fans expecting much more of their team than seems reasonable – to say nothing of the high expectations entertained by an unforgiving club owner or chairman – and so-called easy games against bottom-of-the-table chumps that can end up biting your arse.

This year is no different. We play Chelsea away on Boxing Day with the result that early on Christmas morning when ninety-nine per cent of the country is busy opening presents, going to church, watching the telly in front of a nice fire, or just getting pissed, we're at our training ground in Hangman's Wood, Thurrock. Two days later, on the twenty-eighth, we're away again, to Newcastle, before a New Year's Day game at home to Tottenham Hotspur. Three games in six days. That's not sport, that's a fucking ironman triathlon. When people who are involved in professional football talk about the beautiful game, they generally don't include the Christmas holidays. And whenever I remember that *Boy's Own* story about a friendly football match in no man's land during the First World War between British and German soldiers, I think to myself, yeah, I'd like to see them try that without a goal-keeper who's properly fit and fielding a lazy cunt of a midfield centre who's hoping to get transferred to another club for double his already stratospheric wages during the January window. That's what we call the four-week transfer period that exists in the middle of the season when FIFA says a European club can register a new player. Frankly the whole idea of the January window is a stupid idea – but that's typical of FIFA – because it brings on a garage-sale mentality where clubs try to offload their dead wood and pay over-the-top money for some flash golden boy who might keep them in with a chance of winning something or just staying in their league. Having said all that, there's no doubt that every manager is looking to buy players: the right deal can decide the league title, or save you from relegation. You only have to see which players have been bought in recent January windows to see the value of signing someone halfway through the season: Luis Suarez, Daniel Sturridge, Philippe Coutinho, Patrice Evra, Nemanja Vidic all arrived at their clubs during the January window. If you've ever been part of a housing chain, when a whole series of punters can't buy a new house until they've sold their old one, then you'll begin to appreciate the squeaky-bum complexity of what goes on in January. Personally, I think things were better the way they used to be when the window was always open; but then I am the kind of person who thinks nearly everything about the game was better before Sky TV, instant replays and the 2005 IFAB change to the offside rule made it what it is now.

But there's another, altogether darker reason I don't much like Christmas. Back in 2004, on 23 December, I was found guilty of rape and sentenced to eight years in prison, and you don't have to be the ghost of Jacob fucking Marley to explain how that might exercise a negative effect on anyone's Christmas, past, present and future.

But I'll come back to that later on.

My name is Scott Manson and I am the team coach for London City. Because I always train with the lads I like to set an example, so for me this means no alcohol from 22nd December until the evening of New Year's Day. It's a bit like being a Jehovah's Witness at some dumb WAG's lavish *Hello!* wedding. No alcohol, no late nights, a sensible diet and definitely no smoking; God forbid that I – or more likely, Maurice McShane, the club's fixer – should see one of my players in a magazine behind the wheel of his car coming away from a nightclub on Christmas Eve with a Silk Cut in his hand. I've even handed out a bollocking to a centre forward for getting a dragon tattoo – a Christmas present from his brain-dead wife – on the day before a New Year's Day derby. In case you didn't know, tattoos hurt like shit, plus the inks and pigments can be contaminated and these sometimes cause nausea, granulomas, lung disease, joint infections and eye problems. You've heard of the text in the Bible that says your body is a temple? This is especially true for footballers, and you'd better pray you don't fucking damage yours if you want to keep on being paid a hundred grand a week. I mean it; you want to buy a footballer something nice for Christmas? Get him a box set of DVDs and a bottle of Acqua di Parma. Just don't give him a voucher to cover his temple in graffiti – at least not before we're done with the holiday and early January fixtures.

In the event London City, drew 0–0 against Manchester United, lost 4–3 to Newcastle, won 2–1 against Tottenham – all of which left us ninth in the Premier League – and drew 0–0 with West Ham in the first leg of the Capital One Cup. But none of that seemed to matter – at least not to me – because in the fifth minute of the match at Silvertown Dock against the Tots, Didier Cassell, our first-choice goalkeeper, suffered a serious head injury after colliding with the post in an attempt to save a powerful, curling shot from Alex Pritchard.

The impact makes for sickening viewing; at first everyone thought the sound picked up by the microphone beside the goal was the ball hitting the advertising hoarding, and it was only after Sky Sports had shown the incident several times in slow motion – which must have delighted Didier's family – that people realised the thud you could hear was actually the goalkeeper's skull fracturing against the post. I'm not sure who was more upset, our own lads or the ones from Tottenham.

Cassell was knocked unconscious and he was still insensible when he was carried off the pitch by the St John Ambulance men. Four days later he's still unconscious in hospital. No one is using the word coma – no one except the newspapers, of course, they all have him playing in goal for the team eternal – but with a third round FA Cup tie away to Leeds United scheduled for the weekend, we're already looking to buy a replacement goalkeeper from my dad's old club, Heart of Midlothian, whose creditors think that paying their debts is more important than not conceding goals. Kenny Traynor is a bargain at nine million quid, which is almost two thirds of what the Jambos apparently owe the banks.

Our recently appointed manager, João Gonzales Zarco, spoke about Didier Cassell in his usual enigmatic fashion with all the television cameras and reporters who were waiting on the pavement outside the Royal London Hospital when he and I went to visit him:

'I don't want to talk about replacement goalkeepers. Please don't ask me that kind of question. At this particular time all of our thoughts are with Didier and his family. Obviously we wish him a speedy recovery. All I can say about what happened is that no matter how many plans you make or how much in control of a team you are, life is always putting the ball in the back of your net.' An often emotional man, Zarco wiped a tear from his eye as he added, 'Listen, in football you can't play under the floodlights without there being shadows, and it's essential to know that. Every player, every manager in our league understands what it's like to play under a shadow sometimes. However, I should also like to say this – and I'm speaking now to those of you who have written or said things that shouldn't ever be said when a brave young man is fighting for his life: I'm like an elephant. I don't forget who says what and when. I don't forget. So when all this is over I will trample all over you, wipe my arse with your words and then piss on your heads. The rest of you should always remember that at London City we are a close family. One of our favourite sons is sick, yes. But we will get through this. I promise you, this club will walk in the light again. And so will Didier Cassell.'

I couldn't have put it better myself. I especially liked the part about João Zarco wiping his arse with the words of certain journalists and pissing on their heads. But then I would, wouldn't I? I've no reason to like any of the newspapers. A lot of the journalists I know are troublemakers, only they call it getting a story, as if that justifies everything. It doesn't. Not in my book.

Of course, we didn't know it then, but our troubles at the Crown of Thorns were just beginning.

CHAPTER 2

The Crown of Thorns is the nickname local people have for the City football stadium at Silvertown Dock in London's East End, although the phrase was first used by the sculptor Maggi Hambling, who was the artistic consultant to the building's architects Bellew & Hammerstein. I like her work a lot and own a number of fantastic pictures she painted of the sea. Yes, the sea. They sound crap, I know, but if you saw them you'd see that they are really something special.

The stadium is not dissimilar in construction to the Bird's Nest in Beijing, which was used for the 2008 Olympics, being two structures independent of each other: an orange concrete seating bowl (orange is the colour of the City home strip) and an outer steel frame which really does resembles a crown of thorns. It's the most distinctive building in the whole of east London and cost five hundred million quid to build, so it's just as well the club is owned by a Ukrainian billionaire who must shit money he's got so much of it. According to *Forbes* magazine, Viktor Yevegenovich Sokolnikov is worth twenty billion dollars, which makes him the fiftieth richest man in the world. Don't ask me how Mr Sokolnikov made his Matterhorn-sized pile of cash. Frankly I prefer to live in ignorance about that side of things. All I know is what Mr Sokolnikov told me: that his father worked in a factory that manufactured photographic film in a little Ukrainian town called Shostka, and that he got his first million trading coal and timber, which he then spent on some risky investments that paid off. And don't ask me how he persuaded the FA and the Mayor of London to let him take over the debt on a quartet of old east London football clubs that had gone into administration so that he might relaunch them in the Second Division as London City, either. But money – shed-loads of the stuff – might have had something to do with it. Sokolnikov has spent a fortune regenerating Silvertown Dock and the Thames Gateway, and the football club – which achieved promotion to the Premier League after just five years – now employs more than four hundred people, not to mention the money it brings to a part of London where investment was once a dirty word. As well as the stadium, Sokolnikov has promised that his company, Shostka Solutions AG, will build the new Thames Gateway Bridge that was cancelled by Boris Johnson back in 2008 because it was too expensive; or at least he will when the Labour Party cunts on the planning inquiry wake up and smell the coffee he's making. Right now the project is beset with objections.

When I got home from the hospital to my flat in Manresa Road, Chelsea, Sonja, my girlfriend, came straight to the door with large eyes and a small voice.

'Matt's here,' she said.

'Matt?'

'*Matt Drennan.*'

'Christ, what does he want?'

'I'm not sure he knows himself,' said Sonja. 'He's drunk and in a bit of a state, I think.'

'That is a surprise.'

'He's been here for an hour, Scott. And I don't mind telling you I've had a hell of a job keeping him away from the drinks tray.'

'I'll bet.'

I kissed her cool cheek and squeezed her backside simultaneously. I knew she didn't like Drennan and I couldn't blame her; she'd never known the Matt Drennan I'd once known.

'Scott, you won't let him stay here, will you? Not overnight, anyway. He scares me when he's drunk.'

'He's harmless, angel.'

'No, he's not, Scott. He's a one-man disaster zone.'

'Leave it to me, love. You go and... do something else. You've done your bit. I'll take care of him from here.'

Drennan was standing in the sitting room – but only just – staring at one of the Hamblings: a huge wave, reminiscent of a tsunami, that was about to crash on a Suffolk beach close to where the artist lived and worked. I went and stood beside my old team mate for a while and put my hand on his shoulder to steady him. In the short interval between Sonja leaving the room and me entering it, he'd helped himself to a glass of whisky from the tray and I was hoping to take it away from him if ever he put it down. His shirt was torn and none too clean and there was a large berry of encrusted blood on his earlobe where a diamond stud had once been.

'That looks exactly how I feel,' said Drennan.

His breath smelled like a wheelie bin for mixed glass.

'You're not going to throw up, are you, Matt? Because this is a new carpet.'

Drennan laughed. 'Nah. I'd have to have eaten something to throw up,' he said.

'We could go and get a kebab if you like. And then I could drive you home.'

It had been a long time since I'd visited The Kebab Kid in Parsons Green; these days I was happier with sushi, but I was prepared to go there if it meant keeping Drenno happy.

'Not hungry,' he said.

'What are you doing here? I thought you were spending New Year with Tiffany.'

Drennan regarded me blearily. 'I came to ask how that French lad of yours was getting along. You know, the one who cracked his head? I went to the hospital but they threw me out because I'm shit-faced.'

'I'm amazed they didn't offer you a bed. Look at the state of you, Matt. Did someone else throw you out before that, or is the NHS really as bad as they say it is?'

'I had a tiff with Tiff.' It was something I'd heard him say before. But I had no idea that it had been much more than just a tiff; that Tiff was herself in the same hospital as Didier Cassell, and that this was very likely the real reason Matt Drennan had shown up at my flat.

'She threw a bloody riding boot at me.' He laughed again. 'Just like Fergie. We could have used her in the dressing room at Highbury, eh? I tell you, Scott, that woman has a mouth on her like a fucking blowtorch. Not like that lassie of yours. Sandra, is it? She's a peach. What is it she does again?'

'She's a psychiatrist, Matt. And it's Sonja.'

'Aye, that's right. A shrink. I thought there was something familiar about the way she looked at me. Like I'm a fucking head case.'

'You *are* a fucking head case, Matt. Everyone knows that.'

Drennan grinned and shook his head like the affable mutt he was – most of the time – and then rubbed his head furiously.

'Has she thrown you out again?'

'Aye. She has that. But we've been through worse, her and me. I expect it'll be okay. She'll chew my ear off and I'll have to sleep in the garage.'

'It looks as though she already did,' I said. 'Chew your ear. There's blood on it. I can put something on that if you like. A plaster. A bit of antiseptic cream. A *Sun* photographer.'

'S'awright. It'll be fine. Tiff clouted me with a riding boot, that's all.'

'Normal then.'

'Normal enough, aye.'

Overweight and balding, Matt Drennan cut a forlorn figure. Looking at him now, it was hard for me to believe that it was fewer than ten years since we had both been members of the same Arsenal team. A broken leg had ended Drenno's career at just twenty-nine, but not before he'd scored more than a hundred goals for the Gunners and made himself one of Highbury's heroes. Even today he could show up at the Emirates and have the whole crowd cheering him just by walking onto the pitch. This was more than the bastards ever did for me. Even Spurs fans seemed to like him, which is saying something. Since he'd stopped playing football, however, his life had become a chapbook of very well-publicised fuck-ups: drink, depression, an addiction to cocaine and Nurofen, three months in the nick for drunk driving and six months for assaulting a police officer – I couldn't hold that against him – a flirtation with Scientology, a short and ignominious career in Hollywood, bankruptcy, a betting scandal, a bitter divorce from his first wife and reportedly a failing second marriage; the last I'd heard of him he'd checked himself into the Priory Clinic, again, to try and get himself together. Not that anyone gave it a snowball in hell's chance of success. It was well known that Matt Drennan had dried out more often than a Holiday Inn bath towel. For all those reasons, Drennan was the only footballer I'd ever met whose autobiography was a fascinating read, and that includes my own crappy book. He made Syd Barrett look like the Moderator of the Church of Scotland. But I loved him as if he'd been – well, not my sister, I don't speak to her much these days, but someone important in my life.

'So how is he? You didn't say.'

'Didier Cassell? Not good. Not good at all. He's out for the rest of the season, that's for sure. And right now I'd say you've got a better chance of playing again than he has.'

Drennan blinked as if considering this might be a real possibility.

'Christ, I'd give anything to play a full season again.'

'We all would, pal.'

'Or just one FA Cup Final. A sunny day in May. "Abide with Me". Us against a decent side like Tottenham or Liverpool. The whole Wembley thing. The way it used to be before the Premier League and foreigners and television turned the whole thing into a bloody sideshow.'

'I know. That's the way I feel about it, too.'

'As a matter of fact, it's my intention to make one last headline appearance at Wembley. And then call it a day.'

'Sure, Matt, sure. You can lead the community singing.'

'Seriously.'

Drennan lifted the Scotch to his lips but before it got there

I tackled the glass neatly and carried it out of harm's way.

'Come on. The car's just outside. I'd let you sleep here but you'd only drink all my booze and then I'd have to toss you out on your shell-like, so it's best I take you home now. Better still, why don't I just drive you straight to the Priory? We can be there in less than half an hour. Tell you what, I'll even pay for your first week. A late Christmas present from your fellow Gooner.'

'I might even go, too, but they don't let you read in there and you know me and my books. I get so fucking bored if I don't have something to read.'

As if in evidence of this statement he glanced down at a rolled-up paperback in the pocket of his jacket, as if checking it was still there.

'Why do they do that? Not let you have books?'

'The cunts think that if you read you won't come out of your shell and talk about your fucking problems. As if that makes it better. I'm trying to get away from my problems, not crash into them head on. Besides, I have to go home, if only to get my diamond stud back. It fell out of my ear when Tiff belted me and the fucking dog thought it was a wee mint and swallowed it. He's very fond of mints. So I locked the bastard in the garden shed to let nature take its course, you know? I just hope naebody's let the thing out for a walk. That stud cost me six grand.'

I laughed. 'And I thought I had all the shitty jobs at London City.'

'Exactly.' Drennan grinned and then burped loudly. 'I like it,' he said, pointing to the picture before glancing around the room and nodding his appreciation. 'I like it all. Your place. Your girlfriend. You've done all right for yourself, you canny bastard. I envy you, Scott. But I'm glad for you, too.

After everything that happened, you know?'

'Come on, you stupid cunt. I'll take you home.'

'Nah,' said Drennan. 'I'll walk up to the King's Road and get a cab. With any luck the driver will recognise me and give me a free ride. That's what usually happens.'

'And that's how you end up in the newspapers for getting yourself thrown out of another pub by the landlord.' I took him by the arm. 'I'm driving you, and that's final.'

Drennan took his elbow out of my hand with fingers that were remarkably strong and shook his head. 'You stay here with that nice wee lassie of yours. I'll get a taxi.'

'Straight home.'

'I promise.'

'At least let me come with you some of the way,' I said.

I walked Drennan up to the King's Road where I hailed him a cab. I paid the driver in advance and, when I was helping Drennan into the cab, I slipped a couple of hundred quid in his coat pocket. I was about to close the cab door when he turned and caught my hand and held it tightly. There were tears in his pale blue eyes.

'Thanks, pal.'

'For what?'

'For being a pal, I guess. What else is there for people like you and me?'

'You don't have to thank me for that. You of all people, Matt.'

'Thanks anyway.'

'Now fuck off home before I go and get my violin.'

There was a man sitting on the pavement in front of the ATM. I gave him a twenty although frankly it would have been better if I'd given him the two hundred. The guy in front of the ATM was at least sober. Even as I'd put the money in Drenno's pocket I'd known it was a mistake, just as I knew it was a mistake not to drive him home myself, but that's how it is sometimes; you forget what it's like dealing with drunks, how self-destructive they can be. Especially a drunk like Drenno.

CHAPTER 3

When I got back to my flat I found Sonja preparing dinner in the kitchen. She was an excellent cook and had made a delicious-looking moussaka.

'Has he gone?' she asked.

'Yes.'

I inhaled the moussaka greedily. 'We could have given Drenno some of that,' I said. 'A bit of food inside him was probably just what he needed.'

'It's not food he needs,' she said. 'Besides, I'm glad he's gone.'

'You're supposed to be the sympathetic one.'

'What makes you say that?'

'Because you're a psychiatrist. I sort of thought that it was part of the job.'

'It's not sympathy my patients need, it's understanding. There's a difference. Drenno doesn't want sympathy. And I'm afraid he's all too easy to understand. He wants something that isn't possible. To turn back the clock. His problems will be solved the minute he recognises that fact and adjusts his life and behaviour accordingly. Like you did. If he doesn't, it's plain to see where it will end. He's that rare thing: a self-destructive personality who really wants to destroy himself. He's a classic case.'

'You might be right.'

'Of course I'm right. I'm a doctor.'

'So you say.' I put my arms around her. 'But from where I'm standing you're the best-looking WAG I've ever seen.'

'I'll take that as a compliment even though I regard the idea of looking like Coleen Rooney as anathema.'

'I don't think Coleen knows Ann Athema.'

We were finishing dinner at the breakfast bar and considering an early night when the telephone rang. The caller ID showed it was Corinne Rendall on the phone, Viktor Sokolnikov's secretary. He was not someone I was used to speaking to very much, a fact of which I was sometimes glad. Like many people in football I'd watched the recent *Panorama* special about Sokolnikov, which was where I'd learned of the rumour that he'd inherited his business from another Ukrainian called Natan Fisanovich, an organised crime boss in Kiev. According to the Beeb, Fisanovich had disappeared along with three of his associates in 1996 and it was several months before they turned up in four shallow graves. Sokolnikov denied having anything to do with Fisanovich's death, but then you would, wouldn't you?

'Mr Sokolnikov would like to know if you can take a call from him in ten minutes,' said Corinne.

Instinctively I looked at my new watch – a brand new Hublot – and reflected I wasn't about to say no to the man who'd just spent ten grand on my Christmas present. I, Zarco, everyone on the team, had got a Hublot just like it.

'Yes, of course.'

'We'll call you back.'

I put down the phone. 'I wonder what he wants.'

'Who?'

'Mr Sokolnikov.'

16

'Whatever he wants, don't say no. I've no desire to wake up in bed one morning and find I've been warming my toes on a bloody horse's head.'

'He's not like that, Sonja.' I put some plates in the dishwasher. 'He's not like that at all.'

'If you ask me, they're all like that,' she replied. She pushed me towards the sitting room. 'You go and wait for your call. I'll clear up. Besides, you must be tired after wearing that watch all day.'

A few minutes later, Corinne rang again.

'Scott?'

'Yes.'

'I have Viktor on the line.'

'Viktor, happy new year and thanks again for the watch. It was very generous of you.'

'It's my pleasure, Scott. I'm glad you like it.'

I did like it – but Sonja was right, of course; it was heavy.

'What can I do for you?'

'A couple of things. First I wanted to ask you about Didier. You saw him today, right?'

'He's still unconscious, I'm afraid.'

'That's too bad. I'm planning to go and see him as soon as I'm back. But right now I'm in Miami, on my way to the yacht in the Caribbean.'

At one hundred and ten metres, Sokolnikov's yacht, *The Lady Ruslana*, wasn't the biggest in the world, but it was the same size as an international football pitch – a fact that did not go unreported by the newspapers. I'd been on the boat once and was shocked to discover that just to fill the fuel tanks cost £750,000 – which was a year's pay for me.

'He's a strong lad. If anyone can make a recovery it's Didier Cassell.'

'I hope so.'

'What about Ayrton Taylor?'

'The head that turned out to be a hand?'

'That's right.'

During the same match against Tottenham, Howard Webb, the referee, had awarded a goal to London City when our centre forward, Ayrton Taylor, appeared to head it in from a corner. But almost immediately, while everyone else in our team had been celebrating, Taylor had quietly spoken to Webb and informed him that the ball had actually come off his hand. Whereupon Webb changed his mind and awarded a goal kick to the Tots, which was the cue for our own fans to abuse both Webb and Taylor.

'Was what he did right, do you think?' asked Sokolnikov.

'Who, Taylor? Well, what happened was clearly visible on the television replay. And the man scores ten out of ten for sportsmanship for having owned up to it. That's what the newspapers said. Perhaps it's time there was more sportsmanship in the game. Like when Paolo Di Canio caught the ball instead of kicking it for West Ham at Goodison, back in 2000. I know João thinks differently, but there it is. I saw Daniel Sturridge put one in for Liverpool against Sunderland in 2013 that quite clearly came off his arm, and it was obvious from the furtive way he looked at the linesman that he knew it wasn't a proper goal. But that goal stood and Liverpool won the game. And look what happened to Maradona in the '86 World Cup match against England.'

'The hand of God.'

'Precisely. He's one of the greatest players ever to kick a football, but it certainly hasn't helped his reputation in this country.'

'Good point. But Webb had already given the goal, hadn't

he? And an accidental handball is held to be different from a deliberate one.'

'Law five clearly states that the referee can change his mind until play has restarted. And it hadn't. So Webb was quite within his rights to do what he did. Mind you, it takes a pretty strong referee to do that. If it had been anyone but Howard Webb I expect the goal would have been allowed to stand, in spite of what Taylor said. Most refs hate to change their minds. It was lucky, I guess, that we won the match 2–1. I might not be so happy about what he did if we'd dropped two points. But you know, I wouldn't be at all surprised if Taylor wins the Player of the Month on the strength of that confession. It's the sort of fair play the FA likes to shine a spotlight on.'

'All right. You've convinced me. Now tell me about this Scottish goalkeeper, Kenny Traynor. Zarco says you've known him for a while. And that you've seen him play.'

'Yes, I have.'

'João wants to buy him.'

'So do I.'

'Nine million is a lot of money for a goalkeeper.'

'You'll be glad you spent nine million on a goalkeeper if we're in a penalty shoot-out at a European final. It was the Bayern goalkeeper, Manuel Neuer, who saved Lukaku's penalty and delivered the Germans the 2013 UEFA Super Cup. He almost won the Champions League for them against Chelsea the previous year. Christ, he even scored one himself in the shoot-out. No, boss, when push comes to shove you don't want to find we've got Calamity James in goal.'

Calamity James was what Liverpool supporters had called David James – a little unfairly – when he'd played for them.

19

'When you put it like that, yes, I suppose you're right.'

'Traynor's the Scotland number one. Not that there's much choice up there, mind. But I saw him make a diving save against Portugal at Hampden that the Scots still talk about. Cristiano Ronaldo hammered one from eighteen yards that was going into the top corner all the way, but I swear Traynor must have launched himself twenty feet through the air to fist that ball over the bar. Watching it you'd believe a man could fly. Check it out on YouTube. The Jocks don't call him Clark Kent for nothing. He's a nice lad. Quiet. Not at all chippy like some north of the border. Works hard in training. And he's possessed of the biggest, safest hands in football. His dad is a butcher in Dumfries and he's got his mitts from him. As big as bloody hams, they are. And his hand–eye coordination is superb. When he did the BATAK Challenge he scored 136. The record is 139.'

'If I knew what that was—' said Viktor.

'Not to mention his clearance kick. That boy has a boot on him and no mistake.'

'I've seen some of the films and I agree he's good. I'd just feel more comfortable about buying him if Denis Kampfner wasn't his agent. The man's a crook, isn't he?'

Restraining my first impulse, which was to mention something about the pot calling the kettle black, I agreed. 'Agents? They're all crooks. But at least Kampfner's a FIFA-registered crook.'

'As if that makes a difference.'

'It's like evolution, Viktor. Agents seem to fulfil a need and I guess we have to tolerate them. Like those birds that sit on the backs of rhinos and peck the ticks out of their ears.'

'Ten per cent of nine million is a little more than a tick.'

'True.'

'So maybe I'll bring in my own agent to handle it. Zarco thinks I should.'

'I thought that's why we had a sporting director. To help make deals like this.'

'Trevor John is more of a club ambassador than a deal-maker. He helps promote the club and makes it look good when, thanks to the BBC, I don't. Between you and me, he couldn't buy a bag of potato chips without paying too much for it.'

'I see. Well, it's your choice who you trust to make a deal, Viktor. Your choice and your money.'

'For sure. By the way, did you see the programme? *Panorama*?'

'Me? Unless it's football or a decent film I never watch telly. Least of all crap like *Panorama*.'

'Just so you know, I'm suing them. There wasn't a word in that programme which was true. They even got my patronymic wrong. It's not Sergeyevich, it's Semyonovich.'

'All right. I understand. They're a bunch of cunts. You won't find me arguing with that. Will you be at Elland Road to see the match against Leeds on Sunday?'

'Perhaps. I'm not sure. It depends on what the weather is like in the Caribbean.'

CHAPTER 4

City's training ground, at Hangman's Wood, was the best of its kind in England, with several full-size pitches, an indoor training facility, a medical and rehabilitation area, saunas, steam rooms, gymnasia, physiotherapy and massage rooms, a number of restaurants, an X-ray and MRI clinic, hydrotherapy pools, ice baths, an acupuncture clinic, basketball courts and a velodrome. There was even a TV studio where players and staff could be interviewed for London City Football Television; Hangman's Wood was, however, strictly off-limits to press and public on a daily basis, something the media hated. High walls and razor-wire fences surrounded our football pitches so that training sessions could not be subject to the attentions of tabloid photographers with tall ladders and long lenses; in this way bust-ups between players, or even between players and managers, which are sometimes inevitable in the highly charged world of modern sport – who can forget the hugely publicised shoving match that took place between Roberto Mancini and Mario Balotelli in 2012? – were kept strictly private.

And in view of what happened on that particular morning at Hangman's Wood, this was probably just as well.

Not that there was usually much to see, as João Zarco preferred to leave training sessions to me; like many managers, he liked to observe the proceedings from the sidelines or even through binoculars from the window of his office. Matters of match fitness and teaching football skills were my responsibility, which meant I was able to develop a more personal relationship with all the players; I wasn't one of the lads, but I was perhaps the next best thing.

João Zarco controlled the club philosophy, team selection, match-day motivation, transfers, tactics and all of the hirings and firings. He also got paid a lot more than me – about ten times as much, actually – but then with all his style, charisma and sheer footballing nous, he was probably the best manager in Europe. I loved him like he was my own older brother.

We started at 10 a.m. and as usual we were outside. It was a bitterly cold morning and a hard frost still lay on the ground. Some of the players were wearing scarves and gloves; a few were even wearing women's tights, which, in my day, would have earned you a hundred press-ups, twice around the field and a funny look from the chairman. Then again, some of these lads turn up with more skins creams and hair product in their Louis Vuitton washbags than my first wife used to have on her dressing table. I've even come across footballers who refused to take part in heading practice because they had a Head & Shoulders advert to shoot in the afternoon. It's that sort of thing that can bring out the sadist in a coach, so it's just as well that I happen to believe you'll get further with a kick up the arse and a joke than you will with just a kick up the arse. But training has to be tough, because professional football is tougher.

I'd just done a *paarlauf* session with the lads, which always produces a lot of lactic acid in the system and is a very quick way of sorting out who is fit and who is not. It's a two-man relay and a team version of a fartlek session – one man sprints two hundred metres around the track to tag his partner, who has jogged across its diameter and who now sprints again to tag the same partner, and so on – that leaves most men gasping, especially the smokers. I used to smoke, but only when I was in the nick. There's nothing else to do when you're in the nick. I followed *paarlauf* with a heads and tails routine where a player runs with the ball towards the goal as fast as he can and then shoots before immediately turning defender and trying to stop the next guy from doing the same. It sounds simple and it is, but when it's played at speed and you're tired it really tests your skills; it's hard to control the ball when you're also running flat out and knack-ered.

Along the way I offered explanations for why we were doing what we were doing. A training session is easier when you know what the thinking is behind it:

'If we're fit we can open up the pitch, and create space. Making space is simply a matter of breaking the wind and the spirit of the man trying to mark you. Get eyes in the back your head and learn to see who is in space and pass the ball to him, not to the nearest man. Pass the ball quickly. Leeds will defend deep, and dirty. So above all be patient. Learn to be patient with the ball. It's impatience that ends up giving the ball away.'

Zarco was more involved with the training session than usual, shouting instructions from the sideline and criticising some of the players for not running quickly enough. It's bad enough to be on the end of that when you're out of breath; it's something else when you're almost puking up from exertion.

When the drill was over Zarco walked on to the pitch and instinctively the lads gathered round to await his comments. He was a tall, thin man and still looked like the strong, fearless centre back he'd been in the 1990s for Porto, Inter Milan and then Celtic. He was handsome, too, in a rugged, unshaven kind of way, with sleepy eyes and a broken nose as thick as a goalpost. His English was good and he spoke in a weary, dark monotone but when he laughed, his was a light falsetto, almost girlish laugh that most people – myself excluded – found intimidating.

'Listen to me, gentlemen,' he said quietly. 'My own philosophy is simple. You play the best football you can, as hard as you can. Always and forever, amen.'

I started translating for our two Spanish players, Xavier Pepe and Juan-Luis Dominguin; I speak pretty good Spanish – and Italian – although my German is near fluent, thanks to my German mother. I could tell this was going to be a bad bollocking. Zarco's worst bollockings were always the ones given quietly and in his saddest voice.

'This kind of thinking won't ever let you down, not like any of those other guys – Lenin or Marx, Nietzsche, or Tony Blair. But in the whole of life on earth, there is perhaps no philosophical mystery quite as profound and as inexplicable as the one of how you can manage to lose 4–3 when you were 3–0 up at half time. To fucking Newcastle.'

The less wise started to smile at that one; big mistake.

'At least I thought it was a mystery.' He smiled a nasty little smile and wagged his finger in the air. 'Until I saw this morning's poor excuse for a training session – Scott, no offence to you, my friend, you tried to make a silk purse out of a sow's ear, as always – and it suddenly occurred to me as if an apple had fallen on my head why this had happened. You're all a bunch of lazy assholes, that's why. You know why a lazy asshole is called a lazy asshole? Because it's not good for shit. And an asshole that's not good for shit isn't good for anything.'

Someone sniggered.

'You think that's funny, asshole? I'm not making jokes here. You see me laughing? You think Viktor Sokolnikov pays me millions of pounds a year to make fucking jokes down here? No. The only people making jokes around here are you people when you kick a football. Nil–nil against Manchester United? That was a joke. Let me tell you, it's not just nature that abhors a goalless draw, it's me, too. We can't win unless we score and that's all there is to it, gentlemen.

'Now, as many of you know, I read a lot about history so that my team can make it. Which is crazy because you people aren't fit to make the tea on the bus home, let alone history. Seriously. I look at you all and I think to myself, why did I bother coming to manage this club when they don't even bother to try? Yesterday, some prick of a journalist asked me some crap about what makes a good manager. And I said, winning, you idiot. Winning is what makes a good manager. Now ask me a better question that doesn't suck like the last one; ask me what should be the aim of a good manager and I will give you a longer answer for your readers. I will write your copy for you, you prick. As always I was doing his job for him, okay? Because that's the kind of helpful guy I am. Zarco is always good copy. The aim of a good manager in football is to show eleven assholes how to play as one man. But today I think this task is beyond even me. Each manager in this league is a product of the era in which we live, but in my opinion I'm the only manager who can raise himself up above the ordinary thinking of his time. I can make the impossible happen, it's true. But I'm not Jesus Christ and today I think that even I can't make the biblical miracle of getting eleven assholes to play like one man.

'The biggest assholes I've seen this morning are you, Ron. You, Xavier. And you, Ayrton. Lazy is what you are, which is to say lazier than the others. Lazy with the ball and lazy when you don't have the ball. If you can't find the ball then find space. You remember Gordon Gekko in that movie? Greed is good. That's what he said. And that's what I say, too. Be greedy to get the ball back from the opposition, Xavier. By any means necessary. Ron, you should want the ball the way you used to want your mama's tit.'

'Yes, boss,' said Ron Smythson.

'Which is probably last week in your case, Ayrton. You play like a stupid baby. Not a man. Look at you. Bootlaces undone, socks hanging down – why don't you suck your thumb as well, like little Jack Wilshere? You're not even out of breath, my friend. I look at you and I see an asshole that's not good for shit. An asshole that's not even worth fucking. And another thing, Ayrton: playing football for the love of the game and because you once read a poem about being an English gentleman is a luxury that even Viktor Sokolnikov can't afford. You want to play football this way you'd better go and play for Eton College or Harrow or one of those other homo schoolboy sides where they play up and play the game because they really want to win the Battle of Waterloo. But don't do it for London City. Better still, go and suck some cock at FIFA and maybe they'll give you a fair play award. Me, I'm not interested in that shit. If you have to get a hard-on to poke the fucking ball in the net with then you'd better do it. And I don't care if you ruin your chances of ever having children in order to score a goal

– that's what you'd better do, my friend. That's why you're being paid a hundred grand a week. To win. So the next time the ball comes off your hand and goes in the net you'll swear on a stack of Holy Bibles it came off your head or your foot or you're out of this fucking football club. Do I make myself clear?'

'Fuck you,' said Taylor. 'I don't have to take that kind of bullshit from you or anyone.'

I closed my eyes for a moment. I knew what was coming now. I thought I did, anyway.

'Yes you do.' Zarco took two steps forward, stood in front of poor Taylor and shoved him. 'Yes, you fucking do, you stupid child. My job is to talk. And part of your job is to listen. Even when it's what you don't want to hear. Especially when it's what you don't want to hear. Which in this particular case is that you've got to try harder.'

'Fuck off.'

It had been a while since anyone had really seen Zarco raise his voice in what was popularly known – with apologies to Phil Spector – as the wall of sound. Possibly it really wasn't as loud as it seemed, on account of the fact that Zarco usually spoke quietly; but it was loud enough when he was right in your face and you were close enough to see the plate on the roof of the big man's mouth, not to mention what he'd eaten for breakfast.

'Try harder!' he screamed. 'Try harder! Try harder!'

The best thing to do in these circumstances was close your eyes and take it; I'd seen some take it and cry afterwards – big men, hard men. Now Taylor was a senior player, a hard lad originally from Liverpool, and not used to people screaming in his face, so he turned and walked away, which was possibly an even worse idea than answering back.

Zarco picked up the nearest thing to hand, which happened to be a plastic training cone, and hurled it at Taylor. The cone hit Taylor between the shoulder blades and almost knocked the man off his feet, which had him coming back at Zarco with strangler's hands and real malice in his eyes.

'You fucking bastard,' he screamed as some of the other players caught him by the arms and held him close. 'I'll fucking kill him. I'll fucking kill that smart bastard.'

Zarco just stood there as if he hardly cared if Ayrton Taylor came at him or not and it was easy to see how, when he was a centre back at Celtic, he'd taken a punch almost without flinching from the Hibernian centre forward, Billy Gibson – a punch that had cost him two teeth. Gibson had been sent off, but not only had Zarco not retaliated, he had stayed on the pitch and even headed the winning goal. Famed for his brutal scything tackles, Zarco had put many a player back into the stands and it was no surprise that the Bleacher Report still listed 'Butcher Zarco' as one of the hardest men ever to play soccer, 'because of his chops'.

'You're dropped,' said Zarco. 'Dropped for being a cunt. You're always tweeting things to your seven thousand followers. Now tweet that, you childish cunt.'

But this wasn't the end of it; the very same afternoon Zarco put Taylor on the January transfer list and I quickly formed the conclusion that the Machiavellian Portuguese had engineered the whole incident so that he could make an example of a senior player to encourage the others. So much for sportsmanship in the beautiful game, you might say. But Zarco was right about one thing: Ayrton *was* lazy – perhaps the laziest player in the team. There were quite a few who thought that Didier Cassell might not have been injured if Alex Pritchard had not been allowed the space to shoot because Taylor hadn't tackled him the way he should have done. Besides, everyone knew we had younger strikers who were just as able as Ayrton Taylor and on less than half the money. Sometimes getting rid of one player can be as effective a way of improving the team as buying a new one.

When I got back to my office I made a note of what Zarco had said, not because I disagreed with him but because I used to jot down as much of what he said about football as I could remember – especially the more colourful stuff; one day, I was planning to write a book about the Portuguese. Most football bios are as dull as arseholes, but that was one thing you couldn't ever say about my boss. Next to Matt Drennan, João Gonzales Zarco was easily the most fascinating figure in English football and, probably, European football too. He didn't see that, of course, and probably he would have disapproved of me writing anything at all about him – even a note in the programme. Zarco might have been outspoken but he was also a very private man.

That night I watched *MOTD2* and there he was again, outspoken as usual, only this time Zarco – who was a Jew – had been asked about the 2022 FIFA World Cup, in Qatar:

'Speaking for myself I don't really want to visit a country where I can't drink a glass of wine with a friend from Israel, perhaps. Or a gay friend. Yes, I have gay friends. Who doesn't? I am a civilised person. Being civilised requires that you are also tolerant of people who are different. And who enjoy a drink. Maybe too many drinks. That is everyone's choice, unless you live in Qatar. Perhaps Qatar will be different in ten years' time. But I doubt it. Meanwhile I read in the *Guardian* that almost a hundred Nepalese workers have already died on construction sites in Qatar. Think about that.

A hundred people are dead just so one little country can host a meaningless football tournament. This is madness. It's a meaningless tournament because it's no longer anything to do with football and everything to do with big money and politics. To my mind the last World Cup that meant anything was won by West Germany in 1974, which was also the host country that year. Since Argentina, in 1978, everything has been one big sick joke. There should never have been a World Cup held in a country that was a dictatorship like that one and where the cup was won by cheating.

'But everything about this host country Qatar strikes me as wrong. It's a well-known fact that to be a woman in an Arab country is not easy. So perhaps it's a good thing that the main stadium in Qatar looks like a giant vagina. Certainly it strikes me as ironic that the biggest vagina in the world should now be in Qatar. Personally speaking, I am in favour of vaginas. I started my life in one; we all did. And I think it's about time that an Arab country faced up to the fact that half the world has a fanny.

'Also, you have to wonder why a country where you can be flogged for drinking alcohol wants to play host to a lot of English, Dutch and German football fans. But am I surprised that FIFA picked Qatar? No. I'm not at all surprised. Nothing about FIFA ever surprises me. Maybe no one told them it gets very hot in Qatar. Even in winter it's too hot to do anything very much except flog some poor man because he's gay. Now I hear that the Qataris are planning to use solar power to cool the effect of the sun's rays in their newly built stadia; but I don't think solar power can cool the allegations of bribery quite so easily. Of course, it's easy to make me shut up about all this. You just have to pay me a million dollars like some of those FIFA officials. On second thoughts, make it two million. Then you know what? I, too, think everything in 2022 will be extremely wonderful.'

That was typical of João Zarco. The man was always good copy, although sometimes he said too much; even he would have conceded that. Sometimes he said too much and people kicked back. Literally. In a now infamous interview on Sky Sports, Zarco described the Irish football pundit and former player-manager, Ronan Reilly – who was sitting alongside him at the time – as 'a piece of crap' and 'someone who couldn't run a train set let alone a football team'. Reilly replied that Zarco had the biggest mouth in football and that one day the Portuguese would put his foot in his mouth, and if that didn't happen then Reilly would gladly oblige with his own foot. A week or two later, at the BBC Sports Personality of the Year after-party in the ExCel Arena, the two traded punches and kicks and had to be separated by security staff. But not everyone Zarco criticised publicly was able to fight back like Ronan Reilly.

Take Lionel Sharp, who refereed a UEFA match we played against Juventus last October – an away tie that City lost. Interviewed on ITV after our 1–0 defeat, Zarco half suggested that Juventus – who are not without form in the skulduggery department – had 'influenced' Sharp at half time to give a penalty in the second half. Sharp was subsequently the subject of a lot of vicious trolling on Twitter, which caused him to take a fatal overdose of sleeping tablets.

Love him or loathe him, João Zarco was always interesting.

CHAPTER 5

After a hard training session at Hangman's Wood I have an ice bath and a sports massage, but a good sports massage given by the club's full-time masseur, Jimmy Gregg, is always excruciatingly painful. Jimmy has fingers like fire-tongs. That's why they call it a sports massage: because you have to be a bloody good sport to endure that level of pain without punching Jimmy in the face. And the older I get the more painful it is. Much as I try to behave like a Spartan and stoically take the pain without a sound, I always squeal like a frightened guinea pig. Everyone does. And because footballers will gamble on anything, bets are often taken among the lads on who can endure thirty minutes on the table without uttering a groan or a moan; until now no one has come through the experience without uttering a sound. Jimmy takes pride in his work. I don't think there's anyone who would disagree with me when I say that there are occasions when the massage seems worse than the training session. Perhaps that's why they call Jimmy's treatment room the London Dungeon.

So sometimes when I get home and before I go to bed, Sonja sets up a massage table in my bathroom, puts on a pair of stiletto-heeled shoes, a little white tunic that doesn't quite cover her stocking-tops and tiny G-string, and plays the rub-joint whore, with the happy ending included. She has wonderful, light fingers and has fully mastered the technique of touching without quite touching, if you know what I mean. But if the caressing touch of her hands is magical – and it is – it can't begin to compare with her sweet and loving mouth; she likes to drink a very cold martini before putting my cock in her mouth, and the combination of the alcohol, her lips and her teeth is nothing short of transfiguring. Christ ascending into heaven could not have felt better than I feel as she waits patiently for my ejaculations to end in her mouth, and she always swallows every last drop as if it's the most expensive Manuka honey.

'Now that's what I call therapy,' I said as I climbed down off the table and stepped into the shower beside her. 'If they ever put that on the National Health the whole of fucking Romania will be living here.'

After that I slept like a hibernating bear. My iPhone started ringing, just before midnight.

Normally I switch off my phone at night and put the landline on answer-machine; sports reporters think nothing of ringing you up at all hours to ask you this or that. That was before Twitter, mind. Nowadays the press are lazier and just use player tweets for all the 'tributes were being paid' quotes they could ever need. But during the January window I tend to pick up the phone at all hours, in case it's related to a transfer. Players' agents are more nocturnal than their clients, as befits their vampire-like nature. Some of the best deals I've helped make have been as a result of midnight negotiations.

I have individual ring tones for different people, of course. Viktor Sokolnikov has the Red Army singing a famous Russian folk song called 'Kalinka'. Zarco's is the Clash song 'London Calling'. Sonja has the Pointer Sisters' 'I'm So

Excited'. But this time it was none of these. The Stranglers song 'Peaches' meant that it was Maurice McShane, after Ian McShane who was in *Sexy Beast*; Maurice was City's life-coach and fixer and the club's first line of defence in any off-the-field crisis. It was his job to help our overpaid and often naïve players do everything from open an offshore bank account to pay off some skank who they'd knocked up. This meant that Maurice was one of the busiest men at the training ground. Players tend to bring problems to the coach that they wouldn't dream of mentioning to the manager; only now they bring them to Maurice, who some-times – if the matter is serious – brings them back to me. It had been my idea to hire Maurice; I'd met him in the nick and in the five months we'd been together at City we'd already seen off several scandals. I won't go into these right now. Suffice to say that we never did anything illegal. Just stuff that kept some of our stupid fuck-head players out of the newspapers, for one thing or another.

I went into the bathroom, closed the door, and sat down on the toilet. I think this is what they call multi-tasking. There were several texts from a variety of sports reporters asking me to call them but these I ignored, for the moment; better to get it from the horse's mouth, I thought, already imagining some scandal involving Ayrton Taylor, mouthing off to a newspaper perhaps. Or getting himself into trouble with another player's wife, again; he wasn't such an example of good sportsmanship when it came to shagging someone else's missus.

'What's up, Maurice?'

'I thought you should know, as soon as possible,' said Maurice. 'A pal who works for the Met has just given me the heads-up on this. And I think you ought to prepare yourself for a shock. The police have found a body hanging from the railings along Wembley Way.' He paused. 'It's Drenno. He's only gone and hanged himself.'

'Oh, fuck, no,' I said. 'The stupid, stupid bastard.'

We were silent for several seconds.

'You know his wife is in the same hospital as Didier,' said Maurice.

'No, I didn't.'

'Drenno beat her up quite badly.'

'Christ. Has she been told?'

'Yes. The press are there. And given your high-profile friendship it's safe to imagine that they'll be outside your flat before very long.'

'Like a pack of vultures,' I said. 'To pick over the entrails.'

'That's what generally happens in these situations.'

'Look, I'll tweet something,' I said. 'And release a statement to the City press office at Silvertown Dock. And to Arsenal. Fuck. He was here, you know. The day before yesterday. Pissed as usual.'

'Do you want me to tell the police?'

'No, I'll do it. But find out who's heading up the inquiry, will you? And text me a number? I don't want to explain myself more than once to these bastards.'

'They're bound to ask. So I'll ask: was he suicidal when you saw him?'

'No more so than usual.' I sighed because then I remembered what he'd said. 'But he did say something about making one last headline at Wembley. But I had no idea – Jesus, so that's what he meant. Oh God. The stupid bastard.'

'Scott.'

'Yes?'

'I'm sorry. I know you were fond of him.'

'No,' I said. 'I wasn't fond of him at all, Maurice. But I did love that man.'

I rang off, wiped the tears from my eyes, washed my face and looked at myself in the bathroom mirror. I knew what the guy who was looking back at me was thinking, because he looked angry; he was thinking – Drenno came to you for help but you were too dumb to see that; too dumb or just too lazy. You thought you were being such a fucking hero volunteering to take him to the Priory and offering to pay for his first week of treatment, didn't you? Christ, that was generous of you, Scott. The man needed a friend. Somewhere to stay for a couple of days until he was ready to face the music. He must have known he was going to be arrested for the assault on Tiffany; he'd been cautioned for that before. And you let him down. When you needed a friend, Drenno was there for you – when no one else would give you the time of day; but when he needed someone, where the fuck were you? Christ, he even visited you when you were in the nick. Anne didn't. Your own wife. In the eighteen months you were inside, Drenno was the only one who visited you, apart from your parents and the lawyers. That's the kind of friend he was. He came to visit you when everyone in the club told him to stay away.

'I'm sorry,' I said to the guy in the mirror, wishing it was Drenno. 'I am so, so sorry.'

Being sorry won't bring him back, you bastard. One of the finest, most naturally skilled midfielders this country has ever produced – certainly the best you ever played with – and now he's gone, aged just thirty-eight years old. What a fucking waste.

'I'm sorry, Matt,' I said and started crying again.

'What's wrong?'

I turned to see Sonja standing in the doorway. She was naked. In the bathroom mirror she looked as perfect as a woman can look and if I'd had a golden apple I'd certainly have given it to her. I felt like Caliban standing next to Miranda. Or something callous and ugly, anyway.

'It's Matt,' I said. 'He's hanged himself.'

'Oh, my God, Scott. I'm so sorry.'

She hugged me for a second and then sat down on the toilet.

'That's awful.'

'He was just thirty-eight,' I said, as if somehow that made it worse.

'You mustn't blame yourself,' she said.

'But I do blame myself. He needed help. That's obviously why he came here the other night. Because – because he had nowhere else to go.'

'Yes, he did need help but the help he needed was the professional kind. Frankly, I've been expecting this for a while. He was ill. He should have been in a hospital. His family should have had him sectioned a long time ago. And you know, I think we'll find out that it wasn't just depression that he couldn't play football any more that caused him to kill himself. I'm sure there was something deeper that lay at the bottom of all his psychological issues. I wouldn't be at all surprised if we find that Matt's childhood was marked by instability and tragedy. Perhaps even the suicide of someone who was close to him.'

'Thanks.' I nodded. 'And you're right, actually. His brother killed himself – threw himself in front of a train when he was fifteen. And there was some other stuff, too, that he didn't like speaking about. Like when his best friend and drinking buddy, Mackie, cleared off and joined the army;

Drenno was always rather lost without Mackie there to share his exploits. He's been fucked up all his life, one way or the other.'

'Come back to bed,' she said. 'And let me take care of you.'

'I will in a while.'

She kept hold of me for a minute. 'You're a good man,' she said. 'A decent man. That's why Drenno came here. Because you're the kind of decent man a man like him needed to cling onto.'

'I still find that hard to believe. I mean, after everything that's happened in my life.'

'Believe it,' she said. 'Because it's true.'

I nodded. 'Yeah, well if it is, it's mostly down to you, Sonja. You make me a better person.'

I went into my study, turned on my computer and then switched my phone to mute when it started ringing again: someone from the *Sun* I didn't want to speak to. Then I logged on and spent an hour writing something kind but probably anodyne about Matt on Twitter – how could you describe a great character like Drenno in 140 characters? – and composing an email to the Arsenal press office with a quote for the Gunners website. A few minutes later I got a text from Maurice with the name and number of the police officer dealing with the inquiry into Drennan's death: Detective Inspector Louise Considine LLB from Brent Police, 020 8733 3709. On the BBC News website there was a famous picture of Drenno celebrating after scoring a goal for Arsenal against Aston Villa in 1998, but the sole fact beyond what I already knew was that when he'd hanged himself he'd been wearing his white number eight England shirt – probably the only one he hadn't yet sold on eBay.

Sonja was right, of course; it was less of a surprise that Drennan had killed himself than that players like Gary Speed or Robert Enke should have done it, but I'd always hoped and believed that my old team mate might turn his life around. After all, I was living proof that you could come back to football after a disaster. Wasn't I?

I sat in an armchair with my iPad and spent another hour watching a selection of Drenno's best goals on YouTube. These were some of the sweetest strikes I'd ever seen and a few of them had had an assist from me, which was nice, but the accompanying music – Pink Floyd's 'Shine On You Crazy Diamond' – while wholly appropriate for a man like Drenno, did nothing for my spirits. And I started to weep once again.

I was about to go back to bed when I noticed another text from Maurice, asking me to call him urgently. So I did.

'What now?' I asked.

'Sorry to call you again, and so late, but I'm at the Crown of Thorns,' he said. 'And I think you ought to get down here as soon as. Something's happened. Something unpleasant.'

'Like what?'

'Not on the phone, eh? Just in case. Walls have ears.'

'They wouldn't dare. Not after paying me all those damages for hacking my phone.'

'They might, you know.'

'It's two thirty in the morning, Maurice. I just lost a good friend. And we've got a training session at ten.'

'So let someone else take it.'

'You really think I need to come to Silvertown Dock? Tonight?'

'I wouldn't have called otherwise.'

'No one's dead, are they?'

'Not exactly.'

'What the fuck does that mean?'

'Look, Scott, I can't handle this on my own. I can't get hold of João Zarco, Sarah Crompton, and Philip Hobday is away on Sokolnikov's yacht.'

Philip Hobday was the London City chairman and Sarah Crompton was the club's public relations officer.

'I really don't know what the fuck to say here,' he continued. 'And I'm going to need to say something. You'll understand why when you get to Silvertown Dock.'

'Say something to who?'

'The fucking press, of course. They were here before the police. It looks as if some fucker from Royal Hill tipped them off.'

'Royal Hill? What's that?'

'Greenwich Police Station. Look, trust me, it's important you get here and as soon as possible. Seriously, Scott, this is a situation that is going to require some delicate handling.'

'I'm not sure I'm the right man for that job. Especially with the press. Where they're concerned I feel like I'm wearing boxing gloves when I speak to them. But I take your point. You're right, you're right. If it's serious, you need me the same way I need you.' I glanced at my watch. 'I'll be there within the hour.'

CHAPTER 6

In the event it took only half an hour to drive the ten-mile journey from my flat off the King's Road to the East End. There aren't many people on the road at that time of the morning but the press were there in force when I arrived. As I approached the gates of the club car park they surged towards the Range Rover to see who I was. At the same time I wondered what was so interesting at Silvertown Dock that it could have diverted them from going to Wembley Way; I didn't know it at the time but Wembley Way was equally popular with journalists that night. There are more newspapers and television stations in England looking for a good story than you might think. Especially when it's a story about football.

I drove up to the gates of the club car park and waited for our security men to let me in. It was raining heavily now and while I was waiting I switched off the windscreen wipers just to deny the many waiting photographers a better shot of my tired and probably miserable face. The floodlights were on inside the stadium, which was very strange at nearly three in the morning.

'Scott! Scott! Scott!'

Since I had no idea of what to expect when I got inside the stadium I thought it best not to say anything. That suited me just fine as I don't like talking to the papers any more than I like talking to the police. Sarah Crompton was always trying to persuade me to be a bit friendlier to the press but old habits die hard; whenever I get doorstepped by reporters or papped by some monkey with a Canon I feel half inclined to hand out a taste of what Zinedine Zidane gave to Marco Materazzi in the 2006 World Cup Final. Now that's what I call a headline.

I found Maurice McShane waiting impatiently for me at the players' entrance, next to the riverside and the special private marina where Viktor Sokolnikov sometimes arrived at the stadium aboard a thirty-five-metre Sunseeker sport yacht. Maurice was a big fair-haired man with a beard and a voice like someone shovelling grit. To my surprise he was with the head groundsman, Colin Evans, who Sokolnikov had enticed away from the Bernabeu at great expense: Colin Evans was generally held to be the best groundsman in Europe and the City pitch always won all sorts of awards for its excellent condition.

'The fuck's going on?' I said. 'What are you doing here at this time of night, Colin?'

Colin shook his head, growled, clearly speechless with anger and led the way out through the players' tunnel and onto the pitch. He was fit-looking and young for a groundsman – no more than thirty-five – and wearing the same kind of City tracksuit I was wearing, he could easily have passed for a player.

'You'll see soon enough,' said Maurice.

'Sounds ominous.'

The stadium always looked fantastic for an evening fixture when all the floodlights were on. They made the orange seating look a very appetising and Christmassy shade of tangerine, while the grass seemed to shine like a rare emerald;

and for our sixty thousand seated supporters that's exactly what it was: something very precious, hallowed even. Small wonder that every so often we had requests from fans who wanted to have a relation's ashes scattered on the pitch. Colin would never have allowed such a thing, of course; apparently it's very bad for the grass but not so bad for the flowers. Colin's roses always won prizes.

He led us along the halfway line, through the centre circle to the spot where several policemen were standing as if about to kick off a game. Normally I could never make that walk without a feeling in the pit of my stomach that I was about to play a match; on this occasion, however, I felt as empty as the stadium itself. Drenno's death was still very much at the front of my mind. For a moment I thought I was about to see a dead body. But I certainly wasn't expecting to find what I saw now.

'What the hell?' I put a hand to my mouth and rocked back on my heels for a moment.

'Nice, isn't it?' said Maurice.

A hole had been dug in the centre of the pitch. I say a hole, but it was obviously a grave, about six feet long and at least two or three feet deep.

A stranger wearing a fawn-coloured duffel coat came towards me; he was holding a police identification card in front of him.

'I wonder if I might have a word with you now, gentlemen,' he said. 'My name is Neville, Detective Inspector Neville, from Royal Hill.'

'Give us a minute here, will you, Inspector?' I asked. 'Please.'

I led Maurice and Colin a few paces away so that the detective wouldn't hear our conversation.

'When did this happen?' I asked.

'I came out here just after midnight,' said Colin. Originally from the Mumbles, in Swansea, he spoke with a strong Welsh accent. 'We recently had some electric fox-proof fences fitted to stop them crapping on the pitch at night. The lads hate it if they slip in that shit; it's much worse than dog shit – the smell stays with you for days afterwards. Anyway, I was out to check that they were working properly and I noticed that someone had left some tools scattered across the pitch: a couple of spades and a fork. That's when I found it.'

I picked up a spade, glanced at the initials on the handle: LCC and then tossed it aside.

'How the fuck did they get in here?' I said. 'It's supposed to be ticket only.'

Colin shrugged. 'They probably slipped in during the day, when the doors are open to the building contractors, and hid in the stadium.'

'Building contractors? What are they doing?'

'We're having one of the bars refurbished,' explained Maurice.

I grunted. I could hear the internet joke now: thieves broke into Silvertown Dock to raid the trophy cabinet, but left empty-handed.

'What kind of a bastard would do this, Scott?' complained Colin.

'Colin,' I said. 'How long have you been in the game? You know what some of these bastards are like. A rival team's supporters could have done this. But with the results we've had since Christmas it could just as easily be our own fans – for fuck's sake, our own lot aren't exactly nice. Have you heard the kind of verbal poison that gets yelled from these terraces?'

45

'Well, it certainly wasn't a fox,' observed Maurice. 'I mean, I know foxes are cunning 'n' all but I never saw one who could dig a nice rectangle like that. Not without a ruler.'

'And as for you,' I told Maurice, 'sure it's serious and a pain in the arse, but it could have waited until the morning, couldn't it? I mean, it's just a fucking hole in the ground.'

Maurice McShane was a former solicitor who'd been disbarred for professional misconduct after it was found he'd used an anonymous account to tweet some insults about another barrister. He'd also been a successful amateur boxer, almost winning a bronze medal in the light heavyweight division at the 1990 Commonwealth Games in Auckland. Maurice was a good man to have around when someone was in a difficult spot, and as able to sort things with his fists as he was with a wad of cash. He said nothing; instead he took out his mobile phone and showed me a text he'd received from a reporter on the *Sun*:

Mozza. Would you care to comment on the suggestion being made that the grave in the middle of your pitch is a Sicilian-style message for your prop, Viktor Sokolnikov, whose former partner, Natan Fisanovich, turned up in a shallow grave in 1996, having been buried alive? At least that's what it said on Panorama. *Gordon.*

There was a similar text from the *Daily Mail*; and I dare say if I'd bothered to look at the texts arriving every minute on my own mobile phone I'd have found something along the same lines.

'Would I like to comment?' Maurice uttered a nervous laugh. 'No, I fucking wouldn't. Not particularly. Nor is it a conversation I'd feel comfortable about having with Viktor Sokolnikov. Especially as he's suing the BBC because of what was said on *Panorama*. Isn't that right?'

'That's what he told me.'

I put a couple of pieces of Orbit in my mouth and started chewing fiercely as if I were about to do my imitation of Sir Alex Ferguson, which had become a very popular turn of mine on the team bus.

'But I do think Viktor should know about this as soon as possible,' said Maurice. 'So he can respond to it in whatever way he thinks appropriate. You know him better than I do, Scott. And I'd prefer it if you or Zarco were to tell him what's happened here. This is well above my pay-grade.'

'Yes, I see your point.' I glanced back at Detective Inspector Neville. 'By the way, who brought him along and said he and his size fucking twelves could come here and walk on our grass?'

'I'm afraid that was me,' admitted Colin. 'Sorry, Scott. I was so upset when I saw that hole. But it is criminal damage, so I thought I should tell them. I mean, we do want to catch the bastards who did this, right?'

'Never ever bring the filth into this club without speaking to me, to Zarco, or to Phil Hobday first. Got that, Colin? Once you involve the filth in this club's affairs it's as good as sending an email to Fleet Street. Undoubtedly it was a copper who texted a mate on the *Sun* or the *Daily Mail* about this. Hey, guess what? Someone's only gone and dug a fucking grave on the pitch at Silvertown Dock. That's a two-hundred-quid tip. Maybe more if it's a front page. If it wasn't for them being here with their fucking cameras we could have put out that it was just a hole and not a grave at all. We might still do that if we can get that rozzer in the duffel coat to cooperate.'

'Yes, I see that now.'

'No worries. Can't be helped. Look, here's what we're all

47

going to say. We're going to say it looks like the work of some disgruntled fans. Kids, probably. And we're going to piss on that Sicilian message stuff from an enormous height. The last thing Mr Sokolnikov needs right now is more wild speculation about who and what he is. The people who committed this outrage probably couldn't even spell Sicilian. Got that?'

Maurice and Colin nodded.

'More importantly, Colin, I want you to start thinking about if and how and when we can repair the pitch. We're at home again to Newcastle in ten days.'

'Believe me, I hadn't forgotten.'

'Right then. Let's talk to that rozzer.'

I walked towards the policeman.

'I'm sorry for keeping you waiting, Inspector,' I said. 'Especially at this late hour. But I really think we've wasted your time. Apologies for that, too. It seems obvious to me that this is the work of yobs. Disgruntled fans, so called. That's nothing we're not used to at a football club. I can't imagine you'll be surprised when I tell you that we get threats all the time and that very occasionally they manifest as vandalism. It's regrettable but not uncommon.'

'What kind of threats?' asked the inspector.

'Emails. Tweets. The occasional poison-pen letter. Boxes of shit in the post. You name it, we get it.'

'I'd like to see some of these, if I may.'

'I'm afraid that's not possible. We have a policy of not keeping anything like that. Especially the gift-wrapped turds.'

'May I ask why, sir?'

'Yesterday's shit smells bad, Inspector.'

'I meant the letters and the emails, of course.'

Detective Inspector Neville was thin with a hooked nose

that made him look like he had a permanent sneer on his face. To my keen but cold ear his sounded like a Yorkshire accent.

I shrugged. 'We don't keep that kind of thing because frankly there's so much of it. Really it's simpler just to erase or destroy anything that's threatening or insulting. Just in case a player who's been threatened or abused sees it and is disturbed by what he's read.'

'I'd have thought anyone would have a right to know if he's been threatened, sir.'

'You might very well think that. But we take a different attitude. Some of these lads are very highly strung, Inspector. And one or two of them are none too bright. Even threats that are patently absurd can exercise a strongly negative effect on a weaker-minded player at a Premier League football club. And we wouldn't want that, would we? Not with a third round FA Cup tie against Leeds on Sunday.'

'Nevertheless, a crime has been committed here.'

'A hole in the ground? That's not exactly seven-seven, now, is it?'

'No, but with all due respect, sir, that's no ordinary hole in the ground. For a start, there's the shape. And then there's the obvious financial loss. As holes in the ground go, I imagine this is an extremely expensive one. Wouldn't you say so, Mr Evans?'

The detective inspector obviously knew the kind of person he was speaking to. What groundsman doesn't moan about the state of a pitch? But even before he started to answer I wished I'd told Colin to play down the cost of the damage to the police. His being Welsh only seemed to make this worse as Colin's manner was very considered and deliberate.

'A hole like that?' Colin shook his head. 'Let's see now.

The whole pitch cost nearly a million quid to lay down. So, frankly this is nothing short of a bloody disaster. In an ideal world we'd rip the whole surface up and start again. But halfway through the season we'll have to make do with patching it up as best we can, I suppose. Of course, even before you think about the grass there's the under-soil heating system that stops the pitch from freezing at this time of year. That's been damaged and will have to be repaired. And the grass – well, it's not just grass, you see. Artificial fibres will have to be sewn into the pitch alongside the grass so that the roots can wrap themselves around the nylon fibres. Then there's the fact that at this time of year it's not easy getting new grass to take hold. So we'll need to run the grow lights around the clock. That's expensive as well. I wouldn't think there would be a lot of change from fifty grand to repair this. Seriously. The damage might be even more than that if the pitch still remains unplayable in ten days' time. What with the gate 'n' all. An average ticket price of sixty-two quid means that the total match day income is around six million pounds.'

'So the cost of the damage might be anything between fifty grand and six million?' said Detective Inspector Neville.

'That's about the size of it, yes,' agreed Colin.

Neville looked at me and shook his head. 'Well, sir, I'd say this is as clear a case of criminal damage as I've come across in a long time. And since a crime has clearly been committed here then I'm bound to investigate it. Which is what the insurance company would insist on, I'm sure, if Mr Sokolnikov were to make a claim for this. They always do, you know.'

'Those figures might seem like a lot to you and me, Inspector,' I said. 'But it's not a lot to someone like Viktor

Sokolnikov. I'm sure he'd much prefer just to pay for the repairs himself and avoid as much embarrassing publicity as possible. Which, if things had been done properly, ought to have been avoided. You know, it's a mystery to me how the press managed to get here before the police. I'm sure no one here would have given them the heads-up.'

'Are you suggesting that someone from Royal Hill station told them?'

'I'm suggesting that if it transpires that the press were tipped off by someone from your station then Mr Sokolnikov will want to know why. Especially since it has been drawn to my attention that the press is already suggesting there might be some link with organised crime back in Mr Sokolnikov's home country of Ukraine. That's the kind of sensational reporting that we'd much prefer to avoid. Which we could still avoid, I think. Look, why don't I just arrange for an executive box to be made available for our next home match so that a dozen of your officers from Royal Hill can come along and enjoy the game? You'll be our guests and you'll have a nice day. I'll make sure of it.'

'You mean if I were to forget all about this?'

'That's right. We'll just tell the press that the reports of a grave being found in the centre of London City's football pitch have been greatly exaggerated. In fact, I insist on it. Come on. What do you say? Let's just forget about it and go home. Doesn't that sound like common sense?'

'What it sounds like is bribery,' Neville said stiffly. 'At the risk of repeating myself, a crime has clearly been committed here, Mr Manson. And it's beginning to look as if you really don't want the police here at all. Which I admit does puzzle me, since it was someone from the club who summoned us here tonight.'

'I'm afraid that was me,' admitted Colin.

'He made an honest mistake,' I said. 'And so did I when I offered you the tickets. I think I must have assumed that you were the kind of bloke who had something better to do than look into the mysterious case of the hole in the ground.'

'You know what I think? I think you're one of those people who just doesn't like the police. Is that what you are, Mr Manson?'

'Look,' I said, 'if you want a police medal for this then go ahead, be my guest. I was just trying to save you the effort of wasting police time on something that will almost certainly turn out to be a random incident of vandalism. And to save the club owner a bit of unnecessary embarrassment. But when did that sort of thing ever matter to the Met? Look, I think we've told you all we know. It sounds to me as if maybe we've got even less time to waste here than you have.'

'Yes, you said. An FA Cup third round match against Leeds.' He smiled. 'I'm from Leeds myself.'

'You're a long way south, Inspector.'

'Don't I know it, sir. Especially when I listen to someone like you. I'm just trying to do my job here, Mr Manson, sir.'

'And so am I.'

'Only for some reason you're making mine difficult.'

'Am I?'

'You know you are.'

'Then go home. We're not talking about *The Arsenal Stadium Mystery* here.'

'That's an old black and white film, isn't it?'

I nodded. '1939. Leslie Banks. Piece of shit, really. Only interesting because the film stars several Arsenal players of the day: Cliff Bastin, Eddie Hapgood.'

'If you say so, Mr Manson. Frankly I've never been much of a football fan myself.'

'That was also my impression.'

Detective Inspector Neville paused thoughtfully for a moment and then pointed at me. 'Wait a minute. Manson, Manson. You wouldn't be... ? Of course. You're that Manson, aren't you? Scott Manson. Used to play for Arsenal, until you went to prison.'

I said nothing. In my experience it's always best when you're talking to the police.

'Yes.' Neville sneered. 'That would explain everything.'

CHAPTER 7

Before I tell you anything about what happened to me in 2004 I should first tell you that I am part black – more of a David James or Clark Carlisle than Sol Campbell or Didier Drogba, but I think it's probably relevant in view of what happened. In fact, I'm sure it is. I don't consider myself black but I am a keen supporter of Kick it Out.

My dad, Henry, is a Scot who used to play for Heart of Midlothian and Leicester City. He got picked for Willie Ormond's Scotland squad and went to the World Cup finals in West Germany in 1974 – the year we came so close. Dad didn't play because of injury, which is probably how he found the time to meet my mother, Ursula Stephens, who was a former German field athlete – at the 1972 Munich Olympics she came fourth in the women's high jump – working for German telly. Ursula is the daughter of an African-American air force officer stationed at Ramstein, and a German woman from Kaiserslautern. I'm happy to say that both my parents and my grandparents are still alive.

After finishing his career in football my dad set up his own sports boot and shoe company in Northampton, where I went to school, and in Stuttgart. The shoe company is called Pedila and today it generates almost half a billion dollars a year in net income. I earn a lot of money as a director of that company; it's how I can afford a flat in Chelsea. My dad says I am the company's ambassador in the world of professional football. But it wasn't always like that. Frankly I wasn't always the ambassador you would have welcomed in your executive toilet, let alone the boardroom.

In 2003, aged twenty-eight, I joined Arsenal from Southampton. The following year I went to prison for a rape I didn't commit. What happened was this:

Back then I was married to a girl called Anne; she works in fashion and she's a decent woman but to be honest, we weren't ever suited. While I like clothes and am happy to drop £2k on a Richard James suit, I've never much liked high fashion. Anne thinks that people like Karl Lagerfeld and Marc Jacobs are artists. Me, I think that's only half right. So while we were still living together we were already drifting apart; I was sure she was seeing someone else. I was doing my best to turn a blind eye to that, but it was difficult. We didn't have any children, which was good since we were headed for a divorce.

Anyway, I'd started seeing a woman called Karen, who was one of Anne's best friends. That was mistake number one. Karen was the mother of two children and she was married to a sports lawyer who had cancer. At first it was just me being nice to her, taking her out for the odd lunch to cheer her up, and then it got out of hand. I am not proud of that. But there it is. All I can say in my defence is that I was young and stupid. And, yes, lonely. I wasn't interested in the kind of girls who throw themselves at footballers in nightclubs. Never have been. I don't even like nightclubs. My idea of a nightmare is an evening out with the lads. I much prefer dinner at The Ivy or The Wolseley. Even when I was at Arsenal the club still had a reputation for some hard drinking – it wasn't just silverware that the likes of Tony

Adams and Paul Merson helped earn for the Gunners – but me, I was always in bed before midnight.

Karen's house in St Albans was conveniently close to the Arsenal training ground at Shenley, so I'd got into the habit of dropping in to see her on my way home to Hampstead; and sometimes I was seeing a lot more of her than was proper. I suppose I was in love with her. And perhaps she was in love with me. I don't know what we thought was going to happen. Certainly we could never have imagined what actually did happen.

I remember everything about the day it happened as if it has been etched onto my brain with acid. It was after one post-Shenley visit, a beautiful day near the end of the season. I came out of Karen's house after a couple of hours to find that my car had been nicked. It was a brand new Porsche Cayenne Turbo that I'd only just taken delivery of, so I was pretty gutted. At the same time I was reluctant to report the car stolen for the simple reason that I guessed my wife, Anne, would recognise Karen's address if the story got into the newspapers. So I jumped on a train back to my house in Hampstead, thinking I might as well report the car stolen from somewhere in the village. Mistake number two. However, no sooner had I got back home than Karen rang me and said the car was now standing outside her house again. At first I didn't believe it, but she read out the registration number and it was indeed my car. More than a little puzzled as to what was happening, I got in a taxi and went straight back to St Albans to collect it.

When I arrived there I couldn't believe my luck. The car wasn't locked but it didn't have a scratch on it and, anxious to be away from Karen's house before her husband came home, I drove off telling myself that perhaps some kids had taken it for a joy-ride and then returned it, having had second thoughts about what they'd done. Oddly enough I'd done something like that as a kid: I stole a scooter and then returned it after a couple of hours. It was naïve of me to think that something similar had happened here, I admit, but I was just happy to be reunited with a car I loved. Mistake number three.

Driving home I noticed a knife on the floor of the car and, not thinking straight, I picked it up. Mistake number four. I should have tossed the knife out of the window; instead I put it in the compartment underneath the armrest. I was so pleased to recover a car I thought had been stolen that perhaps I did exceed the speed limit here and there; then again I wasn't driving dangerously or under the influence of drink or drugs.

Somewhere near Edgware I noticed a car in my mirror flashing me and ignored it, as you do; London is full of half-wit drivers. I had no idea it was actually an unmarked police car. The next time I looked, near Brent Cross, the same car was still in my mirror only now it had a cherry on top. And still not suspecting that anything very bad had happened, I pulled over. You can imagine my surprise when two police officers accused me of speeding and failing to stop; I was handcuffed, arrested and taken to Willesden Green where to my greater horror I found myself being interviewed about a rape. A man 'answering my description' and driving my car – the victim remembered the marque and half the registration number – had picked a woman up at a service station on the A414 and then raped her at knifepoint in nearby Greenwood Park.

There was no doubt my car had been involved; some of the victim's hairs were found on the headrest, her knickers were in the glove box, and there was other circumstantial evidence, too. Her blood and my fingerprints were on the knife, of course; and in the same glove box as the victim's knickers the police found a packet of condoms I'd bought at a garage in Shenley. The receipt was still in the ashtray. The sales assistant at the garage remembered me buying them because he'd seen me on *MOTD* mouthing off about some stupid incident in a match against Tottenham. More of that in a moment. Anyway, there were two condoms missing from the packet. The rapist had used one on his victim; I'd put another in my wallet when I'd gone to visit Karen, but I wasn't about to tell the police this because I was still hoping to spare her and, more importantly, her husband. I figured the last thing he needed was his wife providing me with an adulterous alibi while the poor bastard was having chemo. Mistake number five.

The victim – Helen Fehmiu, who was Turkish – wasn't at all sure that it was me who'd raped her, however. Her attacker had punched her several times in the face, so hard she had a detached retina, but she thought he was perhaps black or 'a bit foreign-looking' which was good coming from her, quite frankly. She was darker than I am. Helpfully the police arranged for Mrs Fehmiu to see my picture on the back pages of the newspapers, where I'd been apologising for my conduct after the Tottenham match. One of their players took a dive when I tackled him and the ref awarded a very dubious penalty that resulted in me shouting in his face, which earned me a well-deserved red card. Arsenal versus Tottenham is always a highly emotional fixture, to put it mildly.

Anyway, Mrs Fehmiu thought it *might* have been me who'd raped her, and what with that and the forensics in my car the cops then interviewed me for sixteen hours, at the end of which they typed up a transcript that bore absolutely no relation to what I had said on the tape. In the typewritten transcript I admitted more or less everything; I even admitted 'doing an O.J.' and trying to shake off a police car that was in pursuit of my vehicle. In short they verballed me, confident that the quality of the recording made of the interview was so poor that the jury wouldn't be able to make out what was said, which proved to be the case. Indeed, the jury was so persuaded by the police transcript that it managed to hear me saying things on the tape that were never even there to hear. Weird but true.

Meanwhile it transpired that the police had managed to 'lose' the only piece of evidence that was vital to my defence: a used condom that was found in Greenwood Park on the day of the rape and in the spot where the victim said she'd been attacked. That condom would easily have cleared me.

The newspapers were involved, of course, and before I came to trial the tabloids did their bit for English justice; having already concluded that I was 'a monster', and 'revealing' that my nickname at Highbury was Norman Bates on account of my psycho-like personality on the park (which was a blatant lie), they managed to rake up the fact that I was already technically a rapist. As usual it wasn't what they said, it was what they didn't say. They managed to find an ex-girlfriend in Northampton with whom I'd had sex a few days before her sixteenth birthday. They neglected to mention that I was just eighteen at the time and that she and I had been going out for more than a year; her father – who was none too keen on someone he described as having 'more than a touch of the tar-brush' about him, i.e. me – had found out that we'd slept together and even though he wasn't living at home with his daughter at the time, he threatened to have me charged with statutory rape. It hardly seemed to matter that this same girl volunteered to be a character witness in my defence.

In spite of this, and after a December trial that lasted two weeks, I was found guilty at St Albans Crown Court on the day before Christmas Eve 2004, and sentenced to eight years in prison.

I was sent to Wandsworth nick. In case you didn't know, it's the largest prison in the UK. They've had a lot of cricketers in there – for match fixing – not to mention Oscar Wilde, Ronnie Kray and Julian Assange but, surprisingly, I was Wandsworth's first Premier League footballer. Things went all right for me in the nick – everyone likes talking about football in prison, even the governor – and I made a lot of friends in Wandsworth. There's all sorts in the nick, not just criminals. Some of those blokes I'd trust more than I'll ever trust any copper again. It's one reason why today I'm involved with the Kenward Trust, which assists the resettlement of offenders.

Certainly things went better for me than they did for poor Mrs Fehmiu, who lost the sight in one eye. Three months after the trial she killed herself. I, on the other hand, spent my first year in Wandsworth doing a correspondence course in sports management because I knew eventually that I was going to be cleared.

Eighteen months after I went inside, Karen's husband died of cancer. But frankly I had no idea that his dying would take quite so long. That's a pretty fucked-up place to find yourself in, psychologically; hoping that some poor bloke whose wife you've been shagging will die so that you can get out of prison, but that's pretty much how I was feeling at the time. Straight away she contacted the police to explain that on the afternoon of the rape she'd been with me. But the police said the case was closed and told her to go away.

So she took her story to the *Daily Telegraph*, who started to campaign for my release. Almost immediately they discovered that Inspector Twistleton, who had led the inquiry into Mrs Fehmiu's rape, was facing sixty-five disciplinary charges including an assault on a black police officer. It soon became clear that not only was Twistleton a racist – in view of some of the words he'd used in my cell, this was no surprise to me – he was also a member of the National Front. Incredibly, the condom used in the rape was now 'found' by someone in Willesden Police Station and even after eighteen months there was enough DNA there to clear me of any involvement.

Three judges at the Court of Appeal quashed my conviction and I was released from the cells at the Royal Courts of Justice the same day. Subsequently eight newspapers paid libel damages to me totalling almost a million pounds. The police were also ordered to pay half a million pounds in damages for false imprisonment, although on appeal these were reduced to one hundred grand because I had chosen to omit telling the police that Karen could have provided me with an alibi. Not that the money was important. The damage was done. My playing career was over and even without knowing about Karen my wife had divorced me.

On my release I decided I needed to get away from England. For a while I went to live with my grandparents in Germany, and then I went to study at the Johan Cruyff Institute in Barcelona, which opened in 2002. I'd done a BA in Modern Languages at Birmingham University so I spoke a bit of Spanish, and in Barcelona – my favourite European city – I did a one-year course in Sports Management and then an eight-month postgrad in Football Management. In 2010 I obtained my UEFA certificates and accepted a trainee coaching role with Pep Guardiola at FC Barca. In 2011, I became the first team trainee coach at Bayern Munich and worked with Jupp Heynckes, who was an old friend of my dad. He was part of the West German squad in 1974 although, like Dad, Jupp was injured and spent most of the tournament on the bench.

I've thought about poor Mrs Fehmiu a lot, however; the only time I ever saw her was in court and I felt her pain. A couple of years ago I got involved with another charity called Rape Crisis; I help to fund a Rape Crisis Centre in Camden, because the way I see it I was a victim of Mrs Fehmiu's rapist too. Of her rapist, of the newspapers, and of the Metropolitan Police.

I try not to be bitter about what happened. I tell myself that to some extent it was my own fault. And yet I still feel a sense of grievance. I know I should get over it and put it all behind me and perhaps, in time, I will. Of course it's one thing giving good advice to others in such matters, it's something else when you try to take that advice yourself. But here's one truth I have learned that I try to pass on to all my players: when the worst has already happened, nothing can hurt you. That's as true on the football pitch as it is in life. Because there is always a next time.

I am not a philosopher of football like João Zarco, you understand. To me, managing a football team is just common sense with a scarf on.

62

CHAPTER 8

The next day I went back to Silvertown Dock and took another look at the hole with Colin Evans and João Zarco. It was cold and the sky above the stadium was a dispiriting shade of January grey. The rain and the police had gone but not the picket of reporters, who'd already gone to town on Drenno's death and the Sicilian message that had surely been sent to Viktor Sokolnikov. Fortunately I hadn't had to tell him about it because he'd read the story online and told me he thought the idea of such messages to be preposterous.

'Where I come from, if you want a man dead you don't warn him by sending him a message,' he'd said. 'And certainly not one as theatrical as this. It's like something from the pages of a book by Mario Puzo. I appreciate you calling, Scott, and your concern for my reputation. But don't worry about me. I can assure you, I am very well protected.'

This was true; Sokolnikov never moved without at least four bodyguards. One of them was a former Russian boxer, covered in tats, who looked like Vinnie Jones' ugly big brother.

Now, Zarco stared into the hole and shook his head.

'Football,' he said. 'It's tribal, of course. And this kind of thing is what tribes do, isn't it? It took billions of years for man to evolve from being a beast and a savage, but it only takes ninety minutes on a Saturday afternoon for all of that to come undone.' He looked at Colin. 'Can you fix this little divot, Colin? Before the Newcastle match?'

'It won't be easy,' said Colin, 'but I can fix it, yes. It takes seven to ten days for a new pitch or a bit of turf to bed in. But what about the police, boss? I reckon I could get myself into trouble here. This is a crime scene, isn't it? Suppose that bloody Inspector Neville finds that I've filled in his hole? Suppose he comes back here this morning?'

Zarco pulled a face. Sometimes his face was as rubbery as a comedian's.

'To look at the hole again?' he said. 'It's just a bloody hole in the ground, isn't it? Besides, it's not his hole, it's our hole. And it doesn't belong in the middle of a football pitch.'

'Listen to him,' I told Colin. 'He sounds just like Bernard Cribbins.'

Colin knew I'd made a joke although he didn't understand it. I make a lot of jokes like that, which nobody understands. That's what happens when you get older. Zarco didn't understand it either, but then he was Portuguese.

'Fill it in and repair it,' I told Colin. 'I'll take full responsibility. You can tell him that. But before you do fill it in maybe you should dig down a little. It could be that when you disturbed the people who excavated this, they were actually filling the hole in again.'

'I don't follow you, Scott.'

'Humour me, will you, Colin? Usually when people dig a grave it's because they want to bury something in it. Something, or someone.'

'You don't mean…?' The Welshman glanced at the grave in horror.

'I do mean, Colin. I do mean.'

Zarco grinned. 'Perhaps Scott is expecting you to find Yorick in this grave,' he said.

'Who?'

'Terry Yorick,' I said. 'Defensive midfielder for Leeds United. His daughter Gabby used to do the football on the telly. Nice-looking bird. Great pins. I don't watch it nearly so much now she's gone.'

Zarco laughed at Colin's continuing incomprehension and walked back towards the players' entrance. I followed him closely.

'Alas, poor Terry Yorick,' I said. 'He was Welsh, too. Poor bastard.'

'To be or not to be. You know, with an attitude like that I think maybe Hamlet followed a football team.'

'FC Copenhagen, probably.'

'So, Scott. Today's fitness and injury reports? You got them?'

'On your desk, boss.'

'Good.' Zarco's phone bleeped. He checked the screen and nodded: 'Paolo Gentile. Excellent. Looks like we've now got ourselves a Scottish goalkeeper. Let's hope he's as good as you said he was. Now all we need is a translator. I couldn't understand one fucking word he said. Except that one. Fucking.'

'I'll translate. I speak good Scottish.'

'That's a relief.'

'I thought Denis Kampfner was handling the transfer.'

'Viktor doesn't trust him, so he brought his own agent in. Paolo Gentile.'

'He's your agent, too, isn't he?'

'Yes. What of it?' Zarco's phone bleeped again. 'Now who's this? The BBC. *Strictly Come Dancing*. They want me for the new series. I keep saying no and they keep offering more money. As if.'

'I bet you're quite the twinkle-toes.'

'I hate that shit. I hate all those stupid shows. Me, I'd rather read a book.'

I glanced back over my shoulder and saw that Colin was already in the hole and digging.

'Poor Colin,' I said. 'Get him on the subject of grass seed and he'll talk for fucking hours, but I don't think he's read a book in his life.'

'He reads. He has a book in his office toilet.'

'Oh?'

'Yes. Mind you, it's a pretty crappy book. I think maybe when he runs out of toilet paper... It's your book. *Foul Play.*'

I grinned. 'At least I wrote mine, boss.'

Zarco laughed. 'Fuck you, Scott.'

'You know, it's a pity I didn't think of it before,' I said. 'But I kind of wish I'd persuaded one of the lads to get in that grave before we looked at it with Colin just now. We could have chucked a bit of earth on top of someone and given that Welshman the fright of his bloody life.'

'After what happened to Drenno last night? I worry about you, Scott. Really I do.'

'Drenno would have been the first to see the funny side of a joke like that. That's why I loved him.'

'You have a very sick sense of humour.'

'I know. That's why I'm your team coach, boss. A sick sense of humour is absolutely bloody essential when you're training a squad of overpaid young cunts. Fucking with them keeps their feet on the ground.'

'True enough. Look, I'm very sorry about Drenno. I know you two were friends. He was a great footballer.'

'Just not very sensible.' I shrugged. 'Sonja thinks it was inevitable that something like this would happen eventually. In fact, she almost predicted it.'

'See if she can predict the result on Sunday. I could use a little help from the spirits.'

'She already did. We're going to win 4–0.'

'Good. Buy her a late Christmas present from me, will you?'

I sighed. 'I'll never forget Drenno's Christmas present to me when we were playing at Arsenal. A bottle of sun-tan lotion.'

We were still laughing as we reached the tunnel. But the laughter faded a little as we heard a shout and Colin came running after us, holding a square object in his hands.

'You were right, Scott. There was something in that grave. This.'

'It's not a grave,' I said. 'It's a hole. Just remember that.'

He handed me a framed photograph. The glass was smeared with earth and mud but the person in the picture was clearly identifiable. It was a photograph of João Gonzales Zarco, the one that was on the cover of his autobiography: *No Games, Just Football*.

Zarco took the framed photograph from my hands and nodded. 'This was in the hole?'

Colin nodded. 'Last night's rain must have brought some earth down on top of it. That's why we didn't see it then. We might never have found this. It's lucky you suggested digging down a bit, Scott.'

'Isn't it?' I said, doubtfully.

'It's a good picture,' observed Zarco. 'Mario Testino took this shot. I look like Bruce Willis, yes?'

I said nothing.

'Don't look so worried, Scott,' said Zarco. 'I'm not in the least bit concerned by this kind of thing. I told you: there are times when football supporters are like savages. At the Nou Camp, we had a pig's head thrown on the pitch when Luis Figo was taking a corner. And you should see those crazy bastards at Galatasaray, Coritiba and River Plate. They probably get this kind of thing all the time. But it's England where I work and where I make my living, not a country where a man who plays football sometimes goes in fear of his life. The values of this country are good ones. And the people who did this are the exception. What worries me more is Leeds, tomorrow. They're always a good cup side. Manchester United 1972. Arsenal in 2011. Tottenham in 2013. And the best FA Cup Final I ever saw was a recording of Chelsea versus Leeds in 1970. Now that was a fucking football match.'

Colin nodded. '2–2 draw. Which Chelsea won in the replay. First one since 1912.'

Zarco grinned. 'You see? He does read.' He handed the picture back to Colin. 'You hang onto this. A keepsake. Hang it above your desk and use it to frighten the rest of the ground staff.'

'Shouldn't we tell the police about this?' said Colin. 'Finding your picture in the hole, I mean.'

'No,' said Zarco. 'Don't tell anyone about this or the press will be all over it. It's bad enough that they know I've been asked to go on *Strictly Come Dancing* without them knowing about this, too. And don't for Christ's sake tell Mario Testino. He'll have a fit.'

'My wife loves that programme,' confessed Colin. 'You should go on it, boss.'

'With all due respect to your wife, Colin, I'm a football manager not a fucking *bandido burro*.'

He checked his phone once more. 'Fuck,' he said. 'My builder – again. I swear that man calls me more than my wife.'

Zarco had bought a house in Pimlico and was having extensive building work done, including a new façade designed by Tony Owen Partners from Sydney, Australia. The façade included an ultra-modern-looking Möbius window that had proved less than popular with Zarco's neighbours and, of course, the *Daily Mail*. From the artist's impression I'd seen in the newspaper the new façade looked to me like the J. P. Morgan Media Centre at Lord's Cricket Ground.

'That's because your wife is at my house,' I said. 'To get some peace and quiet, not to mention some good sex. And to get away from you. She hates you just like everyone else.'

'This architect was Toyah's idea, not mine,' said Zarco. 'I tell her, you want a house that looks Australian then go and live in Australia. This is London. This is where I live, this is where I make my living. Let's have a house that looks like a London house, not the Sydney fucking Opera House. But this isn't good enough for her and as usual Toyah gets her way. I swear, this woman is more difficult than any footballer I have ever had to deal with.'

'That's why we love them, isn't it? Because they're not fucking footballers. They're women, who smell nice and who have nice legs. That's why we buy them expensive Christmas presents.'

'Who says I buy her an expensive Christmas present? That's you, Scott, not me. I don't buy women presents. I don't have time. You're the one who likes to buy presents.'

'You must have bought her something, surely?'

Zarco grinned. 'Toyah's married to Zarco. She doesn't need a Christmas present.'

CHAPTER 9

Elland Road, the home of Leeds United FC, is no place for the faint-hearted in January. Even on a midsummer's day the area is as bleak as the hair on a witch's tit, but in winter a northwest wind whips off the Yorkshire Dales and seems to take the spirit right out of you. Doubly so when you consider that the stadium is right next to Cottingley Crematorium and they do say that sometimes, when the wind is blowing in the right direction, you can catch the pungent whiff of an afternoon service of remembrance. The beautiful game was rarely ever played in Leeds and certainly never when Billy Bremner was the Leeds captain back in the seventies, a time when Leeds United was one of the dirtiest sides in football. And I have the marks on my shins to prove it wasn't much better in the nineties and noughties, when David O'Leary was the manager and the likes of Jonathan Woodgate and Lee Bowyer were there.

Although my father knew Billy Bremner very well – Bremner captained Scotland at the 1974 World Cup – I met the man only once, not long before his untimely death in 1997. I mention Billy Bremner because I think there's something very wrong about the statue of Billy that stands outside Elland Road. It's only my opinion, but Billy Bremner looks like he's black. In reality the diminutive Scotsman, who was born near Stirling, was a pasty-looking white man with red hair. I don't know why the Billy outside Elland Road should appear to be black but it's as if he's been partly cremated in the crematorium nearby. The hair is the right colour, as it happens, and so is the Leeds shirt, but every time I see it I have a laugh because I'm sure Billy would have fucking hated it. Even the statue of Michael Jackson that used to stand outside Craven Cottage is more true to life than Billy's statue; weirdly, Billy is blacker than Michael is, although maybe that's not so strange. Anyway, Billy just looks creepy, like a shitty piece of sculpture by Jeff Koons, or a statue of a saint you might see in a shrine in Cuba or Haiti, as if he might come alive to put the fear of God and voodoo into any team turning up to play Leeds at Elland Road. Maybe that's the idea. If so then it might work even better if the supporters were to carry it round the pitch before the match, because it certainly wasn't working for Leeds when London City went there for the third round FA Cup tie.

Nothing was. Not even a spectacularly tasteless song about Zarco from Leeds fans.

It was Leeds United's second loss in a new year that was only seven days old and their worst result since losing 7–3 to Nottingham Forest in March 2012. Christoph Bündchen, replacing Ayrton Taylor up front as our number one striker, gave City fans a very late Twelfth Night present of five golden goals in an eight-goal rout of Leeds United that proceeded without reply. This was the biggest win in our club's history and it was doubly fortunate that Viktor Sokolnikov had flown back from the Caribbean aboard his private Boeing 767-300 just to see the match.

Bündchen was City's hero but Juan-Luis Dominguin also scored two, and this was after Xavier Pepe made a forty-yard strike that was the first of the evening and already looks like being the goal of the season – a top-drawer goal conjured from absolutely nothing, which departed his right foot like an arrow from a longbow. There was nothing speculative about Pepe's incredible strike: by contrast, Andrea Pirlo's curling goal for Milan against Parma in 2010 seems like a long shot, in its full idiomatic meaning. Pepe's shot was something else: head down, with every sinew of his muscular body engaged, he knew exactly what he was doing and the ball flew as straight as a high-velocity bullet. By the time the Leeds goalkeeper, Paddy Kenny, had started to move for it, the football was already in the top corner of his net. Small wonder that Pepe was recently ranked by Bloomberg as the seventh best footballer in Europe.

But it was Christoph Bündchen who gave the Leeds manager nightmares, and perhaps not just him. Bündchen is only twenty-one years old and has yet to be picked for his home country of Germany, and this prompted me to think that if the German manager, Joachim Löw, hasn't yet found a place in his team for a player of Bündchen's goal-scoring ability, then Roy Hodgson's England had better watch out for the rest of the German team. It's true that Christoph's first goal was a well-taken penalty after a clumsy challenge brought Pepe down in the box when the score was 'only' 3–0. But the next four goals scored by the young German were nothing short of sublime, and at one stage it seemed as if it were Leeds United versus Christoph Bündchen, who, incredibly, doesn't seem to have been ranked by Bloomberg at all. What made this even more satisfying to me was that I had persuaded Zarco to pay the German club FC Augsburg just four million quid for the boy when we joined City in the summer.

It wasn't that Leeds failed to take their chances; in truth they only ever seemed to have one chance in the whole match and that was soon after Pepe's goal when Lewis Walters intercepted a nonchalant pass by the City centre back, Ross Field, and chipped our reserve goalkeeper, Roberto Forlan – who had little else to do all evening – only to find our captain, the ever-reliable Ken Okri, hack his effort off the line.

At half time it was 4–0 and the lads seemed to take Zarco at his word when he told them to go and enjoy themselves and do the same in the second half as they had done in the first.

After that Leeds were seldom threatening. The fifth goal came within seconds of the game restarting when another scorching shot from Pepe was well saved by Paddy Kenny; he then rolled the ball out to Kevin Beech, who found Bündchen on him in a flash. Beech attempted a desperate square pass to Stefan Signoret but Bündchen read it as if it had been written on the advertising hoarding in six-foot-high letters, intercepted the ball at speed, sold the poor keeper a sweet dummy and then toed the ball across the line. 5–0.

Bündchen's third goal was pure magic and was made more impressive by the near superhuman length of his stride. Bündchen is well over six feet tall and looks more like a defender than a striker, which makes him very intimidating when he's running flat out at you. Scornfully hurdling trailing legs that looked like obvious penalties if they'd brought him down, and selling dummies as if the Leeds players were toddlers in highchairs, the German must have changed direction three times before he found the space for a shot that he seemed to dig out of the grass, and which left the poor keeper dumped on his backside with his head in his hands. For all the world it looked as if he was just checking he could still hold onto something round. Zarco ran the length of his technical area in celebration, threw himself onto his knees and slid for several yards, ruining the trousers of a good suit and looking like someone who was already in training for *Strictly Come Dancing on Ice*.

With fifteen minutes still to go many of the Leeds supporters were making for the exits as if they were passengers on the *Titanic*, only the lifeboats were gone, and when Leeds conceded a stupid free kick, it's unlikely that any of them were that surprised when Bündchen stepped up to take it and promptly scored again, blasting the ball cleverly underneath the feet of the players' wall, which jumped as one to try to head it clear.

We were still celebrating that one in the dugout when Christoph scored the last goal of the match. In truth it was comedy gold: Paddy Kenny cleared his line only to gift the ball to Dominguin, who volleyed it to Bündchen as if recognising a player who was on the form of his life. The German *wünderkind* proceeded to run straight at the goalkeeper with the ball balanced on his head until, just as the keeper reached him, he dropped the ball onto his toe and tapped it in.

It's generally held that the FA Cup is not what it used to be, that the bonus money in the Premier League means that no one much cares about the FA Cup any more, but that's not how it seemed to us. A cold January evening in Yorkshire never felt as good as it did to me that night in Leeds. We took the ball with us when we boarded the coach to take us to Leeds Bradford International Airport and awarded it to Christoph, who – showing a sense of diplomacy far beyond his years – promptly gave it to the club's absurdly grateful Ukrainian proprietor. As we drove away it seemed to me that Billy Bremner was shaking both his fists at the sky and the capricious gods of football.

On the coach I was already having to deal with a list of

injuries as long as the faces of the Leeds supporters we'd seen outside the ground. The worst of these was our centre back, Gary Ferguson, whose ankle had locked up again.

'There's no diffuse idiopathic skeletal hyperstosis,' explained Nick Scott, the team doctor. 'He's just knackered. So that's all right.'

'Fucking hell,' I said, knowing full well that Ferguson, who was a Scouser, was sitting right behind me. 'The only part of that I understand is him being an idiot.'

'He's probably got some osteophytes floating around in the joint which are causing his ankle to seize up.'

'That explains why his passing was so shit,' I said.

'Thanks a lot,' said Ferguson. 'I was trying me best.'

'I know, that's what made it so fucking painful to watch.'

'We should get it X-rayed this time,' the doctor told me. 'I think we've reached the end of being able to treat this with anti-inflammatories.'

'Or we could just shoot the poor bastard,' I said. 'Might be kinder. Cheaper, too.'

Osteophytes. We used to call these bone spurs, or parrot beaks, but whatever you call them the effect is the same: they severely limit joint movement and cause extreme pain. I knew what that was like as my own ankles were none too good after a decade playing the game; sometimes I count myself lucky that I went to prison and I didn't play on into my thirties with the help of corticosteroids injected into my ageing joints. As it is I hobble through my flat in the morning like I'm looking for my Zimmer frame. A few years ago I saw Tommy Smith giving a speech at a dinner; I was shocked that Liverpool's hardest ever club captain now needs sticks or a wheelchair to get around. It's a hard truth but even today being an athlete can fuck you up.

'Talk about a Pyrrhic victory,' I said to the doc. 'It's the curse of Billy Bremner.'

'Who's Billy Bremner?' asked Ferguson.

'Black bloke, used to play for Leeds,' I answered patiently.

'And what's a Pyrrhic victory?'

I saw no point in giving a history lesson to someone who thought that Napoleon was a type of brandy and that Nelson was a fucking wrestler. It's true I have a university degree, though it's a 2:2 from Birmingham, not a First from Oxbridge, but while I reckon I possess an above average intelligence, next to some of the lads on our team I'm Richard fucking Dawkins.

'It means a win that's so bloody good it gives you a hard-on,' I told him.

Even before we reached the airport the weather suddenly changed for the worse. The team coach felt like our own little snow globe.

CHAPTER 10

We were late getting back from Leeds. The flight was delayed by the snow. As usual my mind was buzzing after the match and it was almost 2 a.m. when I finally went to bed. I took the bed in the spare room so as not to wake Sonja, who sleeps like a cat. When I woke up the following morning it was with the knowledge that she'd already gone to work – she has a practice in Knightsbridge shrink-wrapping people who have eating disorders: people who are fat, or anorexic – and that there was someone ringing my doorbell.

I slid out of bed, hobbled to the entryphone and found a woman staring up at the camera. For a moment I thought it must be one of Sonja's patients except that she was neither thin nor fat; in fact, she was just right.

'Mr Manson?'

'Yes?'

'I'm sorry to disturb you, sir. But we did make an appointment for ten o'clock this morning. My name is Detective Inspector Louise Considine, from the police station at Brent. I'm investigating the death of Matt Drennan.'

'Right. I'm sorry. Had a late night. You'd better come up.'

I buzzed her in, threw on a pair of jeans and a sweater, and poured some bottled mineral water into my one-touch, bean-to-cup coffee machine. At nearly four grand it was the pride and joy of my kitchen. I couldn't cook very much, but I could make a delicious caffè latte.

She was better-looking than most coppers I'd seen, and believe me, I've seen a lot. Wholesome-looking and frankly a bit fairy-like, she had long fair hair, big blue eyes and a nose that was sort of pointy. She was wearing a short grey coat and leather gloves.

'Did you forget? That we had a meeting? Oh dear, I'm sorry. You certainly look like you forgot.'

'We had a match yesterday. And the flight back was delayed by snow. Please. Take off your coat and have a seat.'

'Thanks.'

'Want some coffee?'

'Yes, please, if you're making it. Milk and no sugar.'

I nodded and flicked a switch on the machine.

'That looks impressive,' she said. She sounded posh – too posh to be a copper.

'It does everything except wash the cup afterwards.'

She shrugged off her coat and went to inspect some of the paintings on my walls.

'This is good,' she said, examining a largish picture of a thuggish-looking man with a shaven head and raised fists. He looked like a bare-knuckle fighter. 'He's rather frightening, isn't he?'

'That one's by Peter Howson,' I said. 'Scottish artist. I bought that painting to remind myself of what it was like to be in prison. There were several times when I found myself sharing a cell with blokes just like him. People who were always ready to put a fist down your throat for no good reason. Every time I look at it I tell myself how incredibly lucky I am. Lucky that I was able to put all that behind me. Unlike nearly everyone else who comes out of the nick.'

'It's a nice place you've got here, Mr Manson. You have very good taste.'

'You mean for someone in football.'

'You must be rich to live round here.'

'I only work in football,' I said. 'I make money from something else that doesn't require me to do anything at all.'

'Yes, you're a director of Pedila Shoes.' She smiled. 'I Googled you. It was easier than tapping your phone or having you followed twenty hours a day. These days police work is mostly done with the aid of web-crawlers and hyperlinks, html and meta-tags.'

'That explains why you don't look anything like a copper.'

She smiled. 'How is a copper supposed to look, then?'

'Not like you. You look like you just finished your law degree.' I smiled. 'I read your business card. Or at least a picture of it on my iPhone. LLB, wasn't it?'

She raised an eyebrow at me. 'I do have flat feet. And I can say fuck a lot. If that helps.'

I brought her the coffee and then sat down opposite her.

'It makes two cups at once. Fuck.'

'Time is precious.'

'Isn't it?' She tasted her coffee and nodded with appreciation. 'Mmm. Good, too.'

'Java beans. From the Algerian Coffee Stores, in Soho.'

'I love that place. I should warn you: I'm liable to come here again. This is much better than my local coffee shop.'

'And I should warn you, I don't much like the police.'

'Yes, I know. I was warned about that by my chief inspector. And from what I've read about you I'm lucky this coffee isn't poisoned.'

I smiled. 'I should wait and see, if I were you, Miss Considine.'

'I don't blame you at all for thinking ill of the police. I'm sure I'd feel the same way if I'd been wrongly convicted of something.'

'I was fitted up. That's what happened.'

'But the Met is very different today from how it was, even a few years ago.'

She had a sexy way of talking, as if she knew the effect her voluptuous mouth had on things as ordinary as words; every sentence seemed to end in a pout. She sipped her coffee and glanced around the room again.

'I'll take your word for it.'

'Please do. I was very sorry to hear about Mr Drennan. But if I'm honest, it seems that I only ever knew him as someone who was famous for being drunk and getting himself into one scrape after another. It's hard for me to connect someone as clownish as him with top-level sport.'

'What you have to remember is that a lot of footballers – and I do mean a lot – are just overgrown schoolboys. Every team has someone who's as much of a comedian as Drenno was. But there are very few teams that have someone as talented as him. In his day Drenno was perhaps the most outstanding player in the country. Look, there are a lot of wankers in football – just watch *Soccer AM* – but Matt Drennan wasn't one of them.'

'Yes, I read your tweets about him. And watched some of his goals on YouTube.' She shrugged as if she was hardly impressed with what she'd seen.

'Do you follow a team?'

'Chelsea.'

'It figures.'

'Does it? Oh dear. That makes me sound very predictable. Unlike Matt Drennan. I mean, I know he was your friend and I'm sorry to say this, but to me he always looked like an accident waiting to happen.'

'Not like that.'

'No?'

'I certainly never expected him to go and hang himself, if that's what you want to know.'

She nodded. 'It is, among other things.'

'I expect there will have to be a post-mortem and an inquest,' I said.

She nodded again.

'Will I have to give evidence?'

'Perhaps. Did you know his wife, too?'

'Yes. I was at the wedding. Actually, I was at both his weddings.'

'She says she'd already thrown him out. For good this time, according to her. And that was before he beat the shit out of her.'

'So I believe. How is she, by the way?'

'At home now. Avoiding the newspapers and the newspapermen who are camped out at the bottom of her drive.'

'I tried calling her, but...'

'She's not answering the phone. Now, I appreciate that this might be difficult for you, but I need to ask you some questions about exactly what happened when Drennan was here. After all, you were one of the last people to speak to him before he killed himself. At least according to Maurice McShane you were. It was on your behalf that he contacted us, wasn't it?'

'Yes. It was. I wanted to help with your enquiries.'

'Of course.'

'And I think I was, probably, one of the last people to see Matt.'

I told her precisely what had happened.

'So he was drunk and he was depressed,' she said.

I nodded. 'Definitely. I even offered to drive him to the Priory. I could see he was in a bad way. But he wouldn't let me. I mean he was pissed, but he wasn't that pissed. Not by his standards. I mean he wasn't legless. Besides, he'd been before – to the Priory – and it didn't work.'

'Did he say what he was depressed about?'

'How long have you got? The fight with his wife would have depressed him. He'd lost his diamond stud, from his ear – like I told you. He told me she'd thrown a boot at him but he didn't say he'd assaulted her. I suppose that might have resulted in a custodial sentence because he'd assaulted her before. That would have depressed him, too.' I shrugged. 'What else? Not being able to play football any more. Getting older. His health. Drinking again. Being broke. Life in general. It's a typical football story, I'm afraid. Look, he certainly didn't mention that he was going to kill himself. But if he had I'm not sure what I could have done about it.'

'You could have kept him here and talked him out of it, perhaps.'

'Clearly you didn't know Matt Drennan. You couldn't talk him out of an off-licence or a last game of bar-billiards, let alone what you're suggesting, Miss Considine.'

'So he didn't say anything to you about his best friend from Glasgow, Tommy MacDonald.'

'Mackie? No, nothing at all.'

'You know he was in the army. In Afghanistan.'

'Kind of. Hey, has something happened to Mackie?'

'Sergeant Thomas MacDonald was blown up on patrol in Helmand Province last Tuesday.'

'Christ.'

'He died later on, in hospital.'

'No, I didn't know that.' I nodded. 'But it certainly explains a great deal about Drenno's mood. He never really talked all that much about Mackie. At least not to me. But I know he and Mackie were close. You might even say they were partners in crime, since they were always in trouble for one thing or another: fighting, vandalism, practical jokes that went too far, general bad behaviour. It was nearly always drink-related. When Mackie joined the army I think my old club Arsenal were more than a little bit relieved. They figured he was a bad influence on Drenno. But actually I'm sure it was the other way round. Mackie joined the army to get away from Drenno and the drinking. At least that's what Drenno always said.'

'Did you know Sergeant MacDonald?'

'I met him a few times. I couldn't say that we were friends, though. We weren't. I didn't like him, to be honest. I'm sorry he's dead. He served his country and you have to respect anyone for that.'

'Why didn't you like him? Any particular reason?'

I shrugged. 'Like I said, I thought he was a bad influence. Frankly I was very surprised when he went into the army. He'd spent a lifetime sponging off Drenno and he was the most ill-disciplined sod you could hope to meet. A typically belligerent Scot. It was hard to see why he should suddenly have decided he wanted to do something like join the army. Unless it was just to get away from Drenno.'

'Tell me, what was Matt Drennan wearing when he came to see you?'

'You mean was he wearing an England shirt?'

'No, I mean what was he wearing?'

'Leather jacket. Jeans. Trainers. Plain white shirt. There was blood on the collar. And on his earlobe. I already

83

explained that. *Was* he wearing an England shirt when he hanged himself?'

'I'm really not at liberty to say.'

'It was in the *Daily Mail*.'

'Then it must be true.'

'Why do I get the feeling you're not being straight with me, Miss Considine?'

'One: you don't like the police – you said so yourself, Mr Manson. And two: I'm not being straight with you because I'm here to ask questions, not to provide you with answers. Sorry. This is a police inquiry into a man's death. Even if it looks for all the world like a suicide, there are still rules of evidence I have to observe. As a police officer I operate to a different standard than the *Daily Mail*. Look, all I'm trying to do is build a picture of Matt Drennan's last few hours so that there's no room for any doubt that he killed himself. And in case that seems a rather laborious matter of dotting the "i"s and crossing the "t"s, it is; however, we live in an age of conspiracies and it won't be long before someone who read a book called *Who Killed Kurt Cobain?* Or *Who Killed Princess Diana?* Or *Who Killed Michael Jackson?* is tempted to write a book called *Who Really Killed Matt Drennan?* That's what I'm hoping to avoid. For his sake. For the sake of his family and friends.'

'Fair enough. And I appreciate you saying so.'

'I'm glad you think so. I certainly wouldn't like you to sue the Met again because of my incompetence or dishonesty.'

I nodded. 'I'm beginning to see why they sent you to see me.'

'Oh, good. Then we're making progress.'

'You are. I'm not sure about the Met.'

'Do you mind if I ask you a question you might find a little insensitive?'

'You mean the comments about Drenno being a waste of space weren't?'

'I didn't say that.'

I shrugged. 'Be my guest.'

'Thank you. Well then, it's this. I'm puzzled. You have a university degree. You speak several languages. You live in a fifteen-million-pound apartment in Chelsea. Why would someone as obviously successful as you, Mr Manson, still have a friend who was as big a loser as Matt Drennan?'

'That's not insensitive. It's just a little ignorant of what football is about, Miss Considine. You see football is an international club, a fraternity – a bit like the Freemasons. Wherever you go it's almost inevitable that you'll run into someone you once played with, or against. Matt Drennan was my team mate. What's more, he was the only team mate who came to see me when I was in prison. He came even though he'd been advised by the people who were trying to manage his image *not* to come. At that time it was me who was the loser, not him. I was scum. A rapist. That picture by Peter Howson. That's what people thought of when they thought of me. Everyone but Drenno. Not many people know it, but Drenno lost a sponsorship deal with a pharmaceutical company because he came to see me in the nick. So, for all his faults, he had a good heart and I loved him for it.'

She nodded and placed her coffee cup on the low table in front of her.

'Thanks for your help,' she said. 'And thanks for the excellent coffee. By the way, did you win yesterday?'

'Yes. We won. 8–0.' I smiled. 'That's good, by the way. Very good. In case you were wondering.'

CHAPTER 11

In the week leading up to the Newcastle match, Kenny Traynor arrived at the club and gave his first interview on the Press Bureau TV Sports Channel. Our new goalkeeper was a big fair-haired lad with an easy smile and an accent that was as thick as the head on a pint of heavy. When he spoke it was like listening to Spud in *Trainspotting*. As a result Zarco insisted on my appearing with them in front of the invited newsmen, *to translate*, which added a usefully comic touch to these dull proceedings. Otherwise it was the usual bullshit about how Traynor was 'really looking forward to the challenge of the Premier League and working with a world-class manager like João Zarco'. Asked why he had decided to join City instead of another club like MUFC, Traynor made no mention of fifty thousand quid a week, but instead talked about the quality of the squad and the attractions of living in a great city like London. Asked what he thought he could achieve at a club like London City – which is more or less the same question, when you think about it – Traynor declared he wanted to keep a clean sheet for as long as possible and to help City to win the Premier League. Champions League... FA Cup... Zzzzz.

Traynor and Zarco were also filmed in the doorway of Hangman's Wood holding up Traynor's new silver goal-keeping shirt with his name on the back. That's the thing I hate most about football: the clichés. You can't blame the players for that – they're just kids, most of them; Traynor's only twenty-three and he doesn't know any better. No, I blame the fucking reporters for asking the same old tired and predictable questions that produce these clichéd answers.

Things got a little more interesting when Bill Fleming, an old warhorse of a reporter from STV in Glasgow, suggested that it was extremely insulting to Scots viewers to have what Kenny Traynor was saying 'translated into English', as if they were ignorant of the language. Zarco paused for a short moment and then asked me to translate what Fleming had said, which got a big laugh. I think he understood perfectly well, but Zarco's comic timing was always excellent. He waited for me to repeat Fleming's complaint and then smiled.

'I don't mean to be insulting,' said Zarco. 'But I have been told that it's not just the Portuguese who have a problem understanding Scottish people. It's English people, too. So where is the insult in having a translation? That is something I don't understand. Scott Manson is from Scotland and I understand everything that he says. You, Mr Fleming, you are from Scotland but I don't understand anything of what you say. You say you speak English, and I will take your word for it, but this is not how it sounds to me. Maybe the problem is not with me but with you, my friend. Maybe you should learn to speak better English, like Scott here. Perhaps this is something Kenny will also achieve while he is playing at London City. I don't know. I hope so, for his sake. To make yourself understood in a foreign country is not so difficult, I think. Everyone here seems to understand me all right. But I'm no Professor Henry Higgins and I don't care about the rain in Spain. For sure I can help to make Kenny a better goalkeeper, but I'm the wrong person to offer him speech elocution on how he can make himself understood. Maybe if he opens his mouth a little when he speaks it will be better, I don't know. You should try that yourself, Bill.'

To his credit Kenny Traynor kept on smiling good-naturedly while his new boss was speaking. Lots of people were laughing but they did not include Bill Fleming.

Later that day I found myself translating again, this time from German. Our new star striker, Christoph Bündchen, came to see me in my office at Hangman's Wood. He spoke good English but told me that he preferred to speak in German, in case anyone overheard our conversation.

'Is something the matter, Christoph?'

'No, not at all,' he said. 'But I wanted to have your advice about something.'

'Sure. What is it?'

'First of all I want you to know how much I love this club, and how much I like living in London.'

My stomach lurched a little; Christoph Bündchen was quite likely a star striker in the making, and one we had bought cheaply, but where was this going? What was he going to tell me? That he was a compulsive gambler like 'Fergie Fledgling' Keith Gillespie? A secret boozer like Tony Adams? A compulsive gambler *and* a secret boozer like Paul Merson? Or had he already been tapped up by Chelsea – who had form for this, of course – or one of the other big clubs? Not that I had much time for the FA's farcical rule against tapping up: good players were always going to be tapped up. Tapping up – approaching a player contracted to another club without its permission – has always been part of the game. I smiled thinly and tried to contain my jangling nerves.

'That sounds ominous. Please don't tell me you want a

transfer to another club. You've only just got here and made your mark. We need you, son.'

'This is very difficult for me, Scott.'

'Look, if it's about pay then I've already spoken to Zarco. He's confident that we can get you another ten grand a week.'

'Thank you, but it's not about money. Or a transfer. It's about something else. I don't really feel I can be who I am. I'm different from these guys.'

He folded his arms defensively, stood back on one heel and then tapped his lips with a forefinger, like Samir Nasri making his famous shush gesture. (I still don't get why he does that – who the fuck is he telling to be quiet? The fans?)

'Different? How?'

'When I was playing in Augsburg I was living in Munich.'

'I know. That's where we met, remember?'

'Yes, but do you want to know why I was living in Munich?'

For a brief moment I wondered if he was a neo-Nazi and then rejected the idea; Christoph only looked like a Nazi.

I shrugged. 'Munich is a nicer city than Augsburg. At least that's my own impression.'

'Have you heard of a part of Munich called the Glockenbachviertel?'

'Yes, I think so. It's the trendy part. Lots of art galleries. I often used to go there and look for paintings.'

Christoph nodded. 'There are lots of gay people living in that part of Munich.' He paused for a moment. 'That's why I was living there, Scott. Because I couldn't live the way I wanted in Augsburg. What I mean to say is I was living in Munich with a man.'

I felt my spirits sink. This was going to be coaching football at its most challenging. The only gay footballers who'd ever stepped out of the closet as far as I was aware were Thomas Hitzlsperger and Justin Fashanu, and Fashanu committed suicide, which wasn't exactly an encouraging precedent for anyone else in the game who felt moved to declare his homosexuality.

'Right. I see.'

'It's just that Mr Zarco said some things the other day on television about the Qatari World Cup – about having gay friends – which was very encouraging. And I thought that perhaps it might be all right to be gay at this club. Unlike my last club, where I had to live a kind of lie about who and what I was. Which is hard, you know?'

I winced a little at the mention of Zarco and the Qataris. Since his comments about the 2022 World Cup the London City press office had been besieged with threats from anonymous Arabs; we'd had three bomb threats at Hangman's Wood. Meanwhile the Qataris continued to deny any impropriety and FIFA's executive committee in Zurich had complained to the FA about Zarco; as a result of this the FA had felt obliged to cancel their invitation to Zarco to become a member of its England team think tank. Zarco's response to all this would certainly have been to repeat his allegations had Phil Hobday not told him to button it.

'Look, Christoph, if you're asking me for advice on being gay, I can't give you any. I have one or two friends who are gay but none of them are in football. But if you're asking me what I think you're going to ask me...'

'Should I tell the guys in the team I'm gay? That's what I want to know. That's what I'd like.'

'Then the answer is no, absolutely fucking not. Don't ask me to justify it, Christoph, because I can't, but being gay is just not acceptable in football for the simple reason that the game is the last bastion of open bigotry and homophobia. There are no openly gay footballers in any of England's top four divisions. Of course that's not to say there are no gay players. Everyone knows who they are, or thinks they do, but those players keep it quiet for one simple reason: fear. Not of the other players, but fear of the abuse an openly gay player would receive from the fans. Right now there are lots of fans on terraces all over England who still sing songs about the Munich air crash and about the Hillsborough disaster, and who make gassing noises towards Tottenham fans who are all presumed, wrongly, to be Jews. In my time in football I've heard these bastards sing songs about Sol Campbell's mental breakdown, Dwight Yorke's disabled son, Karren Brady's miscarriage, the floods in Hull, and the excellent public service done by various murderers including Harold Shipman and Ian Huntley. All of which means that there's quite enough shit that they can throw at you already without giving them anything more. That's why you can't tell anyone, Christoph. Wear a pair of rainbow football laces if it makes you feel any better; there are at least some straight players who've done that. Otherwise you have to keep this quiet. You'll be committing career suicide if you say something now. I know this is not what you wanted to hear, but I'm sorry, that's just how it is.'

Bündchen sighed. Looking at him now it was hard to believe the young German could be gay; then again, I never notice these things. Sonja claims she can tell, but I never can. A small part of me wanted to applaud him for his desire to be so open, but mostly I felt I'd told him how it was. Individually most football fans would probably tell you they couldn't care less about someone's sexuality, but on the terraces, a different mood prevails. The Germans have a word for it: *Volksgeist*. It means 'the spirit of the people', and the spirit of the people usually collects around the lowest common denominator.

'Look, you have a wonderful talent and on the basis of what I saw the other night against Leeds, you have a fantastic future ahead of you, Christoph. You could do anything in the game. You could play for your country, make a great deal of money and get right to the top of football. And having got there – who knows? In a few years it could be you who leads from the front and who changes things for the better. I for one hope they do change. But you're at the start of your career and right now my advice to you is never to talk about this with anyone but me at this club. Anyone at all. The fewer people who know about this the better.'

'I see.' He shrugged. 'It's disappointing.'

'I'm sorry, Christoph. Truly I wish I could tell you something different. But best keep it quiet, eh? At least until your career is over. And then talk about it. The same way Thomas Hitzlsperger did.'

He nodded. 'All right. If you think it's best.'

I breathed a sigh of relief as he went out of the door.

But Christoph Bündchen wasn't the only one at London City with a secret that had required me to play counsellor. The fact that Zarco was having an affair with Claire Barry, who was the club's acupuncturist, had become common knowledge at Hangman's Wood – so common that I had felt prompted to speak to him about it. Me, of all people, offering him advice on the wisdom of having an affair with a woman who was herself married. Claire was a decent woman but her husband, Sean, was a bit of a thug; and if he wasn't he knew plenty who were. He ran a private security company that did a lot of work in the Gulf States, which meant he was frequently away; he also employed a lot of people who were used to solving problems with violence.

'People are beginning to talk about you and her,' I'd said over the Christmas holidays, which is a very busy time for an acupuncturist at a football club, as you might perhaps imagine. 'Tell me to fuck off and mind my own business if you like, but I'm your friend. You've been good to me and I wouldn't like to see anything happen to you, João. The press would love to give you a going-over for something like this. Remember what happened to John Terry. They think you're an arrogant bastard and they're just waiting to catch you out. So why don't you cool it for a while? I'm not telling you to forget her. That's up to you. All I'm doing is telling you to keep it zipped for a while. Just to put people off the scent.'

He listened quietly, and then nodded. 'You're right, Scott. You were quite right to tell me. And thanks. I'd no idea this was well known at the club. I appreciate it, my friend. And I'll certainly do as you say. I'll tell her it's got to stop.'

Of course, Zarco completely ignored me. How do I know that? I don't for sure. But a couple of days before the Newcastle game I noticed he had a packet of single-use, sterile acupuncture needles on his desk. He saw me pick them up and offered an explanation before I could even mention it.

'Claire's been showing me how to treat my own knee,' he said, taking the needles out of my hand.

'In here?'

'Yes, in here.'

'You mean you sit in here and stick needles in your own knee?'

'Yes. Of course. What else would I be doing with these needles?'

'I don't know.'

Like a lot of ex-players Zarco suffered from painful knees and acupuncture was able to provide a more effective and safer form of pain relief than drugs and creams. That wasn't what was suspicious. It was him dropping the needles in the bin while he was talking that made the explanation sound so lame it needed crutches. It looked like someone getting rid of evidence and frankly, given the number of strokes he pulled, he ought to have been a bit better at it. For example, I knew he had three mobile phones: one for work, one for play and one for something else. The play phone and the one for something else he kept in a drawer in one of the filing cabinets in my office and took them out when he needed them; we both knew without him having to ask that this was fine with me. This was just one of his funny little ways and something you had to put up with if you were ever going to be a trusted friend of Zarco's. You've heard of mate's rates; well this was mate's traits.

'You should get her to show you how to do it,' he said. 'Maybe you could treat your ankle in the same way. There's no need to be squeamish about needles, you know. It's just one prick.'

For a brief irresponsible moment I considered telling him that he was the only prick I knew about before I thought better of it; he was the boss, after all, and if he was still shagging Claire Barry, it was none of my business.

Nor was it any of my business when, one afternoon, I dropped into a BP service station near Hangman's Wood to put petrol in my Range Rover. Now the club had an account at the nearest Shell garage and Viktor Sokolnikov always picked up the tab for everyone's fuel, a perk the taxman knew nothing about and which was worth several hundred pounds a week, especially when you were driving a Ferrari or an Aston Martin, as most of the players did at City. Consequently, no one ever went to the BP garage about three miles further on where they had to pay for petrol. No one except me, that is, for I had always been scrupulously honest in all my dealings with the Inland Revenue and I always paid for my own fuel. Untaxed perks were definitely not my thing. When you've been to prison you never want to go back there.

Zarco was sitting in his left-hand drive Overfinch Range Rover – identical to my own – which was parked next to a white Ferrari. He was having an animated discussion with the owner of the Ferrari, who I recognised immediately. It was Paolo Gentile, the agent who had handled Kenny Traynor's transfer. Now when you're a coach you see a lot in and around a football club that turns out to be not your business, and sometimes, if you want to keep your job, you learn to keep your fucking mouth shut. I learned that in the nick.

So I drove away again without even stopping.

CHAPTER 12

'You're a bloody little genius,' I told Colin Evans.

Colin blushed. He and I and Zarco and Viktor Sokolnikov were standing on the centre spot at Silvertown Dock. I'd brought a ball and had already bounced it several times just to see how it moved on top of the newly repaired surface. Then I tossed the ball in the air and began to play keepy-uppy, all the time trying to test what the spot felt like underneath my feet. I couldn't tell that anything was different.

'Yup,' I said. 'It's perfect.'

'Amen to that,' said Zarco and clapped the Welshman on the back. 'You've done a great job, Colin. I'm really very appreciative.'

'We aim to please,' said Colin.

Viktor was comparing the picture that I'd emailed to his iPhone with the ground we were standing on. 'Incredible,' he said. 'You wouldn't know there had ever been anything wrong here.' He chuckled. 'You know, the next time I have a dead body to bury quickly and without a trace, remind me to contact Colin. We can do it right here.'

I almost gasped. That was typical of Viktor Sokolnikov: making a joke out of a rumour that would have been acutely embarrassing to anyone else. Then again he was in a very good mood about something that wasn't anything to do with the pitch. His face was tanned and he was wearing an enormous Canada Goose coat that would not have looked out of place worn by Sir Ranulph Fiennes at the South Pole. In spite of the bitter January cold he was smiling broadly.

'Come to think of it,' he added, 'I wouldn't mind being buried here myself. As mausoleums go, I think the Crown of Thorns would be perfect.'

'Why not?' said Zarco. 'You paid for it, Viktor.'

'But I'd have to do it in secret,' said Viktor. 'The local council would never give me planning permission to get buried here. Not without a great deal of arm-twisting. And bribery, of course. You always need that. Even in this country.'

'We'll bury you in secret, if that's what you want. Won't we, guys? Just like Genghis Khan.'

Colin and I nodded. 'Sure. Whatever you want, Mr Sokolnikov.'

Viktor chuckled. 'Hey, take your time there. Reports of my death have been greatly exaggerated. I'm in no hurry to be under the ground. Let's think about burying Newcastle here tomorrow before it's my turn.'

'After the Leeds match?' said Zarco. 'We're unstoppable. Xavier Pepe's goal was probably the best goal I've ever seen in all my years as a manager. And Christoph Bündchen already looks like a star. The team is riding high, right now. Those Newcastle boys will be crapping themselves.'

'Let's hope so,' said Viktor. 'But we mustn't be overconfident, eh? We have a saying in Ukraine. The devil always takes back his gifts. I hear that Aaron Abimbole is going to be fit.'

Before signing for Newcastle in the summer, Aaron Abimbole had played for London City, and Manchester United, and AC Milan. In fact he collected clubs like some people collect air miles. The Nigerian was one of the highest-paid players in the Premier League and generally held to be one of the most temperamental, too; when he was good he was very, very good but when he was bad he was total crap. Abimbole's leaving London City – during Zarco's first tenure at the club – had been acrimonious, and prior to his departure relations with the Portuguese manager, who had bought him from the French club Lens, had become so bad that Abimbole had set fire to Zarco's brand new Bentley in the club car park.

'So what?' said Zarco. 'This particular Aaron doesn't have a brother called Moses, so I don't think we have anything to worry about.'

'He's already scored twenty goals for Newcastle this season,' said Viktor. 'That's twice as many as he scored for us when he was here. Maybe we should worry about that.'

'He's lazy,' insisted Zarco. 'I never saw a lazier player, which is why clubs don't keep him. He only scores when it's up his back to do so but he never tracks back. Not like Rooney. You have Rooney, you have a great striker and a dogged defender. When you have Abimbole all you have is a lazy cunt.'

Clearly the United fans had thought the same way as Zarco; I remember watching him play for MU against Fulham and the fans singing, *'Abimbole, Abimbole, He's a lazy arsehole, And he should be on the dole'*. You had to laugh.

'Besides,' added Zarco, 'Scott here has a brilliant plan to fuck with his mind. Wait and see, boss. We're going to put the hex on him.'

'I'm glad to hear it.'

Viktor glanced at his watch; unlike the rest of us he wore a cheap Timex. The first time I'd seen it I'd checked it out on Google in case it was actually a valuable antique, but it cost just £7.50, which was another reason why I liked Viktor – most of the time he wasn't in the least bit flashy; my suits from Kilgour were probably ten times more expensive than his. He was wearing the coat because it was cold. Only the billionaire's Berluti shoes were expensive. And the Rolls-Royce Phantom in the car park, of course.

'And now I'd best be going,' he said. 'I have an important meeting in the City. See you guys at the match on Saturday. Don't forget, João, you're coming to that pre-match lunch I'm hosting in the executive dining room for the RBG.' RBG was the Royal Borough of Greenwich.

'I wouldn't miss it for the world, boss,' said Zarco, drily.

'Good. Because you're the trophy guest,' said Viktor. 'At least you would be if we had any bloody trophies.' Laughing, he walked back to the players' tunnel, leaving the three of us staring at our much cheaper shoes.

'Cheeky bastard,' said Zarco.

'He's in a good mood,' I replied.

'I was just thinking the same thing,' said Colin.

'I know why, too,' said Zarco. 'This morning the RBG planning committee is going to announce that it has granted permission for the new Thames Gateway Bridge. It's going to be worth a lot of money to Viktor's company because they are building it, of course. That's why he's bringing the RBG council here for lunch on Saturday. To celebrate.'

'But he's paying for the bridge, isn't he?' I said. 'Rather a lot if the newspapers are correct.'

'He's paying for some of it, yes. But don't forget, the Thames Gateway is going to be a toll bridge. And the only bridge between Tower Bridge and the QEII Bridge. That's exactly ten kilometres of river either side of where it will be built. Fifty thousand vehicles a day – that's what they estimate. At five pounds a time, that's two hundred and fifty grand a day, gentlemen.'

'Five quid? Who's going to pay that?' asked Colin.

'It costs six quid to get across the Severn Bridge into Wales.'

'Surely it should be six quid to get out of Wales,' I muttered.

'It's only two quid to go through the Dartford Tunnel,' persisted Colin.

'Yes, but it takes forever,' I said.

'That's right,' said Zarco. 'So you do the math. They reckon the new bridge will make more than eighty million a year, just in tolls, and pay for itself in less than five years. You see? It only looks like philanthropy for five years, then it starts to look like very good business. He owns the bridge for the next ten years after that, before he gives it as a gift to the people of the RBG; but by then he'll have made at least eight hundred million. Maybe more.'

'No wonder he's smiling,' I said.

'He's not smiling,' said Zarco. 'He's laughing. All the way to the Sumy Capital Bank of Geneva. Which, by the way, he also owns.'

'That must come in handy when you need an overdraft,' said Colin.

'Did you hear that?' Zarco shook his head and smiled, wryly. 'Trophy guest, indeed. He never misses an opportunity to have a little dig at me.'

'Talking of having a dig,' said Colin, 'that copper came back here, to the Crown of Thorns. Detective Inspector Neville. He wasn't very pleased to see we'd filled in and grassed over the hole.'

'What did he expect us to do with it?' snarled Zarco. 'Play around it?'

'He said we should have let him know we were going to fill it in. That it was evidence. That they hadn't had time to take a photograph.'

'I'll send him a photograph of a hole,' I said. 'Only it won't be a hole in the ground.'

'What did you tell him?' asked Zarco. 'The cop. You didn't tell him about *my* photograph, I hope.'

'No, of course not. Look, all I told him was what Scott told me to tell him. That he took full responsibility.'

'What did he say to that?'

'He said that suing the Metropolitan Police successfully had made you too big for your boots and that it was time someone took you down a peg or two.'

'He said that?'

Colin nodded.

'The cunt. You're sure it was me he was talking about and not João?'

Colin nodded again.

'Hey, don't drag me into this,' said Zarco. 'I've enough enemies already.'

'You've noticed that too, huh?'

CHAPTER 13

João Zarco had been on the front of *GQ* and *Esquire* and was frequently voted the best-dressed man in football; on match day he cut a very dapper figure in his Zegna suits, cashmere coats and silk scarves. Sometimes he seemed to be as famous for his designer stubble, his Tiffany cufflinks and his bling watches as for his candid thoughts about football. Perhaps that's not a surprise; these days you don't just judge a club by results but by the style of the manager, and if you doubt that then ask yourself this: if you were obliged to support a club because of the manager, who would you choose? José Mourinho or Sir Alex Ferguson? Pep Guardiola or David Moyes? Diego Simeone or Rafa Benitez? AVB or Guus Hiddink? These days it's not just the image rights of players that are important to football clubs; how a manager looks can actually affect the club's share price. Winning is no longer enough on its own; winning while looking good is the essence of the modern game.

I like good suits but I think it's important that, unlike the manager, the coach dresses like his players on a match day. Besides, it looks a bit weird if you take charge of the warm-up in a tailor-made whistle that cost five grand. I don't like tracksuits very much but I always wear one on the day of a match; picking training cones off the pitch and doing mountain climbs alongside the lads is just easier in a tracksuit.

London City is nicknamed Vitamin C because the club colours are orange and because it's good for you; no one in east London gives a fuck about Ukraine's Orange Revolution in 2004, which is why the club colours are orange in the first place. A lot of modern kit looks like it was designed by the art class in a primary school. You expect African World Cup sides to wear shirts that look like shit, and even a few Scottish ones, but not big European sides. Was there ever a worse kit than the one Athletico Bilbao wore in 2004, which looked like some fat bloke's intestines?

City's kit was designed by Stella McCartney, and so were the tracksuits. I don't mind the kit so much: the orange makes your players easy to see on the park, and on a foggy night in Leeds that can be a real advantage. It's the equivalent of playing golf with an orange ball; it seems that seventy-three per cent of golfers find a vividly coloured ball easier to see in flight and on the grass. Come to think of it, that must be why I'm so crap at golf.

In truth, Sonja likes the City tracksuits better than I do. It helps that hers is a size too small and when she wears it she looks just like Uma Thurman in *Kill Bill: Volume 1*, only without the Hattori Hanzō sword. But when I'm wearing an orange tracksuit I look like a fucking carrot. We all do. Which is why some rival supporters call us cat shit; apparently some cat shit is orange. You learn something every day.

When Sonja puts her tracksuit on it's all I can do not to put my hands inside her bottoms, so I usually don't bother trying to resist the temptation; unless it's the day of a big game when, out of solidarity with my players – who are supposed to refrain from sex on the day of a match in order to keep their testosterone levels high – I do my best not to touch her. Testosterone helps players remain aggressive and it's generally held that aggression helps sportsmen to win. Of course, Sonja knows I find her sexy when she's wearing the tracksuit and, on a match-day morning, she often wears it anyway and then goes out of her way to be sexually provocative; I don't know what else you'd call it when she wears the tracksuit bottoms a little too far down her butt and with a tiny bit of dental floss that masquerades as a pair of knickers. Then again she never has knickers like that on for very long; not when I'm around.

You wouldn't believe how different Sonja looks when she goes off to her Knightsbridge consulting rooms to listen to girls discuss their eating disorders – anorexic girls on Tuesdays and Thursdays, fat girls on Mondays and Wednesdays: it wouldn't ever do for them to be in the same waiting room. She doesn't think my jokes on that subject are very funny, however.

Sonja wears a lot of nice Max Mara suits, good shoes and stockings. It's her Dr Melfi look, which I find almost as sexy as her arse in an orange tracksuit. Unlike a lot of the girls she treats, Sonja has a great-looking arse – she works out a lot – and if I mention her arse so fondly it's because the part of me that's still a player seems to find it easier talking about how attractive and sexy my girlfriend is than saying how much I love her, which I do. Like a lot of men in football I find it hard to discuss my feelings; being a shrink she's aware of that and makes allowances. At least I think she does. She knew I was already upset about what had happened to Didier Cassell and then to Drenno, which was why I didn't talk about it; and until the day of the Newcastle match I really thought that the worst had already happened. But in truth it hadn't, not by a long chalk.

I expect Ukrainians like Viktor Sokolnikov have all sort of poetic proverbs and sayings for it, but where I come from we just say this: that troubles come in a packet of three.

CHAPTER 14

Zarco and I always picked the team in his office at Hangman's Wood before boarding the coach to Silvertown Dock. Organising a squad of overpaid, often intellectually challenged young men can be like herding cats and it's always better if everyone arrives at the stadium as a team to avoid any confusion.

There's a lot of bullshit talked about choosing the tactics before you choose the team but here's a truth: unless you want to rest someone for a more important fixture you always pick the very best players available to you. It's really that simple. Anything else is just Fantasy fucking Football. The press loves to speculate that one player has been picked at the expense of another – to cause trouble, if they can – but if someone has been left on the bench there's usually a damn good reason, and more often than not it's simply to do with fitness and attitude. Attitude is even more important than fitness because even when a player is fully fit, he'll sometimes get it into his head that he's not playing well. And if there's one thing that a manager or a coach is paid to do, it's to try and fix whatever is going wrong in a player's mind. To that extent it's useful living with a psychiatrist, as she gives me some good tips on motivation.

Of course, now and then you get a player who pulls a sickie and claims that he's not fully fit, although this isn't nearly as common these days. Thankfully physios are better able than ever to find out if a player is bullshitting you about a niggling muscle or hamstring, and to treat it, too: electrotherapy, ultrasound, lasers, magnetotherapy, diathermy and traction therapy can fix a lot of problems in a short period of time. If all else fails you can always inject some cortisone into a joint that's giving pain, and few players are even remotely keen on that solution; the truth is it hurts to have a needle pushed four or five millimetres into a leg. It hurts like buggery.

After we'd picked the team, Zarco left early in his own car to attend Viktor's lunch, grumbling about how he had better things to do on the day of a match than meet with a lot of Greenwich planning officers and town councillors. Apart from that he was in a very good mood and loudly confident that we were going to stuff it to the Toon.

I waited for the team to show up at the training ground and boarded the coach with them. There are always one or two who manage to be late and in those cases I have to order them to pay a fine. But today was different; two players were late for the team coach but these were my two Africans – Kwame Botchwey and John Ayensu were both from Ghana – and I had a very good reason for wanting them on my side so for once, fines were not imposed.

We arrived at Silvertown Dock at about the same time as the Newcastle team and let them go in first in order to avoid confusing the sports reporters, who were waiting in the players' tunnel to watch the yobs walk into the dressing room. In their woolly hats and big Dr Dre headphones, and dragging carry-on luggage containing all their personal items, our yobs looked much like the Toon yobs. Besides, I had an extra reason to want to keep the two teams apart for as long as possible.

Fit or not, everyone in the team is obliged to turn up for the team coach on a match day; that's how it works. Even the players who are injured or on the transfer list like Ayrton Taylor are required to put in an appearance, although generally speaking they can remain in their normal clothes. In Taylor's case this seemed to involve looking like a tramp, which, after the match, was going to cost him a fine: at Silvertown Dock it's jackets and ties for players who aren't playing through injury or for disciplinary reasons.

I shook hands with the Newcastle management and coaching team: Alan Pardew, John Carver, Steve Stone and Peter Beardsley. I have a lot of time for Beardsley. People talk about Lionel Messi but, in his prime for the Toons, Beardsley was very like Messi. Like him, Beards could beat three men, get tripped, stay on his feet and score a beauty with either foot. Christ, he even looked like Messi. Some of these arrogant young bastards today should be honoured just to be on the same coach as Peter Beardsley.

Team sheets were exchanged and I gave theirs and ours to a club spokesman to read them out to the waiting reporters. As usual it was all filmed for London City TV and must have made some very boring television; then again, some fans will watch anything to do with football.

Feeling the butterflies now – I always get them before a match, even more now that I'm no longer playing – I went along to our dressing room and waited for Zarco to show up and do his pre-match talk. He was pretty good at this kind of thing. There was no one better at understanding and motivating men; he inspires loyalty and players just want to do well for him. If he hadn't been a football manager he'd have made a very good general, I think. But not a politician: he was much too direct and straight-talking to be a politician, although in my humble opinion what this country needs most is someone to tell us that we're all a bunch of lazy cunts.

The game was supposed to kick off at 4 p.m. but it was now nearly three and Zarco still wasn't here, so I picked up the dressing-room landline and I was about to call the dining room when Phil Hobday put his head around the door; he might have been club chairman but he wasn't above running the odd errand for Viktor Sokolnikov. Phil was smooth and talked the same language as Viktor; he was fond of comparing football clubs to big companies like Rolls-Royce, or Jaguar, or Barclays Bank. For Phil, London City was a company just like Thames Water. I'd learned a lot from Phil Hobday.

'Do you know where João is, Scott?'

'No. As a matter of fact I was just calling the dining room to tell him to get his arse down here.'

Hobday shook his head. 'He was there until about an hour ago, when he took a call and left. When he didn't return we thought he must have come down here. Viktor's pretty angry that he just buggered off like that without saying goodbye to any of his guests. Even he's gone to look for him.'

'Well, Zarco's not in here as you can see. Although I rather wish he was.' I shrugged. 'I take it you've called his mobile.'

'Tried. Several times. But it's pointless. The signal here on a match day is awful, as I'm sure you know.'

I nodded. 'Sixty thousand people trying to get reception. You might just as well get a word from God.'

'Is it possible he went to say hello to the Newcastle manager?'

'That's highly unlikely. There's not much love lost between those two. Besides, it's not considered appropriate to go into the other side's dressing room before a match in case you hear anything you shouldn't.'

'Talking of which – look, you don't think...'

Hobday beckoned me outside the dressing room for a moment.

'You don't think he's with – with her?'

'Who would that be, Phil?'

'Come on, Scott. Stop trying to cover for him. You know exactly who I'm talking about: our lady of the needles – Claire Barry. I know she must be in the ground because I just saw her old man in one of the hospitality bars upstairs.'

'Honestly? I'm sure he's not with her. Look, nothing is more important to João Zarco before a match than the match itself. You know that. Not Greenwich Borough Council, not her, not a quick shag in a broom cupboard. If he's not with you then this is where he would be.' I frowned. 'You are telling me everything, aren't you, Phil?'

'What do you mean?'

'He's not had another row with Viktor and walked out? You know what he's like. Sometimes he can be quite petulant.'

Phil shook his head. 'No. Absolutely not. They were the best of friends, upstairs. Really.'

I shook my head. 'Look, perhaps he got caught short, or something. Maybe he's in the bog. I'm sure he'll turn up. This is an important match. I'd look for him, only I've got to take charge of the warm-up. I'll call Maurice and see if he can find him. If anyone can, he can.'

'All right. Thanks, Scott.'

Phil went back to join Viktor's important guests, who were probably tucking into their lunch. Hobday didn't drink, himself, which was a pity as Viktor always served the best wines in the executive dining room. I could have used a large glass of Puligny-Montrachet myself.

I called Maurice on the landline and explained the situation.

110

'I'll get straight on it,' he said.

'And make sure you check the bogs, in case he's had an accident.'

I think that was the first time it crossed my mind that something might have happened to Zarco. He was a strong, fit man but you read all kinds of things about managers having heart attacks – almost half the football managers in the English league have had significant heart problems: Gérard Houllier, Glenn Roeder, Dario Gradi, Alex Ferguson, Joe Kinnear, Barry Fry, Graham Souness. As high-pressure jobs go, football management is one of the worst. When you're a player you can run that feeling off as soon as you go on the pitch; but a manager has to sit there and take it. Just look at Arsène Wenger's face during a game at the Emirates and tell me that he's a man who's relaxed about watching his team; and Arsenal are doing well right now.

I took the lads outside for the warm-up and tried to concentrate on the game in hand; the music on the loud-speakers in the ground hardly helped: it was Puff Daddy's 'I'll be Missing You'. By now I was certain that something must have happened to the Portuguese. Hadn't I seen him rubbing his arm and his chest that same morning as if he was in pain? I also spent some time checking out the opposition, who were warming up in the other half. Aaron Abimbole was playing and always reminded me of Patrick Vieira, the way he dominated the midfield: tall, with quick feet, good technique, aggressive and very brave, he was everything you want in a player. Well, almost. He had two faults: he was a greedy cunt and he was fucking lazy; sometimes he just wasn't in the mood, and that was why City had let him go. But that afternoon he already looked like he was itching to score against his old club, which left me starting

111

to get a pain myself. This was some extra pressure I didn't need.

After we'd warmed up I brought the lads back into the dressing room hoping to find Zarco there, but in the doorway I met Maurice, who was shaking his head.

'Can't find the cunt,' he murmured.

'Keep looking.'

Maurice nodded. 'Tell you what, though. There are some right bastards out there if he has gone missing.'

'What do you mean?'

'Unfriendly faces. That is, unfriendly to Zarco. Sean Barry for one.'

'He's a City supporter. Why the fuck would he be unfriendly?'

'Because he knows that Zarco's been banging his missus. That's why.'

'Shit. Look, Maurice, I don't have time for this. Call him at home. Call him at the fucking Ivy if you have to, just find him.'

I turned to face the dressing room.

'Right,' I said, 'listen up. The boss is feeling a bit Uncle Dick so I'm going to do the talking today. That means I talk, and you listen. Got that?' I repeated this in Spanish and then spoke in English again, doing the same all the way through my team talk:

'All right, here's the deal. Normally I'd be telling you that the number one threat out there this afternoon is going to be Aaron Abimbole, and to mark him like you were tied to him with a piece of red rope. But instead we're going to fuck with his mind and here's how. We're going to neutralise him. And this goes especially for you, Kwame, and for you, John.'

They both nodded keenly.

'The last time we played those Geordie boys I noticed you two were very friendly with Aaron, even though he wasn't playing. That was fine. I get that. You're friends. But this is a big game and this time it's going to be different. The fact is that man still feels just a little bit guilty about the way he left this club for more money. I want to exploit that feeling. So, when we're in the players' tunnel waiting to go out onto the park I want you to blank him, like he was Idi Amin and Charles Taylor and Laurent Kabila and Jerry fucking Rawlings all rolled up into the one shithead. Kwame and John will tell the rest of you ignorant bastards who those guys are later. Don't get me wrong. Aaron is a nice fellow. I never met a nicer one. But being in England has not been easy for him. He's never settled and it's my impression that he misses home a lot. Seeing you two African lads here today is a little touch of home that he appreciates. Only you're going to disappoint him, okay? After the game you can be as friendly as you like with him. But when you see him outside in the tunnel I want you to treat him like herpes. This goes for all of you. You don't shake his hand. You don't smile at him. It won't matter quite so much when he gets the cold shoulder from the white guys. But from Kwame and John it will fucking hurt. This is his old club, see? He thinks he can come back here with no hard feelings. Well, we have to make him think again about that. And just to rub it in I want you to treat the rest of those Toons like they were your best friends when you're in the tunnel. All of them. It's just Aaron I want singled out for special treatment. When he goes out on that park I want to see his bottom lip quivering like someone just stole his fucking train set.'

Kwame and John thought that this was a great idea – they were laughing and grinning at each other.

'That big stupid bastard is going to be so pissed off after the game when we tell him,' they said.

'Yeah, don't tell him it was my idea. I've got enough on my plate this afternoon without having to worry about him sticking one on me.'

'What about the official team handshake?' asked Kwame. 'Do we blank him then, too?'

'Absolutely, yes,' I said. 'Like he was fucking invisible.'

Minutes later, in the tunnel, I watched carefully as our players lined up quietly, ready to walk onto the pitch. Aaron Abimbole swaggered out of the Toon dressing room, no doubt feeling quite at home, grinning his big grin and glad-handing one or two officials; and he looked genuinely taken aback when he offered a brother's handshake to Kwame Botchwey and the Ghanaian turned the other way. I could almost hear him swallow his disappointment as John Ayensu did the same. But he kept grinning for a few moments longer as if he couldn't quite believe what was happening.

'S'a matter with you guys? What's wiv the dis?' asked the Nigerian. 'Something wrong wid you?'

Ayensu ignored him and bent around Abimbole to shake the Newcastle goalkeeper's hand.

Since his arrival in London Abimbole had managed to learn some Brixton black man argot; he was a quick learner.

'What's cracking, bruv? Break it down for me, man. How come you trying to flex on me?'

By now Abimbole didn't know where to put himself and looked about as isolated and lonely a figure as if he was already on another transfer list: even his own Newcastle team mates seemed to sense that something was wrong and started to blank him, too, which was strange. The two Ghanaians had played their parts to perfection, so much so that I thought Aaron Abimbole was going to cry; and he was the last man to leave the tunnel.

But for a while it was a tactic that looked as if it had gone badly wrong. With just ten minutes of the game gone, Aaron Abimbole scored with a skilful chip when he saw our bright new goalkeeper off his line. It was a sucker goal and left me feeling a fool for having spent nine million quid on someone who looked like he was still keeping goal at Tynecastle, where skills like Abimbole's were in much shorter supply. So much for the Scotsman's idea of keeping a clean sheet for the rest of the season. Fuck off.

Now Abimbole was pumped up like a car tyre with a score to settle against his old club and threatened again just three minutes later. This time our new signing made a great save that spared everyone's blushes and it's fair to say that while anyone could have saved the Nigerian's first shot, no one but Traynor could have saved his second; suddenly the nine mill looked like a much better spend.

And then – 'innocent face' – it all went spectacularly wrong for Aaron Abimbole. For several minutes he was everywhere – you couldn't have asked for a better work rate – and yet to my mind he needed to calm down: it was almost like he needed to prove himself, not just to the Newcastle fans but also to the City fans, too, who booed every time he went near the ball. I could see Alan Pardew felt the same. On the edge of his technical area he was shouting at Abimbole to stay in position and to pace himself. But the Nigerian wasn't listening to anything except the blood roaring in his curiously shaped ears.

A couple of minutes later, having read Dominguin's pass to Xavier Pepe on the edge of the box as if it had been sent by Western Union, Abimbole launched himself from behind at the little Spaniard with both feet, all his not inconsiderable weight, and more studs showing than an England ruck; he virtually chopped the other man's legs in half. I've seen riders come off superbikes at Monza who were moving slower than Abimbole was when he intercepted Pepe. It wasn't so much a sliding tackle as an assault with intent to commit actual bodily harm and the referee didn't hesitate, showing him a straight red card that brought the whole of Silvertown Dock to its feet, cheering wildly for although we were a goal down, you could see the effect on the Newcastle players at the Nigerian's dismissal. I might have felt sorry for the boy if I hadn't been so concerned about Xavier Pepe, who had yet to move after the tackle.

Fortunately he wasn't injured and was soon hobbling around on the touchline; four minutes later he was back on and scored the equaliser when he ran onto a pin-point pass from Christoph Bündchen. After that Newcastle struggled to cope with the one-man deficit; City peppered the Toon box with shots and by half time we were a goal up.

As we went back into the dressing room there was still no sign of João Zarco and Maurice McShane was looking worried.

'And?'

Maurice shook his head.

'I've looked everywhere.' He shrugged. 'Well, not every-where. It's a capacity crowd here today: sixty-five thousand people. It's Where's fucking Wally out there on the terraces, Scott. But I've looked everywhere that's obvious and quite a few of the less obvious places, too. I've phoned his wife, his agent, his ghost—'

'His ghost? What do you mean by that, Maurice?'

'The bloke who wrote Zarco's book, *No Games, Just*

Football. Phil Kerr. He's here this afternoon. He's always bloody here. Loser. I've called Claire. I've even called his builder. I've also had a quiet word with the police to see if they can help to find him. I've done everything but make an announcement on the Crown of Thorns PA.'

'Don't for Christ's sake do that,' I said. 'The press will wet their pants if they think he's gone AWOL.'

'I think the cat's out of the bag on that one, Scott. Sky Sports have noticed he's not in the dugout. Those penguins have been indulging in an orgy of speculation about where the fuck he is.'

'Any bright ideas from Jeff Stelling?'

'Only that we should send Chris Kamara to look for him. Kammy knows everything about being fucking lost.'

'Very funny.' I smiled. 'No, it is. If I wasn't so frazzled now I might even laugh. I feel like Charlie Nicholas' haircut.'

'It's been suggested that he's walked out. That he and Viktor have had some kind of barney and that João threw all his toys out of the pram and just buggered off.'

'If that were true Phil Hobday would have said something. And he didn't.'

'Fair enough. But those two have history. Everyone knows it. Even Chris Kamara.'

'Look, try some of the hospitality boxes. Get the security boys to help you. But don't make a big deal out of it. Just say Zarco's left his mobile phone in the dressing room and we don't know how to get hold of him. Better still, have them search the terraces with the Mobotix, as if we were looking for a hooligan.'

The Mobotix video system comprised seventy-seven high-resolution cameras providing cutting-edge crowd management and security. It worked well during our matches and it was a pity it hadn't been switched on when someone had dug a grave in the centre of the pitch.

When we went back on for the second half the Toons were still moaning to the officials about the sending-off, but there was little they could do about it now. Aaron Abimbole was already in a taxi and on his way home, which suited me very well. Pardew had substituted a couple of players and moved to a 3-5-1, but the game was already beyond them and fifteen minutes into the second half Bündchen scored two in quick succession, and that was the way it ended: 4–1.

I was dreading the post-match interview on Sky Sports. They were paying for the game and that meant we had to put someone in front of their cameras. I didn't want to do it but I had no choice since, in Zarco's absence, there was no one else. I knew Geoff Shreeves was going to ask me about where Zarco was and I really had no idea what I was going to tell him. Shreeves could be terrier-like with his questions and I just hoped he would let go and that I wouldn't do a Kenny Dalglish and lose it on live television. Being a Scot that's always a possibility.

'That's a great result, Scott, and many congratulations on the win, but the bigger talking point today, I'm sure you'll admit, is the absence of João Gonzales Zarco from the City dugout for the whole of the match. Can you end the speculation about exactly where your team manager was this afternoon, Scott? And perhaps where he is now?'

'I'd love to, but I'm afraid I can't, Geoff, as I have absolutely no idea myself. It's a mystery. The fact is I haven't seen him since eleven o'clock this morning.'

'There's a strong rumour going around the Crown of Thorns that he and Viktor Sokolnikov have had another

118

major falling-out and that João has walked out of the club. Would you like to comment on that?'

'I'd much prefer to comment on today's win, Geoff; I'm delighted with the way we played today. From being a goal behind to 4–1 is a bigger story, if you'll permit me to talk about that for a moment.'

'But João Zarco is a mercurial, not to say controversial character. And it would be entirely typical for him to do something like that, wouldn't you say?'

'I disagree, it wouldn't be typical at all. João Zarco has always been totally professional in the way he's managed this club. Look, Geoff, I would dearly like to tell you where João is right now. The fact is that no one seems to know. Now, as far as I'm aware there has been no disagreement between João and Mr Sokolnikov. I'd go so far as to say that relations between them are excellent, right now. I think I should also say that we're a little worried that something might have happened to João Zarco, which is why we're conducting a search of the whole ground. So if anyone does have information about his whereabouts, we'd appreciate it if you could get in touch. And perhaps you'll let me know if you hear anything, Geoff.'

'Of course, Scott.'

Finally we managed to talk about the game, but my mind wasn't on Kenny Traynor's cock-up and the magnificent save with which the Scotsman had redeemed himself, the goals we'd scored, or the sending off; all the time I was thinking about Zarco and wondering if his disappearance might be connected with the photograph of him that Colin had found at the bottom of the grave dug in the pitch.

And I don't mind admitting it, I was worried.

CHAPTER 15

In spite of our 4–1 victory and the fact that London City had gone sixth in the table, the atmosphere in the dressing room was a little subdued after the match as the lads sensed that something bad was happening.

Either we'd lost a great manager or we were about to lose one – nobody was quite sure which it was.

But we still got back on the coach as usual and went back to Hangman's Wood so the players could receive treatment on tired and injured limbs. Xavier Pepe had two enormous bruises on his calves from where Aaron Abimbole had tackled him, and Kwame Botchwey had a thigh strain that looked like it was going to keep him on the bench for a couple of weeks. As the bus drove away from Silvertown Dock I could see all these illuminated faces staring at their little smartphone screens like bees in a hive and I thought it best to issue a firm policy about Twitter.

'Listen, there's enough speculation as it is about where Zarco has got to without your bloody tweets. So how about giving your thumbs a rest tonight, eh, lads? We'll know what's happened to the gaffer soon enough. What we don't need are any fucking conspiracy theories for tomorrow's back pages.'

Back at Hangman's Wood the club physio told Pepe, Botchwey and several others to soak in an ice bath. I'd read a new study which said that ice baths after exercise may not be effective in aiding recovery; all our own anecdotal evidence suggests that they are and until we receive proof that they don't work our players will continue to take them, but they are hard-core and players taking ice baths need carefully monitoring as spending too long in one can cause a variety of health risks including anaphylactic shock and an abnormal heart rate.

I might not have had an ice bath at Hangman's Wood but I did feel a profound sense of shock and experienced an uncomfortable sensation in my chest when Phil Hobday telephoned me on my mobile at about seven thirty that same evening with some really bad news.

'Scott? I think you should prepare yourself for a shock. João Zarco was found dead at Silvertown Dock about half an hour ago.'

'Jesus Christ's arsehole. What was it? A heart attack?'

'It's rather hard to say exactly what killed him. But definitely not a heart attack, I'll say that much. He looked like he'd been pretty badly beaten up.'

'You've seen the body?'

'Oh yes. His head was bashed in and – it was awful. Anyway he's dead.'

'Where was he found?'

'One of our own security men discovered the body in a sort of maintenance yard inside the outer steel structure – the actual crown of thorns part of the stadium. It's pretty out of the way, which is why we didn't find him sooner. The uniformed police were here already, of course, but a scene of crimes unit and some detectives are on their way here as well. It's now a murder inquiry.'

'Does Toyah know?'

'Yes. And I just called Viktor at home. He was pretty shocked about it, I can tell you.'

'I'll bet. Jesus Christ. So am I.'

'Scott, I'd like you to tell the players, if you would. And I think it would be best if all of them stayed home tonight as a mark of respect to João. The press have got wind that something serious has happened here and I don't want any of our lads out on the piss and getting himself in the *Daily Mail*.'

'Of course. I'll tell them and read them the riot act.'

'And they'd better cancel whatever plans they may have had for tomorrow as well. I know it's a Sunday but I'm sure the police will want to question everyone who spoke to Zarco today.'

I thought for a moment.

'Phil, there's something I need to tell you. Look, perhaps I'd better come into Silvertown Dock and do it.'

'Tell me now and let me decide that. There's no point in you being here unless you have to be.'

I told Phil about the photograph of Zarco we'd found in the grave, and how Zarco had asked Colin and me to keep it quiet.

'How come the police didn't see it when they were here?'

'Because the police are the police. Their hands are usually dirty enough without getting mud on them, too.'

'You're right, Scott,' said Phil. 'I think you'd better come in and tell the police about this yourself. Under the circumstances I think perhaps Ronnie Leishmann should be here as well.'

Ronnie Leishmann was the London City Football Club lawyer.

'What circumstances are those?'

'You, of course. And you saying things like what you just said about policemen with dirty hands. I think it would be best if you could learn to moderate your dislike of the police while they're investigating what happened to Zarco.'

'Fair enough.'

'By the way, where is the picture now?' asked Phil.

'In Colin's office. João told him he could keep it as a souvenir.'

'Well, that's something, I suppose.'

'I'll be there as soon as I can, Phil.'

As I ended my call with the club chairman I got a message from Didier Cassell's wife: our French goalkeeper had recovered consciousness at last. This was good to know but it wasn't enough to sugarcoat a bitter pill like the one I was about to give the team. Nothing was going to be enough for that.

I had gathered everyone who was at Hangman's Wood in the players' bar. I suppose one or two of them had seen into my eyes, watched my Adam's apple, and already understood the worst.

'Ladies and gentlemen,' I said. 'In any other circumstance but the one in which I am standing here now, the news that Didier Cassell, our team mate and friend, has recovered consciousness and is likely to make a full recovery would be cause for great celebration. But Didier would be the first to tell you that there are no celebrations tonight. Not for him. Not for me. Not for us. Not at this club. And not for anyone who loves the great game of football. Because what I have to tell you now is that João Gonzales Zarco is dead.'

There was a very audible gasp and one or two of the players sat down on the floor.

'I can't tell you very much about what happened. Not yet.

Suffice to say that the police will want to speak to every one of us here, tomorrow. But what I can say now is this. A grief ago, when I lost my friend Matt Drennan, I thought I knew exactly what the acute pain of bereavement felt like. But I was wrong. For much as I loved Drenno, I find now he's gone that I loved João Zarco even more. João wasn't just my boss, he was also my friend; and not only that but my mentor, my inspiration and my example, the only true philosopher I ever knew, and the greatest football manager that ever lived.

'I look around this room now and I'm very proud to see Englishmen, Scotsmen, Irishmen, Welshmen, Frenchmen, Brazilians, Spaniards, Germans, Italians, Ghanaians, Ukrainians, Russians, Jews and Gentiles, whites, blacks – all of us playing as one man for the same team. But that isn't what João Zarco saw. Not at all. Zarco didn't see different races, or different creeds; he didn't hear different languages. He didn't even see a great team when he looked at you people. When he was with us what he saw and heard was something very different. Something inspiring. What João Zarco saw when he looked at you all was the true family of football, his family and mine. And what he heard was only ever this: that we all speak the same language – a language spoken all over the world, in every country, and under every god; a language that unites us; it is the language of love for this beautiful game.

'Right now we are also united in this terrible, unsupportable loss. United in mourning. United in our remembrance of our footballing family's true father. This is a special day, ladies and gentlemen. Remember it always, as I will. For this was the day, not when Zarco died, but when his family wiped the floor with a great team. He can't be with us to acknowledge that victory. But I promise you he sees it and he honours it, as I know you will honour him. And I ask you not to go out tonight but to stay at home and remember him in your prayers; and to remember all of us who have suffered the loss of this man we loved, this beautiful man from Portugal.'

I didn't say anything else; in truth I couldn't say anything at all, not any more. So without another word I went out to the car park and got into my car. For a moment I just sat in the snug silence of the Range Rover's wood and leather interior, and then I wept.

And when I had finished weeping I drove west, to Silvertown Dock.

CHAPTER 16

East London. A Saturday night. Horrible January weather. The air full of sleet and snow as if the city were witnessing a returning ice age; the black River Thames a huge slimy anaconda and as cold as death itself. Wet, dirty cars jostling for space and the kinder sentiments of Christmas and New Year all disappeared now, crushed underfoot by the costly imperatives of living in the most expensive city on earth, or just thrown out like a dead Christmas tree. People hurrying into pubs and off-licences to drink as much as possible before diving into evil-looking nightclubs. The smell of beer and cigarettes and exhaust fumes mixed up into one thick, yellow, all-pervading fog. Ugly buildings dark and derelict and unfeasibly old, as if any one of them might have known the feet of Dickens or even the hand of Shakespeare. And then the unmistakable silhouette of Silvertown Dock. The Crown of Thorns was well-named; sharp, intricately plaited, cruel and jagged, the outer shell of steel looked vaguely holy in the dark, as if the bleeding and battered head of our Lord might appear within it at any moment, looking perhaps more than a little like João Zarco.

The police were in force at Silvertown Dock and so were the TV cameras and newsmen. It looked like a repeat performance of the night Drenno had hanged himself, and I wondered why they didn't just use the same pictures of me arriving at our ground that they'd taken then. I must have looked just as miserable that evening as my rear-view mirror told me I did now.

I parked my car, walked into the stadium and thought of how the last time I was here, I hadn't known that Zarco was dead. Instinctively I made for the executive dining room; it was the obvious place for the police to use as a base for their investigations. Along the corridor leading to the dining room there were pictures of Zarco looking at his most enigmatic and handsome. I still couldn't believe that I wasn't going to see him again, muffled against the cold in his trademark N.Peal zip-up and cashmere coat, his face unshaven but still handsome, his thick grey hair the same colour as the steel structure outside.

A security guard said something and I shook his hand, as if I were on automatic pilot.

'Thanks,' I muttered.

In the executive dining room Phil Hobday, Maurice McShane and Ronnie Leishmann greeted me in the doorway and then turned to face the several strangers who were seated around an Apple Mac on a large circular table: designed by the artist Lee J. Rowland, the surface of the table was made of leather and resembled a football – the old kind, with the laces in the middle. On an earlier occasion Phil Hobday had told me it cost a whopping fifty thousand pounds. Since its arrival in the executive dining room it had been signed by everyone who'd played or coached at London City Football Club, including Zarco and myself.

The photograph of Zarco that we'd found at the bottom of the grave in the pitch was wrapped in polythene and lying on the table with an evidence number stapled to the corner.

A carefully groomed, androgynous woman in her forties,

with short, almost white hair and a strong but equally pale face stood up. Good-looking in a MILFish sort of way, she wore a violet dress and a dark blue tailored coat. She was holding an iPad, which made her seem efficient and modern.

'This is Scott Manson, our team coach,' said Phil Hobday.

'Yes, I know,' said the woman quietly.

'Scott, this is Detective Chief Inspector Jane Byrne, from New Scotland Yard.'

'I know you're feeling very upset, Mr Manson. I know because we were all just watching your very moving speech on YouTube.'

'What?'

'Yes, it seems that someone recorded it on a mobile phone and uploaded it while you were driving here.'

'That was supposed to be private,' I murmured.

'Bloody footballers,' said Phil. 'Some of them haven't got the sense they were born with.' He shook his head wearily and then pointed at a drinks trolley with so many bottles and glasses it looked like the city of London. 'Would you like a drink, Scott? You look as if you need one.'

'Thanks, I'll have a large cognac, Phil.'

'How about you, Chief Inspector?'

'No, thank you, sir.' She handed me her iPad. 'Here. See for yourself.'

I looked at the iPad and saw a paused picture of myself near the end of my little eulogy about Zarco; the title tag was *A Tribute to João Zarco: 'The greatest football manager that ever lived', by Scott Manson*. Someone called Football Fan 69 had uploaded it.

'It was a fine speech, Scott,' said Ronnie. 'You should be proud.'

'Fifteen thousand views already,' said Maurice. 'And it's been up there for less than an hour.'

'It was supposed to be private,' I repeated dumbly, handing her back the iPad and taking a large cognac from Phil Hobday's outstretched hand.

'Nothing about João Zarco is private now,' said Jane Byrne. 'At least not until his killer is caught.'

'His killer?'

'That's certainly what it looks like,' she said. 'The body was quite badly beaten up.'

With a movement of her hand she invited me to sit down. She spoke very clearly and very deliberately as if she were speaking to someone who wasn't very bright. Or perhaps she just realised that I was still feeling numb with shock.

'I'm in charge of this investigation,' she explained, and introduced some of the other policemen who were also present in the room – names that went in one ear and out the other.

She watched me carefully as I drained the glass and let Phil pour me another.

'I know as little as you about what happened, so if you don't mind, Mr Manson, I'll ask the questions for the present.'

I nodded again as she hit an app on her iPhone that would record our conversation.

'When and where did you last see Mr Zarco?'

'This morning at about eleven o'clock. We were at the club's training facility in Hangman's Wood where, as usual on the day of a match, we picked the team; then he left to attend a lunch here, in this room. At least that's where he told me he was going.' I sighed as it began to hit me again. 'Yes, that was the last time I saw him. And also the last time I spoke to him.'

'What time did he arrive here?' she asked Phil.

'About eleven thirty.'

'What was his mood when he left Hangman's Wood?'

'He seemed to be in an excellent mood,' I said. 'We had a good result against Leeds in the week and we both thought we were going to win this afternoon. Which we did.'

She glanced at Phil. 'And when he got here? How was he then?'

'Still in a good mood,' Phil confirmed. 'Never better.'

'I shall want to interview everyone who was at that lunch,' she said.

'Of course,' said Phil. 'I'll fix it.'

Jane Byrne looked at me. 'Mr Hobday has told me about the grave that was found dug into the pitch about ten days ago. And I've read the police report of that incident. According to the investigating detective, Detective Inspector Neville, you weren't very cooperative with that inquiry, Mr Manson. Why was that, please?'

'It's a long story. Let's just say that I was more inclined than your detective to think it was just a hole that had been made by vandals and an inevitable corollary of the kind of fanatical support that clubs get in the modern game.'

'It looks like you were wrong, doesn't it? Especially in view of the fact that a photograph of Mr Zarco was found in the grave. This photograph.'

'It looks like it.'

'It looks like the photograph, or it looks like you were wrong?'

I shrugged. 'Both.'

'Why did you choose not to inform DI Neville about the discovery of this photograph?'

'Like I say, the police missed it when they were here and

130

it didn't seem worth bringing them back again. I figured if they'd really been doing their job properly they'd have found it in the first place. Anyway, it really wasn't my decision. After all, it wasn't a photograph of me we're talking about. Zarco was the boss around here. That's what being a football manager means, Chief Inspector. He said jump, we said how high. Quite literally, sometimes. So it was very much down to him what we did when we were here. And he said we should forget all about it.'

'So he didn't seem alarmed by it?'

'Not in the least. You have to remember this: that threats against football managers are an occupational hazard. Speak to Neil Lennon at Celtic, or Ally McCoist at Rangers – they'll tell you.'

'But they're in Glasgow, aren't they? This is London. Things are a little less tribal down here, surely?'

'Perhaps. Which is probably why Zarco didn't take it seriously when we found his picture in that grave. And why he chose not to report the matter to Detective Inspector Neville.'

'But now he's dead and here we are with a mystery.'

'Yes. It would seem so. The Silvertown Dock Mystery.'

'What do you mean?'

'Nothing,' I said.

'No, say it.'

'It's just that there was a film made donkey's years ago. A creaky old black and white movie called *The Arsenal Stadium Mystery*, in which a player gets murdered.'

'I must check that out on DVD.'

'I could give you my own copy. But to be honest, I wouldn't bother. It really is very old and not at all relevant.'

'Have you any ideas as to who might have killed Mr Zarco?'

'None at all.'

'Are you being serious?'

'Yes. Look, this is football, not organised crime.'

'Really? Come on, Mr Manson. From what I've read and heard João Zarco was a man who'd made a lot of enemies.'

'Who doesn't make enemies in football? Look, I'm not going to sit here and say who they were. Zarco was a man of strong opinions. Sometimes his passion for the game of football upset people. But enemies who might have killed him?' I shook my head. 'I have no idea.'

'Enemies like who, for instance?'

'Please. I just lost a very close friend. And this on top of the suicide, not so very long ago, of another man I was also fond of. Matt Drennan. Perhaps you'll ask me again when I'm thinking straight. But at this particular moment in time I'm not really in the mood to provide you with a list of possible suspects. Perhaps in the morning.'

'Don't you want us to find out who killed him?'

'Of course I do.'

'Then the sooner you feel inclined to help the sooner we'll catch whoever killed him.'

'That's a matter of opinion.'

'Ah.'

'What?'

'Now we're getting to it,' she said. 'To the real reason you don't want to help us with our inquiry, perhaps.'

'With all due respect, and under the circumstances, I think Mr Manson has been more than helpful so far,' observed Ronnie Leishmann.

'That's your opinion,' said the Detective Chief Inspector. 'Mr Manson's hostility to the police is a matter of public record.'

132

'As is the hostility of the police towards me,' I said. 'I believe the same public record will show that the police consistently lied about me in court and conspired to have me falsely imprisoned. And by the way, just in case you feel like you want to wrap this case up very quickly, I have an alibi for the whole of today. There were more than sixty thousand people out there who were watching me all afternoon. Not to mention two and a half million people on telly. When they weren't watching my every move I was in the dressing room with the team. I like to get naked with other men, if you were wondering.'

She seemed about to say something, and then smiled.

'I'm sorry,' she said. 'You're perfectly right, of course. And I apologise. If I'd been through what you've been through then I suppose I might very well feel the same way about the police as you do. It's perfectly shameful what happened to you, Mr Manson. Really it is. Look, let's start again, shall we?' She stood up and held out her hand. 'Jane Byrne. Will you accept my word that I'm not here to protect the reputation of the Met but to apprehend Mr Zarco's killer? And may I offer my sincere condolences on the death of Mr Zarco?'

I took her hand. 'You know, you're the second police officer I've met who seems like a nice person.'

'You mean there are two of us? Christ, who's the other?'

'Detective Inspector Louise Considine, from the police station at Brent.'

'Maybe you just prefer police officers who are women.'

'There might be something in that. Anyway, she's the officer investigating Matt Drennan's suicide.'

'Well, that's a sort of crime, I suppose.' She frowned. 'At least it used to be. By the way, how well did you know Zarco?'

'Zarco? As well as anyone, I suppose. I've known him since I was a boy. Back in the nineties, when he was playing for Celtic towards the end of his career, Zarco was the first footballer to endorse a pair of Pedila boots. Pedila is a sports shoe company owned by my father.'

'And how did you come to work with him?'

'I got my UEFA certificates in 2010 and accepted a trainee coaching role with Pep Guardiola at Barcelona. Then, in 2011 I became the first team trainee coach at Bayern where I was working with Jupp Heynckes, who was another old friend of my dad. Then, when Zarco came back here in the summer, I agreed to be his assistant manager.'

'How do you mean, "came back here"?'

I smiled. 'I'll let Mr Hobday explain that, I think.'

'Oh, Zarco was manager at this football club before,' explained Phil. 'Seven years ago. Before we were in the Premier League. He managed it very successfully, too. It was João who helped get us promoted. And then he left.'

'Why?'

'Um, he was sacked, by Mr Sokolnikov. They had very different ideas as to how to run this club. As you might expect, they're both very strong personalities, which meant that they didn't really get on that well. Not back then. We had a series of managers after that. But none of them worked out as well as Zarco and the fans kept on demanding his return. So that's what happened. Second time around they got on famously. Wouldn't you agree, Scott?'

I nodded. 'Both of them got older and richer,' I said. 'Became a little wiser, perhaps.'

'I shall want to speak to Mr Sokolnikov,' said Jane Byrne. 'Tomorrow, I think.'

'Of course,' said Phil, 'just tell me when and I'll arrange it.'

'By the way,' I said. 'Zarco's wife, Toyah.' I shook my head. 'Don't ask her to formally identify the body. She's rather highly strung. I'll do it.'

She nodded. 'If you like. Since you say you knew him so well.'

'Tomorrow I'll answer all of your questions,' I said. 'Anything you like. And so will the players. Well, you've already heard what I told them, on your iPad. I'll assemble the players and playing staff at Hangman's Wood and then bring them here on the team coach.'

'Thank you. Shall we say ten o'clock?'

I looked at Phil, who nodded.

'Until then,' I said, 'I have one request. I'd like to see where it happened.'

She was quiet for a moment, thinking about it.

'I don't want to leave any flowers or a teddy bear,' I said, 'I just want to see the spot where he died and then say a short prayer for him.'

She nodded. 'All right. But give me a few minutes to sort that out with the CSU.'

'Fine,' I said. 'There's something I want to get from my office anyway. I'll come back here and find you. All right?'

Jane Byrne glanced at her watch. 'Nine o'clock, okay?'

'Yes.'

Before going to my office I went into the men's toilet to splash my face. Drinking those two cognacs had been a mistake.

When I came out again I saw Jane Byrne in the corridor. She had her back to me; she was on her mobile and ducked into the ladies' toilet so that she could hold a private conversation. I paused outside the door for a moment and then pushed it gently open. There was a wall that ran halfway between the door and the cubicles. I could hear her on the other side, walking up and down while she was speaking; on the tiled floor her high heels sounded higher than I remembered them. Quietly, I stepped through the door and listened to what she was saying. Where the police are concerned it's always a good idea to know what they're up to. And since Jane Byrne was at that moment the only woman in the building, I felt sure I wouldn't be discovered.

The Detective Chief Inspector's accent had changed. There was more south London in it now, and rather more malice in what she was saying than perhaps even I had expected:

'. . . beat the shit out of him, apparently. That's what it looks like, anyway. Zarco's head was pretty badly swollen... Yes, even more than normal... The CSU says it looks so badly fractured that even if he had survived, chances are he'd have suffered some sort of brain damage... Where was he? That's rather hard to describe. The trouble with modern architecture is that it creates lots of forgotten little places and that's what this looks like. It's a cross between a shaft and an alcove. Concrete floor, steel girders, wire fence but open to the elements and covered in bird shit. The security guy I spoke to said it's a maintenance area but if it is I don't know what they can be maintaining – other than the steel girders that make up the actual crown of thorns. There was a door at ground level... That's right... Yes, an ideal place to rough someone up but then again, whoever did it must have had access to the key because the door was locked... I imagine Zarco did. He must have gone there willingly with whoever it was that worked him over... No, a fall doesn't make sense; there's nowhere I can see that he could have fallen from... Yes... I'm with them now... Well, you know, they're bloody footballers – with most of them there's a peculiar combination of stupidity and ego... I'm dealing with a club chairman who's as slippery as a fucking eel and a team coach who's Derek Bentley channelling the Guildford Four. Yeah, Scott Manson. And I haven't even seen the Russian oligarch who owns this place yet. I'd love to read the Ukrainian police file on that bastard. I bet it's as thick as a fucking toilet roll. That reminds me, Clive – I want all the files on Manson. I want his life story on my desk when I get back to the Yard. Oh, and Clive, I need this bastard softened up a bit to ensure his more-than-willing cooperation. DI Neville – the copper who came here to investigate that grave in the pitch – he said Manson was an awkward bastard. Right now I'm having to lick his balls just to get him to name a few potential suspects. So, get a local patrol car to do a tug on his motor and give him an alco test. He's had two large ones since he's been here. I'll get one of my officers to text over the index in a few minutes. And Clive? See if you can draft a DI Louise Considine from Brent Police onto my team. And Neville, too, if his guvnor will stand it...'

I'd heard enough to know where I stood with the nice policewoman.

I came out of the ladies' and went back along the corridor. Phil Hobday followed me as he exited the dining room; his office was near mine and he said he wanted to make some calls, but halfway there he stopped me.

'When you're through with her,' he said, 'Viktor wants you to drop in to KPG for a talk.'

KPG was Kensington Palace Gardens, the ultra-exclusive road in Kensington where Viktor lived in a seventy-million-pound mansion.

I paused. 'What about?'

Phil shrugged. 'I don't know. No, really, I have no idea.

137

And I wouldn't dream of trying to second-guess Viktor Sokolnikov. It's on your way home.'

'All right.' I glanced at the enormous Hublot on my wrist. 'But I might be late.'

'How long does it take to say a prayer? I didn't even know you were religious.'

'I am if it involves the people I love.'

'So what time shall I say you'll be there?'

I thought for a moment. 'I don't know.'

'Come on, Scott. This is Viktor we're talking about, not a drink in the Star Tavern.'

The Star was the posh pub in Belgravia where occasionally I met Phil for a drink. Calling it a pub at all was a bit like calling Phil's Rolls-Royce a motor car.

'Then tell him ten thirty.'

'All right. And by the way, good work back there, the way you turned that cop around.'

'I wouldn't be so sure about that.'

'Not bad-looking, though.'

'If you like that sort of thing.'

Phil grinned. 'As a matter of fact I do. I like that sort of thing very much indeed.'

'Ambitious, I should say.'

'I like that, too.'

Outside Zarco's door was a uniformed policeman who was checking his mobile phone. I nodded at him and went into my own adjoining office; the poor copper wasn't to know that there was a door connecting Zarco's office with mine and that the minute my door was closed I was through there with the flashlight app on my iPhone to see what I could discover on his desk and in his drawers. I knew there were some sex-toys and bondage paraphernalia – a remote-control vibrator and handcuffs – that no one needed to know about. It wasn't simply the fact that I didn't trust the police to find their own arseholes, let alone Zarco's murderer; it was also that I had his reputation to protect, and not just his reputation but the club's as well. The Met has a habit of selling sidebar stories to newspapers when they're supposed to be doing something else; and the newspapers have a habit of burying the people they've already praised. Like my old friend Gary Speed; once you're dead, and they've said a few nice things about you and wrung their handkerchiefs a bit, then they can say what the fuck they like. Of course, I already had Zarco's 'play phone' and his 'something else' phone in my drawer, but I had to make sure there was nothing that might have left my friend's family having to deal with a tabloid exposé: *The Real João Zarco*, or *The João Zarco Nobody Knew*. Or just as bad, a Twitter storm. Fuck that.

I wasn't bent for myself, but I was quite prepared to be bent for my friends and for my club.

CHAPTER 17

'Bloody hell,' said Maurice. 'Look at that lot, will you?' He nodded. 'They're going to do him proud.'

'Looks like it.'

We were in my Range Rover, leaving London City Football Club for KPG. It was dark and bitterly cold and the air was full of sleet, but hundreds of fans had gathered to pay their tributes to João Zarco, and there were so many orange scarves tied to the gates of Silvertown Dock that it already looked like a sort of Hindu shrine. Some of the fans were singing the club songs – including what else but The Clash?

London calling to the faraway towns, now war is declared – and battle come down...

A few even managed Joe Strummer's werewolf howl at the end of the lyric.

I was silent for a while as the song and the howls stayed in my head, giving me gooseflesh.

'That's the great thing about football,' said Maurice. 'When you go, people like to show their respect. Who else gets that these days?'

'Michael Jackson?' I suggested. 'That hotel we stayed at in Munich. The Bayerischer Hof. They've still got a shrine going outside the front door.'

Maurice winced. 'That's just the fucking Germans.'

'Hey, careful what you say about the Germans. I'm half German, remember?'

'Well then answer me this, Fritz. How come they do that – make a shrine to him – when everyone knows he was a kiddy fiddler? Doesn't make sense.'

'In some ways the Germans – Bavarians especially – they'd prefer not to know about that sort of thing.'

'Yeah, well, they've got a form for it, haven't they?' growled Maurice. 'Preferring not to know about someone's past.'

'I wish he could have seen that,' I said, ignoring the history lesson. 'Zarco, I mean. Not the plastic guy.'

'Did you actually see his body?' asked Maurice.

'Not really,' I said. 'His legs, I guess. Where the body was – it wasn't a very large space. There were three or four CSU officers around him, plus all their gear – spotlights, tripods, cameras and laptops. These days a murder scene looks more like they're shooting a commercial.'

'What a thing to happen to a guy like João,' said Maurice. 'How old was he anyway?'

'Forty-nine.'

'Christ. Makes you think, doesn't it?' He pursed his lips. 'Tragic, that's what it is. Without question. But it ain't a fucking murder.'

'Listen to him: Inspector Morse.'

'At least not a murder in the old sense, that is, with intent. Yeah, it's reasonably foreseeable that if you're handing out some GBH you might kill a bloke. But I don't see any intent here, according to how most blokes round our way would look at this.'

'Keep talking.'

'You remember how it was in the nick. Nine times out of

ten, if someone wanted to kill a bloke, they didn't do it with a beating. They used a blade. Or they strangled him. And if it was on the outside they'd shoot him or have him shot. But they didn't kick the shit out of him. If a bloke dies after a beating then that's a beating that went wrong or simply got out of hand. More like an accident. Manslaughter. No, if you ask me, someone wanted Zarco hurt, but not dead. This was revenge, or a warning, but it wasn't supposed to be goodnight Vienna.'

'I'm no Rumpole but the law says different, I think.'

'Yeah, well, that's the law, isn't it? There's not much common sense in the law these days. If there was we wouldn't be in the EU, would we? We wouldn't have the Human Rights Act and all that shit. Abu Hamza. Cunts like that make a monkey out of the courts in this fucking country.' Maurice paused as some blue light spilled into the Range Rover. 'Talking of monkeys,' he said, 'we've got some law on our tail.'

I checked the side mirror and nodded.

'Let me handle it, okay?'

'Be my guest.'

We pulled up and I lowered the tinted window a few inches.

A traffic policeman presented himself at the side of the Range Rover; he was already holding a breathalyser unit in one hand and adjusting his peaked hat with the other.

'Would you step out of the car, please, sir?'

'Certainly.'

I got out of the car and closed the door behind me.

'Is this your vehicle, sir?'

'Yes it is.' I handed him my plastic licence. 'What seems to be the problem?'

He glanced at the licence. 'You were driving erratically, sir. And you were doing thirty-five miles per hour in a thirty-mile-an-hour zone.'

'If you say so,' I said. 'I really didn't notice the speed.'

'Have you consumed alcohol this evening, sir?'

'A couple of brandies. I'm afraid I had some bad news.'

'I'm sorry to hear that, sir. However, I'm afraid I shall have to ask you to take a breath test.'

'All right. But you're making a mistake. If you'll allow me to explain...'

'Are you refusing to provide a sample of breath, sir?'

'Not at all. But I was just trying to tell you that—'

'Sir, I'm asking you to take a breath test. Now, either you comply or I will arrest you.'

'Very well. If you insist. Here, give it to me.' I took the little grey unit, meekly followed his instructions on what to do and then handed it back.

We waited a few seconds.

'I'm afraid the light has turned red, sir. The sample of breath you've provided has more than thirty-five millimetres of alcohol per one hundred millimetres of blood. Which means you're under arrest. If you'll please follow me to the police car.'

I smiled. 'For what?'

'You just failed the breath test, sir,' said the policeman. 'That's what.'

'Yes, but as I tried to tell you before, I wasn't driving. My friend was.'

'What's that?'

'The car is left-hand drive, you see?'

There was a long silence and I tried not to smile.

The traffic policeman marched around to the left-hand

side of the vehicle and opened the door. Maurice grinned at him.

'Evening, constable,' he said, cheerily. 'I'm teetotal. Diabetic, see? So you'd be wasting your time.'

'Incidentally,' I said, 'this is an Overfinch Range Rover; as well as being left-hand drive it's fitted with Roadhawk – a black box camera system that films what's happening at the front, the rear and both sides of the car. In case of accident, you understand.'

The policeman pocketed his breathalyser unit. His face was the colour of the night sky in that part of London: an artificial shade of dark mauve. He slammed the door shut on Maurice's grin.

'Does it record sound as well as pictures, sir?'

'No, sadly not.'

He nodded grimly and then leaned towards me until he was near enough for me to smell the coffee on his breath.

'Cunt.'

Then he turned and walked away.

'Good night to you too, officer,' I said and got back into the Range Rover.

Maurice was laughing. 'That was fucking priceless,' he wheezed. 'I can't wait to see that again. You have got to put that up on YouTube.'

'I think I've been on YouTube enough for one night,' I said.

'No, really. Or else nobody will fucking believe it. That rozzer was so keen to nick you he didn't even notice that this was a left hooker. Straight up. That was comedy gold.'

'Might be better to keep it in reserve. Another time I might not be so lucky.'

'In the circumstances you're probably right. I thought you

were joking about that bitch back at the Crown of Thorns. But it looks like she's got it in for you, old son.'

'So what's new?'

We drove to the north entrance of KPG on Notting Hill Gate; the south entrance – on Kensington High Street – is reserved for the inhabitants of the royal palace. Not that any of the other houses on KPG looked to be anything less than palaces. I'd say it's the most exclusive road in London but for the fact that anyone can live there, as long as they can afford to pay between fifty and a hundred million pounds for a house, and it's only the presence of the grey and very grim-looking Russian embassy at the north end that lowers the tone a little.

Viktor's house was three storeys of Portland stone with four square corner turrets and had everything except a moat, a flag and an honour guard. You can live in a bigger house in London but only if you're the Queen.

I got out of the Range Rover and leaned through the open window.

'You take the car,' I told Maurice. 'I'll get a cab home. It's not far from here.'

'Want me to pick you up in the morning?'

I shook my head. 'I'll get a cab company to take me in.'

'Call me when you get home, will you? Let me know if he offers you the job.'

'You really think he will?'

'What else could it be?'

CHAPTER 18

I turned and gave my name to the gorilla in the gatehouse. He checked me off on his clipboard and then waved me through. I didn't have to ring the bell; another security man was already opening the polished black door. A butler materialised in a marble hallway that was dominated by a life-size Giacometti sculpture of a walking man as thin as a pipe cleaner and who always reminded me of Peter Crouch. I'd shared this observation with Viktor before and I reminded myself not to offer it again; when you own a famous work of art I expect your sense of humour about who or what it looks like is limited by how much you paid for it – which, in the case of the Giacometti, was a hundred million dollars, so you do the maths. Clearly Sotheby's or Christie's had a more developed sense of humour than anyone.

Anyway, I wasn't really in the mood for jokes. I wasn't in the mood for anything very much except putting my head under a pillow and going to sleep for about twelve hours.

The butler ushered me into a room that was in keeping with the Giacometti, which is to say that it was one of those 'less is more' modern rooms that looks like you're in the new money wing of a national museum; it was only the huge cream sofas that persuaded me I didn't need a ticket and an audio-visual aid. The big black log resting on the fire dogs looked as if it had landed on Hiroshima a split second ago and even the smoke rising discreetly up the enormous chimney smelled reassuringly exclusive – like being in an expensive ski-chalet.

Viktor dropped a copy of the *Financial Times* and came around the sofa, which took a while, and gave ample time for me to admire the Lucien Freud above the fireplace. Although admire is probably the wrong word; *appreciate* is probably more accurate. I'm not sure I could have enjoyed the sight of a reclining nude man with his legs apart every time I glanced up from my newspaper. I see enough of that kind of thing in the showers at Silvertown Dock.

We embraced, Russian style, without a word. The butler was still hanging around like a cold and Viktor asked me if I wanted a drink.

'Just a glass of water.'

The butler vanished.

I sat down, stretched a smile onto my face, just to be polite, and told him everything I'd learned about what had happened. This wasn't much, but still, it seemed more than enough.

Viktor Sokolnikov was in his forties, I suppose, with a receding silvery hairline that was more than compensated for by the amount of hair growing between his eyebrows and on his habitually unshaven cheeks. His eyes were keen and dark and they were the shrewdest I'd ever seen. A little overweight, he had a jowly sort of cheeks with a near permanent smile; and after all he had much to smile about. There's nothing like having several billion dollars in the bank to put you in a good mood. Not that he always was: right now it was difficult to connect this urbane, smiling man with the guy who'd nutted his fellow oligarch, Alisher Aksyonov, live on Russian television after the two got into an argument. I'd watched the clip on YouTube and, not understanding Russian, it was difficult to know what the argument had been about. But there was no doubt that Viktor had effectively given the other, bigger man a Glasgow kiss – good enough to put him down on the deck. I couldn't have done it better myself.

'I was fond of João,' said Viktor. 'We didn't always see eye to eye, as you know. But it was never dull with him. I shall miss this man very much. João was a very special guy. Unique, in my experience. And a great manager. It was a good result today; he'd have been proud. Today of all days I'm glad we won.'

The butler came back with a glass of water, which I drank almost immediately. Viktor asked me if I wanted another. I shook my head, glanced at the huge cock above me and told myself I knew where to get a refill if I needed one. After two large cognacs I was feeling just a little crude.

We talked some more about Zarco, the plans he and Viktor had made for London City, and some of the more outspoken, even outrageous remarks that the Portuguese had uttered, which soon had us laughing.

'Remind me,' said Viktor, 'what was it he said to the guy on Sky Sports when the FA Chairman publicly disinvited him from the England team commission?'

I grinned. 'He called the commission a "knocking shop"; of course he meant to say "talking shop". At least that's what everyone supposed he meant. But that was no mistake. He knew very well what he was saying. Even before Jeff Stelling corrected him.'

'You think so?'

'I'm certain of it. Sometimes he pretended his English wasn't as good as it really was.'

'That's true,' admitted Viktor. 'It was a useful trick. I do it myself sometimes.'

'Anyway, a commission might as well be a knocking shop for all the good that it's going to do English football. Some of us thought it might actually be the FA's job to look into the declining number of Englishmen playing in the Premier League. It's difficult to imagine what the hell else those fat fucks could be useful for. None of the cunts on the FA board of directors has ever played the game professionally, which says all you need to know; quite frankly those self-satisfied bastards haven't done anything to help the English game since they codified the laws of the game at The Freemason's Tavern in 1863. And it doesn't require the establishment of an England team commission to tell you that the biggest problem with English football is the Football Association itself. The FA by name and FA by nature, right?'

Viktor grinned. 'I think maybe you can be quite outspoken yourself, Scott.'

I shook my head. 'Sorry, Viktor. I was starting to rant. Upset, I guess. Pissed, a bit, too. I had two large cognacs at Silvertown Dock. Spirits always make me a bit fightable. That's the Scot in me, I suppose.'

'In that respect at least you are like a Ukrainian or a Russian,' said Viktor. 'But there's no need to apologise. I like a man with strong opinions. Especially when those opinions happen to coincide with my own. That's not a prerequisite for being the manager of London City, although the press would have you think something else. Yes, we had our differences, me and Zarco. But one thing he and I always agreed about was that if ever we fell out again, you were the best candidate to take over as manager.'

'That's very kind of you. And of him.'

'The players respect you and Phil Hobday speaks very highly of you, as did Zarco. You're well qualified – a university degree, all your coaching certificates, you're the most obvious candidate. I only wish I didn't have to do this tonight. But I'm flying to Moscow tomorrow, and I won't be back for several days. We've bought a player. From Dynamo St Petersburg.'

'I didn't know we were in the market for anyone.'

'Not just anyone.'

'You haven't bought the red devil?'

Viktor nodded and I felt my jaw drop. Bekim Develi was generally held to be the best midfielder in Europe; a Turkish-born Russian, he'd been playing for PSG until seventy-five per cent French tax had driven him back to his home town of St Petersburg. Viktor had always been keen to have Develi come to London City – they were old friends, for one thing. But Zarco had rejected the idea – it wasn't like we lacked options in midfield – and as far as I knew Viktor had been obliged to accept the decision of his recently reinstated manager.

'Bloody hell.'

'Yes. I am going to finalise the deal this week. Dynamo owes me money. Rather a lot of money, as it happens, so instead of taking what they owe in cash, I'm taking Develi. But I wanted to talk with you in private before I went. To reach an understanding. Man to man.'

I nodded.

'I'm offering you the job of City manager – at least until the end of the season. Let's see how we get on. You keep us in the Premier League, then that's one reason to keep you on full time. An FA Cup and a top-four finish so that we can qualify for the Champion's League would count for something, too.'

'I would certainly hope so,' I said.

Viktor paused and lit a cigar; it wasn't anything fancy like a Cohiba, just a little Villiger that you could buy at almost any London newsagent.

'But to be absolutely honest with you, none of that is a priority for me.'

'It isn't?'

Viktor shook his head. 'No.'

'Then I'd say that for someone who's the owner of a Premier League football club, you're a very unusual man.'

'Yesterday I might have told you something else. But today I tell you frankly, Scott, I don't give a fuck about cups or titles. There's something at stake here that's much more important to me than anything.'

'I hate to disagree with you, Viktor. For me there's nothing more important than those.'

'I want the people who work for me to be passionate about what they do, certainly. And of course this is why I'm offering you the job. But with some strings attached. It's those strings I'm trying to explain here. You see the one thing I'm really passionate about – more passionate about than football – is my privacy. Nothing is more important to me than this.

'I don't ever give interviews. I avoid the light like I was a vampire. Everyone thinks that the panel glass I sit behind at Silvertown Dock is bulletproof. It's not; it's camera-lens neutralising. It's also part of the London City contract with Sky that they don't do cutaway shots to my seat. I don't go to film premieres or parties very much. But it's not always so easy to keep out of the public eye. Especially with the media you have in this country. And the police you have, too. You of all people know to your cost that the media and the police here have an uncomfortably close relationship. If the police want to arrest someone at six o'clock in the morning, they like to tell the newspapers. But this is not a public service. Someone in the police gets paid for the tip-off. For other stories, also.'

I nodded. 'Where is this going, Viktor?'

'We have a saying in my country: if you send a man out to shoot a fox, don't be surprised if he hits a rabbit. In a murder inquiry the police can go where they want and look where they want. Almost anywhere. So the police won't just be looking for Zarco's murderer. The police will use Zarco's murder as a fishing trip to investigate all of my affairs. Any information they get they'll share with the media. With Her Majesty's Revenue and Customs. With the Financial Services Authority. With the security services – MI5 and MI6.'

'With all due respect, sir, this country is a little different from yours. I know our police can behave disgracefully. But what you're suggesting—'

'Has already happened, Scott. I'm sorry to disappoint you but you see, in the name of national security, this country is much more like Russia and Ukraine than you might imagine. I have my sources in the British government who keep me informed of things that might affect me. I pay very well for this information and it comes from the highest level, so believe me, it can be trusted. Your Detective Chief Inspector's boss is a man called Commander Clive Talbot OBE, and at this very moment he's having a meeting with some shady people in the Home Office.'

'I see. So the quicker Zarco's murder is solved the better.'

'Precisely.'

'I understand.' I frowned. 'Actually, no, I don't. You say you want Zarco's murder solved quickly. Surely that implies we ought to cooperate with the police. I mean, how else are they to find out who killed him unless we help them? I don't see how we can let them hunt for our fox in any other way. If I can borrow your metaphor for a moment, surely the risk to our rabbit is the price we have to pay in order to shoot the fox.'

'Then let me explain. I want *you* to hunt for our fox, Scott.'

'Me?'

Viktor nodded.

'You want me to play detective?'

'I pride myself on knowing the people who work for me and I think that you would also prefer to have things handled as discreetly as possible, out of your loyalty to the club and to Zarco. Am I right?'

I thought of the two mobile phones I'd already taken away from Silvertown Dock and which were now in the bag at my feet. You had to hand it to Viktor Sokolnikov: he had me sussed all right.

'Yes. You are.'

'We both know that Zarco pulled quite a few strokes in his time as City manager. It certainly wouldn't help him and it probably wouldn't help me if some of those strokes were laid bare in the media.'

'Agreed.'

'You're not afraid of the police, Scott. That makes you a very unusual man. That makes you ideally suited to steer your own course in this investigation. To risk their collective displeasure. You understand?'

'Yes. I think I do.'

'I also have the impression that it would give you some pleasure to embarrass the police a little. Am I right?'

'Of course. But look, Viktor, I'm not a policeman.'

'In Ukraine we say that a policeman is just a thief with no manners. In truth, Scott, have you ever really met a policeman you thought was well qualified for the job? No, of course not. Motorists are the only criminals in this country who are regularly caught and prosecuted. Why? Because they have registration numbers. The police will arrest someone for making a racist tweet, or an NHS manager who's fucked up, but try asking them to catch a burglar and they wouldn't know how to begin going about it. We live in a country where it is quicker to order in sushi than to summon the police.'

'It's true I don't like the police any more than I trust them. But detectives have their ways. Investigative techniques. Forensic reports. Informers.'

'I have several reasons for thinking that you can catch Zarco's murderer quicker than the police can, Scott. You are intelligent, well educated, you speak several languages, you're resourceful, you knew Zarco as well as anyone, you know the club, you know Silvertown Dock, you know Hangman's Wood, and you know football. That woman from the Yard – Detective Chief Inspector Jane Byrne: in the days it would take just to bring her up to speed with what *you* know, I'm certain this case could be solved.'

I nodded. 'Perhaps.'

'Forensic reports? I'll get those for you. Believe me, News International aren't the only ones who can pay the police for information. I guarantee to have a copy of the pathologist's report delivered to you before that cop even knows it's finished. As for informers – well, you know the same people the police do. People who've been in prison. Our own club fixer, Maurice McShane, is just such a person. Yes? Perhaps information can be obtained from this world, also. The criminal world.'

'You could be right about that, Viktor. As a matter of fact Maurice has already suggested that Zarco's death was an accident. A beating that went too far.'

I explained what Maurice had said in the car.

Viktor nodded. 'You know, I have a little experience of this myself. Back in Ukraine, in the last days of communism and the beginning of the new republic, there was no company law, no law of contract, no commercial law, so we handled things ourselves. No Mafia, just businessmen. To be honest, Scott, sometimes things went a little too far there as well, you know? So it strikes me that Maurice is probably quite right.'

I nodded.

'I'm glad you agree,' said Viktor. 'But before you say yes, Scott, let me tell you that in addition to everything I've told you, you'll also have two very important incentives to find Zarco's killer that Detective Chief Inspector Jane Byrne and the police won't have.'

'Like what?'

'The manager's job, for one thing. You find out who killed Zarco, and soon – you get the police out of our hair for good – and the City job is yours, permanently. A five-year contract. On the same salary as Zarco. Same bonuses. Same everything.'

'That's very generous, Viktor. And the other incentive?'

'I know you like pictures, Scott.' Viktor glanced up at the painting of the naked man. 'You like this portrait?'

'I hadn't noticed the face very much.'

'My wife, Elizabeth, doesn't like it. She's English, as you know, and she's not what you might call comfortable with the human body. When I first met her she used to wear a swimming costume in the *banya*.'

Banya was what Russians called the sauna.

'Anyway, I paid ten million dollars for this painting, back in 2008. It's worth twice that now Freud's dead. Perhaps more.' Viktor stood up. 'Come with me. There's another portrait I want to show you.'

We walked through the house into his study where, above a Hitler-sized desk, there was a large and very striking portrait of João Zarco. I'd read about the portrait in the London *Evening Standard* at the time of its commission. It was painted by Jonathan Yeo, one of Britain's most collectible young artists.

'Do you like it?' he asked.

'Very much,' I said. 'I didn't know you owned it, Viktor.'

'It was a gift from Zarco. I suppose his idea of a joke – to give me a picture of himself. But it's very fine, don't you think? It was having his photograph taken by Mario Testino – yes, that photograph – which gave him the idea to commission a portrait from a painter.'

I nodded. 'I won't say it's an excellent likeness. That much is obvious. But there is something very lifelike about it. And I like the way that the clothes don't matter all that much – the way they fade away. It seems to make him seem altogether more himself. He's not smiling but there's a real twinkle in his eye, as if he's about to say something else that would get him into trouble.'

'You say more than you know, Scott. When Jonathan Yeo showed the portrait to Zarco he said he didn't like it. Said it made him look too ugly and too grumpy. That's why he gave it to me. But I think it's excellent. I think that in a few years a painting by Jonathan Yeo is going to be every bit as sought after as one by Lucien Freud. Anyway, I want you to have it, Scott. That's the other incentive I was talking about.'

'You're joking. Really?'

Viktor lifted the picture down from the wall; the fact that it was covered in glass made it heavy, so I helped him.

'I'm perfectly serious, Scott. This picture is yours, now, to take home with you tonight. I want you to have this so that every time you look at it, you'll hear João Zarco saying what I'm going to say to you now:

'"Find out who killed me and why, Scott. Find my killer. I didn't deserve what happened to me today. Not ever. So, take control of the game yourself and don't just leave it to other people, like the police. Please, Scott, for me and for my wife, Toyah, you must discover who killed me, okay? Next time you look in my eyes I want to know that you're doing your best to get them. Really, I won't have any peace until you do this for me."'

Viktor could always do a wicked impersonation of Zarco's dry monotone of a voice and, just for a second, this seemed more than mere mimicry.

'That's what he seems to be saying,' said Viktor. 'Don't you agree?'

I stared at the picture now leaning against Viktor's desk. The man depicted was looking right into my eyes, as if he too was asking the same question as Victor Sokolnikov.

'Yes, I do.'

It wasn't quite the ghost of Hamlet's father, but I'll say one thing for Viktor Sokolnikov; he always knew how to get exactly what he wanted.

CHAPTER 19

Viktor's Rolls-Royce took me and the oil painting of Zarco back to my flat in Chelsea, but in truth if it hadn't been for the picture I'd have walked down to Kensington High Street and caught a cab home. When I was a boy I always wanted to own a Rolls-Royce, but now I felt acutely embarrassed whenever I found myself being driven in one. I hated the glances I got when the car stopped at traffic lights. You could see what was going through the minds of the Londoners who looked inside – even in Kensington and Chelsea. *Rich bastard.* *Cunt.* And who could blame them for thinking that about someone who was insensitive enough to ride around in the back of a car that cost ten times the average London wage? It wasn't even all that comfortable. The seats were too hard. That was bad enough but I hadn't bargained on there being a host of reporters and TV cameras outside my home in Manresa Road and I felt doubly embarrassed to be getting out of a Rolls-Royce in front of them, especially with a picture of João Zarco in my hands. In order to get through my own front door I had no choice but to bite my tongue and speak to everyone gathered on the steps and on the pavement, and it was probably fortunate that the effects of the cognac had worn off a bit by then.

'João Gonzales Zarco was without question the best football manager of his generation,' I said, carefully. 'And one of the most truly remarkable men I ever met. It was my privilege to call him a friend and colleague, and the whole game of football is the poorer for his untimely death. He was generous, a gentleman, a lovely man and I will always miss him. I'd like to extend my sympathies to his wife and family and to thank all of the fans who've already paid tribute to Zarco. You might say that I'm about to do the same. As you can see this is a portrait of Zarco, by Jonathan Yeo, and I am going in now to hang it on my wall. Thank you. I have no further comments to make at this time.'

Of course, all of the reporters wanted to know how Zarco had died and if I was going to take over as London City manager, but I thought it advisable to avoid answering any of their many permutations of the same two questions; in spite of that it took several more minutes and the help of the porter to get me and the painting safely through the front door.

When I was finally in my flat I remembered Sonja was away at a conference in Paris and before doing anything I called her, just to feel grounded again. Just to hear her voice felt like the best kind of therapy and it was easy to understand why she was so good at her job – although I have to question how it is that you need a psychiatrist to persuade you not to eat that second doughnut.

Then I called my dad, who was predictably shaken by the news; he and Zarco had been on many a golfing holiday on the Portuguese Algarve, where both of them still had homes.

After I'd spoken with him I set about hanging Zarco's picture in my own study where I keep all my football memorabilia, including a twenty-two-carat FA Cup winner's medal from 1888 – West Bromwich Albion, in case you were wondering – and the shirt George Best was wearing when he scored six against Northampton Town in the FA Cup fourth round in February 1970. When the painting was up on the wall to my satisfaction I sat and looked at it for a while; I kept hearing Viktor's impersonation of Zarco in my head. Now that's what I call psychology.

I called Maurice at home.

'You were right. Mr Sokolnikov offered me the manager's job.'

'Congratulations. You deserve it, my son.'

'Although only as caretaker. Until I fuck up.'

'No pressure, then.'

'It all seems a bit premature to me. I mean, Zarco's not even in the ground yet.'

'Then again,' said Maurice, 'we do have the second leg of the Capital One Cup game against West Ham at home on Tuesday night.'

'Which I suppose we'll have to play. Unless we hear anything from the FA to say we can postpone as a mark of respect.'

'Thrash the arse off the bastards. That's the only kind of respect that Zarco would have wanted from City. 'Sides, it's on the telly, so you might as well forget it now.'

'I suppose you're right. Look, there was something you said this afternoon, when we were searching Silvertown Dock. You said that Sean Barry had found out Claire was shagging Zarco.'

'S'right.'

'How did you find out?'

'Sarah Crompton told me.'

'And how did she know?'

'Because she and Claire are best mates.'

'So why did Sarah tell you?'

'Because... let's just say that I'm good friends with Sarah. All right?'

'Am I the only bloke at Silvertown Dock who's not getting his leg over someone else who works there?'

'No. There's you and there's the German lad, Christoph Bündchen.'

'What about him?' I asked innocently.

'Some of the lads think he's not that interested in girls.'

'Some of the lads are a bit excitable, jumping to conclusions like that.'

'Maybe. But he had a hard-on in the shower, the other day. Now that's what I call fucking excitable.'

'Did Sarah tell you that, too?'

'No. Kwame did. It's not the sort of thing you'd miss, is it?'

'I dunno. I haven't seen it. His hard-on, I mean.'

'Fucking huge, according to Kwame. And he should know.'

'Really.' Changing the subject, I said, 'Sean Barry. He's a bit excitable, too, right?'

'Oh, yeah. Very.'

'So maybe he killed Zarco. Jealous husband 'n' all that.'

Maurice shrugged. 'Maybe, yeah. On the other hand I saw him right after the game and he seemed okay. Chuffed about the result, he was. I mean, he didn't look like he'd beaten the shit out of anyone. Or told someone else to do it, for that matter. What I mean is, he didn't look guilty. But then you never know with a bloke like Sean.'

'You also said there were a few unfriendly faces in the ground when you were doing your Where's Wally this afternoon. Some right bastards, I think you called them. Who did you mean, exactly?'

'I did, didn't I? Let's see now. There was Denis Kampfner

– he was none too pleased when Zarco got Paolo Gentile to be the agent on the Kenny Traynor transfer. Missed out big time on a million quid's worth of commission. Spitting tacks about that, he was. Ronan Reilly. You'll remember the run-in he and Zarco had at the BBC SPOTY.'

'Of course I remember it. It was the only interesting thing that happened all evening. Those things are a pain in the arse.'

'It was a proper scrap they had that night, you know. And I certainly wouldn't have put it past those two to mix it again.'

'True. They're none too fond.'

'Then there was that referee Zarco slagged off: Lionel Sharp.'

'I hope you didn't see him, Maurice, or I'll start to worry about you. He's dead.'

'No, but his son was at the game today. Jimmy, I think his name is. He's in the navy. Marines, I think. Who else? Oh, yeah. Some Qatari lads. Not so much Where's Wally as Where's Ali. Dodgy lot, if you ask me. Connected to some of the powers that be in Qatar, where Zarco's name is shit. They've got one of the executive boxes. Come to think of it, they've got three or four boxes. I've heard they like some coke at half time, and I don't mean the stuff that comes out of a can. Coke and Lamborghinis and enough money to put a ceramic brake on your mouth.'

'Christ, Maurice, you've got more possible suspects there than the Orient Express.'

'And I haven't even mentioned Semion Mikhailov.'

'Who the fuck's he?'

'Ukrainian business rival of Viktor's, apparently. Huge bloke. Head like a fucking bowling ball.'

'What do you know about him?'

'Only that people are afraid of the guy. One of the security guards who operates the Mobicam – a Russian bloke called Oleg – he spotted him sitting in the crowd. Oleg said he was surprised that the Home Office let someone like that into the country. He's top Mafia, apparently.'

'I wonder if Viktor knows he was there.'

'There's not much Viktor doesn't know.'

'Sounds like we're spoilt for choice.' I laughed. 'Is there anyone we left out? Al Qaeda? Lee Harvey Oswald? Fucking hell.'

'It's a funny old game,' said Maurice.

'Look, Maurice, Viktor wants me to play Sherlock here and see if I can find the person who did it before the law does. To save him some aggro.'

'Makes sense. When you've got that much loot you've got plenty to hide as well.'

'He reckons the Home Office are out to get him; and that I hate the police just enough to have the guts to tell them to fuck off.'

'I don't recall Sherlock Holmes saying that to Inspector Lestrade,' said Maurice. 'But fair enough. I guess that makes me Watson, right?'

'If you like. All right then, draw me up a list of possible suspects. People with a grudge who were at Silvertown Dock. Or people who are just villains. And start putting your ear to the pipe. But let's keep all this between you and me. No law for now, eh?'

'I don't like talking to the old Bill any more than you do, boss. Especially after tonight. That woman from the Yard was really trying to bring you into line, wasn't she?'

'I have that effect on women,' I said. 'And while you're at

it, check on Zarco's ticket allocation. Who his guests were this afternoon, if any. It's usually just his family, but you never know.'

'Right you are, boss.'

I spent another hour under Zarco's watchful eye going through the messages and calls on his mobile phones.

Zarco's 'play phone' contained a series of texts to and from Claire Barry. Most of the older ones were spectacularly obscene. *Sexting*, I think they call it. A couple of times I glanced up at his portrait and shook my head.

'You dirty old bastard,' I said. 'What were you thinking of? Suppose Toyah had found these?'

But the tone of their exchanges changed, abruptly, when Claire revealed to Zarco that her husband had discovered the existence of the relationship with the London City manager. Sean's reputation had gone before him and suddenly Zarco's texts became stiff and formal. He told Claire he was breaking it off and it was clear from our acupuncturist's replies that the end of the love affair had caused her considerable heartache – and him, too. It seemed they had been in love with each other, although Zarco – a staunch Roman Catholic – had never made any secret of the fact that he wasn't ever going to leave Toyah. I didn't blame him for fancying Claire, she was a good-looking girl. I sent her a message of condolence – from my own phone – telling her I'd come and see her in the morning, if that was okay.

Meanwhile, I made a note of Claire's mobile number and decided to try and speak with her about what had happened when I next saw her alone at Hangman's Wood.

The 'something else' phone had a flat battery and I didn't have the right kind of charger for it, so I dropped it in my desk drawer; besides, I now had an important job to do as the new manager of London City. I called Phil Hobday to tell him what he already knew; next I called Ken Okri, the team captain, and informed him that I had been appointed the caretaker manager; then I called our first team coach, Simon Page, and asked him if he would take over from me as assistant manager, and when he agreed, I also asked him to take charge of the training session on Monday morning.

'Are the police saying anything about what happened to Zarco? Because there's this rumour on Twitter that he was beaten to death.' Simon was from Doncaster and whenever he spoke I was reminded of Mick McCarthy.

'It seems to be the theory the police are working on.'

'Not everyone loved the man like you and me, Scott.'

'That was just his management style,' I said. 'He didn't mean half the things he said. He was just winding people up. Playing mind games.'

'In any other walk of life but football that might be okay,' said Simon. 'But for a lot of people, you make these kinds of remarks and they don't forget them. They don't forget and they learn to hate. Some of the comments I've seen on Twitter are less than complimentary. "Big mouth had it coming" – that kind of thing. So I'm glad you made that speech about him at Hangman's Wood tonight. I've been watching it again on YouTube. In fact I've watched it several times. It was good what you said, and it helps cancel a lot of those negative comments out, you know? Everyone appreciated it. I just hope I'll be as good an assistant as you were.'

'Thanks, Simon. And you will be. I'm sure of it.'

When we'd finished talking about the team and our next match I switched on my Mac and watched myself on YouTube, the way you do. In truth, I wanted to see if I looked in any way equal to the man from whom I had taken over, who was always a master of man-motivation. Frankly, I had my doubts about that.

Someone behind me had shot the speech on an iPhone – I wasn't sure who and it didn't really matter – but they'd also filmed some of the players' reactions and when I looked at them, it was a shot of Ayrton Taylor that caught my eye. Taylor was the player humiliated by Zarco in front of everyone at the training session before the Leeds game and subsequently placed on the transfer list. He was standing immediately behind Ken Okri and at first I didn't know why, but something about Taylor struck me as curious. Then I realised what it was: as Taylor moved his hair with his left hand I could see that his hand was bandaged.

A good coach knows everything about the injuries all his players are carrying – especially those players who are for sale, because the first thing that happens before a transfer deal can be finalised with a new club is that the player submits himself to a medical – and it puzzled me that Taylor's injured hand should have escaped my eye until now, especially as he was left-handed.

I could have called Nick Scott, the team doctor, and asked him about Taylor's hand, but by now it was very late and I didn't want to disturb him at home in case I'd made a mistake.

So I switched on the television and chose the London City sports channel on the Sky box. Speeding quickly through the tribute to Zarco I finally found what I was looking for – footage of both teams entering Silvertown Dock a couple of hours before the game. I saw myself – ridiculous in my hideous orange tracksuit – leading the players down the tunnel to the dressing room, Ken Okri joking with Christoph Bündchen, Xavier Pepe and Juan-Luis Dominguin lost inside their own Skullcandy, and finally Ayrton Taylor wearing his street clothes. I hit the pause button and with the Sky remote moved the picture forward, frame by frame, until I had exactly the view I wanted. This was a shot of Ayrton Taylor's left hand. Quite clearly I saw him glance at the enormous Hublot on his wrist – the same kind of watch that Viktor had given me for Christmas.

Taylor's hand was unbandaged. Whatever injury he had sustained must have occurred between the team's arrival at Silvertown Dock and my speech at Hangman's Wood, an interval of time during which João Zarco had probably been beaten to death.

CHAPTER 20

João and Toyah Zarco's house in Warwick Square was a ten-minute drive from my flat in Chelsea. Pimlico is quiet at seven o'clock on a Sunday morning and as I drove along the embankment in Sonja's BMW, I hoped I'd be a little too early to encounter any of the photographers and reporters who, according to Toyah's text, had been camped outside her front door until the small hours. I was wrong about that. They were there in force and looked like they'd been there all night. Muttering curses I drove a couple of times around the communal gardens before leaving the car on the opposite side of the square, in front of the large house the Zarcos were converting, and which was covered in scaffolding hidden behind a mural designed to look exactly like the house next door, and that described itself as 'noise-cancelling'. Erected by the builders to forestall complaints from the neighbours, it didn't seem to be doing its job very well; despite it being a Sunday I could already hear the sound of drilling. Texting Toyah to tell her I was approaching her front door, I walked round to the other side of the square and the elegant six-storey white stucco mansion the Zarcos had been renting while the Lambton Construction Company attempted to complete the extensive conversions ahead of schedule.

At the last minute the mêlée of newsmen and women recognised me and, desperate for a syllable of something they could report, they surged round like a pack of beagles as a policeman helped me make my way up the steps where a house door was already opening.

'Scott! Scott! Over here, Scott!'

'Sorry to hear about Mr Zarco, sir,' said the policeman. 'It's a great loss to football. I'm a London City fan myself.'

'Thanks,' I said, and stepped quickly into the hall.

The Sunday newspapers lay, unread, on the black and white tiled floor, which was probably the best place for them. They were full of Zarco's murder, of course, and most of them carried a list of some of the things Zarco had said, as if to say here was why Zarco was killed: he had a big mouth. And there was a small part of me that couldn't disagree with that.

A tall, thin blonde woman wearing black-framed glasses closed the door behind me and let out a deep breath.

'Hello, Toyah. How are you bearing up?'

'Not well,' she said. 'This would be quite bad enough without all that as well.' She nodded at the door. 'I feel like a prisoner in my own home. They've been there all night – I could hear them, chattering away, like they were queuing for seats for the centre court at Wimbledon. Them and that policeman's radio. I wanted to ask him to turn it down but that would have meant opening the door.'

I could hear the grief choking her voice. She shook her head wearily, took off the glasses, wiped her pale blue eyes and then blew her nose with a handkerchief that looked inadequate to the task of coping with so much misery. Putting her thin arms around my neck, she said:

'Not that I could sleep, even if I wanted to – there's so much going on in my head right now. I suppose they're just doing their jobs, but I really don't know what they want. A picture of me looking like shit, I suppose: the grieving widow's tears. It's what sells newspapers, isn't it?' She sighed. 'Oddly enough, it's the neighbours I feel sorry for. On top of everything else they've had to cope with from us since we moved here, now there's this media circus to contend with.'

She smelled of white wine and perfume and she looked very tired. Her strawberry-blonde hair was combed severely back from her forehead and fastened tight with a black scrunchie. Like a lot of Australian women Toyah tried to avoid the sun, but her plain black T-shirt and trousers made her look even more pale than she probably was.

'I'm so sorry,' I said.

'Thank you for coming,' she replied quietly.

'I'll miss him a lot. More than I can say.'

'A friend emailed me a link to what you said on YouTube,' she said. 'That was very nice. And I was thinking... at the funeral, I'd like you to speak about him. If you would.'

'Of course. Anything.'

I took her in my arms and hugged her close as she started to cry. After a while she pulled away and blew her nose again. 'I must look such a sight,' she said.

'What are you supposed to look like when your husband dies?'

'Like Lady Macbeth, I guess. *What's done cannot be undone*. I played that part, you know. At the Old Vic. That was how we met, Zarco and I. It was Patrick Stewart, the actor, who introduced us. He supports Huddersfield Town Football Club. Zarco liked it that he still supported the team from his home town.'

'I know. João told me.'

'Would you like a coffee, Scott?'

'Please. If you feel like making it.'

We went down an open iron staircase and into a huge Bulthaup kitchen that looked as clean and functional as a Swiss laboratory. On the wall was a large painting of the Australian outlaw, Ned Kelly, as imagined by Sidney Nolan. I knew that Zarco had admired the famous outlaw for the simple reason that like Kelly, Zarco saw himself as someone who was very much opposed to the ruling establishment, at least in the world of football. On more than one occasion he had suggested that the best way of improving things in the English game would be 'to buy a guillotine and cut off some heads'.

'Is it just you here?' I asked, looking for the Brazilian house-keeper who was usually hovering around the Zarco home.

'I sent Jerusa home. She always goes to mass at Westminster Cathedral on a Sunday. I'd go myself if I could get out of the door. Besides, it was João who hired her and I'm not entirely sure she's legal, and what with all the cops who were in and out of here last night I thought it best to send her away while this is going on.'

'Probably a good idea,' I said. 'Best not to tempt them.'

Toyah paused in front of the built-in Miele coffee machine and sighed with exasperation.

'I'm afraid I don't know how to make this work,' she said. 'Zarco loved being the barista around here. I've never learned.'

'Here,' I said. 'Let me. It's the same model as the one I have at home.'

She nodded. 'I forgot. Coffee's your thing, isn't it?'

She leaned against the worktop and watched me carefully as I set about operating the machine.

'Was it Detective Chief Inspector Byrne who came to see you?' I asked.

'I don't know. I can't remember.'

'A woman. Looks a bit like Tilda Swinton.'

She nodded.

'Did she tell you how they thought Zarco had met his death?'

'A blow to the head, she said. And there were several other injuries that were consistent with him having sustained a severe beating.' She shrugged. 'There were other things but after that I stopped listening, for a while.'

'I see.'

'She said you'd offered to go and formally identify the body. Is that right? Because I'd give anything not to see Zarco laid out on a slab in a morgue. I've always had this thing about hospitals and the smell of ether. I really think I might faint. It's one of the reasons we never had any children, he and I. I'm very squeamish. The sight of blood just makes me shudder.'

'I have the same feeling about policemen. But, yes, I'll identify him. It's not a problem for me.'

'Thank you, Scott.'

'If there's anything else I can do, please don't hesitate to call me. Manresa Road is only ten minutes away in the car. If you feel you don't want to be alone you can always come and stay there with Sonja and me.'

'Thanks but no, I'd prefer to stay here, I think. At least for the moment. Besides, the police are coming back this afternoon. With more questions, I expect.'

'I get a bit antsy when there's lots of law around,' I said. 'So I'm not looking forward to all that myself. I'm on my way to Hangman's Wood later on this morning. She – Byrne – wants to question everyone who was at Silvertown Dock yesterday afternoon.'

'Sounds a little excessive.' Toyah smiled thinly. 'There were sixty thousand people there yesterday.'

'Everyone in the club, anyway. From the kitman to our star striker. Even Viktor Sokolnikov is going to be interviewed.'

'Good. Because personally I'd put him at the top of a list of possible suspects.'

'How do you mean?'

'Oh, come on. You know. His background in Russia. All of these oligarchs are dodgy, Scott. Viktor Sokolnikov more than most. Speaking for myself I never trusted him. I mean, you don't like to disappoint people like that, do you? I'm quite certain that Zarco was afraid of him.'

'No, he wasn't,' I said.

'Aren't you?'

'No. Not in the least.'

'I'm surprised. You've seen some of the thugs he has around him.'

'They're bodyguards. He has to be careful. Okay, I wouldn't want to tangle with any of them. But Viktor's okay. Really.' I paused for a moment. 'Look, he's asked me to take over as manager, Toyah. I wanted you to be the first to know. Before I told anyone that I've said yes. It all seems too soon to be appointing someone new, but—'

'But there's a Capital One Cup match on Tuesday. Yes, I know.' She nodded. 'I appreciate you telling me, Scott. Just be sure you know what you're getting into. And remember what I told you. That Zarco was afraid of him.'

'Thanks for the warning. But in relation to what, exactly?'

'You remember that Zarco made those remarks about the World Cup in Qatar.'

'Of course.'

'It was Viktor who put him up to it.'

'For Christ's sake, why?'

'I don't know. But I think it was something to do with the naming rights for the Crown of Thorns stadium. But don't ask me to explain about that because I can't.'

'All right. But did you tell any of this to the police?'

'That he was afraid of Viktor Sokolnikov? I might have mentioned it. But I didn't mention the Qataris.'

'What else did they ask you?'

'Nothing specific. It was more general stuff, really. Did we have any threats at home? Any anonymous phone calls? Did he have any money worries?'

'Did he?'

'No, I don't think so. But he never told me things that he thought might worry me. Anyway, she kept asking me about some photograph of Zarco that had been found in a hole in the pitch at the Crown of Thorns. I didn't know anything about it. He didn't tell me. I felt like such an idiot. Did you know about it?'

'Yes. He told me to forget about it. Not to tell anyone. He thought it was just hooligans, and so did I. I expect he didn't want you to worry.'

When the coffee was made I handed her a mug. She kept the hot mug in her hands for warmth and indeed it wasn't very warm in the kitchen. I still had my coat on and was glad of it.

'What did you tell her?'

'About what? Threats? Enemies? That kind of thing?'

I nodded.

'You mean apart from the threats and abuse you guys get during an away game at Liverpool? Or Man U? What was it they used to sing about him at the Stretford End? *One*

174

João Zarco, there's only one João Zarco. With a zarky word and a cheeky smile, Zarco is a fucking paedophile. Charming. I don't know how you stand it, Scott. Really I don't.'

'It's rough out there sometimes.'

'Not that Zarco was any kind of saint. No one knew better than you, Scott, what he was like. He could wind people up like no one I've ever met before. Me included. I probably shouldn't have told that detective that there were a couple of times when I could have killed him myself. But I did and there were.'

She sipped her coffee noisily.

'So, yes,' she said. 'He had his enemies. I'd like to tell you that things were different at home. But we were never going to win any popularity contests around here, either. Since we started work on number twelve we've had numerous complaints. Not to mention several noise abatement actions. Ironic, isn't it? Me having been in *Neighbours* for all those years. Zarco even managed to pick a fight with our bloody builders.'

'What about?'

'They demolished a bathroom in number twelve we'd planned to keep. There were these two Victorian baths, side by side and they just disappeared. Stolen, we think. Anyway, the matter was under dispute until a couple of weeks ago. So it looks like everything has been sorted out. But that hardly seems to matter now.'

'What will you do?'

'Go back to Oz,' she said. 'As soon as the funeral is over. Finish the house and sell it. I can't bear it here. I couldn't feel less welcome in this square if I was a bloody Nazi war criminal.'

I nodded. 'Look, Toyah, I know this is difficult but if you

do think of something – something that you think might help the police find out who killed him – then I'd appreciate a heads-up. It could be anything at all. Anything that strikes you as strange. Anything you didn't know about. Something that might fill in a few blanks, perhaps. As you know I've got a few reasons for distrusting the police and I want to make damn sure that no stone is left unturned in finding Zarco's killer. Even if I have to turn sleuth myself.'

'Good. I'm glad.' She nodded. 'He was right about you, Scott. He always said that you were the most dependable bloke in the whole club. Just make him proud, okay? That's all I ask. Go and win the next one for Zarco.'

CHAPTER 21

I drove back to Manresa Road so that Sonja would have her car when she returned to London from her French conference. We spoke again on the telephone and she told me she was on her way to the Gare du Nord to catch the Eurostar back home, for which I was very glad. Just having her around made me feel better about everything.

As soon as the cab company texted me to say that their driver was in front of the building I grabbed my bag and went outside. It was a bitterly cold January day and the sun was so ill defined in the uniformly white sky that it was almost invisible. With my face shrouded in the upturned collar of my new winter coat – a Christmas present from Sonja – I pushed through the many cameramen and climbed into the back of the people-carrier. I tried telling myself that I was lucky to be working in a sport which could generate this amount of media attention, that if it were any other game but football no one would have been there, but it didn't work. I felt beleaguered and under pressure – not just from the press, but from my new job and the extra responsibilities given to me by my employer. How was it possible that I was going to successfully manage a Premier League football team and solve a serious crime?

The very next moment, as if he had been reading my mind, I got a text from Simon Page asking me if he thought we should be fielding a full-strength side against the Hammers in a competition like the Capital Cup. It was an easily answered question. In spite of what title-hungry fans thought, you always let the money do your thinking for you: staying in the Premier League was worth between forty and sixty million quid a year to a club; a place in the Champions League group stage was worth about twenty-five million quid; the League Cup was worth shit. I wasn't sure if I even wanted us to stay in the competition; with the Mickey Mouse cup, sometimes losing was a better outcome than winning, and as poisoned chalices go the League Cup was more toxic than most. But even worse than winning the League Cup was the prospect of the winner being obliged to play in the Europa League, a competition that amounted to the biggest fucking headache in football. I texted back one word: RESERVES. Who knows: maybe we'd find another star like Christoph Bündchen; but for Zarco sacking Ayrton Taylor, Bündchen would still have been on the bench.

I pocketed my iPhone and turned my attention to my iPad. I'd downloaded the *Sunday Times* to read on the way to Hangman's Wood. There were a few handsome tributes to Zarco from other managers and players but as far as the circumstances of Zarco's death were concerned the writers didn't have much to go on, and quite a bit else of what was printed in that particular newspaper was about the man who was likely to take over from Zarco in the short term, and his own colourful past; in other words, *me*.

I read this with the kind of horrified fascination I might have felt if I had been reading my own obituary, which, given that a small part of me had died with Zarco, was not so far from reality;

Following the murder of João Zarco speculation surrounds

the appointment of a new manager at London City but, in the short term at least, the job seems likely to go to Zarco's 39-year-old assistant manager, Scott Manson. Born in Scotland, Manson is the son of Henry 'Jock' Manson, who played for the Edinburgh football club Heart of Midlothian, and won fifty-two caps for his country. He also played for Leicester City before founding the Pedila Sports Shoe Company in 1978, which today generates almost half a billion dollars a year in net income. Recently Manson turned down an offer from the Russian sports apparel giant, Konkurentsiya, to purchase the company for five billion dollars. Henry Manson was an old friend of the Portuguese manager, who was one of the first players to endorse a Pedila football boot when he was at Celtic.

A director of his father's company, which also earns him a salary of over two million pounds per annum, Scott Manson was a talented schoolboy footballer and played for Northampton Town while still attending the local grammar school. He was a member of the side that won the 1986–7 Fourth Division Championship with a record 99 points.

Choosing a university degree in modern languages at Birmingham University instead of a career in football, Manson played for and coached his university side and was a part-time player for Stafford Rangers, where he was scouted by the famous John Griffin and, upon graduation, joined Crystal Palace as a centre back in 1995 under Dave Bassett. After an unsuccessful season in the Premier League, Palace were relegated and Manson was sold to Southampton where he scored sixteen goals under Glenn Hoddle, and then Gordon Strachan. Southampton did well in the 2001–2 season, and even better the year after when the twenty-seven-year-old Manson was sold to Arsenal. But his career as a player ended when, in 2004, he was wrongly convicted of raping a woman at a service station off the A414 in the London Borough of Brent. Manson served eighteen months of an eight-year sentence before his conviction was quashed by the Court of Appeal, since which time he has been working his way slowly up the ladder of football management as a trainee coach at Barcelona and then Bayern Munich.

Zarco had managed La Braga and the Brazilian side Atletico Mineiro before his first spell at London City, but he was sacked in 2006 after a disagreement with the billionaire club owner Viktor Sokolnikov, and went on to manage AS Monaco before his return to London City in 2013, with Scott Manson as his assistant manager. Manson has a German mother and speaks the language fluently; he also speaks Spanish, French, Italian and Russian, which would be one reason why he might get on well with Ukrainian-born Sokolnikov. Manson, who has an MBA from INSEAD, the international business school in Paris, is generally held to be one of the smartest men in football and shares a luxury flat in Chelsea with Sonia Dalek, who is a consultant psychiatrist specialising in the field of eating disorders, and the author of several books on the subject.

Zarco's death marks the end of a tragic month in English football; two weeks ago saw the suicide of Matt Drennan, the troubled ex-England star who was a close friend of Scott Manson and formerly his team mate at Arsenal.

Sonia Dalek was actually Sonja Halek – her nickname at school had been the Dalek Queen, and I knew she wasn't overly fond of this common misspelling, so I guessed she wasn't going to be pleased to be reminded of that. I was aged forty, not thirty-nine, and I'd scored only fourteen goals while I was at Southampton. I didn't speak a word of Russian, although I'd often wanted to learn. My MBA was from the London Business School and I didn't earn a salary from Pedila, I had a yearly dividend that was very much less than two million pounds. And the Russian company Konkurentsiya had actually offered a billion quid for Pedila after buying a twenty-seven per cent share in the company.

Apart from all that, the story in the newspaper was one hundred per cent correct.

The press were outside the gate at Hangman's Wood, too, but the entrance to the club's training facility was so far away from the low-rise buildings that it hardly seemed worth coming and I almost felt sorry for the bastards. I knew most of the players had already arrived, since the car park looked like the Geneva Motor Show.

We drove up to the entrance where the team coach had just arrived to take us all to Silvertown Dock. I got out of the car; for a moment I looked through the glass wall of the indoor pitch where some of the reserves were having an informal kick-about.

They looked very young – too young to pit against a side of thugs like West Ham – and I was gambling that in spite of being close to the bottom of the table, the Hammers manager would make the same decision as I had: I figured they needed the money from surviving in the Premier League even more than we did.

One player quickly caught my eye – the sixteen-year-old Belgian midfielder, Zénobe Schuermans, who we'd bought in the summer from Club Brugge for a million quid. I'd seen him on video in a friendly against Hamburg when he'd scored direct from a corner kick. It was no wonder that Simon Page rated Schuermans as the most talented sixteen-year-old he'd seen since Jack Wilshere. As I watched he suddenly turned on a performance of skills that properly belonged in a Nike freestyle football commercial; it was mesmerising – the best thing I'd seen since watching Zlatan Ibrahimović play keepy-uppy with a piece of chewing-gum – and for a moment I started to dream about what a kid like him might do for us.

The next second I almost had a heart attack as a stray ball hit the glass wall in front of my face. The impact broke only my chain of thoughts; I turned and walked through the front door.

CHAPTER 22

Several of the older players were waiting patiently inside the entrance and fell silent as I walked in the door. They all looked suitably sombre. A few were already wearing black or sporting black armbands. Simon Page tossed aside the *Mail on Sunday* and jumped up off the waiting area sofa to greet me; Maurice, too. But I couldn't have felt less like the real manager of London City if I'd been carrying a lacrosse stick. I don't think there was anyone who wasn't aware of the fact that the last time we had done this as a team Zarco had still been alive.

It was then that I noticed a Roman Catholic priest was standing beside Ken Okri.

'Is everyone here?' I asked, one eye on the priest.

'Yes, boss,' said Simon.

As soon as I had everyone's attention I told them what they all probably knew, which was that I had accepted Viktor's offer of the manager's job.

'That's really all I have to say for now,' I told them. 'You'll hear plenty from me soon enough. Which reminds me: if you must tweet, then keep it sweet. Right then, let's get everyone on the bus. The quicker we get there the quicker we can go home. And by the way, no headphones or Skullcandy, please. This is the saddest day in the club's history so please, let's make sure that when we get to the dock we look like we recognise that fact.'

'Boss,' said Ken, 'this is Father Armfield from St John's Church in Woolwich. Before we get on the bus, if it's all right with you, the lads would like him to say a short prayer for Mr Zarco. It is a Sunday, you know.'

'Of course,' I replied and bowed my head in prayer, wishing I'd had the nous to think of inviting a priest along that morning. Zarco had been a staunch Roman Catholic, and so was I. It was being a Catholic that helped get me through prison. At least that's what I told myself. The priest was a welcome surprise. But there was more to come when we got on the bus: to my surprise all the lads started to sing the FA Cup hymn, 'Abide with Me'. I was surprised that they knew the words – many of them were foreigners, after all – only until I saw that they had downloaded the words onto their smartphones. I might have joined in myself but couldn't because I was so choked with emotion and, for a moment, I was transported to Cardiff's Millennium Stadium in 2003 and the only FA Cup Final I ever played in. I was hugely impressed with this show of loyalty to Zarco and wished only that Matt Drennan could have been here to hear it, as no one loved the hymn more than he had.

The bus route west along the B1335 through Aveley and Wennington was pretty well known to the residents of east London, and to our surprise – London City was a new club, after all – many had lined the route to pay their respects. Twenty minutes later we were driving through the gates at Silvertown Dock, slowly, so as not to crush the hundreds of fans gathered there, or the many bouquets of flowers that had been laid there as a mark of respect to Zarco. The gates themselves were almost invisible, hidden under a mass of orange scarves. Candles had been lit and the whole area now resembled the scene of some national disaster – a rail crash or royal death.

'Is the chairman joining us?' I asked Maurice.

'Yes.'

'What about Viktor?'

'He's coming later on with Ronnie. He decided it was better to meet them here rather than have them over to KPG.'

'When we get inside you'd better put the lads in the video analysis room,' I told Simon. 'They can watch the Tottenham match while they're waiting for their turn with Chief Inspector Byrne.'

'Right, boss.'

'Maurice? I'll want you with me in my office. We've got a lot to talk about.'

'Too right we have.'

We trooped inside the door of the south entrance where, on a black easel with a black laurel wreath, there was a framed photograph of Zarco – a larger version of the same Mario Testino picture that we had found in the grave.

Uniformed officers and men from the Essex Constabulary were already there, of course. Probably they'd been there all night. The corridor leading down to the crime scene was cordoned off with tape.

Simon led the players along to the video analysis suite, while Maurice and I went upstairs to the executive dining room where I found Chief Inspector Byrne and the members of her team, only now she was also accompanied by the two detective inspectors she had drafted onto her inquiry: Denis Neville, who had investigated the hole in the pitch, and Louise Considine, who was – as far as I knew – still investigating the suicide of Matt Drennan. Both of these events already seemed a long time ago.

I wished Jane Byrne a good morning, trying my best to conceal my loathing; she had conspired to have me nicked for drunk driving, after all. She smiled thinly, no doubt wondering if I was going to mention it. So was I.

'You'll remember Detective Inspector Neville and Detective Inspector Considine,' she said.

'Yes, of course,' I replied. 'Thank you for giving up your Sundays to be here. We're grateful. Detective Inspector Neville?'

'Sir?'

'I'd like to apologise for not being more cooperative when you were here the last time. Perhaps if we'd taken things a little more seriously then you wouldn't be here again now.'

Neville smiled a wry-looking smile as if he didn't quite believe me.

'No, I mean it. But with regard to the picture we found in that grave, it wasn't my call. It was Mr Zarco's.'

'I understand, sir.'

'Are you being looked after all right?' I asked DCI Byrne, politely. 'Getting everything you need? Something to drink, perhaps? Tea, and coffee?'

'Miles Carroll and his staff are being very helpful,' she said. Miles Carroll was the club secretary. 'They've opened up the staff canteen for us.'

'Good. And please order anything at all. Breakfast. Lunch. Dinner. It's on the club.'

'Just to let you know, we've asked everyone who was in the executive dining room yesterday to come back here today. We're going to be interviewing Mr Sokolnikov, Mr Hobday and all of the club's guests from the council. At the same time we're going to be interviewing the players and playing staff in alphabetical order.'

'So I could be in for a wait, is that what you're saying?'

'Actually, no, I was hoping you might sit down with me right now and do what you said you'd do last night.'

'And what's that?'

'Help me identify who disliked him enough to kill him, perhaps. After all, you knew him as well as anyone here.'

'That's correct.'

'Was he always such a big mouth?'

I winced a little at that, but left it alone.

'Zarco was someone who called a spade a spade.'

'I certainly hope not,' she said. 'That would make my job even more difficult than it is already.'

I frowned, wondering exactly what she meant by that remark. 'Excuse me?'

'I mean he does seem to have gone out of his way to irritate people, wouldn't you say?'

'Playing mind games with other teams and other managers was just part of his style. Everyone does it. But Zarco being Zarco, people just paid more attention to it. He was quite a charismatic figure. Good-looking, articulate, well dressed. A breath of fresh air after all the dour Scots managers who used to dominate the game: Busby, Shankly, Ferguson *et al.*'

'If you say so. But this was more than just mind games, I think. I'm sure you'll agree that pre-match wind-ups are one thing, but this must have been something much more serious. With that in mind, Mr Manson, I was hoping you and I could arrive at a definitive list of his enemies.'

'Sure, why not? It will save you the effort of having to look them up on Google, I suppose.'

'Oh, I've already done that.' On her iPad she showed me a dozen names I recognised. 'Here.'

I nodded. 'The usual suspects. Okay. Now all you have to do is round them up. Like Captain Renault in *Casablanca*.'

'Actually, I was hoping you might help me to shorten the list.' She shrugged. 'Or perhaps add a name or two that isn't there already. That's what I meant by definitive.'

'All right.'

'Please. Come and sit down. Talk to me, Mr Manson.'

I followed her to the far end of the room. Out of the irregularly shaped window you could see the equally irregular steel structure that constituted the exterior of the stadium. The rain had turned to snow; I felt sorry for the fans still out there. I sat down on a leather sofa and reread the list on her iPad. Our knees were just touching, which is more than could be said of our respective characters. She wasn't a bad-looking woman, just a cunt.

'Well, what do you think?' she asked.

'About this list? You know, if you were writing a piece for a newspaper about who disliked João Zarco, then you've already covered the bases with most of these names. But there's a healthy difference between disliking someone enough to bad-mouth them, and hating them to the extent that you actively want them dead. Some of these men are highly respected figures in football. This is a game that inspires strong feelings, after all. Always has done. I remember my father taking me to an Old Firm match on New Year's Day. That's Rangers versus Celtic, by the way. This was long before the laughably named Offensive Behaviour at Football and Threatening Communications Act, which sounds like an oxymoron. The ferocity of the historic and religious rivalry between those two sets of supporters was truly something to behold. And it's fair to say that murders have been committed because a man was wearing the wrong colours in the wrong part of town. Having said all that—'

'Is this where you start to talk about the beautiful game?'

'I wasn't going to mention it. But if you're asking me if I believe any of the men on this list could have killed João Zarco then the answer has to be a definite no.' I handed back the iPad. 'If you want my honest opinion, this will turn out to be fans. Newcastle thugs bent on handing out a beating to the opposition team manager. Not these men.'

'I hear what you say,' she said. 'And yet. It would seem that some of the men on my list are given to violence. For example: Ronan Reilly.'

She touched the iPad and opened a file to reveal a photograph of Ronan Reilly. He was pictured with Charlie Nicholas, Jeff Stelling, Matt le Tissier and Phil Thompson; he looked like he was sitting in for Paul Merson on *Gillette Soccer Saturday*.

'Nice suit. Not sure about the earring. What about him?'

'Reilly and Zarco actually came to blows at the BBC Sports Personality of the Year party last year, didn't they?'

'So? Reilly's a hard man with strong opinions. I respect that.'

'He's certainly a quick-tempered one. I've been reading up: in 1992, in the first year of the Premier League's existence, he received more red cards than any other player.'

'I'll take your word for it. But look, that was more than twenty years ago. And I dare say he took most of those for the team. Professional fouls and that kind of thing. The last I heard even the Met wasn't prosecuting people for getting sent off. But time will tell; it's an easy nick.'

'And yet it seems that even when he's off the park Reilly has form for this sort of behaviour. He's handy with his fists, is Mr Reilly. When he played for Liverpool there was an incident at a nightclub where chairs were thrown and another man was assaulted. Reilly was charged with affray.'

'He went to trial and was acquitted.'

'Yes, the trial was in Liverpool,' added DCI Byrne. 'Where he was a very popular man with the red half of the city.'

'It's true,' I said. 'The outcome might have been different with more toffees on the jury. Or if a few bent coppers had testified against him. That always helps with the local clear-up rate.'

She ignored that one.

'And then, before he was on television, he was manager at Stoke City, wasn't he? Where he punched a player in the dressing room and broke his jaw, by all accounts, for which he was almost sacked.' She smiled. 'Honestly, how anyone can call this the beautiful game escapes me.'

'Like I say. Passions run high sometimes. Besides, I think I'm right in saying that the player – who was no saint himself – withdrew the complaint.'

'Reilly was here yesterday. At Silvertown Dock. Did you know that, Mr Manson?'

'Yes, and I'm not surprised. It was a big game. Pretty good one, too, for us.' I shook my head. 'Look, you asked my opinion. And that's all it is. My opinion. I know Ronan Reilly. He's not a bad man. Just one with a short fuse. That fight at the SPOTY – it was just handbags.'

'It looked a bit more than that to me. I've seen the fight on YouTube. Blood was spilled. I could show it to you, if you like. Refresh your memory.'

'No, thanks. I've seen enough YouTube videos for one weekend. So maybe they expected people would pull them apart sooner than they did. Besides, they'd both had a drink. Several, probably. I know I had.'

'And that makes it all right, I suppose, Mr Manson.'

'No. But it makes it easier to understand.'

'Would it surprise you to learn that Reilly was absent from his seat for fifteen minutes during yesterday's match?'

'Have you tried to buy a drink here at half time? It can take a while.'

'Oh, it wasn't then. It was during the first half. You see, Sky Sports has made all their footage available to us, from all of their cameras, so we can time his absence precisely. And he's clearly missing from his seat for a full fifteen minutes at about the same time that people were beginning to realise João Zarco was missing. I could show you that, too, if you like.'

'Fifteen minutes of looking at what, an empty seat? I've got better things to do with my time.'

'Come now, Mr Manson. What could be more important than finding your friend's killer?'

'Look, have you asked Reilly where he was?'

'Not yet. But I intend to ask him this afternoon. I just wanted to get your input first.'

'On what? Reilly's mind? His criminal credentials? Look, I'm just the caretaker manager here.'

'You appear to be taking rather a lot of care right now, Mr Manson.'

'It seems I have to, with coppers like you around, Miss Byrne.'

'By the way, congratulations.'

'On what? Not getting nicked last night? Or landing this job?'

She smiled. 'The job, of course. But beating an alco test, that's a cause for celebration, too. And hey, unlike so many other people in football, you didn't even have to call Mr Loophole.'

'You've got a nerve,' I said.

'I don't know what you mean, Mr Manson.'

'Trying to set me up like that. Don't bother denying it. I know you were behind that little stunt. You and your friend Commander Clive Talbot OBE thought you could soften me up, did you? Make me more cooperative? Next time you use the ladies' loo in this place, you'd best make sure you're the only lady in there. Using the word in its loosest possible sense.'

She frowned as if she was trying to remember if she'd bothered to check all of the cubicles and then coloured a little. 'I see.'

'I'm sorry not to have been more help to you,' I said. 'I don't remember anyone who I think might have killed Zarco. But I have remembered why I don't like the police.'

'As if you'd forgotten.'

'Are we done here? Is that all?'

'Not quite. Mrs Zarco says her husband was having an affair with the club acupuncturist,' said DCI Byrne. 'She's Mrs Claire Barry, isn't she?'

'That's her name.'

'Her husband, Sean, runs a private security company called Cautela Limited. According to Google they just landed a big contract to look after some of the teams for the World Cup in Russia and Qatar. Zarco wasn't very complimentary about the Qataris, was he? Many of the people Cautela employs are ex-MI5, MI6. They could be out of a job if it doesn't go ahead. For that reason they might have been pissed off at him. On both counts. Business and personal. Maybe enough to work him over.'

'You tell me, Miss Byrne. You're the one with all the Home Office connections.' I stood up. 'Just so as you know, João

Gonzales Zarco was my friend. But I really don't care all that much if you manage to find his killer. It certainly won't bring him back. The only things I care about are this football club, its fans, and the match on Tuesday night.'

'You've made yourself very clear, Mr Manson. That being the case, let me be equally clear. I hate football. Always have. I think it is the greatest curse of modern life. Until yesterday the only time I'd been in a football ground was in May 2002 when, as a young WPC, I went to help police a game at The Den. Millwall lost a play-off game to Birmingham City and I was just one of forty-seven police officers who was injured trying to contain the violence that resulted – to say nothing of twenty-four police horses. What kind of person would stab a horse with a broken bottle? Or, for that matter, a young WPC? Namely me. So, I have nothing but contempt for people who go to football. And nothing but contempt for the overpaid adolescents who play the game – not to mention the egomaniacs who manage these so-called clubs. I will find Mr Zarco's killer. I promise you that. But if, while I do it, I can also bring disgrace upon the game and this place, then so much the better.'

'You can do your worst,' I said. 'But I've a feeling it won't be anything to compare with the disgrace the police managed to bring on themselves at Hillsborough.'

CHAPTER 23

'How did that go?' asked Maurice.

'As well as could have been expected. Which is to say not well at all. Detective Chief Inspector Jane Byrne is a piece of work, and no mistake. I think you can safely say we already hate each other.'

'After what happened last night I can't say I'm surprised. But a friend of mine at the Yard says she's headed for the top.'

'The top of what? A pile of shit?'

'That bad, eh?'

'Let's just say she's not a lover of the game. And right now, she seems to like Ronan Reilly for Zarco's murder.'

'I never liked that cunt much myself.'

'Him, or Sean Barry.'

'Sean?' Maurice made a face. 'Actually, I don't think it can have been Sean who killed Zarco.'

'No?'

The phone on my desk rang. It was Simon Page.

'There are two people from the FA here,' he said. 'Apparently they just missed us at Hangman's Wood.'

'The FA? What the fuck do they want?'

'It's the DCO and the FATSO. They want urine samples from four random players.'

The DCO was the Doping Control Officer from UK

Anti-Doping and the FATSO was what we called the Football Association Supervising Officer. They had enormous powers and it was wise to cooperate with them in whatever way they wanted; famously a UK anti-doping team had given the tennis player Andy Murray a drugs test when he was just about to go to Buckingham Palace to collect his OBE.

'They pick their moments, don't they? You'd better give them what they need.' I put the phone down.

'Who was that?' asked Maurice.

'Drug testing. As if having the police here wasn't enough of a hassle. You were saying. About Sean Barry.'

'It seems that finding out about Zarco and his missus prompted him to reveal that he'd had a girlfriend himself. More than one, as it happens. So we can rule out jealousy. Apparently he's more upset about Zarco's death than his wife is. Thinks it's going to damage our chances of winning anything this season.'

'He could be right. I suppose your friend Sarah Crompton told you that, too?'

'Yes.'

'So we're crossing him off our first team list.'

'I reckon.'

'What about that ref's son – Jimmy Sharp? What did you find out there?'

'He's on the bench, too. He's applied to Campion Hall at Oxford University. Wants to study theology as soon as he's out of the Royal Marines. I'm told he wants to go into the priesthood. There was an article about him in the *Daily Telegraph* a few weeks ago.'

'On the face of it, hardly the type bent on revenge.'

'Good cover, though. I mean, if you were going to do someone in it wouldn't half throw them off the scent if they thought you had the hots for Jesus. Don't forget the Reverend Green in *Cluedo*.'

'It's Mr Green these days. He's considered more PC. Apparently the Yanks who bought the rights to the game objected to the idea of a clergyman being a murderer.'

'Stupid cunts.' Maurice laughed. 'Denis Kampfner, I don't know about. Not yet. As for that Russian bloke – Semion Mikhailov – he owns a large energy company, not to mention a bank or two and a Russian football club: Dynamo St Petersburg.'

'That's interesting. Viktor is buying a player from them. Says they owe him money.'

'From what I've heard, I'm not sure which would be worse: owing Mikhailov money, or having him owe you. He's seriously bad, that man. But so far all I've got are a few sharp intakes of breath. He's looking for a house in Chelsea, I've heard. Best place for him, I reckon. But I can't imagine he'd actually misbehave while he was trying to set up home here. Wait a minute, Viktor's not buying the red devil, is he?'

'That's what he says. But keep it under your hat.'

'Good luck to him. They say Bekim Develi liked French grub even less than he liked paying the top rate of French tax. Word is he's put on thirty pounds since he went back to play in Russia.'

'Just what we fucking need.'

Phil Hobday appeared in the doorway.

'How's it going, Scott?'

'It's just beginning to dawn on me how much work I have to do.'

'For anything worth having you have to pay a price, Scott, and the price is always work and self-sacrifice. More than that if you're looking for sporting immortality; in that case it's only necessary that you die a little, maybe twice a week.'

'You won't mind if I borrow that for my next team talk, will you?'

'It's not exactly *Henry V*, but be my guest. The match on Tuesday night – perhaps we should try to get the FA to have it postponed.'

I thought for a moment. 'And fuck up the rest of our season? I don't think so. Maybe we can make Zarco's death work for us, if that doesn't sound too cynical. What I mean is, perhaps we can get the best out of the lads as a mark of respect for Zarco. Besides, I'm sure all the fans would like to mark his passing.'

'Well, you're the boss now,' said Phil.

'That's what I keep telling myself.'

'Difficult decisions. That's what management is all about. Get used to them.'

'Maurice? Go and see if the law's finished at the crime scene, will you? I want to go and take a look at the spot where Zarco died a bit later. And close the door on your way out. I need to ask our club chairman an awkward question. Maybe two.'

'Yes, boss.'

Phil sat down on a sofa arranged along the wall and waited for Maurice to leave my office. Even on a Sunday he wore a well-cut three-piece suit, an Hermès tie and a matching silk handkerchief in his top pocket. Phil was in his early sixties, not very tall with a full head of white hair; he'd started life with a top American law firm called Baker & McKenzie, which, in 1989, became one of the first international law firms in Moscow, and it was there he'd met Viktor during the privatisation of the Volga Automobile

Company. Phil had helped turn Volga into the most popular car-maker in Russia. He might have known nothing about football but he knew plenty about mergers and acquisitions and capital market transactions; and – according to Viktor – he spoke perfect Russian.

'Since you mentioned immortality,' I said, 'maybe now's the time to mention commissioning a statue of Zarco.'

'So, ask Viktor. You'll be seeing quite a lot of him from now on, sunshine. More than you know.'

'Yes, but I figured you were the go-to man for this. After all, there is a statue of you in – where is it now? The Volga factory in Nizhny Novgorod. I mean, who do you go to in order to arrange these things?'

'Do *you* think we should have a statue of Zarco outside the Crown of Thorns?'

'Yes. As long as it doesn't look like the one of Billy Bremner. Especially as that one doesn't look anything like Billy Bremner.'

'I'll mention it to Viktor.' Phil grinned. 'But that wasn't what you wanted to speak to me about in private, was it?'

'No. You know Viktor has asked me to play in a new position that's not exactly our usual 4-4-2. He wants me to become a new sort of midfielder; the clean-up-other-people's-mistakes kind who's supposed to make sure our back four avoid any defensive duties at all.'

'I get it. Someone with positional discipline but full of confidence in his own ability. Keeps the ball for long spells. Works out well for everyone. A bit like David Luiz.'

'I was thinking of it being a bit more like Hercule Poirot.'

'Who does he play for? Anderlecht?'

'Come on, Phil. I'm betting this was your idea.'

'Why's that?'

'Because it's the smart thing to do.'

'Viktor's smart.'

'If Viktor was really smart he'd get a smaller yacht. One that doesn't draw attention, like yours. No, you're smarter. Besides, *The Times* said so when it interviewed you. You were described as one of the most high-profile lawyers in the UK. But from what you said it was my impression that you'd much prefer to be low profile. That you're the grey eminence behind this particular cardinal.'

'You're pretty smart yourself, Scott. I don't know many football managers who know books by Aldous Huxley.'

'There's me and there's Roy Hodgson. Only don't tell anyone. Being smart in football is only one down from being gay. So?'

'You know, it might have been my idea – I can't remember for sure. However, if there's one useful piece of advice I can give you, it's this: at our football club, if you've got a good idea – if there's something important you want done around here – then it's usually best to make sure you let Viktor think it was his good idea first.'

'All right. Was it Viktor's idea to get Zarco to slag off the World Cup in Qatar, or yours?'

'Who told you that?'

'Toyah.'

'Okay.' He nodded. 'It was my idea.'

'Why?'

'You know that we still haven't sold the stadium naming rights. Or acquired a shirt sponsor. But we'd negotiated a deal with a Qatari bank. The Sabara Bank of Qatar. A deal worth about two hundred million pounds.'

'Yes, I can easily see why you'd want to piss them off – sure.'

'As a matter of fact that's exactly what we wanted. To

piss them off, big time. We'd agreed a deal with Sabara. And then, just before the deal was announced, Viktor found another willing sponsor. Jintian Niao-3Q Limited.'

'Catchy. I can see that on a football shirt. But only if we buy a few really fat players – like Bekim Develi.'

'According to Forbes, Jintian is the largest mobile phone operator in China. Bigger than VimpelCom and worth about thirty billion dollars. And they're about to launch a new smartphone and a new 4G network in the UK. Jintian was willing to pay us five hundred million pounds for a ten-year deal. So we hit on a scheme that might persuade the Qataris to change their minds and cancel their sponsorship. That's where Zarco came in with his comments about the 2022 World Cup. It was working, too. The Qataris were royally pissed off with us. And the Doha stadium looked like it was never going to happen.'

'Until yesterday. When Zarco was killed.'

'I fear so. Now the only impediment to their completing the deal has been removed.'

'You know that's a pretty big motive to kill someone right there, Phil.'

'I wouldn't have thought the Qataris had anything to do with it. They were pissed off, sure, but not that pissed off.'

'Two hundred million pounds being the kind of insignificant sum anyone could overlook.'

'I know these guys. I've had dinner with them. This kind of thing just isn't their style.'

'If you say so. Phil, I'm just guessing here, but I assume this is the kind of information we're hoping to conceal from the law.'

'Very much so. It's not that there was anything illegal, mind. It's just an issue of commercial sensitivity.'

'I can see what was in it for Viktor. And perhaps for you. But what was in it for Zarco?'

'Football is becoming more and more expensive, Scott. Three hundred and fifty million quid spent this summer in transfer fees by English football clubs. Another record signing at Real Madrid. That extra sponsorship money from the Chinks would have come in very handy. Even for someone as rich as Viktor Sokolnikov.'

'Every little helps, eh? I bet he shops at Tesco, too.'

'You know in five years, I'm betting three hundred million won't be enough to pay the top transfer fee.'

'You could be right. Let's hope it's us who are doing the selling, eh?'

Phil stood up and walked to the door.

'Before you go,' I said, 'I've got a Russian name for you: Semion Mikhailov.'

Phil stopped halfway there. 'What about him?'

'He was seen in the stadium yesterday afternoon.'

'Seen by who?'

'Someone who works here. I've heard he's dangerous.'

'Very dangerous. But not dangerous to us. And you can take my word for that. Viktor's taking Bekim Develi from him in part-payment for a debt when he travels to Russia tomorrow. Mikhailov isn't about to do anything to spoil that.'

'You know, if I'm going to find Zarco's killer before the cops do then it would help if I knew what you know.'

'Fire away.'

'Did Zarco have any reason to be afraid of Viktor?'

'Why would Zarco have been afraid of Viktor?'

'Not just Viktor, perhaps. You too, Phil.'

'Me? What on earth makes you say that?'

'Because Viktor knows some shady people, people like Semion Mikhailov; and so do you.'

'This is Toyah again, isn't it? You can tell she used to be an actress – she has a very vivid imagination. Look, Scott, why would Viktor and I ask you to look into Zarco's death if we had anything to do with it?'

'Sometimes if you want to stop the other side from scoring, you park the bus in the goal-mouth. Similarly, asking me to look into Zarco's death just frustrates the police, makes it hard for them to get a result. That's how it works. If all we want to do is not concede, then we severely reduce their chances of winning.'

'True. But I think Viktor mentioned bonuses, didn't he? Maybe I need to mention them again. Thanks to your father, you're already minted, of course. But I know you well enough to believe that you're someone who wants to succeed in your own right. This football club is going to be one of the great clubs, Scott. You can achieve great things at London City. Things you weren't ever able to achieve as a player with Southampton and Arsenal. All you have to do is prove that you really want to manage here.'

CHAPTER 24

Just after eleven o'clock Sarah Crompton appeared in my office to show me a draft of the press release announcing that I was to be the new City manager.

Sarah was a great-looking brunette in her forties, slim and elegant, and always dressed in a two-piece suit from somewhere like Chanel or Max Mara. Before joining London City she'd worked at Wieden + Kennedy in Amsterdam, an American-owned advertising agency responsible for Nike's 'Write the Future' campaign, which hit cinemas before the 2010 World Cup. That's the one with a bearded Wayne Rooney living in a caravan because Frank Ribery had stopped his shot going in. Sarah was smart and articulate and while I was speaking to her, even with Maurice McShane still in the room, it wasn't obvious to me what she and he had in common beyond a love of sports; Sarah was an accomplished golfer and with a handicap of just six she could easily beat me. I had a lot of time for this woman. For any woman with a brain like hers. In many ways she reminded me of Sonja.

Since Viktor and Phil had already approved the press release I had little to add to it except the fact that I wasn't 'looking forward to the challenge'. I suggested that 'trying to live up to the example set by one of the great managers of all time' was a choice of words that suited me rather better – there were quite enough clichés in football reporting without me adding to the already enormous ziggurat.

I also told her I didn't want to do any interviews until well after Zarco's funeral.

'I don't want to make your job more difficult or anything,' I said, 'but I'm upset by what's happened and I'll need a little time to get over it. Also, I'll need a little time to grow into the job before I feel even half comfortable talking about myself as the manager of this club.'

'There's a lot of interest from the *Guardian* in you being one of only four black managers in the Football League – you, Chris Hughton, Paul Ince and Chris Powell.'

'I hadn't really thought of it like that,' I said.

'Maybe you should,' said Sarah.

'No,' I told her. 'Players get bought because they're good players, regardless of colour. And managers get hired because they're good managers. I don't for a minute believe that some kind of affirmative action programme by the FA is going to fix anything. If we can get a few players on the board of the FA then maybe things will change for the better – any players, not just black ones. Until the FA stops being a club for footloose royals and fat white businessmen then nothing can happen for the good.'

'So, say that.'

'Maybe when I've got my feet under the table a bit more. When City have won something. Not before.'

'All right,' she said. 'But maybe there's one interview you should do now. Hugh McIlvanney from the *Sunday Times*. You know him, don't you?'

I nodded. 'A little.'

'He sent me an email. A very nice email, actually. He's writing a piece for next Sunday's paper about Zarco and says he'd welcome your input. And let's not forget that he is the best sports journalist in the country.'

I couldn't disagree with that assessment. It wasn't the fact that McIlvanney was a Scot that made me like him, it was his sheer ability as a writer. He never disappointed you. When George Best had died, in November 2005, it had been McIlvanney who'd written the most eloquent appreciation of George in his 'Voice of Sport' column. I still remembered a particularly favourite phrase of mine that he'd written then: 'Trying to explain how or why the sight of men playing about with a ball can hold countless millions in thrall from childhood to dotage is a task beyond rational argument. But we never needed anything as prosaic as logic when George was around.' Amen. Mac hadn't always written kind things about João Zarco – once he'd described his approach to football as 'forensic' and the man himself as 'the reigning master of sporting realpolitik' – but he was always scrupulously fair.

'Yes,' I told Sarah. 'I'll speak to him. But only because it's a piece about Zarco.'

Sarah put out the press release on Twitter and almost immediately I started getting texts from other managers that were an understandable mixture of commiserations and congratulations. From Porto – Zarco's home town – I received an Instagram of the Estádio do Dragão where, underneath a mural of the club's famous dragon, there was now an enormous brooding photograph of Zarco flanked by two members of the Portuguese National Republican Guard. While from Glasgow, where Zarco had ended his career as a very popular player with Celtic, every inch of the green railings that surrounded Jock Stein's statue was now covered with lengths of black ribbon. In the Brazilian city of Belo

Horizonte, where for a while Zarco had managed Atlético Mineiro, the Estádio Raimundo Sampaio – a ground that always reminded me a little of Arsenal's old stadium at Highbury – the pitch was now covered with flowers. It seemed that the man's death had touched people all over the world.

One or two of these texts I answered, but I was rather more interested in reading the hundreds of texts that were on João Zarco's 'something else' mobile phone. Mostly these were to and from Paolo Gentile who, as well as having been Zarco's agent, had been the club's agent, too – at least he had been in the recent transfer of Kenny Traynor. The texts between Gentile and Zarco were undated and often deliberately obfuscating, but it was quickly obvious that Zarco had taken a bung on the Traynor transfer. For a nine-million-pound transfer an agent would have made close to a million quid in commission. That was just normal pay for a top-ten football agent like Paolo Gentile, and indeed he'd made much bigger fees on higher-priced players. When Henning Bauer went to Monaco from Bayern Munich for fifty million euros, Gentile had walked away with a cool five million euros.

Put simply, a bung is an illicit payment made to ensure that a player-transfer deal is completed satisfactorily; a club sanctions a payment to an agent, some of which then gets secretly handed back to a manager in cash. Famously, during the scandal that followed on from the transfer of Teddy Sheringham to Nottingham Forest, Terry Venables alleged that Brian Clough 'liked a bung'. And not very much has changed. Managers and agents are perhaps more careful of the FA and the Inland Revenue these days but, as anyone in football will tell you, illicit payments are more or less impossible to police. I wouldn't ever take a bung myself, but if an agent and a manager decide between them that cash should change hands, then I don't see how it can be prevented.

Zarco and Gentile were wise to be cryptic. The penalties for taking a bung were severe, as the former manager of Arsenal, George Graham, would testify: he was the first and only casualty of the bungs scandal that hit football in 1995. He lost his job and was punished by the FA with a year-long ban from football.

What was less obvious was exactly how and when and in what form the bung on Kenny Traynor was to be paid to Zarco. I had to read the texts several times before I could get any kind of a handle on what had happened between the two men.

CHAPTER 25

Zarco Tuesday 20.45
VS says DK is history; KT's
yours now.

Gentile Tuesday 20.47
KT is cool with that?

Zarco Tuesday 20.48
If he wants to come to SD
he is, yes.

Gentile Tuesday 20.49
I just wish I could have seen
DK's face when you told him.

Zarco Tuesday 20.52
He was very pissed off.

Gentile Tuesday 20.53
Good. Shall I call KT tonight?

Zarco Tuesday 20.54
He's expecting your call at
home.

Gentile Tuesday 21.00
Okay. I will call him now.

Zarco Tuesday 21.03
Good. NB he's Scots. If you
don't understand him his text
English is better than his spoken.

I assumed VS was Viktor Sokolnikov, DK was Denis Kampfner, KT was Kenny Traynor and SD was Silvertown Dock.

Gentile Tuesday 21.45
Okay, I called him. He's good. Watch this space. We're going to talk again in the morning. To finalise details.

Zarco Tuesday 22.00
WTF? Why not tonight?

Gentile Tuesday 22.11
Because he says he feels bad about DK. He's been with DK for a couple of years. Thinks they're friends.

Zarco Tuesday 22.15
You told him that V won't use DK for the deal. End of story. Doesn't trust him.

Gentile Tuesday 22.20
Who does? Of course I told him. Look, don't worry, he'll get over it.

Zarco Tuesday 22.21
I hope so for your sake.

Gentile Tuesday 22.25
Believe me, they always get over it when you tell them how much they're going to get paid per week.

Zarco Tuesday 22.29
I can never understand that. Players get paid monthly like everyone else.

Gentile Tuesday 22.40
Yes, but they can only understand these sorts of figures when you tell them how much per week. It's like they're autistic.

Zarco Tuesday 22.45
I thought autistic people were good with numbers. Like Rain Man.

Gentile Tuesday 22.50
Thick then. All footballers are thick when it comes to numbers. Have to be. Otherwise they wouldn't need agents.

Zarco Tuesday 22.55
True. You have the skill set of the Borgias. Are you by any chance related?

Gentile Tuesday 23.00
LOL.

So far this was all entirely above board, but as the texts became more cryptic and numerical, paradoxically it became more and more obvious that something even dodgier than a straight bung was about to go down.

Gentile Wednesday 13.30
Okay, you have new gk.

Zarco Wednesday 14.00
And?

Gentile Wednesday 14.02
He's very happy. At least I think so. I don't understand everything he says.

Zarco Wednesday 14.06
Makes two of us.

Gentile Wednesday 14.30
There's half a quid in it for you, as discussed.

Zarco Wednesday 14.40
You remember how I want this.

Gentile Wednesday 14.50
Sure. 50k in the hand. Balance in some SSAG with Monaco STCM. Tomorrow no fail.

Zarco Wednesday 14.55
You have contact and a/c details. Get a taste yourself.

Gentile Wednesday 15.25
You sure?

Zarco Wednesday 16.00
Sure. But Friday or Monday too late. Must be tomorrow. Before it's in the paper. Understand?

Gentile Wednesday 16.05
Okay. Understood.

Gentile Wednesday 17.00
All done. Where do you want the 50k?

Zarco Wednesday 17.30
Tomorrow. Usual BP on A13. 15.00

On the few occasions that I'd heard agents and managers talking business, some of them would mention 'a quid' in a kind of shorthand, coded, Polari way, almost as if trying to conceal the real monies that were involved in modern football. A quid was a million quid, just as ten quid was ten million and fifty quid was fifty million. It was yet another reason to despair of the attitude to money in football. With the likes of Eden Hazard, Robin Van Persie and Yaya Touré on £180,000 a week, it was easy to forget that fans could be asked to pay up to 126 quid – real quid, not millions – for a match-day ticket at Arsenal, which represents a quarter of the average weekly wage.

But it seemed that things had not quite gone to plan, and probably explained why I had seen the two men arguing at the service station in Orsett, near Hangman's Wood – which was certainly 'BP on A13'.

Zarco Thursday 15.00
Where ru?

Gentile Thursday 15.02
In traffic. Be there any minute.

Zarco Thursday 15.15
Still waiting.

Gentile Thursday 15.19
More traffic. Be patient.

Zarco Thursday 15.21
Easy for you to say. Did you
buy SSAG? Like I said?

Gentile Thursday 15.22
Yes. No problem with that. But
there was a problem with the
50k. I couldn't get it today.

Zarco Thursday 15.24
WTF? So why am I waiting
here? I told you I needed that
for the weekend. What I
needed it for. Those guys will
be very pissed off if I don't
give them what I promised.

Gentile Thursday 15.25
Arriving.

Zarco Thursday 16.30
That was a waste of time.

Gentile Thursday 16.45
I told you. You'll have it day
after tomorrow. I'll bring it to
the BP.

Zarco Thursday 16.50
Be sure you do.

My first thought was that Monaco STCM was something
to do with AS Monaco FC, the football club, and that SSAG
was perhaps a player, although it hardly seemed likely that
an agent would have been encouraged to buy a player, unless
it was one of those offshore, Tevez-type economic rights
schemes that had given lawyers and accountants so much
well-paid work on the back of a talented footballer; but

things were about to become even more confusing for me and, it seemed, very much more awkward for Zarco, to say the least.

Gentile Friday 18.00
Tell me, did you know that MSTCM is owned by SCBG?

Zarco Friday 18.47
SCBG? Remind me.

Gentile Friday 18.50
Sumy Capital Bank of Geneva.

Zarco Friday 19.00
Fuck.

Gentile Friday 19.15
But surely VS knows what you're making from KT deal. It's why he agreed to bring me on board, isn't it? To give you a taste.

Zarco Friday 19.30
Yes. He knows about that. But he doesn't know I used most of the quid to buy into SSAG. He wouldn't like that.

Gentile Friday 19.37
Okay, but MSTCM wouldn't necessarily tell SCBG about the SSAG purchase. Client confidentiality etc.

I typed a few of these abbreviations into Google on my desktop PC. Monaco STCM was actually Monaco Short Term Capital Management, an investment company wholly owned by the Sumy Capital Bank of Geneva, which was in turn owned by Victor Sokolnikov; and SSAG looked like it was probably Shostka Solutions AG, which – according to the newspapers – was the Sokolnikov-owned construction company that had the contract to build the new Thames Gateway Bridge. According to what I found on Google, SSAG shares had shot up following the news that planning permission for the bridge had finally been granted. And from the texts I'd read it looked as if Zarco had used most of his bung for a bit of offshore insider-trading – to buy into his employer's company before the news that all planning objections to the bridge had been lifted could be made public. Since the announcement, the shares had risen by almost thirty per cent, which meant that if the 'half a quid' mentioned in the texts represented half a million pounds – bar '50k', presumably fifty thousand pounds – then four hundred and fifty thousand invested would have turned into almost six hundred grand. Which is a hell of a return. And thoroughly illegal.

Zarco Friday 21.00
On second thoughts, don't bring 50k to the BP. Prob best we're not seen together in public for a while. Anywhere.

Gentile Friday 22.00
Okay, you're right. Where then?

Zarco Friday 22.10
Use 123 this time.

Gentile Friday 22.13
Okay. Will you be there?

Zarco Friday 22.15
Maybe. Not sure. Before the game I have a lunch in director's dining room with VS and some people from the council. So if I'm not there just leave it where you left it last time.

Gentile Friday 22.25
Will do. Should beat Newcastle.

Zarco Friday 22.45
Scott has good idea to psyche them out. You wait and see.

Gentile Saturday 10.00
Have 50k.

Zarco Saturday 10.10
Glad to hear it.

Gentile Saturday 11.17
On my way to SD.

Gentile Saturday 11.45
Arrived at SD.

Zarco Saturday 11.48
If we meet anywhere in the ground outside 123 just blank me, okay?

Gentile Saturday 11.55
No problem. I'm not going to stay for the match.

Zarco Saturday 12.10
I appreciate this.

Gentile Saturday 12.10
No problem. *Football Focus* thinks it will be a draw today.

Zarco Saturday 12.15
Is that Keown or Lawro?

Gentile Saturday 12.18
Lawro.

Zarco Saturday 12.19
Both good defenders, but Keown is smarter. Besides, you can't have a haircut like Lawrenson's and be taken seriously. Put your money on City.

Gentile Saturday 12.23
I never bet on anything that's not a sure thing.

Zarco Saturday 12.45
Sensible guy.

> **Gentile** Saturday 13.00
> Delivered as promised. Just missed you, I think. Easy as 123. Good luck this afternoon, and enjoy your weekend. I'm off home now. I have to fly back to Italy this evening.

> **Gentile** Saturday 15.15
> A thank you would be nice.

> **Gentile** Saturday 15.25
> Whatever. At airport.

> **Gentile** Saturday 19.00
> Back in Milan. Where the fuck are you?

There were no texts from Zarco after 12.45 p.m. and, according to Phil Hobday, Zarco had left the director's dining room at around 1.05 p.m., after which he hadn't been seen alive again. Where had he gone after that? It was impossible to imagine him being forced to go somewhere against his will without someone noticing. Zarco's face was in a thirty-foot-high mural on the side of the stadium. He wasn't exactly anonymous. Surely someone must have seen him.

These texts begged several other questions, too: if Paolo Gentile had brought a fifty grand bung to Silvertown Dock and left it hidden somewhere for João Zarco, where was it now? Was it even where he had left it? After all, fifty grand is a pretty good reason to beat someone up and rob them. Unless of course he hadn't brought it at all, and they'd quarrelled again. Wasn't it possible that the texts Gentile had sent to Zarco after 1 p.m. had just been a cover? And where better to be now that the police were investigating Zarco's death than safely at home in Italy?

On the other hand, maybe Toyah was right after all, and Zarco had good reason to be afraid of Viktor – a better reason than even she knew. Just what would Viktor have done if he'd found out that Zarco had bought shares in SSAG on an insider tip?

In the hope of learning more – what was 123? Who were the guys he'd needed the fifty grand for? Could they have been sufficiently pissed off at Zarco to have killed him? – I called Paolo Gentile on the number listed on Zarco's mobile phone, but I wasn't at all surprised when the call went straight to his voicemail. I left a message asking Gentile to call me urgently.

By now I had also realised just how sensitive all of these texts were and how dearly the police would have wanted to see what was on Zarco's phone. Of course I knew that I was committing a serious offence by not handing it over – withholding evidence in a murder inquiry carries a prison sentence, and I knew all about what that was like. I had no wish ever to go back to Wandsworth. But Zarco's reputation and that of London City were of greater consequence than this. For the first time in my life I knew the absolute truth of Bill Shankly's famous quote when he was still the manager of Liverpool: 'Some people believe football is a matter of life and death... I can assure you it is much, much more important than that.'

And how.

CHAPTER 26

I went along to the players' lounge where everyone was watching Sky Sports, just for a change – Tottenham versus West Bromwich Albion, the first of three Super Sunday televised matches. In the studio before the match there was, of course, plenty of talk about Zarco's death and my appointment as manager, which the three pundits seemed to think was a good thing. I tried not to pay attention to it but I'd always respected Gary Neville; that back pass to Paul Robinson in the Euro 2008 qualifier against Croatia aside, you had to admire a man who, at the age of just twenty-three, had had the strength of character to tell Glenn Hoddle just what he thought about the faith healer the England manager had brought into the squad.

Every so often an attractive uniformed WPC with a clipboard from the Essex Constabulary would summon one of the players or staff who'd been at Silvertown Dock the day before for a short interview with a detective; but this seemed to be taking a while and some of the lads near the end of the alphabet were impatient to get back home to spend what would have been a rare Sunday with their families. A few of the others were behaving in a rather boorish and tiresome way towards the poor WPC; when she came into the room one of the younger players said, 'Hey, lads, the stripper's here,' and I quickly gained the impression that this had been going on for a while.

'That's enough of that,' I said firmly. 'This woman has got a job to do. Try to remember that this is a murder inquiry and treat her with respect.'

Which was good, coming from me.

Everyone groaned, not because they disagreed with me but because Tottenham, who were just three points behind us in the table, scored first.

'Hey, boss, can you get someone to turn the heating on? It's brass monkeys in here,' someone said. 'We've asked Big Simon but nothing seems to happen.'

Which explained why a moody-looking Ayrton Taylor was wearing a black shearling coat from Dolce & Gabbana which seemed to match his curly, rockabilly hair; on the other hand, since the coat cost seven grand, maybe he just didn't want to leave it lying around for someone to fuck with – give it a haircut, perhaps. I couldn't blame him for that. Players were always pissing around with each other's clothes – cutting the arse out of a pair of jeans, and sometimes far worse. I'd looked at that coat in the shop myself and decided that a) seven grand was far too much to pay for a coat and b) I looked like a tit in it anyway. That was how Sonja came to buy me a nice grey cashmere coat from Zegna. Taylor's hand was still bandaged but he wasn't trying to hide it in his pocket as perhaps he might have done if he really had battered Zarco to death.

'I'll see what I can do,' I said, then I caught Taylor's dark eye. 'Ayrton. Could I have a word with you, please?'

'Sure.'

We stepped outside and walked down the corridor until we came to a bulletproof glass cabinet containing Viktor Sokolnikov's most precious possession – a replica of the famous Jules Rimet trophy that he had bought from the Brazilian Football Confederation for fifty million dollars.

The real one was in a vault in Viktor's bank – but most people believed the one on display at Silvertown Dock was the real thing.

'What happened to your hand?' I asked.

'I punched a locker door yesterday, after the match,' said Ayrton. He was English, from Liverpool, but he'd grown up in Brazil where, in spite of a father who wanted him to become a racing driver, he'd learned to play football.

'Why, for Pete's sake?'

'Because I was frustrated, I suppose.'

'About what?'

'I wanted to play yesterday, of course. There's nothing worse than seeing your team do well without you. Even when you're injured. Christ, you should know that, boss. I just wanted to get on the park and score a goal myself.'

'You still feel that way?'

He nodded at the trophy. 'There's a World Cup coming up soon. The only way I can get picked to play for England is if I'm playing regular football, and scoring goals, but there's not much chance of that happening now.'

'Show me the door,' I said.

'What?'

'The door you punched,' I said. 'Show it to me.'

'Why do you want to see a fucking door?'

'Just humour me.'

Taylor shrugged and led the way downstairs to the dressing room where there were twenty-seven locker doors made of polished oak, each of them behind an individual seat upholstered in orange suede. He led me to the number seven locker, which had Christoph Bündchen's name on it. I opened the door and saw that it was split all the way through the wood, as if it had been struck with considerable force.

'Christ, how hard did you hit it?'

He looked sheepish. 'Hard enough. I used to study karate in my spare time and thought I could still do that kind of stuff. But it seems I can't do that either.'

'Have you had an X-ray?'

'No need. I can tell it's not broken. I bruised the bones, that's all.'

I took his hand by the fingers and turned it over.

'Nice bandage. Who did it?'

'The wife, Lexi. She used to be a nurse. She was waiting at Hangman's Wood for me to drive me home last night. You know I lost my licence a while back. She always picks me up after—'

'Why her and not the team doctor?'

'Because I was embarrassed about it.'

'You're fucking crazy,' I said. 'You could have broken it.'

'I figured it was better than hitting Christoph,' said Taylor. 'Given that it's him who's got my place in the team.'

'True.'

Then he smiled. 'Oh, I get it. You thought maybe it was me who smacked Zarco.'

'Someone did.'

'It wasn't me. Between you and me I hated the bastard, sure. And he probably had it coming. But not from me. Besides, I've got a witness who saw me do this. Manny.'

Manny Rosenberg was the kitman.

'Maybe you hit the door because you'd already hit Zarco. Good way of explaining your hand. You could have hit the door to disguise the bruising.'

'But you don't really think I hit him, do you?'

'Not really.' I glanced at the Jules Rimet. 'How old are you, anyway, Ayrton? Twenty-eight?'

'Yes. This is my last chance.'

'You know we've had offers for you from other clubs?'

'I know. But Fulham and Stoke City don't exactly blow my hair back.'

'Can I be frank with you?' I nodded at the iPhone in his unbandaged hand. 'That's to say I don't want to read anything I say now on Twitter.'

He nodded and dropped the phone into his coat pocket.

'I thought the way Zarco treated you was unfair. But you should never have sworn at him like that. Even though he threw a cone at you. In my day as a player managers did much worse than that. It's good to get angry in football. It's an emotional game. Big Ron Atkinson chased a player around the dressing room at Villa and ended up punching the wrong bloke. Lawrie McMenemy had a ruck with Mark Wright in the showers at Southampton. And when he was at Forest Cloughie punched Roy Keane.'

'Really? Jesus. I can't imagine anyone punching him.'

'Keane says now it was the best thing that ever happened to him. Players do things that piss coaches and managers off – like being lazy in training – and when that happens they deserve a kick up the arse. What happened was my fault. You were a lazy bastard but I should have been the one who kicked your arse, Ayrton. Not Zarco. I was taking the training session and it should have been me who bawled you out.'

'Thank you.'

'You won't get a place in the England squad if you're a lazy cunt – you know that, don't you?'

'Yes.'

'I admire fair play and sportsmanship but there's no place in my squad for anyone who doesn't work hard in training.

If you're prepared to do that, then I want you in my team. As far as I'm concerned, everything that happened between you and Zarco is water under the bridge if you can tell me now that you want to stay here at City and work your fucking balls off for us.'

'Do I want to stay here? I never wanted to leave.'

'And you'll work hard for me?'

'Yes. Yes. You mean it, boss?'

I put my hands on the boy's shoulders and looked him squarely in the eye.

'Of course I mean it. We need an experienced player like you, Ayrton. There's bags of talent here but apart from Ken Okri there's no one in our squad who can steady the younger lads and help to keep them going if we're still behind with five minutes left to play. When we lost 4–3 to Newcastle just after Christmas, you were the only one who was still looking for the equaliser at full time. You may be a lazy bastard in training but in a match you've got that never-say-die attitude that wins games, Ayrton. There's no obligation to win when you're playing football, but there is an obligation to keep trying. That's what the fans believe. And it's what I know. The number of games I've seen won in the last minute—'

'You're right, boss. Arsenal against Liverpool in May 1989, Man U against Bayern Munich in 1999, Man City against QPR in 2012.'

'That's what I'm talking about, son. The really beautiful thing about football is that at any moment, a match can turn the other way. A goal changes everything. The last minute of the game is always, always, without exception, the most important minute of the match; and yet the number of times you see a winning side relax before the whistle has gone.

People used to talk about Fergie time as if by chewing the fourth official out he'd unfairly get a few more minutes of extra time so that Man U could steal the match. Bollocks. It was just that Fergie had schooled his players never to give up. The players saw him walking up and down, getting mad and they knew that he hadn't given up. So they didn't either. That's what people didn't understand. What they still don't understand.'

He smiled and it was the first time I'd seen him smile in ages. 'I'm really off the transfer list?'

'You can play on Tuesday night if Simon thinks you're fit enough.'

'Fucking brilliant.'

Ayrton pulled his phone out of his pocket. 'Can I tell Lexi?'

'Yes.'

'She'll be over the moon, boss. There was no way she wanted to leave London to live in fucking Stoke.'

'But no tweets. In fact, if I were you, I'd stop tweeting altogether. It's only cunts that pay attention to Twitter.'

'Yes, boss. Whatever you say.'

'And no more punching lockers.'

I didn't know it, but I'd just made one of the best decisions of my new managerial career.

CHAPTER 27

I went outside onto the pitch for a cigarette break without the cigarette – to breathe some fresh air and clear my head a little. Mist hung over the stadium like a poison gas rolling across a line of trenches and the east London air tasted fresher than it looked, with just a hint of salt blown in off the last high tide. Just to walk on the pitch made me feel grounded and I longed to run up and down for a while. Instead I fetched a football and for several minutes played keepy-uppy – what the Americans call 'ball-juggling'. It wasn't that I was particularly good at it but, for me, there was always a Zen-like absorption to be found in doing this; it clears the head wonderfully because it's impossible to think of anything else while you're trying to keep the ball off the ground. Sometimes it's as good as meditation; perhaps better, in that it helps to keep you fit as well.

'Get off the fucking pitch, you stupid bastard!'

I looked around to see Colin Evans striding down the touchline like an army sergeant. When he saw it was me, he slowed his stride and checked his anger.

'Sorry, boss,' he said. 'I didn't know it was you.'

'No, you're right, Colin,' I said. 'I shouldn't be on the grass. What with all these coppers around I just had to get outside for a few minutes; and then I couldn't help myself.'

'That's all right,' he said. 'I expect you have a lot on your plate right now.'

'More than I can eat.' I frowned. 'That reminds me: I'm hungry.'

Leaving Colin, I went up to the players' dining room and collected a chicken salad from the buffet, but not before thanking the kitchen staff – or at least as many of them as I could see – for coming in to the dock on what was supposed to have been a day off. Sometimes being a manager is as much about diplomacy as it is about football. As I see it, you have to make up for all the dimwits who surround you. Like those dimwit players at our own club who didn't jump to their feet when Peter Shilton – the player with the most caps for England, ever – came to visit our dressing room. Zarco had gone mad at them for the lack of respect. One hundred and twenty-five caps and an England career that spanned twenty years and they didn't get off their fucking arses.

With my back to the room and sitting at a corner table I'd hoped to snatch lunch without being bothered by anyone, but I wasn't there for very long before Detective Inspector Louise Considine was hovering over me with a coffee cup in her hands and a curious look in her eye.

'Mind if I join you?' She smiled. 'On second thoughts, please don't answer that. I'm so not up to anyone being aggressive to me today.'

'Please do,' I said and for a moment I even stood up, politely. 'No, really. You're very welcome.'

'Thank you.'

'Hard day?'

'Yes, but I don't want to talk about it.'

We sat down. She was wearing jeans and a tailored tweed jacket with a matching waistcoat. The handbag slung over her arm was old but classic: something her grandmother had given her, perhaps.

'So I assume they must have drafted you in for your footballing expertise, Miss Considine? Not that you'd know very much if you support Chelsea.' I frowned. 'Why do you support Chelsea, anyway?'

'Because José Mourinho is the handsomest man in football?' she said. 'I don't know.'

'That was obviously before you met me.'

'Obviously.' She sipped the coffee and grimaced. 'This isn't a patch on the coffee you make at home,' she said.

'I'm glad you think so.'

'Who needs a man to be handsome as long as he makes excellent coffee?'

'It's a point of view. Every man needs a skill, right?'

'So, when they sack you from London City, you can open your own coffee shop.'

'I've only just got the job,' I said. 'It's a little early to be thinking about the sack.'

'Not at City. How many managers has the club had since it came into being? A dozen?'

'Maybe. I never counted.'

'You're number thirteen by my count.'

'I guess I deserve that after my Chelsea remark.'

'Yes, you do.' She smiled and stared out of the window at the pitch. Light filled her clear, perfect blue eyes so that they resembled two matching sapphires. Suddenly I wanted to lean forward and kiss each of them in turn.

'Then if I might mention manager number twelve, for a moment,' I said. 'And the crime scene. Have the forensics people finished down there?'

'Yes. Who should we return the key to?'

229

'You can give it to me,' I said.

She laid a key on the table. I picked it up and dropped it into my pocket.

'Find anything interesting?' I asked.

'No,' she said. 'Not a thing. But then I haven't yet had a chance to go crawling over the ground with a magnifying glass.'

'I suppose you wouldn't say even if you had.'

'Walls have tweets,' she said. 'Especially around here.'

'Footballers and their smartphones, eh? I sometimes wonder what they did before them.'

'Read books, like everyone else. Then again, maybe not. Did you know that one of your players – and I won't say who – is illiterate. He couldn't read his own statement.'

'That's not so surprising. English is a foreign language for a lot of—'

'He is English.'

'You're joking.'

Louise Considine shook her head.

'He really can't read?'

'That's what illiterate means, Mr Manson. Oh, and another of the players thought Zarco was Italian.'

I finished eating and sat back on the chair.

'We have all sorts of nationalities here. Sometimes I have trouble remembering these things myself.'

'Now that I don't believe. You being such a polyglot.'

'I'm half German, remember? And you know what they say: a man who speaks three languages is trilingual, a man who speaks two is bilingual and a man who speaks one is English.'

She smiled. 'That's me. O-level French, and that's it, I'm afraid. I can barely tell my *cul* from my *coude*.'

'Now I know that's not true.'

230

'Maybe.'

'They're like children, sometimes, footballers. Very large, very strong children.'

'And how. Two of them wept like babes: Iñárritu, the Mexican, and the German – Christoph Bündchen.'

'That's nothing to be ashamed of. They're sensitive lads. I wept myself when I heard the news.'

'Yes, I'm sorry for your loss. Again.'

I nodded back at her. 'You know, it's been a while since Matt Drennan hanged himself. But the police still haven't released the body so his poor family can bury him. Why is that, please?'

'I don't really know. I'm no longer on that case. At least not that particular case.'

'Case? I didn't realise it was a case. What's taking so long?'

'These things can take a little time. Besides, the circumstances of Mr Drennan's death have obliged us to reopen a previous inquiry.'

'What exactly does that mean?'

She looked around. 'Look, perhaps this isn't the right place to tell you about it.'

'We can go to my office if you like.'

'I think that might be better.'

We got up from the table and went along to my office in silence. She walked with her bag slung over one shoulder and her arms folded in front of her chest, the way women do when they're not entirely comfortable about something. I closed the door behind us, drew out a chair for her and then sat down. I was close enough to smell her perfume – not that I could tell what it was, merely that I liked it. In spite of who and what she was, I liked her, too.

'So. What did you want to tell me, Miss Considine?'

'I'm sorry to land it on you like this,' she said. 'Really, I am. Especially now. But you'll hear about it soon enough. Tomorrow, probably, when we make it official.' She paused for a moment and then said: 'We're reopening the police inquiry into the rape of Helen Fehmiu.'

I was silent as, for a moment, it was 23 December 2004 and I was back in the dock at St Albans Crown Court, about to be sentenced to eight years in prison for rape. I closed my eyes wearily, half expecting that Louise Considine was going to tell me that I was under arrest again. I lowered my head onto the desk in front of me and let out a groan.

'Not again.'

'I'm afraid so.'

'Christ, why?'

To my surprise she laid her hand on my shoulder and left it there.

'Look, Mr Manson, you're not a suspect so there's no need for you to worry. No need at all. I promise you, you're in the clear. If anything, this is good news for you. You have my word on it.'

I sat up again. 'That's easy for you to say.'

'It really is good news, you know. It will completely remove any lingering suspicion that in spite of your acquittal you might have had something to do with it.'

'I don't understand,' I said. 'Why now? It's been almost ten years. And how does Matt Drennan's death have any bearing on what happened to Helen Fehmiu?'

'Well, you see we found a suicide note in Mr Drennan's pocket. In the note he talked about you. In fact, his suicide seems to have had quite a bit to do with you, Mr Manson.'

'I find that hard to believe.'

'Rather than me try to explain what I mean, the quickest

thing would be if I were to let you read it. The note. I have a PDF of it here.'

She picked up her handbag, took out an iPad and then showed me an image of a handwritten note. I didn't recognise the childlike handwriting but the signature at the bottom with a smiley face inside the capital 'D' of Drennan was familiar, although on a suicide note it struck me as rather strange. Then again, it was quite typical of the man: I imagined him writing the note, then signing it with the smiley face out of sheer habit, as if he'd been signing an autograph for a fan in a pub or outside a football ground. Drenno was never too busy to sign an autograph for whoever asked him. It was one of the reasons why so many people loved the man.

Dear all,

I've come to the end of my rope, if you'll excuse the cliché. My time in football being over now, there doesn't seem to be anything worth living for. My life at the bottom of a glass isn't any kind of substitute for how things used to be when I was a player. I figure it's better to check out before I really fuck up big time. Tiff, I love you, I love you. I am so, so sorry. For everything. But I want to say an especially big sorry to my pal Scott Manson. Feeling guilty at having let you down so badly for all these years. I kept my mouth shut when I should have said something long ago. It was me that put Mackie up to stealing your new car, back in 2004. Just a joke. I knew how much you loved it. But I didn't know Mackie would nick it and then do what he did. It was him that raped that lassie. I couldn't say then because I couldn't grass him up. See, he did time for me years back, in Scotland, when I fucked up the first time. I tried to get him to hand himself in but he just wouldn't do it. Every time I used to see you in the nick it used to cut me to pieces. I *made Mackie join the army to serve his country by way of atonement. He's dead now so it doesn't matter, I suppose. Wanted to tell you the other night but didn't have the guts to look you in the eye, Scott.*

Anyway, that's it for now. Cheerio. See you in God's dressing room.

Matt Drennan

'I've managed to get hold of a photograph of Sergeant MacDonald,' she said, 'and if you'll forgive me I think it's fair to say that he looks not unlike you. He was part Nigerian. It might account for why Mrs Fehmiu was prepared to identify you as the rapist.'

I nodded slowly.

'You're nodding like it seems to make sense,' she said.

'It certainly explains one or two things that have always puzzled me about what happened back then,' I said.

'Such as?'

I told her how my car had disappeared from outside Karen's house in St Albans, and then reappeared again; and how Drenno had visited me regularly in prison.

'He obviously felt guilty,' she said.

'I suppose so. And now I come to think of it, Mackie had a conviction for car theft. Drenno used to say he'd nicked cars, too, when he was a kid in Glasgow, only he never got caught.' I sighed. 'The fucking idiot. Drenno was always playing stupid practical jokes like that. Every day. And I mean every day. Sometimes it seemed to me that he wanted to make people laugh more than he wanted to play football. Once some bloke's wife bought him one of those fat Mont Blanc Meisterstück pens as a birthday present and Drenno filled it with his own piss. Stupid. Juvenile. But at the time very funny.'

'So he must have known that you were having an affair with this woman, Karen, and where your car would be. Did you tell him?'

'God, no. But for all his stupid larks he was actually quite clever, so he must have worked it out. And now I seem to remember that one day he tailed me in his car from the Arsenal training ground at Shenley. I was sure it was him and then I wasn't, if you know what I mean. But it must have been him, I think. I should have known there were no lengths Drenno wouldn't go to for the sake of a practical joke.' I nodded. 'Wait, I remember now. My car keys. He came to the garage with me when I bought the car. He said he was thinking of buying one the same. Maybe he did, for all I know. Anyway, he must have rung up the salesman, pretending to be me, told him I'd lost my key and asked him to order me a spare from Germany. That's the only way they could have done it. If he gave that bastard Mackie a key.'

Louise Considine nodded. 'I know Helen Fehmiu is dead and it won't help her, but rape is a serious crime and we're reopening the inquiry because we have to, although it seems pretty cut and dried. I may have to interview you formally, so that you can tell me the full story again. I hope you'll understand. And I give you my word that when I do, the press won't know about it.'

'Thank you.'

She touched my hand. 'I'm sorry I had to mention it at all. But you had to know the truth about what happened. I think you know that, don't you?'

'Yes.'

'I'm just sorry it's going to change your perception of Matt Drennan.'

I shook my head. 'It won't, you know. I honestly can't

find it within me to condemn him. After all, he's paid a dreadful price. He's dead. That's much, much worse than anything that happened to me.'

CHAPTER 28

Sometimes, modern buildings function in ugly, hidden ways never quite conceived by the men and women who design them. They have their own inbuilt wastelands – leftover spaces which go unseen by the public and which often end up having minor, unplanned, alternative uses. The place at Silvertown Dock where Zarco's body had been found was such a space – a forgotten area that existed in the bird-shit gap separating one independent structure from another – a no-man's-land space between the seating bowl and the outer steel frame. In an attempt to hide this particular space – or perhaps to protect it from illicit use – a crude, triangular gunmetal grey door with a weather-tough Abus padlock had been installed; and stepping through it now I found myself in a similarly triangular concrete spot that was dominated by a long, sloping, polished steel column that reached up through the uppermost branches of the distinctively jagged support structure and into the afternoon sky.

I closed the steel door behind me, sat down on my haunches and looked up and around, trying to picture the dreadful fate that had befallen Zarco. As Jane Byrne had observed, with no windows in sight there was nowhere he could have fallen from – unless he'd jumped off the very top of the building – and it was just the kind of secluded, fag-end place where a savage beating could have been handed out to Zarco without any fear of disturbance. It seemed a lonely, awful place for a convivial man like him to have ended his life. I had hoped in some vague way to connect the scene of the crime with the texts on Zarco's 'something else' phone. Could this be the '123' where Paolo Gentile was supposed to have brought fifty grand in cash?

The key to the door had a plastic tag on the end which read 'SD Outer Ground 28/1', which was a long way from '123'. And since there was no roof, it was hard to imagine that Gentile would have left fifty grand exposed to the elements, even if the money had been inside one of those 'overboard' waterproof hold alls that yachtsmen use. Suppose someone from building maintenance had come in here and found it? There were a few brushes and brooms stacked in the corner which seemed to suggest that might have been a possibility. The keys to the door's padlock – two of them – had been easily located; they were still in the dock caretaker's key-safe. Had there ever been three keys? No one was quite sure, but other such padlocks had been supplied with three.

If I'd hoped to have some great detective moment and somehow 'see' the crime in my mind's eye, it didn't happen. Right then the only insight I had was that I was entirely unsuited to any of the tasks my new employer had given me. I felt cold and more than a little bewildered, especially after Louise Considine's unwelcome news. Things were moving much too quickly for me right now. It was all I could do to remember where I had parked my car. Which was when I remembered that Maurice had done it for me.

I stood up and went outside again, locking the door carefully behind me. I was halfway back to my office when I saw Simon Page striding towards me with a face like a calamity was about to befall us.

'Disaster,' he said. 'Bloody disaster.'

'What is?'

'That stupid fucking German poof has only gone home, that's what's fucking happened.'

'You mean Christoph Bündchen? For Christ's sake, Simon, keep your voice down. If one of these coppers hears you using words like that they'll nick you for whatever it is they nick you for now when you call someone a poof. Hate crime or something.'

'I'm sorry, boss, but I'm at my wit's end trying to find him, that's all.'

'Look, what's the problem? The police said they could go home after they'd been interviewed.'

'Maybe the police did, boss, but UKAD certainly didn't; he was one of the four players drawn at random to give a urine test.'

'Oh fuck, I'd forgotten all about them.'

'That's right. After his interview with the police this morning it seems that Chris buggered off in a taxi back to Hangman's Wood, like everyone else when their interview was over. I told him before he left the room with that WPC to come straight back, but the daft bastard must have forgotten. At least I hope he just forgot. Anyway, the drug testers are about to go home. Unless we can find him in the next fifteen minutes he'll be in breach of the strict liability rule on dope tests and charged with failure or refusal to take the test.'

'You've tried his mobile? And Hangman's Wood?'

'I've tried his mobile, his landline. I've rung Hangman's Wood. I've done everything but send a fucking carrier pigeon to his mum and dad in Germany, so unless he's remembered and is already on his way back here to take the test, he's buggered and so are we without a fucking striker. Because you mark my words that's exactly what's going to happen if that stupid Kraut doesn't take that fucking test. They'll slap a ban on him for sure.'

'We've still got a striker. I had a conversation with Ayrton Taylor an hour or so ago and took him off the transfer list.'

'Thank fuck for that.'

'But you're right, this is serious. Look, I'll come and speak to the doping people now.'

'Don't get your hopes up, boss. These people can be right bastards when they've a mind.'

We went down to the doping control station near the dressing room; all the big clubs have them now. It's just a suite of antiseptic-looking rooms, including a lavatory, some chairs, a table covered in a black cloth, a sink, a box of sample collection bottles, a chiller cabinet containing plenty of bottled water – sometimes you have to drink a lot of water before you can pee – and, on that particular afternoon, an air of crisis. On the wall was a poster that read:

Cannabis →

← Success

Make your choice. It's your career.

Seated under the poster were two men wearing shirts and ties and blue blazers and faces as long as two streaks of dope-free piss. They got to their feet as we came through the door.

'Scott Manson,' I said. 'Acting club manager.'

'Hello,' said a man holding a clipboard. He showed me a plastic identity card on a red ribbon around his neck and then shook my hand. 'My name is Trevor Hastings and I'm the doping control officer with UK Anti-Doping. And this is the Football Association Supervising Officer.'

'Pleased to meet you, gentlemen.'

'Is Christoph Bündchen available to take the test?' he asked politely.

'I'm afraid there has been a misunderstanding,' I said. 'You'll be aware that João Zarco was murdered here yesterday afternoon, and that the police are here now. They've been interviewing the players and playing staff, and it's beginning to look as if Mr Bündchen – who is German and doesn't speak the best English – has confused the meeting he was supposed to have with you, to give a urine sample, with the meeting he had with police officers earlier on today. As far as we can determine he's gone home. We've called him and left messages instructing him to return here as soon as possible. But so far without success.'

The DCO looked at his watch. 'I understand what you're saying, Mr Manson, but I have to inform you that the player was informed he would be subject to a drugs test today, and he has already signed a consent form; so unless the player presents himself for a test within the next ten minutes, he will be in breach of Part 1, Section 5A of the FA's anti-doping regulations, and the penalties set out in Regulation 46 will apply to this violation.'

Simon opened a copy of the FA's procedural guidelines that was lying on the station table and started to look for the relevant section.

'I understand that,' I said. 'But it seems to me that some people might think it a little unreasonable not to cut someone a bit of slack under these extraordinary circumstances. It's been a while since I read the regulations but I do think you ought to reconsider your position here.'

'I'm afraid a breach is a breach. It's for an FA disciplinary commission to decide on whether or not that breach is justified. At a formal hearing.'

'I see.'

'Fucking hell,' said Simon, who always got more Yorkshire when he was angry and upset. 'Have you seen the penalties in Regulation 46, boss? It's a minimum one-year suspension for a first violation. One bloody year. Christ, that could end the German lad's career. And all because of a silly misunderstanding. Listen here, Mr Hastings, you've got to be joking.'

'I don't think Mr Hastings is joking, Simon. He's just doing his job, aren't you, Mr Hastings?'

'Yes, I am. I'm glad you see it that way, Mr Manson.'

'And I think we all recognise the gravity of what might happen here.'

'Thank you.'

'Those regulations are there to uphold and preserve the ethics of sport, and to safeguard the physical health and mental integrity of players. Isn't that right, Mr Hastings?'

'That's correct.'

I gestured towards the regulations in Simon's hand. 'May I?'

Simon sighed a sigh that sounded like there was a large dog in the room and passed them to me.

'Aye, maybe so. All of that times ten with a cherry on top. But it's still bloody unfair to the lad. And I say that as someone who's hated the Krauts all his life.'

'Why don't you go and get us all some tea?' I said to the big Yorkshireman.

'Aye, perhaps I will.'

'Sorry about that, Mr Hastings,' I said, after Simon had gone. 'He's feeling a bit emotional right now. We all are.'

'That's quite understandable.'

'I'm glad you said that.'

'How long have we got before we're in breach?' I asked the DCO.

'Seven minutes,' he said.

I found the relevant section of the guidelines and considered it very carefully; I knew that Christoph's whole career depended on what I said next.

'"The failure or refusal by a Player without compelling justification to submit to drug testing after notification is prohibited,"' I said, reading out the guidelines. '"The expression 'compelling justification' shall embrace, and shall only embrace, circumstances where it would be wholly unreasonable to expect a Player to submit to drug testing in the circumstances pertaining at the time, bearing in mind the limited commitment that this entails."'

'That's right,' said the DCO.

'You know, Mr Hastings, I'm not a lawyer. But I've had considerable experience of the law, not all of it welcome, and I wonder if you've ever heard of the rules of natural justice.'

Hastings shook his head.

'It's a technical term for the rule against bias and the right to a fair hearing. And it does seem to me that the duty – your duty – to act fairly, trumps everything that the FA have written down here. I suggest that any court of law would think it more than a little unfair of you to come here today of all days, a day when we're in mourning for our late manager, and a day when the police are conducting an inquiry which, with all due respect, would seem to take precedence over anything that the FA could fairly ask of us.

'Having said all that, I'd have thought that there are not one but two very good reasons to support a compelling justification argument such as I've just described. And I haven't even mentioned the special relationship that existed between the late Mr Zarco and Mr Bündchen. You see, it was Mr Zarco who brought young Christoph from Augsburg in Germany, and who gave him his big chance just the other night against Leeds United. Mr Bündchen is very upset. Perhaps more upset than any of the other players, I hardly like to mention this to you now – however, you leave me no choice. Earlier on, one of the police officers informed me that Christoph Bündchen wept when he was questioned about Zarco's death. If I'm honest, I'm not in the least bit surprised that he's forgotten that he was supposed to take a drugs test. It might save us all a lot of time and embarrassment if you were to take that into account.'

I'd said enough. In my mind I was already phoning Ronnie Leishmann and instructing him to start preparing the club's legal case for the FA hearing – whenever that might be. I was thinking of Rio Ferdinand in 2003, and the eight-month ban he'd undergone for missing a drugs test, not to mention a fifty grand fine. Everyone in the game knew Rio was as straight as an arrow, but the farts on the FA still went ahead and busted him, making him ineligible for the 2004 European Championship in Portugal. Which the Greeks ended up winning. How did that happen?

'I'll be outside if you need me.'

CHAPTER 29

In the corridor outside the drug-testing station I found Simon speaking agitatedly on the phone.

'Where the fuck are you?' Simon caught my eye and then handed me his phone. 'It's Christoph,' he said. 'Daft bugger says he's at a fucking football match.'

'Where the fuck are you?' I yelled into the phone. I was speaking German now, in case I was overheard. When there are UKAD people about it's best to be a little close-lipped. 'We've been trying to get hold of you for ages.'

'I'm at Craven Cottage,' said Christoph.

'What the fuck are you doing there?'

'I came to see Fulham play Norwich City, with a friend. It's my local team.'

'Don't you ever answer your phone?'

'I honestly didn't hear it until half time.'

'At Fulham? Don't make me laugh. There's never that much noise at Craven Cottage. The neighbours wouldn't allow it.'

'It's true, boss. They're four goals up.'

'You must be on fucking drugs, son. Look, you know you've missed giving a urine test. That's bloody serious, Christoph. You could be facing a ban.'

'Yes, I know. And I'm really sorry, boss.'

'The guys from UKAD are still here, debating your fate.

In five minutes you might have a lot more time to watch football than you could ever have imagined.'

The door to the drug-testing station opened and the two officials from UKAD emerged.

'Hang on,' I said. 'I think we're about to learn if they're going to cite you for a breach of the code, or not.'

I lowered the phone and waited, my heart in my mouth.

Mr Hastings looked at me and nodded what looked like his acquiescence. 'Under these exceptional circumstances it's been decided that no further action will be taken.'

I let out a sigh of relief and nodded. 'Thank you,' I said. 'Thanks for being so reasonable, gentlemen.'

As the two UKAD officials left I almost punched the air and cheered; and so did Simon.

'Blimey. What did you do, boss? Put a gun to his head? I felt sure that boy was fucked.'

It probably wouldn't be the first time, I thought.

In German I said to Christoph: 'Did you hear all that?'

'Yes, boss.'

'Did you forget about the UK doping people or are you just an idiot?'

'I guess I'm just an idiot, boss.'

I frowned. 'What the hell's that supposed to mean? You mean you didn't forget?'

'I went to a friend's birthday party in Soho on Thursday night, you see. A gay party. And by accident I took some tina. Someone slipped it into my drink, I think. For a laugh. At least, that's what they told me. I mean, I really didn't know until it was too late.'

'What?'

So Christoph Bündchen hadn't forgotten about the UKAD officials at all; he'd panicked and taken off because he knew he was guilty. I now realised just how close we'd been to an even bigger, Adrian Mutu-sized disaster; I hadn't a clue what tina was but I assumed it must be a drug of some description and not the kind you could ever have argued was a cold remedy.

'It was a soft drink, I swear. An orange juice.'

'Oh, I guess that's all right then.'

'I've never taken that stuff before. It just happened. And when those two UKAD guys showed up at the dock this morning I freaked out, I guess. I promise it won't happen again.'

'You're bloody right it won't. And don't tell me any more. Not another bloody word. But you are so fucking busted. See me in my office at Hangman's Wood tomorrow morning after training and we'll discuss your punishment. But I can tell you this: don't expect to go home with any bollocks in your Y-fronts.'

I handed Simon back his phone.

'What's he got to say for himself?' he asked.

Simon didn't need to know. A trouble shared is never a trouble halved. Not in football and certainly not with a man like Simon who, in spite of his tall, handsome, silver-fox, appearance was possessed of a hard, gloomy, northern disposition. He wasn't called Foggy for nothing. He had only one expression and that was stoic. Even his smile looked like ice forming on a line of gravestones. Born in Barnsley, he'd played football for Sheffield Wednesday, Middlesbrough, Barnsley and Rotherham United – hence what was truly surprising about him was that he should ever have left Yorkshire. This was entirely due to his much younger Venezuelan wife, Elke, whom he'd met on a trip to Spain where he had a holiday home – it was said that she'd refused to marry him unless he lived in London. I certainly couldn't blame her for that. But Simon hated the south of England almost as much as he hated southerners, and to say he was one of football's hard men was like describing the SAS as butch.

'He said, "*Entschuldigung*",' I replied. 'That's just German for "I was a stupid cunt".'

'That's what I thought it meant.'

I went back to my office where I found Maurice glued to the television set.

'You're not going to believe this,' he said.

I glanced at the screen. It was the weather report.

'After what I just experienced I think I could believe anything,' I said. 'Even a warm sunny day in January.'

'No. Wait a minute and the news will be on again. This is just priceless. The law's only gone and arrested Ronan Reilly.'

'You're kidding.'

'I kid you not.'

'For murder? No way.'

'Dunno. They're not saying. Apparently they went to Reilly's house to interview him and he legged it out of the window. He was doing an O.J. down the drive when they nicked him.'

'Maybe it was to do with something else.'

'Let's hope not, eh? And then we can get back to normal.'

A few moments later Reilly was on screen, being led to a police car in handcuffs. He'd looked better, even on the BBC; he was wearing a wife-beater and had a black eye. The famous scar on his forehead that was the result of a juvenile gang fight was even more pronounced than usual. He did at least seem like a murderer. There were guys in Wandsworth Prison who looked less obviously criminal than Ronan Reilly did.

Maurice laughed. 'I never liked that cunt,' he said.

'Yes, you've made that clear before.'

'And with good reason. He's never had a decent word to say about this football club. Not ever. You think I'm exaggerating, boss, but I'm not. He hates us. Even before Zarco came back here he hated us. Every time he was on *MOTD* he was giving us stick for this and bad-mouthing us for that. I'm surprised he's got the nerve to show his face in this ground.'

And then Detective Inspector Neville could be seen leaving Reilly's home in Coombe Lane without answering any of the reporters' questions.

'Hold up,' said Maurice. 'That's the copper who was here earlier on today.'

'That's right,' I said. 'Detective Inspector Neville.'

'Blimey, maybe it really was Reilly that topped Zarco,' said Maurice. 'I mean, why run away if you're not guilty?'

'I can think of a few damned good reasons.'

'Christ. Who'd have thought? Ronan Reilly a murderer.'

'We don't know for sure that's what it's about.'

'What else could it be? They don't arrest you for nothing, boss.'

'That's certainly not been my own experience.'

We waited a moment and then the Sky reporter mentioned the fight Reilly had had with Zarco at the BBC SPOTY and started to speculate that Reilly's arrest might have something to do with the Portuguese manager's death.

'See?' said Maurice. 'He thinks so, too.'

'Believe me,' I said, 'I've been there. Where Reilly is now, I mean. People jumping to conclusions. No smoke without fire. Guilty until proved innocent.'

'Talk about Super fucking Sunday.'

'You don't know the half of it.' I told him about the UKAD officials and how Christoph had narrowly escaped being busted. 'What is tina, anyway?'

'Crystal meth. Methamphetamine. Popular with PnP boys having a chem session.'

'PnP?'

'Party and play. Crystal meth's a gay drug, popular in the clubs.'

'How long would that stuff stay in your urine?'

'Up to five days, I reckon. Ninety days if they were to use a hair-follicle test to look for it. Which they can, of course. Provided you've got a bit of hair – unlike him.'

Maurice nodded at the TV and laughed cruelly as Sky re-showed the footage of a handcuffed Reilly being led to the police car. It couldn't be denied: Ronan Reilly was a bit of a slaphead. It was hard to connect him with the mop-top and babe-magnet who'd once played for Everton and was married to a former Miss Singapore.

'You just made picking the side for the game against the Hammers a lot easier.' I picked up my phone and started to type a text to Simon. 'If Christoph can test positive for drugs today then he could test positive on Tuesday night. Ayrton can play instead of the German lad.'

'Ayrton? I thought he was on his bike, to Stoke.'

'Not any more. I asked him to stay on.'

Maurice nodded. 'That was smart. We need his experience. It's the one thing that Mr Sokolnikov – for all his millions – can't buy.'

CHAPTER 30

I spent the remainder of the afternoon in my office avoiding the police, fielding calls and texts, drinking tea, and studying the previous Hammers match on my iPad. I'd always liked the Thames Ironworks, as we used to call them at Arsenal – that was their name back in 1895 when the team was formed. I'd nearly signed for them myself, once. You always had the feeling that the Premier League was never quite the same without West Ham, like in 2011. There were plenty of other sides who never looked right in the Premier League, but the Hammers weren't one of them. It was always a tough game when we played West Ham and thanks to the likes of Harry Redknapp and Frank Lampard senior, they'd always had a pretty good Academy – one that had produced nine England internationals, including Bobby Moore – which meant that we were probably in for a few surprises on Tuesday night.

Just before five, when I was getting ready to go home, Viktor put his head around my office door. He was wearing a long brown Canali coat with a fur collar and in his hand was a beautiful Bottega Veneta briefcase.

'How's it going?' he asked.

'Viktor. What are you doing here?' I asked.

'I came to see that woman,' he said. 'Detective Chief Inspector Byrne. To tell her what happened at the lunch yesterday.'

'And what did you tell her?'

'That everything seemed normal. Zarco was his usual ebullient self. I had no sense that this was a man who thought that someone was going to beat him to death. He was in a good mood.'

'You asked me to investigate his murder underneath that copper's high heels. With respect, it might help if you were to afford me the same opportunity to question you a little. After all, you were one of the last people to see Zarco alive. Maybe I can learn something useful I didn't know before. Something you overlooked when you talked to the police, perhaps.'

He glanced at his cheapo watch and nodded. 'Sure. Good idea.'

That was Maurice's cue to make himself scarce again. As he opened and closed the door I caught a glimpse of a couple of Hulk-sized bodyguards outside in the corridor. I thought it best to keep my questions very respectful indeed.

Viktor shrugged off his coat and sat down on the sofa.

'Did you see the news on television?' he asked me. 'About Reilly?'

'Yes.'

'Do you think he killed Zarco?'

'I honestly don't know, Viktor.'

'If you're innocent, why run away?'

'I've been wondering that myself.'

'They used to be friends, he and Zarco. Did you know that? Long before all that stupid business at the SPOTY. When Reilly and Zarco were still playing, back in the early nineties, there was an incident on the football pitch, during a match. Reilly used to play for Benfica. This was at the same time Zarco was playing for Porto. Anyway, words were exchanged and Zarco elbowed Reilly in the face, which almost cost him an eye and ended his season. Indeed, it almost ended Reilly's career.'

'I didn't know that.'

'It's in Reilly's book, which is long out of print so I don't suppose anyone really remembers it now. But I do. I remember it because I remember everything I read. I don't say I have an eidetic or photographic memory. Frankly I don't believe they exist. However, my memory *is* exceptional.'

'Since you remember so much, tell me more about the lunch. About Zarco and how he was the last time you saw him.'

'Like I say, he seemed himself,' explained Viktor. 'Dry and funny, as he always was. And confident about the match, of course. Always confident. Sometimes too confident. He had steak for lunch. And a glass of red wine – just the one. What else? Yes, he had a hat with him, and a pair of sunglasses.'

'A hat? What kind of a hat? Malcolm Allison, Roberto Mancini or Tony Pulis?'

'Malcolm Allison, I don't know. I've never heard of this man. A Roberto Mancini, I think. A woolly hat. Well, yesterday was a very cold day.'

'City colours?'

'Actually no. The orange ones make your head look like a flower pot. A black one. He was wearing the hat and a pair of scary-looking motorcyclist's gloves. With black knuckle armour.'

'He was scared of you, did you know that?'

'Sophocles says that to him who is in fear everything rustles.' Viktor smiled. 'Believe me, Scott, around me there is always a lot of rustling. Everyone seems to hear it. Everyone except me. It's said – mostly by people who are my enemies – that I have ties to organised crime. This is not true; but what is true is that this was not always the case. When I first started doing business in Russian and Ukraine it was more or less impossible not to make deals with so-called Russian Mafia figures. But let me tell you, if I may, something about the Russian Mafia. It does not exist. It never did exist. It was convenient for the racist government in Moscow – Boris Yeltsin's government – to blame all of the country's problems on so-called ethnic gangs: the Georgians, the Chechens, the Tatars, the Ukrainians and the Jews. Always the Jews. But you know mostly these were just businessmen who saw an opportunity and took it in a country where opportunity had not existed in almost a hundred years. Were they greedy? Yes. Were they ruthless? Sometimes. Was I one of these men? Undoubtedly. Did I make a fast buck after the collapse of the USSR? Certainly. Did I do it by means that would not satisfy the SEC or the FSA? Perhaps. Did I ever have anyone killed? No, I did not.'

He meant this little speech to be reassuring, I think, and yet somehow it wasn't. For one thing there were the body-guards outside, and for another there was the simple reality that even if Viktor was just a businessman, he knew plenty of people who operated on the edge of the law.

He grinned. 'Next you're going to be asking me for my alibi, Scott. It's just as well I spent the whole afternoon with those people from the Royal Borough of Greenwich. They'll vouch for me.'

'I'm glad to hear it. Because I think Zarco had a good reason to be afraid of you. He'd done something wrong. Something illegal.'

'So, you know about that.' Viktor's cold, dark eyes narrowed. 'I can see I wasn't wrong about you, Scott. I made the right choice.'

'Let's hope you still think so at the end of this conversation, Viktor.'

'I'm not an idiot. I knew there was a good reason Zarco preferred us to use Paolo Gentile rather than Denis Kampfner for the Traynor transfer. I suspected he was going to take a bung on the deal. Partly it's my fault. Let me explain: you see, a long while back Zarco had begged me for a share tip. I hate doing that kind of thing but he insisted, so I told him about this energy company in the Urals. They'd just had a big find of oil and it was generally held that the shares would go through the roof. I had bought some and so, I believe, did he. Except that there hadn't been a big find of oil, it was all a fraud, and instead the shares went down the toilet. Zarco lost a lot of money. Not as much as I did, but then I can afford it. I felt bad about that. Very bad. He lost at least a quarter of a million pounds, I think. So when he asked if we could use Gentile as the agent on the Traynor transfer I agreed so that Zarco could recover what he'd lost. I even pretended to believe what Zarco told me – that Denis couldn't be trusted. Yes, it's true, I turned a blind eye to being robbed by my own manager.'

Viktor lit a little cigar with a gold lighter. That's the thing about owning your own football club; the anti-smoking laws just don't apply.

'You remember when people first had cars? Well, of course you don't remember it. What I mean is that in 1865 the British parliament passed a series of acts called the Locomotive Acts, which applied to self-propelled vehicles on British roads. A law that was copied in America, by the way. For safety reasons a man with a red flag was obliged by law to walk sixty yards ahead of each vehicle. It's the same with me. My money walks sixty yards ahead of me with a red flag and everyone sees me coming, in the full sense of this figure of speech. Like a patsy, you know? What else do you call someone who always has to pay full price? And no one ever gives me value for money. Not unless I push hard for it, which means, of course, that I am always seen as ruthless. Ruthless and grasping. But only because I want the same value for money as anyone else.

'You're well off in your own right, Scott. Well off and comfortable – but not rich, perhaps. But when you're very rich you get used to people robbing you, my friend. To some extent you learn to put up with it. I've been ripped off by everyone. My PA, my lawyer, my pilot, my driver, my butler, my ex-wife, my accountant – you name it, Scott, they've ripped me off. When you're as rich as me it's an occupational hazard. I suppose they think I'm so rich I won't notice. But of course I do. I always do. It's a sad fact, Scott, but when you're as rich as I am the only people you can trust are the people who don't want anything from you. It was extremely disappointing to find that Zarco was stealing from me. But it wasn't exactly a surprise. It's as simple as that.'

'Not quite.'

The narrow eyes narrowed a little more. He picked a piece of tobacco off his tongue and said, 'Explain, please.'

'When Zarco learned that the planning objections to the Thames Gateway Bridge were about to be rejected by the Royal Borough of Greenwich, he used the money from the bung to buy shares in SSAG. Almost half a million quid's worth.'

'This I didn't know.'

'Him and Gentile.'

'Wait.' Viktor sighed wearily. 'Don't tell me he used the same company to buy the shares that he did to buy those Urals Energy shares? Monaco STCM?'

'I'm afraid he did. It was only later on that he discovered Monaco STCM was partly owned by the Sumy Capital Bank of Geneva.'

'Idiot. If you'll forgive me, this is why people go to prison, Scott. Because they're stupid and they make stupid mistakes.'

'He was afraid you'd find out and that you'd be angry.'

'He was damn right. I didn't know this, Scott. But now that I do, I am angry. Perhaps I would have sacked him if I'd found out. Perhaps I might have been obliged to sack him, you know? It's such a stupid thing to have done. Maybe I would even have hit him.' Viktor smiled wryly as he realised what he'd said. 'Yes, I might have hit him for being greedy, and for dropping me in the shit, which this does. But let me be quite clear, Scott: I would not have had him beaten to death. Insider trading – even by proxy – is a serious matter. Difficult to prove, but serious. And yet not so serious that I would have had him killed. Even so, I shall certainly have to take legal advice in this matter. Just in case it is suspected that I gave Zarco this information so that he might profit from it.'

'How did he find out? Do you have any idea?'

'That's a good question. I'm not sure. Perhaps he saw something on my laptop once, read an email on my iPhone, I don't know for sure. But more importantly now, how did you find out? And does anyone else know about this? In particular, the police?'

'Gentile knows, but that's all. I only know because Zarco used to keep a burner phone in my cabinet drawer, which he used for – well, I assumed it was for making arrangements with his mistress. In fact I think this particular phone was exclusively for speaking with Gentile.'

'And this phone? You still have it?'

'Yes.'

'I should like to see it,' said Viktor. 'It may even be that I will have to give it to my lawyers. Just to protect myself, you understand.'

'I want to speak to Gentile before I do that. I'd like to use it to lever some more information out of him, if I can.'

'Be very careful, Scott. While I'm not connected to the world of organised crime, the same can't be said of Paolo Gentile.'

'You mean, he's linked to the Mafia?'

'Gentile lives in Milan but he is originally from Sicily. A few years ago he was investigated by the Italian authorities for his links to a man called Giovanni Malpensa. Malpensa is the head of a family that controls the Palermo district of Trabia; not to mention a stake in several Italian football clubs. Gentile may not be dangerous but Giovanni Malpensa certainly is.'

'And you still allowed the Traynor deal to be made by this man?'

'You think one agent is any more honest than another? Come on, don't be so naïve. Denis Kampfner has some very crooked friends in Manchester's drug-dealing underworld. This is not surprising, of course, because there's more money than ever in football. It's a whale, tied to the side of the ship that's the world economy. And more money means there are more sharks feeding on it. In 2013 BT paid almost a billion dollars for Champions League and UEFA football broadcasting rights. But do you honestly think that means the game has become any less corrupt than it ever was? On the contrary. Football and money go hand in hand. Football itself has become an important marketing tool – perhaps the biggest marketing tool there is, these days. How else are you to reach the all-important market of men? Life's decision-makers. Whatever the women's groups say should happen, it's still men who make the big financial decisions in any household, which means they're the most important audience to reach. Anywhere in the world. From Qatar to Queensland, football is now the lingua franca of the world. It's why people are prepared to bid so much for World Cup rights, even to the extent of paying millions of dollars in bribes.'

'Which reminds me,' I said. 'I understand we're to be the Subara stadium.'

'Yes, the Subara. It's a little like the Emirates, don't you think?'

'And yet we could so easily have been the Jintian Niao-3Q.'

Viktor made a comic sad face. 'Yes, it's a great pity that isn't going to happen. Unless of course you feel inclined to accuse the Qataris of murdering Zarco, Scott. That would certainly be a game-changer. It would leave the field clear for the Chinese. Again. Of course if you did that you'd be a friend to me.' He laughed a big jolly laugh. 'Not to mention Ronan Reilly. He'd be pleased to have the Qataris accused of murder, too.'

He was smiling but it was hard to know if he was joking or not. That was the thing about Viktor Sokolnikov; he was a hard man to read.

'Look, Viktor. I think I should make one thing quite clear. I'm not going to accuse anyone of murder unless I'm absolutely sure they did it. Not for you, not for Jintian Niao-3Q, not for anyone. Right now, I've no idea who killed Zarco. No idea at all. And I really think it's best I keep any theory in this matter in reserve until I have some pretty hard evidence, don't you?'

'Well, please make sure you let me know first of all. I shall be very interested to hear what you have to say on the subject. Very interested indeed.'

'Thanks for being so frank with me, Viktor.'

'No problem.'

'Since you're being frank, let me ask you one more question.'

'Fire away.'

'That argument you had with Alisher Aksyonov, on Russian TV. When you nutted him in the teeth? What was it about?'

Viktor grinned sheepishly. 'What else but football?'

CHAPTER 31

It was almost seven o'clock when I decided to pack up and go home. I was tired. It had been a long day and I was looking forward to seeing Sonja and doing not very much. Maurice tossed me my car keys and wished me a good night.

'You staying in the office?' I asked.

'Just for a short while,' he said. 'I made a call to a mate, someone I knew in Wandsworth. He's always been good for information. You know, the sort you can't get on Google. And he said he'd call back before seven thirty. I was thinking that if this was a professional job – I mean the meet-and-greet on Zarco – then he'd probably know about it. There's not much he doesn't know.'

'Thanks, Maurice.'

'Careful driving home, boss. It's pretty murky out there.'

I went along the corridor towards the main stairs. It kept you fit walking around and up and down the dock; there were only three floors but at the highest point of the Crown of Thorns the building was almost ten storeys high, a height of more than one hundred feet, and it could take you a full ten minutes to make your way around the entire floor. Some of the security guys and post boys used Segways – those electric stand-up scooters – but I preferred to walk, especially on a day as busy as this one when I'd been unable to get into the gym. Things were much quieter now and almost everyone had gone home. A yard or two ahead of me, a uniformed police officer seemed to be walking in the same direction and, in his wake, I could detect a faint whiff of something sweet and vaguely familiar.

'Are you lost?' I asked, helpfully. 'This place is like the maze at Hampton Court. Each floor looks the same.'

'Looking for the stairs to the main entrance,' he muttered.

'Then you are lost,' I said. 'The main stairs are back the way you just came. This way are the stairs to entrance Z. Which leads to the car park.'

'The car park will do,' he said vaguely. 'That's where I left my car.'

Everything about this copper seemed vague except the smell, which at last came to whichever part of my memory dealt with something as elusive as the proper names for scents. I could never identify perfumes. I never knew the name of the stuff Sonja preferred, but I did know the smell that was coming off the copper's clothes. When you've spent eighteen months in Wandsworth you get to know the smell of marijuana the way you know the stink of your own unwashed body. And there was something else that was strange: the car park I was going to was the players' car park, not the place where the police had parked their own vehicles; that was outside the front entrance.

I came abreast with the man and glanced over at him. He wasn't the copper who'd been stationed outside Zarco's office that morning while detectives conducted a fruitless search of his desk and filing-cabinet drawers. That man was long gone. This one was different. Perhaps a little too different.

'Have you got the time?'

'Sure.'

The man stopped and lifted his wrist, which gave me a chance for a closer look at him.

'Five past seven,' he said.

'Thanks.'

He was tall, with slightly too-long hair, and badly pitted skin on his face, but it wasn't any of this or the dope on his breath that gave me pause for thought; it was the job-stoppers that were tattooed on his knuckles. Back in the nick there were plenty of cons who went in for prison tats, with ACAB being one of the most popular. It stood for All Coppers Are Bastards and was a sentiment with which I heartily agreed. But it seemed unusual that a policeman should have had those four initials on his knuckles; just as it seemed unusual that a policeman from the Essex Police – which was the force on the scene – should have been wearing a badge on his flat cap from the Surrey Constabulary. The cap badges were the same colour, all right – blue and red – but the Essex badge had three scimitars and this one had a lion couchant. I could see why the Essex law had called in detectives from the Yard, that made sense, but I really couldn't understand why the Essex Police should have felt they required the help of the Surrey Constabulary.

I told myself that it wasn't any of my business if a copper should have been sneaking a quiet toke on an upper floor when things were a bit slack; the job was probably very boring. I told myself that maybe the rules about coppers not having tattoos on their hands had been relaxed since I'd had much contact with the law. I told myself that my hatred and distrust of the police was becoming an obsession and that I should tell Sonja and ask her if she thought I needed profes-sional help. I told myself I had enough trouble with the Met without pissing off the Surrey Constabulary as well. I told myself I just wanted to go home and have a nice bath and eat the sushi dinner I supposed Sonja had ordered in for us from the Jap restaurant on the King's Road. I told myself that if he was impersonating a police officer then he'd leg it when I asked to see his warrant card and that I'd better be ready for a thumping.

He nodded and turned away.

'Just a moment,' I said. 'Would you please show me your warrant card?'

'Come again?'

'Your warrant card. I'd like to see it please.'

'Don't need one, sir,' he said. 'Police Act 1996. 'Sides, I'm off duty. My warrant card is in the car downstairs. I was just dropping off some spare forensic kits for the coppers here. I'm not even part of the local force. So it wouldn't be right for me to be carrying a warrant card. If I was arresting you, sir, then I would certainly need my card. Although the uniform is meant to be a bit of a clue for dozier villains.'

'All right,' I said. 'Sounds fair enough. But only if you can tell me what the local force is.'

'You what?'

'Simple. The uniformed coppers here. Are they Metropolitan Police or Surrey Constabulary? And which one are you?'

The man faced me down. 'Look, sir, it's been a long day and I really don't need someone getting clever with me right now. So why don't you just fuck off?'

Now ordinarily I'd say that was standard chit-chat from a copper, and I'd have taken it, too; but not this time.

'You know, if I was impersonating a police officer,' I said, 'in a building where there are lots of coppers, I might have a joint in the car outside, just to calm my nerves a bit. To give me the bottle for the job. Whatever that might be.'

The man shot me a sarcastic smile and then ran for it.

Which was like a hare setting off in front of a racing dog.

As a defender I'd earned my fair share of red cards; sometimes you have to take one for the team. A striker gets through and then you simply have to chop his legs and bring him down – like Ole Gunnar Solskjaer. I'd seen some pretty criminal tackles in my time, too. None worse than Roy Keane in 2001 when he tackled Alf-Inge Haaland. I still remembered the red card the Man U captain had got from David Elleray – again – when he took down the Manchester City midfielder. But that's football, as Denis Law has famously said.

As tackles went, this one was just as high as Roy's, and of course was well off the ball; and it was probably just as well that the fake copper's leg wasn't on the ground when I struck with both feet against his knee, otherwise I could have done him a lot more damage. The man went down and he must have banged the back of his head on the floor, because he lay there stunned just long enough for me to get up and call Maurice on my phone.

A few seconds later the two of us were marching the still-groggy man back to my office for a little Q & A.

A quick search of his pockets revealed another copper's warrant card, not to mention a couple of joints, and an automatic pistol that gave me more than a pause for thought.

'It's a Ruger,' said Maurice, examining the gun carefully.

'Is that fucking real?' I asked.

The fake copper sat down on the chair opposite my desk. 'What do you think?' he sneered.

'It's real all right, boss.' Maurice thumbed out the magazine and inspected the bullets. 'Loaded, too.' He smacked the man on the back of the head. 'What are you fucking thinking of, you stupid cunt – bringing a gun to football? There's tooled up and there's tooled up, but that shooter's just asking for trouble.'

'Fuck off,' said the man.

I was still searching his pockets; wallet, car keys, a map of Silvertown Dock with an X to mark the spot somewhere on the second floor, a couple of grand in new fifties, a mobile phone, and a door key with a number on it.

'Tell you what,' I said. 'It's handy that we've got so much law upstairs. Makes it easy for us. And for you.'

'How's that?'

'Tell us what you were up to, and we'll let you go,' I said. 'Or else we'll hand you over to the filth. It's as simple as that.'

The man moved suddenly for the door but Maurice was there before him – or more accurately Maurice's fist was. It connected with the side of the fake copper's head like a wrecking ball and sent him crashing onto the floor.

'Fuck,' said Maurice, shaking his hand and flexing the fingers. 'That hurt.'

The burglar was still lying on the floor.

'Not as much as it hurt him,' I said. 'He's out cold, I think. Still. Can't be too careful, eh?' I pulled open my desk drawer and found the handcuffs I had taken from Zarco's desk the night before – the ones I guessed he'd used for his sex games with Claire Barry. I took the key out of the lock, dropped it into my pocket and then cuffed the unconscious man's hands behind his back.

'That's handy,' said Maurice. 'Christmas present from the wife?'

'Don't ask.'

'You play your games and I'll play mine.' Maurice chuckled obscenely.

266

We pulled the man back onto a chair and waited for him to stop breathing so loudly and to straighten up again. For a moment we thought he was going to puke so I put a wastepaper bin between his feet, just in case.

'Tell us what you were up to and we'll let you go,' I said. 'My guess is that you've got form for this kind of thing. A professional. Talk to us and you can be on your way.'

'That's a good offer, cunt face,' said Maurice. 'Me and the boss here, we've both done some bird, so we've got no love for the law. You cooperate with us and you can be on your toes again. But stay shtum and we'll hand you over wearing a fucking ribbon on your hat. With this gun in your pocket, you'll get five years.'

The man shook his head. 'I've got nothing to say to you.'

I looked at the key for a moment. According to the plastic identity tag it was wearing this was the key to an executive hospitality box, number 123.

'Is this where you were supposed to go?' I said. 'Box 123? To get something for someone – some money, perhaps?'

'Fuck off, you muppets.'

'Muppet, am I?' Maurice grinned. 'You got that right, sunshine.' He twisted the man's ear. 'And you know what my Muppet character is? Animal.'

'Stay here with him,' I said.

Maurice pushed the magazine back into the handle of the little Ruger.

'No problem,' he said.

'And while I'm out, find out who owns suite 123 and everything about them.'

CHAPTER 32

There were one hundred and fifty executive boxes at London City, all of them on the second floor. For £85,000 – that was the starting price for the present season – you got a private box about the size of a decent caravan, a fully equipped kitchen, a private lavatory, fifteen seats for every competitive home fixture, a support team of elegant hostesses to greet guests and serve food and drinks, a widescreen television and betting facilities. The more you paid the nearer the halfway line you were and the bigger the box was. All the suites were furnished differently, according to the taste – or lack of it – of the person or company owning it. Most were owned by companies like Carlsberg and Google, but the name on the door of suite 123 was an individual and an Arab one: Mr Saddi bin iqbal Qatar Al Armani.

I unlocked the door, switched on the lights and went inside. The room felt cold; colder than it ought to have been. I checked the sliding doors, which were still locked behind the pulled-down roller blinds, then looked around.

Mr Al Armani's suite was furnished like the interior of a private jet – all thick cream carpets, polished ebony panels and expensive white leather armchairs. He probably owned a private jet like this, too. Occupying a whole wall was a silver print of Monte Fresco's famous photograph of Vinnie Jones squeezing Gazza's bollocks, signed by both players

– the poster, not the bollocks – and a framed number ten Argentine shirt belonging to Diego Maradona that had also been signed. On an ebony wood table stood a pile of dinner plates edged in gold, a canteen of gold cutlery, a gold table lighter and several gold ashtrays. The widescreen television on the wall was an 84-inch Sony, which looked as big as the sliding doors that led out to fifteen seats that were just fifty feet above the halfway line. Everything looked like it was of the very best quality, even though the taste left something to be desired in my own eyes; I don't much care for all that Bin Laden bling.

It was obvious Zarco had been there; a black woolly hat lay on the table and his Dunhill chestnut leather grip was on the white leather sofa. I opened the bag, half hoping I would find fifty grand and Zarco's lucky football scarf inside it – which was still missing – but apart from a pair of motor-cycle gloves, it was empty.

I went into the lavatory; there were gold fittings on the sink and on the cistern, and on the wall an aerial photograph of the Al-Wakrah in Qatar – the so-called Vagina Stadium.

Opening the door to the kitchen, I switched on the light and walked the length of the room to the window. I opened the cupboards and the fridge, I even opened the dishwasher, which was switched on and had run a cycle, because a little light on the door indicated as much. There were three coffee cups in there, which wasn't much washing up to have warranted switching it on. Glancing around, I saw a pair of grey steel Oakley sunglasses that lay on the worktop. I picked them up. They were Zarco's. I knew that because I'd bought them for his birthday; I had told him they matched the colour of his hair, which they did. Otherwise I'd found nothing that left me any the wiser as to why a man with a gun would have taken the risk of impersonating a police officer to get in here.

On the face of it I couldn't see why anyone would have burgled the suite. Not for an empty bag. I weighed the cutlery in my hand – at best it was dipped, and hardly worth the risk. The framed Maradona shirt wasn't worth more than a few hundred quid; after all, he'd signed so many. At fifteen to twenty grand the telly was probably the most expensive thing in the suite, but it weighed a ton and wasn't exactly the sort of thing you could tuck under your coat.

The only interesting fact I'd discovered was that the suite was owned by an Arab who appeared to be from Qatar. Why had Zarco arranged to have Paolo Gentile come here, of all places, with fifty grand? After all, the Qatari who owned the box was hardly likely to think fondly of a man who had been so vocal in his opposition to a Qatari World Cup. And you could just tell that fifty grand was chump change for a man like that. None of it made sense.

I sat down and noticed that the stereo was still on; I turned up the volume and found myself listening to TalkSPORT. Don't get me wrong, I like TalkSPORT; most of the pundits know what they're talking about. Especially Alan Brazil and Stan Collymore. But this was one of those post-mortem phone-ins when football fans would ring in with their opinions on the weekend's games. Their comments were always the same: x should be sacked, y should never have been bought, and z was rubbish. TalkBOLLOCKS would have been a better name for what most of the fans calling in had to say.

I turned it off, picked up Zarco's bag and his hat and his sunglasses, locked the door of 123 behind me and went back to my office.

The fake cop was where I had left him, handcuffed on the chair, staring morosely at the floor. There was a little bit of blood on his nose; I found a tissue and wiped it, but only to prevent it from dripping on the carpet.

With the man's gun lying on the desk, Maurice was in front of my PC.

'Has he said anything?' I asked.

'Not yet.'

'What did you find out about suite 123?' I asked.

'The suite is owned by an Arab gentleman from Qatar,' said Maurice. 'Mr Saddi bin iqbal Qatar Al Armani from the Bank of Subara and, according to Forbes, he's worth six billion dollars. Mr Al Armani has owned one of the top-price boxes here for the last three years, although he doesn't actually appear to be a very keen fan of football. He hasn't been to a match since the beginning of the season. Probably too busy finding oil and shitting money. Not that this is at all unusual at our club. There's at least half a dozen others who own a hospitality suite who've never shown up to a game. Wanker bankers, mostly. No wonder the fucking fans go mad when they see so many empty seats going begging. Some of these rich bastards have probably forgotten they even own these boxes. Not surprising when you think about it. Eighty-five grand when you're worth several billion dollars? What's that? A fucking pizza.

'Yesterday wasn't an exception to Mr Armani's general no-show rule. None of the tickets allocated to Mr Armani shows up on the computer as having been used. And whoever João Zarco went to see in that box it doesn't look like it was a man with a towel on his fucking head.'

'Possibly that's why he went there,' I said. 'Because he knew it wasn't going to be occupied. A nice quiet place for

271

Gentile to leave a bung and for Zarco to collect it. Only I don't think he did. He took a bag there all right. This bag. But the bag was empty.'

'So maybe the bung didn't get paid after all,' said Maurice. 'And Zarco went looking for Gentile. Found him somewhere. Dragged him into that maintenance area to give him a piece of his mind and got more than he bargained for.'

'And no one recognised him?' I shook my head. 'Wearing this hat and these sunglasses I can easily see how he made it to the executive suite without attracting attention. But he seems to have left them there. Who owns the suites on either side of 123?'

Maurice typed out the numbers on my keyboard. '122 is owned by a Chinese gentleman called Yat Bangguo. Runs something called the Topdollar Property Company. 124 is owned by Tempus Tererent Inc. They're the people who make games for people like Xbox and PlayStation. Including *Totaalvoetbal 2014*. The Tempus Tererent people were there yesterday, used all their tickets; Mr Bangguo only used half his tickets. 121 is owned by Tomas Uncliss.'

Tomas Uncliss was the previous manager for London City when they'd been in the Championship League; he'd been sacked unceremoniously by Viktor after a few unlucky results.

'All of them had catering and hostesses. Might be an idea to speak to some of those girls and see if they noticed anything unusual in 123.'

'Have you ever spoken to one of those girls?'

'Can't say I have.'

'Most of them aren't English; and about the only footballer they would ever recognise in a million years is David Beckham. Still, it couldn't do any harm, could it? See what you can find out.'

'Sure thing, boss.'

I looked at our prisoner. 'What do you think, Mr...?'

Maurice pushed back from my desk and handed me a driving licence and a Tesco loyalty card.

'This cunt's name is Terence Shelley. Lives in Dagenham. And he shops at Tesco. Apart from that I know fuck all about him.'

'Well, every little helps, doesn't it?'

I picked a football off the floor and bounced it hard on the back of Shelley's head.

'Hello! Is anyone at home? Talk to us, Mr Shelley, or you're the Sweeney's fucking dinner.'

Shelley said nothing.

'I'm tired. My friend here is tired. So I tell you what we're going to do: we're going home, he and I. But we're going to leave you somewhere safe overnight to reflect upon your situation. Manacled to a nice heavy kettlebell. All right? That is unless you talk to us, now. So, what do you say?'

'Bollocks,' said the man.

'You know something, Terry?' I said. 'I can call you Terry, can't I? You should be on TalkSPORT.'

CHAPTER 33

Sonja didn't much care for football and tended to spend most weekends alone, at her own flat in Kensington. This was just as well as Saturdays and Sundays are always the busiest times at a football club. If we played on Saturday she would come around on Sunday morning; and if we played on a Sunday she would arrive on Sunday night. It was an arrangement that seemed to suit us both very well.

I was especially looking forward to seeing Sonja after her shrinks' weekend in Paris. As a leading authority on eating disorders she was much in demand as a speaker at practitioners' conferences. But whenever she was away I felt a definite lack of equilibrium in my life, as if something important was missing from what kept me going; you might say that without her I had too much football, that she was the vital ingredient in the *Gestalt* that made me a complete man. But to put it much more simply, she made me happy. We always talked a lot, mostly about books and art, and we joked a lot, too – we shared a sense of humour, although sometimes it did seem that I had the lion's share of it. We were also very attracted to each other, which meant that we always had great sex. I never knew a woman who enjoyed sex with me as much as she did. She was keen on games and on trying to find ways of pleasing me in the bedroom. Not that this was very difficult but for a number of reasons

– the affair I'd had when I was married, the fact that I'm in a very physical profession and because I am very fit being the most important ones – she thought that I was also highly sexed, when in fact I don't think I am. I was just as happy with what you might call main course sex as I was with the many sauces and pickles she was fond of devising. Frankly I think that if anyone was highly sexed it was her. She couldn't get enough of it but, like a lot of blokes in football, I was often too knackered to have sex every night of the week – which she'd have liked, I think. In fact I'm sure of it.

Before she'd gone to Paris she'd told me that she was going to visit a lingerie shop called Fifi Chachnil in the rue St Honoré to buy something seductive to wear for me just as soon as she was back in London. She was always doing things like that and while I never asked her to, I have to confess I never tired of seeing Sonja in sexy underwear. In fact I had come to appreciate it very much. I suppose I liked her wearing it because it was the absolute antithesis of my own very masculine world of liniment and sweat, jock straps and shin pads, muddy boots and Vaseline, dubbin and compression shorts. The lingerie she bought and wore was improbably, impossibly small and delicate and lacy and utterly feminine, or at least so it seemed to me. And of course she had the most fabulous figure. Her bottom was quite perfect and she had a stomach like a washboard. For a woman who spent a lot of time in an office she was very fit indeed. Whenever she dressed up – as she usually did when she returned from a weekend away – she would light lots of tea lights and scented candles and answer the door wearing something diaphanous and wispy. After the weekend I needed a bit of that, but more importantly I needed a lot of love from the woman I loved; the death of Zarco, and the

275

revelations about Drenno's friend Mackie – not to mention the crisis with the UKAD people and the pressure I was getting from everyone – had left me feeling very raw indeed.

I turned into Manresa Road and saw the lights on in my flat, which lifted my spirits. In my mind's eye I was already stepping out of a hot bath into a large towel to be dried carefully by her. At the same time I saw that the press had gone from outside my building. Now that Ronan Reilly had been arrested they had other fish to fry. I breathed a sigh of relief, parked the Range Rover in the underground car park and already happy to be home, I rode the lift eagerly up to my floor. My only regret was that I'd not bought flowers – a white orchid, perhaps; she was very fond of orchids – or some sort of present. I loved buying her presents.

But as I opened the front door I knew immediately something was wrong. For one thing there was no scented candle on the hall table; and for another the Louis Vuitton Bisten 70 suitcase I'd bought her for Christmas was standing on the floor, next to the matching beauty case I'd got for her birthday. I'd joked that I was planning on turning her into a proper WAG, which she thought was very funny, but in truth there was never any danger of that happening; Sonja was much too clever to be something as pejorative as that. I picked the Bisten up by the handle to check the weight; it was heavy, too heavy for a weekend in Paris. Besides, I knew she'd been home to her own flat already.

Another reason I knew something was wrong was that the television was on; she seldom ever watched television and certainly not the news, which she said was mostly disasters and sport. Sonja only watched television when she was trying to take her mind off something at work. A patient. Or a paper she was preparing for a journal. She was wearing a rather businesslike two-piece suit with a pencil skirt, and a white shirt, which was the very opposite of what I'd thought she'd be wearing. She got up when I came into the sitting room – that was another bad sign, I thought; it was as if something formal was about to happen. Which of course it was. Nobody ever sits down to give you bad news.

'I'm sorry I'm late,' I said, warily. 'But since this time last night it's just been one thing after another. But all that can wait, I think. It looks as if you've got something important to tell me.'

'I suppose I should congratulate you,' she said, 'on your new job.'

I hesitated. 'Thanks, but I've got a feeling that in about five minutes congratulations are going to seem like the wrong word. I'm looking at you, baby, and I can tell that I'm about to see a card come out of your pocket. So say what's on your mind, eh? Before you lose your nerve for whatever this is about.'

'Okay, I will.'

'Thank you.'

'Now that you've been given this job, Scott, I've got a feeling that we're going to see even less of each other than we do already. And, well, the fact is, I want a bit more than that during the weekend. The fact is, I want a lot more than that.'

'Such as?'

'You remember that Nike ad we saw in the cinema? With all the famous footballers and the Elvis Presley song?'

'A little less conversation, a little more action?'

She nodded. 'That's the very opposite of what I want in life. And what I need from a man. My man.'

'I see. At least I think I do.'

277

'And it has to be said that in the bedroom things aren't very good, either. At least not for me. You're always tired, Scott.'

I nodded. 'I can't deny that.'

I went to my cigar humidor and took out a cigarette. Once a week – usually it was a Sunday night – I smoked a single cigarette, which always felt like a real pleasure. Used like that – just a couple of puffs, the way South American Indians had smoked the stuff – tobacco seemed to have almost medicinal qualities. 'You don't mind, do you?' I asked, lighting up. 'But, under the circumstances…' I let out a sigh that was one third smoke and two thirds disappointment. 'You know how to pick your moments, Sonja, I'll say that for you.'

'Don't feel sorry for yourself, Scott. It really doesn't suit you. You're not the type.'

'No, you're right. I'm just tired, that's all. As per usual. But actually, to be honest I don't understand, Sonja. Really, I don't. I thought we made a pretty good couple. At least I did when I looked at you. I even managed to like myself when I was with you, which, believe me, takes some doing.'

But what I was actually thinking was this: I couldn't believe I was never again going to see her naked, or get the chance to marry her, even, and that seemed too much to bear.

'Listen, this won't help at all, but I'll try to explain it to you, Scott. I owe you that much. I love you, and maybe you love me, but I can't ever be part of the most important thing in your life, which of course is football. I've tried, believe me I've tried my best to like it, but a while ago I realised it just wasn't going to happen, no matter how hard I tried. The fact is I can't be interested in the very thing that's about to take even more of your time than it does already, if such a

278

thing were possible. You do see that, don't you? I used to think it was just a game but it's not, it's much more than that, with you and with a lot of other men like you. It's a way of thinking about the world. A philosophy of a kind. And why not? It seems to work for a lot of people. It's no accident that the Premier League is like a mini-FTSE of successful companies. It's pure capitalism. The strong survive and the weak get relegated.'

'No,' I said. 'You make it sound almost Darwinist.'

'Oh, but it is. You're just a kind of selfish gene, that's all. Yours is a football-centred view of evolution. Because football is what everything comes down to with you, Scott; results, the team, the next match, the January window, a good cup run, the closed season, the top four, relegation, three points, a penalty not given, a red card that should have been. It's never ending and unrelenting and I can't take part in it because I feel nothing at all for it except the wish that the last match really could be the last match. And if what I've said doesn't make any sense to you, then forget it and we'll make it just this: even though a large part of me wants to stay with you, Scott, I can't stay because I won't be a football widow like the rest of those women you call the WAGs.'

'No one's asking you to be like that, Sonja.'

'Maybe you're not. But the imperatives of your job certainly are. And have you ever wondered why the WAGs are the way they are? Why they occupy themselves with shopping and fashion and hair extensions and manicures and boob jobs? Of course you haven't. But I have. Those women are desperately trying to make their stupid boyfriends and husbands pay some attention to them, that's why. They're trying in vain to compete with the most jealous mistress or wife of them all, which is football itself. Well, I won't be a part of that. I have my own life, my own interests, my own ambitions – and they don't include a good run in the FA Cup. We'll both have some bad nights for a while but we're both grown-up enough to know that will pass.'

Some fucking Sherlock I was, I told myself. What chance did I have of spotting Zarco's killer when I hadn't even been able to spot the disappointments felt by the woman I loved.

'Jesus, baby, it sounds like you've been saving this up for a while.'

'Maybe I have. Maybe I was just waiting for the best time to say it. The best time for me, that is. You see, I met someone in Paris. He's just a businessman. Don't worry, nothing happened between us. I wouldn't ever do that to you. But I will be seeing him again. Maybe nothing will come of it. Who knows? But on Saturday he goes to the theatre and on Sunday he likes going to Tate Britain. And he's never been to a football match in his life.'

'So he's the guy.'

'Make a joke of it, if it makes you feel better.'

'It doesn't. But I thought it was worth a shot. I would try to persuade you to change your mind, Sonja, but after a speech like that I can see it would be pointless. You've thought this out. Which is more than I have. Perhaps I should have done. So, I'm sorry.'

'You'll be fine, Scott. You're strong. Very strong.'

'Am I?' I took a last puff of my cigarette and then stubbed it out. 'Right now I don't feel very strong.'

'Of course you are. Just look at the way you smoke. Two or three puffs off one cigarette a week. Your strength astonishes me, sometimes. You know, if it was anyone else but you I wouldn't be leaving you right now; not after the twenty-four hours you've just had.'

I smiled. 'You noticed that.'

'I read the newspapers.'

'Do you now?' I pulled a face.

'At least I do when you're not around to look disapproving. Is there a law against reading the *Mail on Sunday*?'

'No, but perhaps there ought to be. There's a law against everything else that's unwholesome in this country.'

CHAPTER 34

After a miserable night I was up early to visit Silvertown Dock before driving on to Hangman's Wood. It was a very cold morning and I was a little worried about Terence Shelley who we'd locked up in the maintenance area, the same one where Zarco had been found dead. Even in a policeman's coat and uniform he would have spent a very uncomfortable Sunday night in the open air, handcuffed to a twenty-kilogram kettlebell. But if he had I doubt he could have felt as bad as I did after the events of the previous night. I hadn't felt as bad as this since my first night in the nick.

On the way I listened to the news on the car radio. Ronan Reilly had been released on bail, which was the clearest indication yet that the police did not suspect him of murder. It seemed that plain-clothes police had arrived at his house in Highgate hoping to question the *MOTD* pundit about Zarco's death and found a party in progress; mistaking the police for other guests, an unnamed female had admitted them to the house. Apparently it was Reilly's birthday, which might have been why he'd decided to celebrate with several prostitutes and a quantity of cocaine; this was probably also the reason why he'd decided to climb over the wall of the back garden and run away, in the hope of denying any knowledge of what was happening in his house. I felt almost sorry for Reilly because if there's one thing the BBC doesn't like – even on grown-up programmes like *MOTD* – it's pundits who use prostitutes and cocaine. Does anyone remember Frank Bough? I rest my case. But I still smiled as I tried to imagine how Zarco would have greeted the morning news. Zarco would have loved it.

Toyah called and left a message for me to call her back; she sounded like she still hadn't been to bed. Death is like that. It stops you from sleeping, which, even when everything is rosy, can seem a little too close for comfort to being dead. I was feeling too sour to speak to her; too sour and more than a bit sorry for myself. But I was trying to get over my troubles; just about the last thing Zarco had said to me before I left my flat that morning was to pull myself together.

'Come on, Scott,' he said as I'd stared at Jonathan Yeo's uncanny portrait of the Portuguese manager now hanging on the wall of my study. I'd been online to look at some of the other portraits Yeo had painted and thought the one of Zarco was as good if not better than the picture he'd done of a rather haunted-looking Tony Blair. 'You'll get over it, just like Sonja said you will. You had some good times, you and her. That's the way to look at it. And don't hold it against her. What she said was right. Football is football and nothing else matters very much; not to guys like you and me. That's why we're in the game, right? If we cared about anything else we'd be lawyers and bankers and fuck knows what. Me, I should have your troubles. Don't you think I'd like to be around to have a nice girl like that dump me? Sure I would. And we both know you'll get another soon enough. Handsome guy like you. Fact is you probably already know the girl you're going to sleep with next. That's how it works. Never forget, always replace – that's what my father used to tell me when a girl gave me the sack. It's good advice. Sure you loved her and maybe she loved you, like she said, but in six weeks you'll wonder why the hell you ever cared. Besides, you've got other fish to fry right now. Find out who killed me and why, Scott. Find my killer. I didn't deserve what happened to me, no more than you deserved to be dumped by Sonja. So, please take control of the game yourself and don't just leave it to other people, like the police. For them this is just another job. Please, Scott, for me and for Toyah, you must discover who killed me, okay? Really, I won't have any peace until you do this for me.'

When I arrived at the dock there was a police boat parked by the marina and several divers bobbing up and down in the Thames. I didn't envy them but I did wonder what they were looking for.

Maurice had already released our burglar and brought him back to my office where, still handcuffed, he was warming up with a cup of tea. Steam was emerging from the cauldron of his manacled hands, which were still trembling with cold, and he seemed to be as grateful for the heat from the mug as he was for the hot drink inside him. Secretly I was relieved that the man looked none the worse for wear but, for the sake of appearances, I decided to play the hard guy. I'd seen enough real hard men in Wandsworth to carry this off without any self-consciousness.

'So, you didn't freeze to death after all,' I said. 'Maybe now you'll talk to us, you stupid cunt.'

He sipped his mug of tea and nodded his alacrity. Cold had turned his nose the shape and colour of a tomato and had it not been for the gun he'd been carrying I might have felt sorry for him. In Wandsworth some of the old lags had always said that you should never carry a gun unless you're prepared to use it.

'Because if you don't start talking you can spend the rest of the fucking day where you already spent the night. Freezing your nuts off outside.'

'You'll really let me go if I tell you?' he asked.

'You have my word. You can even keep the money you were paid. I'm assuming the two grand in fifties was your fee.'

'What about my gun?'

'Would you have used it?'

'Just for show. Made a noise if necessary. I'd use blanks but you can't get them; there's just no call for them these days.'

'That's a comforting thought,' said Maurice.

'You can have the gun back, too,' I said. 'But not the bullets. We'll hang onto those, just in case you come back here with an attitude.'

'Fair enough, guvnor.'

'But don't dick us around with any lies. My girlfriend dumped me last night and I'm not in the mood to be patient.'

He finished his tea, replaced the mug on my desk and shook his head. 'I should have known better than to rob someone from me own fucking club. S'right. I'm a City fan meself. So I had my doubts, yeah? It felt unlucky. Any other London club – the Yids, the Arsenal, Chelsea, Fulham, the Hammers – I'd have been laughing to do a job there. But not City.'

'More facts, less fart,' I said.

'I'm just saying I didn't want this job, that's all. It felt unlucky. But the guy who paid me to do the job – an Italian bloke, called Paolo Gentile – he was paying good money.'

'Gentile. It figures.'

'Anyway, he told me to collect a package that was in suite 123. I was on my way there when you spotted me.'

'You're lying,' I said. 'I already searched that suite from top to bottom and found nothing.'

'Yeah, but did you check the fridge? Inside the freezer cabinet?'

'No.'

'That's where it is, apparently. The package I was supposed to grab. Job couldn't have been simpler, you'd have thought. A quick in and out. But it's always the easy ones you fuck up, not the jobs that require some planning.'

'Whose idea was the Plod uniform?' asked Maurice.

'Mine. The Italian bloke said the place would be swarming with law 'cos of Zarco's murder, so I thought I'd be all right dressed like this. Blend in, like. I thought no one would face down a copper. Not even another copper. Rented it off a mate who's a real rozzer, in Teddington, I did. Cost me two hundred quid. Never gave a thought to the fucking cap badge until you mentioned it.'

'Blimey,' said Maurice. 'The old Bill these days is getting to be like Berman's and Nathan's.'

'All right,' I said. 'Then what?'

'There's a FedEx box in my car, with a waybill already filled out for an address in Italy and everything. Business documents, it says. That's what I was told, anyway. I was to put the package from the freezer in the box and take it to the FedEx office in Dartford first thing this morning. Unit 14, Newton's Court. Apparently they open at 7.30 a.m. It was all on account so I wouldn't have to pay anything.'

'How did you get the job?'

'On the phone. Friend of a friend.'

'And you spoke to Gentile? On the phone?'

'S'right. He was in Milan, he said. It wasn't even stealing, he said. It was him what put the package there in the first place.'

'What about the key to the box? How did you get that?'

'From Mr Gentile's offices in Kingston. Really that was the only part of the job that involved any breaking and entering. I had to get in there on Sunday morning and collect the key from his office drawer. And two grand in fifties that was in the cash box. Straight up, guv, that's the God's truth. All of it, I swear.'

'All right,' I said. 'Wait here with my friend.'

CHAPTER 35

I went back up to the suite, opened the fridge and plucked the freezer door towards me. The package was there, just like Terence Shelley had said it would be – a large Jiffy bag that was wrapped in a thick plastic bin bag. I opened it up and found ten pink bricks of nice new fifties. The bricks of notes were a little hard but none the worse for a weekend below zero. Hot money never felt so cold. It was clear Shelley had spoken the truth; if the FedEx box was in his car as he'd said it was then I'd send him on his way like I'd promised. Quite apart from the risk to Zarco's reputation the last thing I wanted was Detective Chief Inspector Byrne upsetting our new goalkeeper by asking him about the details of his own transfer.

The chain of causation was beginning to seem clear enough, too. Zarco would have known that the Qatari guy who owned suite 123 wasn't likely to be using it for a while and figured he could use the room as his letterbox. Gentile would have taken the fifty grand to the suite and left it in the fridge freezer, as instructed in Zarco's texts; but when the news of Zarco's death broke the Italian agent must have realised that only he and Zarco knew about the bung and figured that he might as well try and recover the money. It was just sitting there, getting cold, and with the key it would have been easy enough, but at the same time Gentile couldn't have risked leaving the cash there for much longer as there was a match against the Hammers on Tuesday night and, unlike Zarco, he had no way of knowing if suite 123 would remain unoccupied by its usual owner.

It was time I spoke to Gentile, so I called him on my mobile and on this occasion he answered.

'Scott,' he said, 'I was just about to phone and congratulate you. It's too bad about João. He was truly one of the greats and I shall miss him a great deal. But I hope you and I can do business together in the future.'

I'd met Paolo Gentile on several occasions; it was hard to be the assistant manager of a top English football club owned by a billionaire and not have met Paolo Gentile. Where there is a huge picnic laid out on a perfect lawn there are also wasps, and Gentile was one of the largest and most persistent. FIFA seemed to have him under permanent investigation but nothing ever stuck. And unlike most English football agents, who couldn't have looked less like their clients, Gentile was smooth and cool and strikingly handsome, in a very Italian way. He always dressed well, in Brioni, and his many white Ferraris were his trademark and just the thing to excite the impressionable and usually car-crazy young men who were the subject of his relentless human trafficking. Incredibly thin – he seemed to survive on a diet of tennis, cigarettes and coffee – Gentile had a hooked nose that lent him the profile of some Renaissance princeling or Doge of Venice. And he was just as cunning as either.

My Italian was usually better than his English but on this occasion I wanted him to be the one who was paying close attention and so I sat down on the sofa and continued the conversation in my own first language.

'That all depends, Paolo,' I said. 'You see, I've just been

having a little chat with a friend of yours. Terry Shelley. I caught him raiding the fridge here yesterday evening. It seems as if he was trying to find you a late-night snack. That's what fifty grand is to someone like you, isn't it, Paolo? A snack.'

'Terry Shelley. I don't know him, Scott. Unless he's the boy who plays up front for QPR.'

'Nobody plays up front for QPR, Paolo. If they've any sense they sit back and defend. And if you've any sense you'll sit back and try to do the same. Only the ball's already in the back of your net, old son. It only remains for me to decide on the proper course of action. Whether to involve FIFA or the Metropolitan Police. After all, there is a murder inquiry going on here at Silvertown Dock. And you were trying to get hold of what the police might consider to be vital evidence that might shed some light on who killed João Zarco.'

'I had nothing to do with what happened to Zarco,' said Gentile. 'Really, I am as mystified by what happened as you probably are. But you know that already, of course. Otherwise you wouldn't be calling me like this, would you? And you must also have the money, too. Perhaps you have even decided to keep it for yourself. I certainly couldn't stop you. So the only question is what else do you want, Scott?'

'Some information.'

'Perhaps I can help you. But let's be quite clear. It's you I'm speaking to, right? Not the police.'

'You know about me and the police, Paolo. We're not really on speaking terms. Haven't been for a while.'

'Yes, I thought that was still the situation. I just wanted to hear you say it. In Italy we have a different attitude to the police than you do in England. You make jokes about the law-abiding Germans but I think no one in Europe is quite as law-abiding as the English.'

'You're forgetting I'm half German, half Scots.'

'That's true. So then, let's talk. What do you want to know?'

'I know about the insider share deal with SSAG. And to be fair I should inform you that so does Viktor Sokolnikov.'

'That's a pity. Is he going to inform the Financial Services Authority?'

'Probably not if he can avoid it. Viktor likes to keep a low profile where he can. He's going to speak to his lawyer before he does anything. But even if he did speak to the FSA you can probably blame what happened on Zarco.'

'Thanks for that, Scott. I appreciate the heads-up.'

'Look, the only thing I don't know about is the cash part of the bung. What he wanted it for. And what the urgency was. So, tell me about Saturday morning.'

'Are you turning detective at the same time as you become the new City boss? I've heard of total football. What's this? Total football management?'

'You might say I'm playmaking here, yes. Making space for the truth, perhaps. I figure it's my job to sort things out here as quickly as possible. Not just the football, but the rest of it, too. The unsolved murder of a club manager is very bad for player morale.'

'True.' Gentile paused long enough to light a cigarette and inhale sharply. 'So then. We'd done business like this before, Zarco and I. He would use an executive box when he knew it wasn't going to be occupied. It was convenient for him and convenient for me, too. I went to the box, as instructed. I left the bung in the icebox, as instructed. Zarco wasn't there when I got there; and he wasn't there when I left. That's all I know about Saturday morning.'

'And why did he want the cash? I mean, he seemed to be

in a hurry for it. In his texts he said he wanted it for the weekend.'

'That's true, he was. But I don't know why. Look, why does anyone want cash, Scott? Paper is nice to have around. You put it in your safe and you use it for holiday expenses, to pay the babysitter, to give to your mama at Christmas. Lots of managers like a bit of cash in hand. Literally. They're old-fashioned like that. You'd be surprised who else likes a bung; it's not just the usual suspects. It's like drugs and sport. Nobody takes drugs until they get caught and even then it's a mistake, someone else's fault, a cold remedy that turned out to be something bad. It's the same with bungs. Everyone is against it until they get one. And is it any wonder with all the money that's sloshing around football right now? BT pays out nine hundred million pounds for broadcast rights to the Champions League and right the way down the food chain there are people saying, *dov'è la mia parte?* Where's my slice of the big pizza? That's just economics, Scott. The law of supply and demand. Except that Adam Smith forgot about the law of television sport and the law of two hundred grand a week and the law of insatiable greed. You can't change that. All you can do is take advantage of it.'

'Did Zarco mention he was scared of anyone? I'm wondering if he wanted the fifty grand to pay someone off. Someone who'd threatened him, perhaps. I take it you heard about the grave that was dug in our pitch, with Zarco's photograph at the bottom of it?'

'He said something about it, yes. But it didn't seem to have scared him. He thought it was just hooligans. Frankly he was rather more alarmed that Sokolnikov might discover the fact that he'd bought shares in SSAG. That he'd get fired, or worse.'

'What did he say? Can you remember?'

'Most of our communication was done by text, you under-stand. For reasons of confidentiality. But he did say something about it in a conversation we had. On Saturday morning. He called me from Hangman's Wood and said something to the effect that he wouldn't be surprised if he was found floating in the Thames when Viktor found out what he'd been up to.'

'He actually said that?'

'I thought he was joking. And to be fair he was laughing when he said it. But maybe I was wrong. Maybe it was fear making him laugh, yes? On the other hand, if Viktor Sokolnikov was going to take him out I can't imagine he'd have done it at the dock. With his money and connections he could surely have arranged something a little more discreet. His kind of money buys you a lot of discretion.'

'So it would seem. What about the room itself? Suite 123.'

'An Arab's idea of luxury. A bit like a cabin on a luxury yacht. What can I say?'

'No, I meant was there anything unusual about it that you noticed?'

'Unusual? No. Well, maybe a couple of things, yes. The dishwasher was on. That struck me as odd, for a suite that wasn't supposed to be in much use. And there was a pair of sunglasses on the floor. I assumed they were Zarco's and I put them on the worktop.'

'So he'd been there already when you turned up.'

'Yes. Just to make absolutely sure the room was empty, probably. His leather bag was on the sofa.'

'Anything else?'

He paused. 'That really is everything I can remember.'

'All right.' I thought for a moment. 'By the way, what have you heard about Bekim Develi? He's coming here.'

'The red devil? It's news to me. But if he is moving to London I'm not surprised. At a match against Zenit a couple of weeks ago, one of Dynamo's black players was getting abuse from the crowd and Develi made a citizen's arrest during the game. He went into the crowd and hauled a fan out – a man he claimed had been one of the ringleaders. He was pretty rough with him, too. Almost started a riot. The fan was sent to prison and Develi's had death threats ever since.'

'He should fit in very well around here. Getting death threats is par for the course at Silvertown Dock.'

After my call with Gentile was concluded I stepped into the kitchen, placed Zarco's Oakley sunglasses on the tiled floor and opened the curious-looking window – like one of the awkward rhombus-shaped windows in that talking shop for the awkward-squad that is the Scottish Parliament. Several pigeons flew away in a loud flurry of wings that made my heart leap in my chest for a moment. There was talk of employing a hawk or a falcon to control the pigeons at the dock; apparently they were very effective and, as far as I was concerned, it couldn't happen soon enough. If only we could control players as easily. Then I walked back to the kitchen door and turned to face the room. You might say I was trying to see things just as Paolo Gentile and Zarco had seen them. I'd watched Inspector Morse do something vaguely similar on the telly and figured it certainly couldn't do any harm. I checked the bin but it was empty; what's more it looked clean as a whistle.

In a framed colour photograph hanging on the wall the former Emir of Qatar, Sheikh Hamad, and his glamorous wife, Sheika Mozad, were pictured holding the World Cup under the proud eyes of FIFA's diminutive president, Sepp

Blatter, a man whose knowledge of football was doubtless enhanced by his having been the former General Secretary of the Swiss Ice Hockey Federation. Mr and Mrs Rich were smiling proudly and looked like two cats that had got all the cream. It was always nice to remember that the future of football was in such safe hands as these.

I leaned out of the window and stared up at the pale winter sun. It wasn't the view of Silvertown Dock that made me yawn but the fresh air. From my current vantage point the outer part of the stadium was closer to the inner structure than on the ground floor. I could almost have reached out and touched one of the cross beams. I looked down through the polished plaited steel to the ground, about fifty or sixty feet below the window, and then glanced back at the fifty grand that lay on the worktop. What the hell was I to do with a fifty grand bung? I could hardly give it to the police or keep it myself, as Gentile probably assumed I would do. Of course, strictly speaking it was money paid to Gentile and Zarco that should never have been paid at all, which made it Viktor's more than anyone's. It seemed almost pointless to reimburse a man for whom fifty thousand was less than 0.0006 per cent of his total wealth, but it looked as if this was probably what I was going to do.

My phone started to ring. It was Phil Hobday.

'I believe Viktor promised you sight of an autopsy report,' he said.

'Yes. I was wondering if he was serious about that.'

'Viktor never makes idle threats,' said Phil.

After what Paolo Gentile had told me that wasn't exactly what I wanted to hear at this particular moment, and I reflected that the chairman might have chosen his words more carefully.

'Is this from your source in the Home Office again?'

'Actually, no. Since March 2012 all forensic work in the UK is contracted out to the private sector.'

'That doesn't sound very reassuring.'

'Maybe not. Anyway, it's here in my office if you want to come and get it. In fact I wish you would. I'm afraid I opened the envelope before I knew what it was. And now I'm rather wishing I hadn't.'

'I'll be there in five minutes.'

CHAPTER 36

While Maurice escorted a grateful Terry Shelley out of Silvertown Dock, I got up and locked the door to my office before making myself a very strong cup of coffee with the Nespresso machine that sat on top of the filing cabinet. If there'd been any brandy around I might have added some of that to my mug instead of milk from the refrigerator. I figured I needed something strong inside me if I really was going to play detective for the whole nine yards, and it was impossible even to imagine catching Zarco's killer without knowing the exact circumstances of how the man had met his death. I could see no way of avoiding it. Ignoring a text from the *Guardian* soliciting my opinion on the absence of black goal-keepers in top-class football – why was it, for example, that City had chosen a Scot instead of the 'equally talented' Hastings Obasanjo, or Pierre Bozizé? – I settled down to read.

I hadn't ever seen an autopsy report or had anything to do with one before. In fact, I hadn't even seen a dead body, unless you count the guy in the next cell at Wandsworth Prison who got a shiv in his neck and died later in hospital. The closest I'd come to seeing an autopsy had been on the telly when the almost infamous German anatomist Gunther von Hagens had dissected a cadaver 'live' on Channel Four television; it had been fascinating to see the human muscu-lature in close detail. I was of course especially fascinated to see those more vulnerable parts of the human leg that give all footballers problems from time to time: the anterior cruciate ligaments, the knee cartilage, the hamstrings and the groin. I remember gasping that something as simple as a length of tendon at the back of the knee could be so fucking painful when it tore, and that an Achilles could reduce you to a whimpering puppy when it snapped. For me it was like my teacher at school explaining how the Pythagorean theorem works infallibly; or, in the case of the anterior cruciate ligament, doesn't. Some of those Creationist bastards in the US who are forever arguing 'intelligent design' – I'd like to see them do that while trying to play on to the end of a match with a torn adductor muscle.

But while there had seemed a purpose to the carnage wreaked upon a human body by von Hagens, and a genuine investigative value to his carving up a cadaver like a pig carcass in a butcher's shop, what I was reading now seemed like something altogether different. The pale, rubbery bodies von Hagens used had hardly appeared to be human at all, more like something from the special effects guys at Pinewood Studios – perhaps because they had been emptied of the one thing that had made them human: life itself. And turning the pages of my friend's autopsy report felt uncomfortably personal, even transgressive. I hadn't ever sat in a steam bath with any of von Hagens' cadavers, or embraced them fondly at Christmas; I hadn't enjoyed a good dinner with any of them, or joined them in joyous celebrations as our team won a match; I hadn't known them for most of my life. I hadn't spoken to them less than seventy-two hours ago. It was a little like the computer guy taking your PC to bits in order to fix it – with all of the inside bits laid improbably open for inspection – except of course that no one was going to fix João Gonzales Zarco now. I suppose the moment when it hit me for the first time that Zarco really was dead and wouldn't be coming back – that my friend and mentor was gone forever – was when I saw a photograph of him lying on the pathology table with a Y-shaped suture zippered up the front of his pale and naked corpse.

What a waste, I thought; what a waste of a spectacularly talented man.

I tried to ignore the many other colour photographs and to concentrate mostly on the text, which was of course written in cold and scientific legalese. The tone was measured, matter-of-fact, dispassionate, like a medical textbook, with very little use of the past conditional tense and almost nothing supposed. Wounds and injuries were simply described and evaluated in an efficient way that rendered them less extraordinary and perhaps, for the detective at least, easier to deal with.

Had Detective Chief Inspector Jane Byrne attended João Zarco's autopsy? According to the notes, this had taken place during the course of a single hour the previous afternoon. I didn't envy her if she had. There were better ways to spend your Sunday than listening to the sound of a sternum being snipped open, or the sight of a human crown being removed with a saw like the top of your boiled egg. Perhaps she was used to it. She certainly looked like she was. You can get used to anything, I suppose. More than likely she'd have freaked out at the sight of a badly broken leg on a football pitch, though; I'd seen more than my fair share of those and I don't think there's a more traumatic sight in sport. I'd seen several players faint at the sight of a career-ending leg break. What I was looking at now was bad enough but I owed it to Zarco to steel myself to keep reading. Unfortunately there was no cortisone injection I could give myself in order to carry on turning the pages.

Poor Zarco. The pictures of his body, as found by Phil Hobday and the security guards from the dock, showed a man who looked like he had played ninety minutes in goal with his clothes on. These had been examined first and it had been concluded that the body had been clothed at the time of death; the pathologist had matched his injuries to the blood stains on Zarco's white Turnbull & Asser shirt, his grey Charvet silk tie, and the beautiful black silk coat from Zegna he'd been wearing on the morning of his death. Two grand, it cost him. But it did not look quite so beautiful now after he had crawled some way along the wet ground and several pigeons had come and crapped on him. The knees of his suit were almost as dirty and I was reminded of the night when we had beaten Arsenal and Zarco had 'done a Wayne', celebrating with a massive slide on his knees that took him from the technical area right down to the corner flag. Of Zarco's lucky club scarf – from a shop called Savile Rogue, it was made of cashmere – there was no sign.

The injuries to his body were all blunt trauma injuries, mostly to the head and upper torso, consistent with a severe beating; a violent impact to the front of the skull had resulted in a depressed fracture that had been the most probable cause of death. From the shape of the head fracture it seemed more than likely that Zarco had been struck with a blunt instrument although, so far, no murder weapon had been found.

Which probably explained the police divers in the Thames.

The right-hand side of the chest area was badly bruised, several of the ribs cracked, and his fingers and knuckles badly bruised as if he had fought back. And, underneath the fingernails of his right hand, the pathologist had found minute traces of skin and blood that were not Zarco's. This did not surprise me. Zarco had never been the type to turn the other cheek; certainly not as a player. Once, when he'd been playing for Celtic, he'd responded to a couple of hard punches from the Rangers player Nwankwo Nkomo with a well-placed and rather more effective head-butt that had broken Nkomo's nose. Even as a manager of La Braga, Zarco had had his fair share of brawls and fisticuffs, most famously in the tunnel at the San Siro when he'd mixed it with Howard Page, the manager of AC Milan, with the result that FIFA had banned them both from the touchline for several games. Zarco was no shrinking violet and I couldn't see that anyone taking a swing at him wouldn't have received something in kind.

The pathologist also found several blue woollen fibres underneath Zarco's fingernails that could not be matched to anything that the Portuguese had been wearing at the time of his death and which, it was implied, might have come from an assailant's clothing; this seemed to suggest the possibility that Zarco had grabbed hold of the lapel or the collar of whoever it was that had attacked him. Also consistent with a violent struggle having taken place was the way Zarco's tie had been found around his neck; it had been knotted much too tightly, almost as if an assailant had used it to try and strangle him with.

Traces of Zarco's vomit had been found on the ground; this was thought to be consistent with his having sustained a hard blow to the stomach.

Of more palatable interest to me were the contents of Zarco's pockets, and there were colour photographs of these, too: his regular mobile phone – the one his wife knew about – some loose change, a money clip, a wallet for credit cards, a set of keys – which didn't include a key to the door of the maintenance area where his body had been found – a wedding ring, a leather Smythson notebook in which he would write things during a game, the hard box for his Oakley sunglasses, a Mont Blanc pen, a business card from a councillor with the Royal Borough of Greenwich, a piece of white moulding from a ceiling (rather strangely), a gold coin, a Silvertown Dock pass which had been on a silk lanyard around his neck, and the Hublot watch and light blue prostate cancer silicone band that had been on his wrist.

After Zarco's father, José, died of prostate cancer, Zarco had become a tireless supporter of Prostate Cancer UK. Growing a terrible moustache every November to help raise funds was only a small part of what he did for this charity, which had already tweeted their grief on learning of his death.

On the ground surrounding the body were found several brooms and brushes, a couple of buckets, and some window-cleaning equipment. Small litter included eleven cigarette ends – most of which were English or American brands, although one was Russian – some spent matches, a button, a few copper coins, a McDonald's wrapper, several old City ticket stubs, a Styrofoam Starbucks coffee cup, a football programme, a month-old copy of the London *Evening Standard*, and an empty half-bottle of vodka. None of this looked like it was going to provide the vital clue that would solve the mystery of Silvertown Dock.

I closed the report and locked it in my filing cabinet before unlocking my office door again. Rather shamefully, perhaps, my first reaction on having finished reading the report was to congratulate myself on being alive when someone else – someone close to me – was not; but this, in the great scheme of things, is really all you can ask. To be around when others have had their heads bashed in is not much of a philosophy, but in the absence of something better it serves just as well as anything else.

CHAPTER 37

When the training session at Hangman's Wood was over I sat down with Simon Page and some physio reports and made the team choice for the match on Tuesday night. Christoph was out of the team in favour of Ayrton, and we had some of the more experienced players, like Ken Okri, at the back, but the rest of the side was taken from our reserves and under twenty-ones. At their pre-match press conference the Hammers had announced that they intended to field a full-strength side for the Capital One Cup match. Since the last cup won by West Ham had been the UEFA Intertoto Cup in 1999 – an out-of-season competition that was generally held to be a joke – and before that the FA Cup in 1980, when they'd defeated Arsenal, the club had decided that they owed it to the supporters to actively compete for some silverware.

I was surprised at this decision; then again, it's an easy mistake to make – to pay attention to what the fans want instead of what's best for the team. I decided that we were going to stick to our guns – the young guns, that is. But my mind really wasn't on team selection. I kept on thinking about Zarco's sunglasses on the floor of suite 123 and what they were doing there.

I had a theory, but as with all good theories I needed to conduct an experiment in order to test it. I rang Maurice.

'I want you to do me a favour,' I told him. 'There's a place called the Mile End Climbing Wall, on Haverfield Road, in Bow. I want you to go and buy some rope.'

'Don't do it,' said Maurice. 'You're too young to die.'

'Two hundred feet of rope, to be exact. In fact, I want everything you'd need to go climbing on the Crown of Thorns. A helmet, a padded harness, the rope, and someone who knows how to use that gear. If Sir Edmund Hillary is knocking around tell him there's two hundred quid and a pair of tickets in it for him if he'll come back to the dock with you. Otherwise, bring back anyone else who looks like he knows his ice axe from his elbow. I need two things from him: one is to lower me safely out of a high window; the other is to keep his mouth shut. If there's no one prepared to help we'll just have to work it out ourselves. But I want to do this today before it rains or snows again.'

'All right. Will do. It's your neck. What's this about, boss?'

'I'll explain everything when I see you.'

A couple of hours later Maurice was back at the dock accompanied by a thin, intense-looking man with red hair and a beard; he was wearing a green Berghaus fleece and carrying a large coil of rope and a rucksack full of gear. His name was Sean and he was from Bethnal Green, which is of course where a lot of great Alpinists have hailed from. I was still wearing my tracksuit and a pair of trainers from the training session at Hangman's Wood. I led the two men up to suite 123 and closed the door behind us.

'What is this room, then?' asked Sean.

'Private hospitality suite. Belongs to some guy from Qatar.'

'Really? Looks like the inside of my dad's Jaguar.'

I showed Sean into the kitchen and then opened the kitchen window.

He peered out of it and nodded, circumspectly. 'That's about a fifty-foot drop.'

'About that, yeah. I figure twenty feet to the descending cross beam and then another thirty or so to the ground.'

'You're serious about this, aren't you?'

'Very.'

'That cross beam looks a bit awkward. You wouldn't want to have to climb on it. Especially in this weather. It looks slippy.'

'Probably.'

'What the fuck's the point of it, anyway? The beam, I mean. In other words, does it have a function?'

'It's modern architecture,' I said. 'There's no function. Just form.'

'So what's this all about?' he asked. 'Are you an adrenalin junkie or did you just drop your mobile phone out of the bleeding window?'

'Let's just say I'm doing it because it's there.'

'Comedian.' Sean smiled a thin sort of smile. 'Everyone thinks they're Mallory and Irvine these days. You ever done any climbing before?'

'Only the stairs,' I said.

'Got a head for heights?'

'I guess we'll find out.'

'True.' Sean sighed. 'Two hundred quid and a couple of tickets, right?'

I nodded and handed over the money and the tickets for the Hammers match, which had been in my pocket.

'Paid in full.'

'Cheers, mate. I'd have preferred tickets for Tottenham, myself, but I 'spose these'll do, yeah. Thanks.'

All the time he kept glancing around as if checking out his surroundings.

Sean went out of the kitchen and into the sitting room. He pointed at the sliding door.

'What's out there?'

Maurice lifted the roller blinds and then opened the door to reveal the stadium seating and, in the centre, the pitch.

'Ah,' said Sean. 'Now that's what I'm looking for.' He pointed at some of the seats in front of the hospitality suite. 'First principle of climbing: find something stronger than yourself to tie a rope onto. These seats will do fine.'

When he'd finished tying the rope onto the seats he fetched the climbing harness from his backpack and fed the long piece of webbing around my waist, through the buckle, and then back again; with the two leg loops he did much the same. He checked the three buckles were fastened to his satisfaction and then tugged a loop in front of my navel towards him.

'This is the belay loop,' he explained. 'The single strongest point of the harness. And the bit that's going to attach you to life. Are you left-handed or right-handed?'

'Right-handed.'

He attached a karabiner to a belay device and clipped it onto the belay loop. Then he took a bite of rope and forced it through the bottom of the belay device. 'This lower part of the rope is your brake,' he explained. 'The brake hand is your right hand and that never comes off the line. Not for a moment. The guide hand on the upper part of the rope is your left hand. You're safely tied in now.'

'I'm beginning to think my two hundred quid is well spent,' I said.

'Hopefully you won't ever know just how well,' said Sean. 'Now all you have to do is belay.'

Having showed me the basics of belaying, and letting me practise a little, we were ready to go.

'If you start to fall too quickly then bring your brake hand – your right hand – down between your legs and the bend in the rope will arrest your descent. Understand?'

'I understand.'

He handed me a helmet and I strapped it on. A few minutes later I was out of the window and leaning back with both hands on the brake rope, as instructed. Each time I loosened my double grip on the brake rope I could descend.

'Take your time,' said Sean. 'A couple of feet at a time until you get your confidence.'

From the kitchen window I let out the rope in short increments until I was standing on tiptoe on one of the main beams on the crown of thorns. And now that I was there I was able to inspect the steel surface of the descending beam more closely and confirm what I had strongly suspected: that Zarco had actually fallen from the window of the kitchen. He'd hit the main beam on which I was standing, then slid round and down at an angle, shifting a trail of dirt and bird shit from the polished steel.

I sat down, let out some more of the guide rope and followed the trail along the beam on my arse, down and around, like a child descending a water slide, until about forty feet further on, the trail in the dirt and bird shit moved abruptly to the left, and then terminated. It was here that Zarco must have slipped off the beam and fallen a second time, this time onto concrete about twenty feet below, where Maurice was now standing, to confirm what I now knew for sure: that Zarco hadn't been beaten up and that all of the injuries detailed in the autopsy report were surely consistent with a fall from the kitchen window of suite 123.

Given that you couldn't actually see the window – any window – from the ground, it was an easy mistake for the police to have made; I'd made the same mistake myself when I'd first seen the crime scene. But crime it was, not an accident, or even a suicide: Zarco might have been worried that Viktor Sokolnikov was going to find out about his insider dealing, but he certainly wasn't the type to throw himself out of the window. I couldn't ever imagine him committing suicide. Besides, on Saturday morning he'd been in a good mood. He was always in a good mood before a big game. Especially one he thought we were going to win.

No, someone had pushed him out of that kitchen window. Pushed him to his death. It was the only possible explanation for how his sunglasses had come to be found lying on the floor by Paolo Gentile.

CHAPTER 38

After Sean had gone, and I was alone again with Maurice in suite 123, I told him about the fifty grand I'd found in the freezer and then explained my theory about what had happened to Zarco: that someone had pushed him out of the kitchen window.

'There's a tiny blood stain on the beam immediately below this window,' I said. 'That must have been how he got the blow to his head.'

'Makes sense,' said Maurice. 'It certainly explains why the door on that maintenance area was locked from the outside. Because no one opened it.'

'And it explains why no one spotted someone as famous as him going down there in the first place; because he didn't. At least not using the stairs.'

'But why do you believe that Paolo Gentile found the sunglasses exactly like he said he did?' asked Maurice. 'Maybe he was lying. Maybe he and Zarco argued about something. The bung, perhaps. Maybe it was him who pushed Zarco out of the window.'

'It's true they'd argued about the bung before,' I said. 'I saw them arguing about it at a service station in Orsett. But the bung was paid, after all. The cash part, anyway. So they could hardly have argued about that.'

'Yes, but he did fuck off to Milan that very same day. He

didn't even hang around for the match. And that's exactly what I'd have done if I'd topped Zarco. Caught the next flight home. Once someone is in Italy, it's not so easy getting them back here to face charges. If you've got money there you can give the Italian law the runaround. Look at Berlusconi. He's got away with it for years.'

'I still don't buy it, Maurice. It was Zarco who persuaded Viktor Sokolnikov to use Gentile on the Kenny Traynor transfer, instead of Denis Kampfner. Viktor was a golden goose for an agent like Gentile. There's no telling how many golden eggs Zarco could have persuaded our mega-rich proprietor to lay for our Italian friend. I just don't see Gentile doing it. He had too much to lose by killing him.'

'All right. That makes sense.'

'Now Viktor, on the other hand...'

'Don't tell me you fancy Viktor for it,' said Maurice.

'I don't know. Maybe. There's a YouTube video of him nutting his fellow oligarch, Alisher Aksyonov, live on Russian television. He looks like he means it, too. If Viktor had found out about Zarco buying shares in SSAG he might have been angry enough to hit him.'

'But he was with the people from RBG when Zarco went missing, wasn't he?'

'Only some of the time. On Saturday afternoon, before the match, when Phil Hobday came to tell me that Zarco had gone missing, he told me that Viktor was looking for him, too. But yesterday, when I spoke to Viktor in my office, he told me he was with the guys from RBG for the whole afternoon. One of them is mistaken. Or lying.'

'Fucking hell, Scott. Be careful. You've only just got this job.'

'Listen, someone was in here with Zarco. I think whoever

it was sat down and had a cup of coffee with him. There were just three mugs in the dishwasher, which was still on the first time I came in here. A dishwasher cycle's a pretty good way of getting rid of your fingerprints. So, suppose that Viktor found Zarco in suite 123; maybe they sat down over a coffee and Zarco decided to confess all to Viktor, who went nuts. Frankly, who could blame him? On the evidence of what's on YouTube there's no doubt that Viktor can handle himself. And that he's got a temper. By his own admission he used to be a rather more hands-on businessman than he is now. That is, hands on someone's coat lapels.'

'Yeah, but why would he ask you to investigate Zarco's murder if he was the one who did it? Doesn't make sense.'

'I've been wondering about that. But it's not like I'm Lord Peter Wimsey, is it? I'm just some cunt in a tracksuit. So perhaps I was only supposed to muddy the waters for the police and stop them from finding out that he killed Zarco himself. Which, so far, has worked rather well, wouldn't you say? I mean the cops don't know shit about what really happened. They're outside, playing Jacques Cousteau, looking for a murder weapon – a blunt instrument that doesn't even exist. The only metal pipe that hit Zarco on the head was the one weighing several tons below the kitchen window. Without what I know, the cops don't know anything very much. They don't know about this room, Paolo Gentile, the bung on Kenny Traynor, the cash in the freezer, the shares bought in SSAG, and the fact that Zarco was feeling nervous about Viktor Sokolnikov. At least he was according to Toyah. She's afraid of him, too. And here's another thing, Maurice.'

'Oh, fuck. I don't think I want to know.'

'Viktor gives me the job of replacing Zarco as manager of London City. One of the top jobs in football. I'm on the same money as Zarco, plus bonuses. Viktor even gives me a valuable portrait of Zarco to help sweeten the deal. To incentivise me, he says. Now suppose I do find something out. Something that incriminates Viktor himself. What do I do? Naturally I don't go to the cops. He knows I hate the cops. According to Viktor, that's one of the very reasons he asked me to play sleuth for him. Because he knows I won't rat him out to the law. So if I do find something, the chances are that I'll then do one of two things. Either I'll have it out with him and he'll persuade me to keep my mouth shut; perhaps he'll try to bribe me, I don't know. Or I'll suppress the evidence altogether in the interests of my oh-so-generous employer and of course my own bright future with this football club.'

'Hold up a minute.'

'What?'

'There's a third alternative here that maybe you ought to consider, boss. That Viktor Sokolnikov doesn't bribe you or persuade you to keep your mouth shut. Instead he puts the frighteners on you. He threatens you. Some of those body-guards who work for him, they're very scary guys. I was in the steam room at Hangman's Wood with one of them and he's got more fucking tattoos than a beach in Ibiza. Proper Russian Mafia tattoos, too. None of that "Mum" and "Dad" and "Scotland Forever" bullshit. These are tattoos that mean stuff to those in the know. You mark my words, boss: if you have it out with Viktor you might just disappear. This is the East End of London, remember? People have been disappearing round here since the princes in the Tower. Someone shoves you in that river one dark night, you might never be seen again. It's not just me who thinks so. That's what the Leeds fans were singing about Zarco when we went to Elland

312

Road. Remember? The fans might not have known about Zarco's photograph in the grave we found out there, but it didn't stop the flat-capped bastards from filling in the gaps, so to speak. *He's getting murdered in the morning/ Ding Dong the bells are gonna chime/ Vic and his mafia/ Will soon fucking have ya/ And get you to your grave on time.'*

'I'd forgotten that.'

'All I'm saying is, be a bit careful, yeah? This isn't handbags on the pitch with Mario Balotelli, boss. You're up against someone with a very murky past. I watched that *Panorama* special on Viktor. He's got more skeletons in his fucking cupboard than the Museum of Cairo. So, promise me you won't accuse him or anything daft like that, not without speaking to me first, eh?'

'Fortunately all the evidence is very circumstantial,' I said. 'So unless I find some real hard evidence I'm not about to do anything crazy.' I shrugged. 'But the fact is, I'm still going to have to consider my position here.'

'How do you mean?'

'I mean that if I do finally conclude that the person who killed João Zarco was the proprietor of this club then I can hardly remain here working for him. That would be impossible. Quite apart from anything else I'd always wonder if the reason I got the job was to keep me on side. But the fact is, I loved Zarco. I might not be able to tell the police about it but I couldn't be around someone who'd killed Zarco, or had him killed. You do see that, don't you? It would be a betrayal of my friendship for Zarco. He may not always have been entirely honest but he was always a good mate to me. And that's what counts, Maurice.'

'Would he have done the same for you? I don't know.'

'It's what I think that matters, Maurice. It's my bloody

conscience that's affected here, not Zarco's. When I was in the nick I read Dante's *Inferno*. Being in a hell like Wandsworth it seemed appropriate. Dante places Brutus and Cassius in the worst part of hell because they chose to betray their friend, Julius Caesar, rather than their country. I feel much the same way about Zarco.'

'All right, I get that. But how will you decide? If Viktor's guilty?'

'I don't know. I suppose I'll keep my ears and eyes open for some clue as to his guilt or innocence. And then, when I've thought about it for a while, I'll make my decision. To leave this club, or to stay.' I shrugged. 'That's something real I can do. There won't be a big reveal in the fucking dining car or the library when I've decided what really happened. I'll just resign. Simple as that.'

CHAPTER 39

A little later on, Detective Inspector Considine appeared in my office doorway. She was wearing a black coat and a little black dress. She had very bright red lipstick for a police-woman and she looked smiley and nice.

'I'm beginning to feel like the bad penny,' she said. 'Always turning up.'

'You know, I've never really understood what that means.'

'I suppose you'd have to understand the value of a penny, first. And it strikes me that you don't. Haven't done for a long while. Not with a flat like that in Manresa Road.'

I smiled. 'You like my flat, don't you?'

'Who wouldn't? It makes my own flat look like a broom cupboard.'

'Drop by sometime and I'll make you another coffee.'

'I'd like that. Listen, there are two reasons for my being here now. One is to apologise for yesterday; I'm afraid I was rather abrupt in the way I told you that Matt Drennan's friend had raped Miss Fehmiu. That must have come as quite a shock to you. Not to mention your friend's part in covering it all up. I'm sorry about that. Really I am. I was only doing my duty in telling you, but—'

'Forget about it. Like you say, you were only doing your job.'

'Honestly? I could have handled it better.'

'Apology accepted. And the other reason?'

'You're going to hate me.'

'No, I'm not.'

'Another equally unpleasant duty, I'm afraid. Only this time I'm going to do my utmost to handle it with more sensitivity.'

'Which is?'

'Maybe you don't remember, but you volunteered to identify Mr Zarco's body.'

'Oh Christ, yes, I did, didn't I?'

'I'm sure you can think of a hundred things you'd rather do this afternoon. But it is important. A legal requirement. Fortunately, his body isn't so very far away from here, in East Ham, so I can drive you there myself. Now, if it's convenient. Later, if it's not.'

I glanced at my watch. 'Now is good, as it happens.'

'All right then. Let's go.'

She made a quick call to the mortuary to let them know we were on our way. Every time I saw her I liked her a little bit more. Maybe it was because she was posh; I like posh, good-looking birds. But mostly it was because she was clever. I followed her outside to a black Audi TT and got in. A minute or so later we were heading north away from the dock and up East Ham High Street.

'All I really know about you is that you studied law,' I said. 'Did you ever want to be a lawyer? Or did you just watch too many episodes of *Inspector Morse*?'

'Actually I really wanted to be a vet, but I abandoned that idea because I used to faint at the sight of blood. I'm still pretty squeamish sometimes.'

'Forgive me, but a career in the police doesn't seem like an obvious alternative. Especially under the present circumstances.'

'True. Most of the time I'm okay with these things. And I absolutely adore working in the police. It's just now and then that something makes me feel a bit dodgy. I've got several strategies for dealing with it. Bodies, I mean. What about you? Will you be all right with this? With seeing Mr Zarco's body?'

'I'll let you know when I see him.'

'What, you mean you've never seen a body before?'

'You make it sound like I should have done. I'm only forty, for Christ's sake. My parents are still alive and so are my grandparents.'

'Oh, I see. I thought when you volunteered it had to be because you were cool with this kind of thing.'

'I volunteered because I hoped to spare his wife, and because I've known him longer than she has. But I'm not in the least bit cool about it, Miss Considine. In fact, you might tell me one of your strategies for dealing with your squeamishness, just in case I go wobbly on you.'

'It's just a bottle of smelling salts. *Sal volatile*. I keep some in my handbag. I know it sounds a bit old-fashioned of me but it's actually quite scientific, you know. They give it to weightlifters before they compete in the Olympics because the ammonia triggers an inhalation reflex and activates the sympathetic nervous system; and this elevates the heart rate, blood pressure and brain activity, thus counteracting the faint. Before I see a body I just take a whiff of the stuff and I'm usually fine. Now it's just another tool in my forensic kit.'

'Well, if I keel over don't forget to loosen my clothing, will you? I'm a bit old-fashioned myself. Besides, I like to wake up with a smile on my face.

'You're very funny, do you know that?'

'I'm glad you think so.'

When we got nearer the East Ham Mortuary, she pointed left and said, 'I think West Ham Football Ground is about half a mile that way, on the Barking Road.'

'With all the stiffs in their team it's certainly handy for the mortuary.'

'You're playing them tomorrow night, aren't you?'

'Yes. It's the second leg of our semi-final match in the Capital Cup. Would you like to come as my guest? We can have dinner afterwards in the director's box.'

'I can hardly say no if I'm to be your guest, can I? But what if you lose – won't you be in a filthy temper? Throwing football boots at people and that kind of thing? You might throw a boot at me. I wouldn't be at all surprised after yesterday.'

'That's Sir Alex Ferguson you're thinking of, Inspector. Besides, we're not going to lose. We're going to win. And I promise not to be in a filthy temper. But bring your smelling salts, just in case.'

'Are you planning another inspiring team talk, is that it? Like the one on YouTube.'

'When they win it won't be for me, it will be for João Zarco.'

'That might work for the team. But it won't work for me. I think if I come to the match it had better be because I'd like to see you smile some time. And only if you promise not to tell anyone that I'm coming. I'd hate the news that I was at your game to get as far as Stanford Bridge.'

'It's Stamford Bridge. And I don't believe you've ever been to a game of football in your life, Miss Considine.'

Just beyond a park she pulled up on a double yellow line in front of a small sixties-style building that most resembled a public library, with what looked like a little chapel on the end. There was a fence and a hedge and a large oak tree in the garden. She smiled a disarming smile.

'All right, it's a fair cop. I haven't. And I lied about supporting Chelsea. But it cannot be denied that José Mourinho is a very handsome man. Very handsome indeed.'

'I can deny it, Miss Considine. I can deny it on a stack of Bibles.'

'It's Louise. If I'm going to switch allegiance from José to you, I think we'd better be on first-name terms, don't you?'

'Agreed. Louise.' I smiled. 'Is this just to make me feel better before we go in there?'

'You'll have to wait until tomorrow night to know for sure,' she said.

She got out of the car, opened the gate and then pulled onto a short driveway.

Inside the door of the mortuary she handed me a little glass ampoule covered in cloth.

'Ammonia gonna say this once,' she said. 'Just break it under your nose if you feel faint.'

A mortuary official greeted us. He was small and balding with a gold tooth, and had an Arsenal pin in his lapel, which struck me as brave so close to Upton Park. He showed us into a room with a curtained window.

'You ready?' asked Louise.

I nodded.

She broke one of the little white ampoules under her nose and inhaled sharply. The atmosphere in the room was suddenly filled with a strong smell of ammonia and then she was gasping and blinking like she was in bright sunshine and knocking on the window glass.

The grey curtains parted to reveal Zarco's body lying on a trolley. Most of him was under a green sheet but I could have wished his head had been covered, too. He had been such a handsome man – every bit as handsome as José Mourinho, whom he had known well, of course, since they were both Portuguese. His habitually unshaven face was badly bruised and his skull bashed in like a discarded plastic water bottle. It was the only part of his face that had any colour; the grey hue of the remaining part made him look like an extra in a zombie movie. But it was Zarco all right – I recognised the grey Brillo-pad hair, the sulky mouth and the broad nose; I'd have recognised that nose anywhere. I'd seen it hovering over a glass of good red wine often enough, savouring the bouquet like a true connoisseur. I remembered the dinner we'd had at 181 First, a restaurant in Munich, when he'd come to offer me the job at London City, and the two-hundred-euro bottle of Spätburgunder he'd ordered to cement the deal, and how much he'd enjoyed that particular red wine. I remembered how the restaurant was in the Olympic Tower and that it had been a revolving room, and the fantastic 360-degree view of Munich it had afforded us, and how even now I could remember our table and the way that it, and the whole restaurant, had turned, and how I'd drunk too much that night – we both had – and then the whole world was spinning until the moment when Louise, bless her, had something under my nose and I was reeling away from the ammoniac smell and her hand and the next world's window.

'Are you all right?' she asked as I staggered through the mortuary door.

Outside in the fresh air I wiped a tear from my eye and nodded. 'It's him,' I said. 'It's Zarco. Sorry about that.'

'Don't be.' She took my hand and kissed it quickly. 'Come on. I'll take you back to Silvertown Dock.'

CHAPTER 40

On my way home from the dock to Chelsea I dropped in to see Zarco's widow again. It wasn't as if I had anything particular I wanted to tell her but after not taking Toyah's call that morning I'd called her back, several times, without success. I'm not sure who else she had to rely on, apart from Jerusa the housekeeper, but I was determined not to abandon my friend's widow just because I didn't like her that much. Like a lot of Australians in London she was a little too contemptuous of Britain and its awful weather for my taste, which begged the question: if you don't like it, then what the fuck are you doing here? The one time I'd been to Australia I'd enjoyed myself a lot; at the same time, however, when you were there it was easy to see why so many Australians came to live in London. The weather was actually the least important part of why anyone chose to live in London. Apart from the weather everything was better than in Australia. Especially the football.

I rang the bell without success. The copper guarding Toyah's door recognised me from before and told me she was still at home but that he hadn't seen her all day, which worried us both, a little, so he allowed me to shout through her letterbox; and when eventually she came downstairs and let me into the house, I found her wearing a long silk dressing gown and it was obvious that she'd been in bed.

'I'm sorry,' I said. 'I was starting to get a bit concerned. So was the copper outside.'

'I'm not the type to do myself in, Scott. Not for any man. And certainly not for one who was cheating on me with some little bitch at Hangman's Wood.'

'Did the cops tell you that?'

'They didn't need to. I knew what he was up to. I knew and I learned to look the other way because I figured it wasn't going anywhere, okay? Don't get me wrong. I loved Zarco. But there were times when he couldn't keep it zipped. And to have an affair at work? That was just stupid.' She lit a cigarette. 'Would you like some tea?'

I took off my coat and we went down to the spaceship of a kitchen, which gave me a welcome opportunity to change the subject.

'I'm sorry I woke you up, Toyah.'

'That's all right. I took a pill after I called you this morning and I've been asleep ever since. Really, it's lucky you woke me up. I've got so much to do.' She glanced at her watch. 'And apparently very little time in which to do it. Jesus, I had no idea it was so late. I must have slept for eight hours.'

'That's good,' I said. 'It's probably the best thing there is for grief.'

I was looking forward to going to bed myself; Sonja had sent me a neutral sort of text, saying that she hoped I was all right and I replied that I was, but thoughts of Louise Considine notwithstanding, I knew I would feel a lot better as soon as I was fast asleep.

'I identified his body,' I said. 'About an hour ago. I thought perhaps you should know.'

'Thank you. I appreciate you doing that. I know it must have been very upsetting for you.'

I shrugged that off.

'Have the police got any ideas yet?' she asked. 'About who killed Zarco, and why?'

'I don't know.'

'What about you?'

'No,' I lied. 'Nothing yet. But it's early days.'

She poured the tea and we sat down at the long wooden table.

'You asked me to tell you about anything unusual that happened,' she said. 'Something that might fill in a few blanks, you said. Well, there was something. My builder came round, Tristram Lambton. He's been handling the work on number twelve. He said he'd come to pay his respects, but it wasn't long before he mentioned the real reason he was here. He asked me if Zarco had left an envelope for him.'

'An envelope?'

'I hate to mention this right now, Mrs Zarco, he says when he's finished being sympathetic, but your late husband had agreed to pay me in cash for some of the building work. Did he leave something for me, perhaps? An envelope?'

'How much cash?'

'Twenty thousand pounds, he said.'

'That's pushing any normal envelope,' I said. 'I know builders like cash in hand, but twenty grand needs two hands. Maybe three or four.'

'Tell me about it. But I can't honestly say I was entirely surprised. Zarco had all sorts of fiddles going, as you probably know. He was a typical Portuguese. Always making bloody deals, he was. It was meat and drink to the man. A right Del Boy.' She took an angry puff of her cigarette. 'Anyway, I told him that Zarco hadn't mentioned any cash to me but I went and checked the safe, just in case. But there wasn't any envelope. At least not one containing thousands of pounds. And Tristram said something like, well, if you do come across it, then please let me know. And I said that twenty grand wasn't exactly the kind of sum that I was likely to find in Zarco's sock drawer. And that's how we left it.'

I nodded. 'What kind of guy is this Tristram?'

'Posh boy. Nice-looking. Plenty of money and a Bentley. Good builder, though. Our architect seems to rate him very highly. And so did Zarco.'

'I'll speak to him,' I said. 'I'll speak to him after I've had my tea.'

'Thanks, Scott. I appreciate it.'

I stayed another fifteen minutes for appearance's sake. The house felt odd without Zarco's loud voice and his laughter. Even the cat was looking a little bewildered. I used Toyah's lavatory, put my coat back on, went outside and walked around to the other side of the square.

It was dark and well past the usual going-home time for builders, but from the lights and noise behind the Lambton Construction mural that hid the façade of number twelve it was plain that they were still working hard. I could hear what sounded like a carpenter at work, hammering one nail after another into some wood. I went through a wooden gate in the side of the mural and down the side of the house, which had been largely transformed by the addition of a huge modern window. I walked down a flight of stone stairs and found myself facing a man wearing a hoodie under a hard hat with a roll-up in his mouth and a plank on his shoulder.

'Here,' he said in a thick foreign accent, 'what you up to, sunshine? You nicking tools or something?'

'No, I wasn't nicking tools.'

''Cos people nick our tools and the boss he say it's us. Threaten to take it from our wages.'

'No, that's not what I want.'

'What do you want? You here to complain? Because I just work here, see?'

'I'm looking for Mr Lambton. I'm a friend of Mrs Zarco.'

The man's dark eyes narrowed. 'Sure, I know you,' he said. 'You're the football guy. Scott Manson. Used to play for Arsenal – I remember. Now you manager of City. Me, I like Arsenal. They good team. Better than City, I think. Arsenal is cake your mother makes. Home-made. Good cake. City is cake you buy in shop. Not as good. More expensive, too.' He took a last puff on the roll-up and then threw it into the house. 'Hey, you got any tickets?'

'No, I don't. And I'm still looking for Mr Lambton.'

'There's two Mr Lambtons. Brothers, see? Tristram and Gareth. Which one you want?'

'Tristram.'

'Okay, you wait here and I find him.'

He put down the plank and walked into a maze of scaffolding that was lit by a bare bulb, leaving me alone with my thoughts, which were a knot of this and that. If I'd had a little more time I might have been able to think things out, to perceive what was significant, and to separate what was important from what was not. Being a cop on the Zarco inquiry might have presented them with a few more challenges if they'd been facing a full-strength West Ham on Tuesday night. There was no doubt about it, I was feeling under pressure. In Toyah's loo I'd glanced at a newspaper article about the fun of being a fantasy football manager, and I'd thought, if only football was all you had to deal with then the job might seem as fun as that; it's all the other shit that life throws at you – your girlfriend dumping you, the Inland Revenue telling your accountants that they think you owe them more tax, fucking reporters camped outside your house, gay players taking drugs, one of your oldest pals hanging himself – that makes the job so fucking difficult.

I took my iPhone out of my backpack, in the hope that I might deal with some of the shit heaping up at my door. An email I'd been composing for Hugh McIlvanney about João Zarco looked unimprovable, so I sent that, with a copy to Sarah Crompton. Jane Byrne wanted to stage a reconstruction of Zarco's last moments with the help of *Crimewatch*, at our next weekend home fixture. I said yes to that. Another one from UKAD invited me to a meeting at the FA head office so that my memory could be refreshed regarding drug-testing protocols. Stupid sods. Could I do an interview with *Football Focus*? Fuck off; I'd already said no to *Gillette Soccer Saturday* and TalkSPORT. I had an old mate from Southampton who'd been given the manager's job at Hibs and did I have any advice for him? Knowing Edinburgh, I did: don't let the bastards get you down.

Then I scrolled through some texts: the Rape Crisis people wanted a donation, to which I said yes, and Tiffany Drennan informed me that Drenno's funeral would be on Friday, to which I also said yes. Viktor had sent me a text saying he would be back from Russia in time for the match on Tuesday night, and that Bekim Develi would be coming with him; and the red devil himself had sent me a text in which he told me he was looking forward to playing for City and felt sure that ours would be a very successful relationship. I texted him back a one word 'Welcome'. Meanwhile, on my iPad, I quickly Googled Warwick Square and discovered that it had its own website, with an active residents' association and a useful table of property prices. Flats were a staggering two million quid, while what few houses there were for sale started at a cool eight million.

It never surprises you what your own house is worth, but it always surprises you the price that other people want for their houses.

'Can I help you?'

The man looking at me was thirtyish, thin, and about six feet tall; he wore a brown Crombie coat with a velvet collar and a yellow hard hat.

'I'm a friend of Zarco,' I said.

'Yes, I know,' he said. 'I've seen you on the telly, haven't I? On *A Question of Sport*.'

'You've got a good memory. Is there somewhere we can talk?'

'What about?'

'I understand you went to see Mrs Zarco,' I said. 'About some money you say you're owed. Twenty thousand quid, to be exact.'

Tristram Lambton hesitated.

'It's all right,' I said. 'You say you recognise me off the telly? Well, that should reassure you I'm not from the Inland Revenue or the Home Office. I don't care who you're employing on the site and how you're paying them. I'm here to help Mrs Zarco, if I can.'

'There's my car. Let's talk there.'

The Bentley was silver grey with all the extras; when you shut the door it sounded like you'd walked through the entrance of a very exclusive gentlemen's club. It smelled like one, too; all leather and cigars and thick pile carpets.

'I didn't know that Mrs Zarco wasn't aware of my arrangement with her husband,' said Lambton. 'I felt really awful about it afterwards. But I thought, widowed or not, the best thing for her now would be to complete the building project as quickly as possible so she can flog the place and get on with her life. Which does seem to be what she wants to do. Frankly the whole job has been a bloody nightmare from start to finish.'

'That's certainly the impression I got. But what was your arrangement with Mr Zarco?'

'The Zarcos have been getting a lot of complaints about the building work from the neighbours. In particular the people at number thirteen, next door – as you can imagine. Which means that I've been under a lot of pressure from the Zarcos to get this building finished as soon as possible. And the only way I can get the lads to work the overtime I'm asking them to do in order to make that happen is to pay them double time, in cash. Money really does talk to these boys. That was my arrangement with Mr Zarco. He'd pay the double time himself. The weekends, too. On Saturday he was supposed to stump up the twenty k that would help me to get things finished before the end of March, which is ahead of schedule, I might add. But you know what happened. It's really too bad. I liked him a lot. Now I've no idea what I'll do. I mean, that's the end of the double overtime and working on a Sunday.'

'Not necessarily.'

I'd anticipated this moment. In Toyah's lavatory I'd separated the bung money into two amounts: twenty grand and thirty grand. The twenty grand was still in the Jiffy bag, the rest was in a compartment in my backpack.

'Here,' I said. 'The twenty grand he was planning to give you.'

'That's brilliant. I know it sounds a lot, but these Romanian boys are hard workers and worth every penny. I mean they really do want to bloody work, unlike some of our own. But don't get me started on that.' He laughed. 'Now if you can just sort out Mr and Mrs Van de Merwe at number thirteen, everything will be perfect.'

'What would you suggest?'

'Seriously?'

CHAPTER 41

Pimlico is like Belgravia without rich people. The folks in Pimlico aren't exactly poor, it's just that much of their wealth is tied up in the value of their flats and houses.

Number twelve was an end-of-terrace property; the house next door was a six-storey white stucco mansion from the early nineteenth century with a fine Doric portico and a black door that was as polished as a guardsman's boots; or at least it would have been if it hadn't been covered with a fine layer of builders' dust. There was a blue plaque on the wall but it was too dark for me to identify the famous person who had once lived there. But I knew the area quite well; Gianluca Vialli had lived around the corner when he'd been player-manager of Chelsea until 2001, and if anyone deserved a blue plaque it was him: the four goals he'd scored against Barnsley were among the best I'd ever seen in the Premier League.

I pulled the old-fashioned doorbell and heard it ring behind the door, but I think I might have heard it ring in Manresa Road.

At least a minute passed and I was about to give up and go away when a light went on in the portico; then I heard several bolts being drawn and a largish key being turned in a probably Victorian lock. The door opened to reveal an old man in a brown corduroy suit. He had a sort of Dutch painter's beard and moustache that was white but stained with nicotine, and wild grey hair that seemed to be growing in several different directions at once so that it looked like the Maggi Hambling seascape on my wall. On his nose was a pair of half-moon glasses and around his neck was a loosely tied beige silk scarf. He had one of the weariest faces I think I'd ever seen – not so much lined as cracked; you wouldn't have been surprised to see a face like that shatter into a dozen pieces.

'Mr Van de Merwe?'

'Yes?'

'Forgive me for interrupting you,' I said. 'My name is Scott Manson. I wonder if I might come inside and talk to you for a moment?'

'About what?'

'About Mr Zarco.'

'Who are you? The police?'

'No,' I said. 'Not the police.'

'Who is it, dear?' said a voice.

'Someone about Mr Zarco,' said Mr Van de Merwe. 'He says he's not the police.'

His voice, no less weary than his face, sounded a bit like someone looking for a channel on a shortwave radio. And his accent sounded vaguely South African.

A woman as anxious-looking as a stolen Munch scream came into the hall; she was old and small with a mountain of fairish hair and wore a thick white sweater with a South African flag on a breast that was as large as my backpack.

'You'd better come in,' said the man and shuffled to one side, which was when I noticed he had a crutch to help him walk.

The hall was dominated by a film poster for a creaky old

movie called *Passport to Pimlico*, an Ealing comedy from a few years after the war. The old couple looked as if they'd been in it. On a table was a blue glass figurine, possibly Lalique, of a semi-naked woman; some opened mail for a Mr John Cruikshank MA lay next to it. There was a strong smell of furniture polish in the air and a large pile of newly washed yellow dusters on the stairs.

They ushered me into a large sitting room full of furniture that had seen better days but possibly a couple of world wars, too. There were books and paintings and everything looked like it had been there for a very long time; a thin layer of more recently acquired dust covered the back of long leather sofa they invited me to sit on. A younger woman, quite good-looking, wearing jeans and a fleece, was seated at the opposite end. She noticed me wiping my fingers on my hand and, immediately producing another yellow duster, angrily set about wiping the sofa.

'This is my daughter, Mariella,' said Mr Van de Merwe. 'Mariella, this is Mr Manson. He wants to ask us some questions about poor Mr Zarco.'

Mariella grunted, irritably.

'Not exactly questions,' I said. 'Is it just the three of you here?'

'That sounds exactly like a question,' said Mariella.

'It was just small talk,' I said. 'Maybe a bit too small for some.'

'My son-in-law John lives here too,' said Mr Van de Merwe. 'He's away at the moment.'

'Would you like a drink, Mr Manson?' asked his wife. 'A sherry, perhaps?'

'Yes, please.'

All three of them went out of the room, leaving me to

stare at the ceiling for several minutes. Through the wall I could hear the sound of one of Lambton's Romanian workmen hammering nails, and then someone started with a drill. It was easy to see why the Van de Merwes had felt moved to complain about the noise; listening to that for twelve hours a day would have driven me mad. All the same it was hard to imagine them harassing a tardy postman, let alone a gang of Romanian builders, as Lambton had alleged.

They arrived back as a little trio – Mr Van de Merwe bearing a single glass on a silver tray, his wife carrying a bottle of sherry, and their daughter holding a plate of sliced ham.

'Is that a Stanley Spencer?' I asked, pointing at a painting on the wall.

'Yes,' said the old man.

'It's nice,' I said, with considerable understatement; Spencer was one of my favourites.

'Mr Zarco liked a drop of sherry,' explained the old man. 'Particularly this Oloroso. Which goes well with Iberian ham.'

I tasted the sherry; it was delicious. 'When was Zarco last here?' I asked.

'Several weeks ago. And on more than one occasion. He came to apologise for all of the building work next door, which has been going on for the best part of six months now. Quite intolerably. Well, you can judge for yourself if anyone could live with that noise from first thing in the morning until eight at night. At our time of life you look forward to peace and quiet. For reading and listening to music. It wouldn't be so bad if we were deaf, but we're not.'

'Yes, I can quite understand how irritating it must be,' I said. 'And you have my sympathy.'

Mariella spotted another cloud of dust falling from the ceiling onto the sideboard and went after it fiercely with the duster.

'We tried to reach some accommodation with him about it,' continued Mr Van de Merwe. 'But I'm afraid we failed.'

'What sort of accommodation?'

'A financial settlement,' said Mr Van de Merwe. 'We had hoped we might all go back to South Africa for a while. That's where we come from, originally.'

'From Pretoria,' his wife said, helpfully. 'It's really lovely there at this time of year. Around twenty-five degrees. Every day.'

'But the air fares are very expensive,' continued her husband. 'And so is accommodation. Even a cheap hotel costs a lot of money.'

'Do you know South Africa, Mr Manson?' asked Mrs Van de Merwe.

'A little. I was there for the World Cup in 2010. My ears are still recovering from all the vuvuzelas.'

When the old couple looked at me blankly, Mariella said, 'The lepatata mambus.' She looked at me and shrugged. 'That's the proper Tswana name.'

'I see.'

'Pretoria is very beautiful at this time of year,' repeated Mrs Van de Merwe.

'Couldn't you have gone somewhere else?' I said. 'Somewhere nearer, perhaps, like Spain? It's warmer there than it is here at this time of year. And cheaper to get to.'

I started to stuff my mouth with the ham; that was delicious, too, and would maybe save me from having to make dinner. Now that Sonja was gone my enthusiasm for doing anything but make coffee in the kitchen was much reduced.

'We've never really liked Spain,' said the old man. 'Have we, dear?'

'We don't speak the language,' said his wife. 'South Africa was the only real alternative for us.'

'Mr Zarco did make us an offer,' said the old man, 'to cover the expenses of our temporary relocation, but it simply wasn't enough, so we turned it down. I think he thought we were trying it on. But we really weren't, you know. It was all most disappointing.'

'Look,' I said. 'Do you mind me asking how much money he did offer? To compensate you for all you've suffered while the work has been going on?'

'Ten thousand pounds, wasn't it?' said the old man.

His wife nodded. 'Yes. I know that sounds like a lot of money, and it is. But the flights alone were about three or four thousand.'

I made a quick mental calculation, picked up my backpack and took out four bundles of cash. It's always nice being generous with someone else's money. Not that this was entirely my own idea; it was Tristram Lambton who had put the germ of the idea in my head and it seemed as good a way of getting rid of Zarco's bung as anything else I could think of.

'There's twenty thousand pounds,' I said, feeling a sense of relief to have got rid of yet more of Zarco's bung. 'To cover all your expenses, and to compensate you for what you've had to endure these past few months.'

'What?' Mr Van de Merwe's jaw had started to sag in a rather alarming way, as if he'd had a stroke. 'I don't understand. Mr Zarco is dead, isn't he?'

'Look, please don't ask me to explain, but I'm quite sure he'd have liked you to have this money.'

The Van de Merwes looked at each other, bewildered.

'Twenty thousand pounds?' said Mrs Van de Merwe.

'It's very generous of you,' said the old man. 'Of Mrs Zarco. But really—'

'Are you serious?' asked her daughter.

'Very.'

'No, really, we couldn't,' said the old man. 'Not now he's dead. It wouldn't seem fair, somehow. I mean on the television it said the man had been murdered. We couldn't accept it, could we, dear? Mariella? What do you think?'

'Oh, Dad,' his daughter said irritably. 'Of course we can accept it. It only seems unfair. But it isn't unfair at all. After all you've gone through, it's exactly what you and Mum should do.'

'But Mrs Zarco is a widow now,' said his wife. 'She can ill afford this kind of expense, surely. That poor man. What his wife must be feeling now. We should speak to John. Ask him what he thinks.'

'We'll take it, Mr Manson,' Mariella told me firmly.

Her parents looked at each other uncertainly, and then Mrs Van de Merwe began to cry.

'It's all been very trying for my wife,' explained the old man. 'What with the noise and everything. She's quite exhausted.'

'We'll take it,' repeated his daughter. 'Won't we? I think we should. And I'm speaking for John now, too. If he were here he'd say that this is absolutely the right thing to do. Yes, we'll take it.'

The old man nodded. 'If you think so, dear, then yes.'

'Good,' I said. 'I think you're doing the right thing, too.'

I got up to leave with Mr Van de Merwe accompanying me to the door.

'You've been very kind to us, Mr Manson,' he said. 'I don't know what to say, really. I'm almost speechless. It's more than generous.'

'Don't thank me. Thank Mrs Zarco. Only not right now, eh? Perhaps when the work is complete and she's finally living next door, you might thank her then.'

'Yes, yes I will.' He held my hand for a moment too long; there were tears in his eyes, too.

'The blue plaque outside,' I said in the hall, anxious to be gone from my good deed. 'I'm just curious – who was it who lived here?'

'Isadora Duncan,' he said and pointed at the glass figurine on the hall table. 'That's her.'

'The stripper,' I said.

'If you like.' He smiled uncertainly. 'Yes, I suppose she was, really.'

Isadora Duncan wasn't really a stripper; not as such. I knew that. It was just my way of making him think a little less highly of me. That seemed only proper; after all, it wasn't my money I'd just given away.

CHAPTER 42

I shouldn't have been nervous but because this was my first match as the new manager of London City, I was. The previous Saturday's game against Newcastle didn't count; then I'd been talking to a football team that Zarco had picked and which was playing for him. All of the players had wrongly assumed that at some stage Zarco would turn up in the dressing room and hand out praise to those who'd played well and, more importantly, bollockings to those who'd played badly. No one ever wanted a bollocking from João Zarco.

But the game against West Ham was very different and everyone knew it. A manager's first match in charge sets the tone for how his tenure is perceived, not just by the owner and the sports writers, but more importantly by the club's supporters, who are as superstitious as a wagon-load of gypsies. My ex-wife's brother refuses to go to an Arsenal game without his lucky cat's whisker; he's just one of many serious, rational men who follow football but who believe in jinxes and curses and the acts of a capricious God who ordains a win or a loss. A bad defeat in this first match would be like an albatross around my neck. I don't know what Napoleon's opinion of Premier League football was, but he knew the value of luck and I badly wanted to be lucky with my first game in charge. In spite of what Geoff

Boycott says, good luck is the most valuable commodity in sport.

I'd even managed to convince myself that the League Cup was worth the candle; if we beat West Ham we'd be in the final and now that the match was less than an hour away the idea of my first trophy as manager of City was looking much more persuasive. Hadn't the League Cup win cemented José Mourinho's reputation in his debut season as manager at Chelsea, in 2005?

Of course none of this meant I was any less inclined to play a stronger side against the Hammers; I was sticking to my young guns, come what may, with only five of our regular first team players in the side: Ayrton Taylor, Kenny Traynor, Ken Okri, Gary Ferguson and Xavier Pepe. Three of our back four – Ken, Gary and Xavier – were first team regulars, of course, and I was trusting that they would steady the rest, none of whom – with the exception of Kenny and Ayrton – was older than twenty-two. I wasn't and never had been a believer in what Alan Hansen had famously said, that you don't win anything with kids.

Our second youngest player, Daryl Hemingway, who we'd bought in the summer from West Ham's Academy of Football for £2.5 million, was just seventeen. I'd watched Daryl play when he was still at Hainault Road and thought him as promising a midfielder as I'd seen in a long time; he reminded me a lot of Cesc Fabregas. He wanted to show his old club the mistake they had made getting rid of him. Daryl was playing alongside our youngest, the sixteen-year-old Zénobe Schuermans, from Belgium, and Iñárritu, the twenty-year-old Mexican that João Zarco had bought from Estudiantes Tecos, in Guadalajara.

Iñárritu's was an interesting story. The young Mexican

had fled his country after police rescued him from a kidnapping ring tied to the local Gulf Cartel, which had abducted him. Iñárritu had narrowly escaped death when members of the drug cartel filmed him on their phones being dangled outside the window of his apartment building – the ninety-metre-high Plaza building in Cuauhtémoc – in the hope of making his father, who was a wealthy banker with BBVA Bancomer, pay a ten-million-dollar ransom. The kidnappers had actually dropped him – accidentally – and Iñárritu had only survived because he had fallen into a window-cleaning cart a couple of floors below. The Mexican was keen to play although, following a broken leg against Stoke City who were always good at breaking legs, he was still getting himself back up to first team fitness.

Playing 4-3-3 requires enormous stamina from your midfielders, but given our three had a combined age of just fifty-three, I figured they could probably run around all night without much of a problem. Even Iñárritu. I had no real worries about him, either. Iñárritu had been fond of Zarco and wept openly when the news of his death was announced; I knew that if anyone was going to play his heart out in memory of the Portuguese it was the young Mexican.

Of the three up front, Jimmy Ribbans on the wing was returning from a groin strain. There are plenty of players who are right-footed – too many, if I'm honest – but Jimmy was naturally left-footed, which was odd as he was actually right-handed. They say left-footers are a dying breed but they're often very good technically, and the importance of having a great left-footer in your team cannot be overstated; most teams will try hard to hang onto a good one. Messi is a lefty and so are Ryan Giggs, Patrice Evra and Robin Van Persie. But Jimmy had a good right foot, too, and we usually played him on the right side, which made his sweet left foot even more unpredictable. As a defender I always found natural lefties more difficult to deal with and perhaps the best of these was Giggsy.

On the left wing was Soltani Boumediene, a twenty-four-year-old from Israel who was almost as good with his left as he was with his right: nicknamed the Comedian, for obvious reasons – he was indeed a bit of a joker – Soltani had previously played for Haifa and had been Israel's most prominent Arab footballer before joining Portsmouth, from whom City had bought him during the garage sale that followed Pompey's relegation from the Premier League in 2010.

Ayrton Taylor was, of course, our centre forward. The newspapers said he'd lost his mojo and had no chance of playing for England again, but although it was five weeks since Ayrton had scored a goal – at least a goal that was not disallowed – I knew that he was keen to show that the sports writers were mistaken. I was confident that his disciplinary problems were behind him. I suspected that these were mostly the result of the relentless ribbing he'd endured at the hands of his team mates following an incident in a London night-club when two girls had spiked *his* drink with Rohypnol and, back at his flat, had photographed him on their iPhones in a state of disarray; they subsequently sold their story and the pictures to a Sunday newspaper. It was, they famously remarked, like taking candy from a baby. Footballers are a merciless lot and for several weeks afterwards Ayrton had found his shearling coat pockets filled with packets of Haribos and lollipops. If anyone was going to score a goal for us I felt it was Ayrton Taylor, despite William Hill, Bet 365 and Ladbrokes giving odds of 4-1 against him scoring at all.

Odds like that were too good to miss, even for me, especially as I still had ten grand of Zarco's bung left in my bag.

'You want to be careful, boss,' Maurice said when I told him what I was planning to do with the money. 'This isn't a five-pound Yankee. If Sportradar or the FA finds out you've got ten bags of sand on with a bookie then they'll have your guts for fucking garters.'

He was right – what I was doing was expressly forbidden by the FA's betting rules but we'd done it before, of course. *Everyone* in football was betting on games, week in week out, and provided you never did anything as bent as betting against your own team there was, in my opinion, nothing wrong with this. It's no different to what boys in the City do all the time.

'I take it you want me to use our mate Dostoyevsky,' he said.

Dostoyevsky was what we called a professional punter whom we'd met in the nick. For five per cent of a bet he'd put a house to let for anyone, on anything.

'Of course. For the usual commission. Besides, if I win, the money isn't for me. It's for the Kenward Trust. An anonymous donation. Seems appropriate somehow, don't you think? That some old cons should profit from a dodgy bet?'

Maurice laughed indulgently. 'That sense of humour of yours, boss. One day it's going to get you in trouble.'

'I'm an old con myself, Maurice. What do you expect?'

'On the other hand maybe you should mention it in the team talk before the match. They might play a bit harder if they know you've got ten k on Ayrton Taylor.'

'This is Zarco's night, Maurice, not mine. It might be me giving the team talk but it's him they're going to be playing for. They won't be in any doubt about that, I promise you.

The minute they walk into that dressing room they'll know exactly what this match means. Not just to me, but to anyone who supports this football club. Anyone who fucks up tonight is going to have to explain himself to Zarco, not me. You see, he's going to be there, Maurice. Zarco's going to be with us all in that dressing room.'

CHAPTER 43

Zarco might have been dead but I was certain that the Portuguese's memory could still inspire the City team to victory. And not just his memory. I didn't blame him, but Maurice probably thought I was crazy, or, even worse, that I was going religious on him – that I was going to tell him that Zarco's spirit would actually be present in the dressing room. Of course I didn't believe this any more than he did; however, I did want the players to think something like that, which was why, before any of the players arrived in the dressing room – while Manny Rosenberg was still laying out the kit – I went in there with a hammer and some nails and hung Zarco's portrait on the wall. I'd brought it with me from Manresa Road especially for this purpose.

Manny was a tall, thin man with thick, white hair and heavy black glasses; he looked like Michael Caine's older brother. Sounded like him, too.

He was about to lay the black armbands on each shirt when I stopped him.

'I'll give those out tonight if you don't mind, Manny,' I said.

'As you wish.' He handed them over.

'I want to make this feel personal,' I explained.

'I take it that picture's not permanent,' he said, with one eye on the portrait. 'I wouldn't want to leave anything as nice as that in here. You know what these sods are like. Balls getting kicked around. Boots thrown. So-called practical jokes.'

'No, it's just for tonight.'

'Wise.'

Manny nodded and gave it a longish appraisal. 'Who did that, then?'

'An artist called Jonathan Yeo.'

'I know. He's the Tory politician's son. I read about him in the paper. That's a good portrait, that is. Lad's got talent. Not easy to capture with a brush, a man like João Zarco and what made him tick, but he's done it very well, so he has. Soft twinkly brown eyes, big broad nose, sulky mouth, with just a hint of a sneer. Face like an African tribal mask, when you think about it. Hard as fucking wood but full of mischief, too. There was always so much going on behind the eyes, you know? Like now. I mean you can look at this painting and tell exactly what's in Zarco's mind.'

'What's in his mind, Manny? Tell me. I'm interested.'

'Easy. He's thinking if these overpaid cunts don't win this fucking match tonight out of respect for my memory I'm going to haunt the bastards forever. I'll sit in their fucking Ferraris and their ridiculous Lamborghinis and scare the cunts off the road and into a ditch. And they'll deserve it, too.'

I grinned. 'Maybe you should do the team talk, Manny.'

'Nah. They're so gullible they might actually believe me. Besides, you'll know what to say, Mr Manson, sir.'

'I hope so.'

Of course, I'd thought long and hard about what I was going to tell the players. Every word, every inflection of my voice would be important. I knew they would be looking for something extra from me tonight, a reminder of who and what they were playing for. And as I looked into Zarco's eyes now I could hear the advice he had once given me about how a manager talks to his players. I was grateful to Manny for reminding me of what Zarco had said:

'I've heard a lot of dressing-room team talks in my time, Scott. We both have. Most of them were a joke – David Brent in a tracksuit, a shop-steward on a soapbox, a travesty of what it means to manage players. You know why? Because most managers and coaches are stupid, ignorant men, who've had no real education and possess no imagination. Can you picture some of our own players becoming managers? Jesus Christ, they can't even manage their pet dogs, let alone men. Their brains are in their feet. They haven't got the words – at least not ones that don't have four letters. I don't know why but a lot of guys in football think they've got to behave like that marine drill sergeant in *Full Metal Jacket*. Fuck this, fuck that, kicking lockers, punching the air. Ridiculous. Embarrassing. Futile. When I was a player and I heard this kind of thing I wanted to laugh, every time. This kind of talk is going to motivate me? I don't think so. You shouting in my ear like I'm some guy in the army is going to make me score a goal? Not a chance. Half the time I think maybe the managers are shouting because they really don't know *what* to say. They're angry because they don't have a solution to the problems they see on the pitch.

'Sure, sometimes you have to be a bully, but motivating players is something else. To motivate men in sport is like motivating people in any other walk of life. You need two things. First thing is you need to understand people and you can only do that by listening to them; too many people talk but they don't listen first. Listening is essential. Get to know your players; talk to them quietly and with respect; and treat them like individuals. Like human beings. Second thing you need is to have earned people's respect. People respect experience, and mostly that means experience of life itself. Now I don't know many men who have as much experience of life as you, Scott. After all that's happened to you, I see a man who other men will always listen to. Sure, you played professional football for years, you've been where they are, but this is the very least you can expect of a manager. That he's done the job himself. More important than any of this is that you've survived the worst things that life can throw at you and come out the other side. You're a survivor. This makes you a man that other men will listen to. Even me.

'But when you do speak, what will you say? Actually, speaking to players is simple; you have to say a lot but in as few words as possible, because they have very short attention spans. You have to make every word count. Simplicity is the most sophisticated motivational tool in the world. It takes real intelligence to know *what not to say* as well as what needs to be said. I'm not talking about doing it in a hundred and forty characters but frankly, men who can say what needs to be said in less than a thousand words are the best men in football.'

A couple of hours before the game Simon Page arrived with the team from Hangman's Wood; full of noise and jokes and excited to be playing a match they trooped into the dressing room but gradually fell silent when they saw me already sitting there below the portrait of Zarco. I was wearing a black suit, a white shirt and a black tie and I probably looked like a funeral director. At least I hoped I did.

The lads changed into their kit and waited quietly for me to say something. For once nobody had his ears full of music or a PS Vita in his hands; I think if I'd even seen one of these stupid handheld game consoles I'd have thrown it into the bin. This was no time for games. But I wasn't ready to say anything yet. I wanted my words still to be ringing in their ears like the noise of the crowd as they waited in the tunnel. Instead I handed each man his black armband, told him to wear it on his left arm and reminded him that there would be a minute's silence on the pitch before the match.

Just before the team went out onto the pitch with Simon to warm up, Viktor arrived in the dressing room with Bekim Develi. They'd just flown in to the nearby London City Airport on Viktor's private jet. Silvertown Dock was the only ground in the country you could fly to and be in the stadium within twenty minutes. He was dressed for Russian cold in a long-haired beaver coat and Develi was wearing something similar; these two bearded men looked like the Brothers Karamazov.

The dressing room always stiffened when Viktor appeared; he was essentially a shy man and in spite of his lavish generosity he lacked the common touch. Maybe it was the fact that he was Ukrainian or maybe it was because he was sometimes embarrassed to be quite as rich as he was, but sometimes Viktor expressed himself a little awkwardly.

'I just came down to wish you luck tonight,' he said, 'and to introduce you to Bekim Develi, who I think you will all agree is certainly the best midfielder in Europe. Now that the objections to Bekim's coming to this club have been thrown out of the window, he's joining us from Dynamo St Petersburg, where as many of you will know he was on loan from Paris Saint-Germain.'

I wasn't sure what Viktor meant by this remark. After all he wasn't to know that I had discovered – more or less – the way in which Zarco had really been killed. Was it possible that he was unconsciously referencing the manner of Zarco's death? A Freudian slip, or something like it? A tasteless joke, even? Surely not. It wasn't long before Viktor's words started to feel like a piece of grit in my shoe.

'At a press conference tomorrow,' continued Viktor, 'Bekim will be introduced to the world as our last and, with due respect to Kenny Traynor, our most important January signing. Before then I'm sure you'll all want to make him feel very welcome at London City, just as I'm sure you're going to beat West Ham tonight.'

Viktor certainly saw his gift to me hanging on the wall of the dressing room, but he didn't mention Zarco at all; perhaps he was leaving that to me. But it surprised me a little, as did the fact that Viktor was wearing Zarco's lucky scarf, the one I'd looked for in suite 123.

Bekim Develi shook hands with everyone as they went outside to warm up. He was a tall man – well over six foot – powerfully built and handsome, too, with a square shovel of a red beard and fortunately not nearly as fat as had been rumoured; but he smelled strongly of cigarettes and I hoped he wasn't a smoker. I shook his hand and handed him a black armband.

'What's this?'

'I'm surprised you have to ask. Didn't Viktor tell you?'

'Tell me what?'

Just as I was about to say something rude to our new star signing Viktor came over and started speaking to Develi in Russian. Although I don't know the language, it was quite clear to me that Zarco's death was news to the footballer, which left me in little doubt that in spite of having shared a private jet from St Petersburg to London, the two men simply hadn't discussed it. I was astonished by this.

'That's Zarco's lucky scarf,' I said as I handed Viktor a black armband.

'Is it?' he asked nonchalantly.

'It's from Savile Rogue,' I said, pointing out the JGZ written on the logo, just in case anyone nicked it. 'They make cashmere football scarves.'

'Cashmere, eh? I wondered why I liked it so much.'

'Perhaps, if he'd been wearing it, then he might still be alive,' I said pointedly. 'Where did you find it?'

'He left it in the executive dining room on Saturday,' said Viktor. 'I took it with me when I went to look for him. I thought someone ought to wear it tonight. Just in case we need any luck. Do we? Need any luck tonight?'

'Of course we do,' I said. 'Because if we lose, luck, or the lack of it, will be the best way of explaining why the other side won.'

CHAPTER 44

'When I came out of prison one of the first things I did was to go on holiday to Nîmes in France – and while I was there I went to see a bullfight in the Roman amphitheatre they have in the city. I loved every bloody minute of it. And not just me. I've never seen a stadium so packed, the people so overwhelmed, so blinded with sunny tears and emotion. I told someone here about it – some twat from the BBC – and they were very disapproving, the way people are about bullfighting; they said, "That's not a sport." And I said, "You're right, it's not a sport, it's not something you watch or enjoy, like a game of fucking tennis; no, it's something you feel in every fibre of your body because you know that at any moment, the matador could easily slip or make a mistake and then there would be a black Miura fighting bull putting all its half-ton weight into the stiletto tip of one lethal horn as it bears down on that man's thigh. Of course that's not a fucking sport," I said, "it's so much more than just a sport. It's life in the moment, because the future is promised to no one."

'It's the same with football, guys. We only pretend that it's a fucking sport, in order not to frighten women with this, our passion for the game. The truth is that sports are for children on a summer's day, or idiots with stupid hats who go to flirt with chinless wonders wearing tailcoats and maybe look at all the pretty horses. Because if you were to walk out there now and ask any one of our supporters if they are here to be entertained or to see anything pretty, I promise they'd look at you like you were fucking crazy. And they'd be right to do so. They'd tell you that they haven't paid seventy-five quid for a seat *to be amused*. Some of you people are on a hundred thousand pounds a week. But football is worth so much more than that to those people outside. A hell of a lot more. To most of those men and women this team is their whole fucking life and the result of any match means *everything* to them; everything.

'So let me enlighten you, gentlemen: nobody at this club is playing for a hundred grand a week. You're playing so that our supporters can go to work tomorrow morning and feel a sense of pride that their team won in grand style last night. And any man who thinks differently ought to put in for a transfer right now because we don't want you at Silvertown Dock. It doesn't matter who they are – players or supporters – it's believers we want here. The believers, gentlemen: that's who we play for. That's what we are. We're men who believe.

'If this sounds a little religious, that's because it is; football is a religion. I am not exaggerating. The official religion of this country is not Christianity, or Islam, it's football. Because nobody goes to church any more. Certainly not on a Sunday. They go to football. Take a walk around this building some time, guys, and listen to the prayers from our believers. That's right; this is their cathedral. This is their place of worship. This team is their creed. If that sounds blasphemous I apologise, but it's a fact. This is where the believers come to commune with their gods. Every week I look up from the dugout and I see signs hanging from the stands that read

352

Have Faith in Zarco. But right now, their faith is being tested, gentlemen. That faith has been severely challenged. Right now, they're feeling a tremendous sense of grief and loss. As I am and as I hope you are, too. Look, I'm not going to give you any Coach Carter bullshit and tell you that this is the most important match in our club's history. I wouldn't insult you. What I will say is this: it's up to just eleven of you to restore that faith. And that's more important than anything.'

I pointed to Zarco's picture on the wall.

'Take a good look at that man before you walk out there. Ask yourself what it would mean to him if you won this game tonight. Really look him in the eye and listen to his voice in your head because I promise you that you'll hear it, as clear as a bell. I think he will tell you this: you're not going to win this game for me, or for Scott Manson, or for Mr Sokolnikov. You're going to win this game for all those believers out there.

'Some of you will struggle tonight. Some of you will not perform to the best of your ability. You know something? I don't care. What I do care about is that you try your utmost and that you do not give up. Not until you've heard that final whistle. In case you never noticed, that's why supporters stay right until the end of the game, because they don't give up. And nor should you. So all of you who are playing tonight will be out there for the full ninety minutes, together as a team, and unless you've got a broken leg don't even think of coming off. I mean it, gentlemen. There will be no substitutions at half time or any time. You are the best that this club can field tonight. So, forget whatever you've read in the newspapers or heard on the radio; I've picked you because I think you're eleven men with something to prove to the fans, to Zarco, to me, and to yourselves. But mostly

I picked you because I think you will beat these guys tonight. I sincerely believe that, which is why no one is coming to help you out. Not the spirit of Zarco, or God, or me. Just them. The believers.'

CHAPTER 45

Every football fan in Silvertown Dock had found a paper square taped to his seat; one side of the square was the club's Ukrainian orange and the other side was black. When the referee blew his whistle to begin a minute's silence for Zarco everyone lifted up his square of paper, flipped it over and the whole stadium turned from orange to black. You could have heard a ticket drop and I was grateful we were playing a class club like West Ham who can always be relied on to respect football traditions. It was very moving to see.

The match was finally ready to start. Wrapped in my cashmere coat, I settled down on my Recaro heated seat in the dugout, with Simon Page beside me, and glanced around Silvertown Dock in wonder. As usual Colin Evans looked to have done a fantastic job. In spite of near freezing conditions the pitch looked like a bowling green on a summer's day, although as things turned out it was a little harder than usual. A message on my iPad informed me that it was a capacity crowd and it certainly looked and sounded that way. The atmosphere in the stadium was quite extraordinary, a strange mixture of grief and excitement. There were tributes to and pictures of Zarco everywhere you looked, and when the minute's silence was completed the home fans began to sing (to the Beatles tune 'Hello Goodbye'), 'João, João Zarco, I don't know why you say goodbye we say hello'. They also sang Pat Boone's 'Speedy Gonzales' ('Speedy Gonzales, why don't you come home?')

An attempt by the Hammers fans to make themselves heard with a spirited rendition of 'Bubbles' proved to be in vain.

My satisfaction at the way things had begun lasted precisely thirty-eight seconds. Ayrton Taylor was dispossessed by Carlton Cole straight from the kick-off, and a quick through ball from him was neatly transferred from Ravel Morrison to Jack Collison, who sent Bruno Haider running swiftly down the right. West Ham's young Austrian striker glanced up as if to cross but he had only one thing on his mind. Right on the edge of the penalty area he stepped inside Ken Okri, and onto his stronger left foot. The shot Haider then curled into the far top corner had so much topspin it might have been struck by Andy Murray and, let down by some horrible defending, poor Kenny Traynor had no chance of getting a hand to the ball. One-nil to them.

The West Ham fans behind our goal were predictably delirious with joy; otherwise you might have been forgiven for thinking that a second minute's silence was under way, such was the reaction of the orange-wearing supporters. I lifted the iPad in front of my face – so that the television cameras watching my every move and scrutinising the succession could not read my lips – and swore loudly several times. But it was a spectacular goal for the young Austrian and given his age and experience he could have been forgiven for taking off his claret and blue shirt and running towards the television cameras to celebrate. Frankly if I'd had a six-pack like that I'd have taken my shirt off too, but the referee felt obliged to give him a yellow card for which he was justly booed, by everyone – even our supporters, who could appreciate the excellence of Haider's strike. Personally, I don't blame the referees but IFAB's stupid law 12 regarding fouls and misconduct, which just ensures that no one gets any advertising without paying for it.

'Well, that's a good start,' I told Simon. 'To be fair it was a pretty speculative shot. The Austrian kid was as surprised as we were when it went in.'

Simon's Yorkshire sensibilities were much less forgiving than my own.

'I think that minute's silence sent our back four to sleep. The dozy cunts. I'm surprised their number ten didn't read them a bedtime story while he was scoring their fucking goal.'

The match restarted and for a while our players kept on troubling the goalkeeper; the only problem was that it wasn't their goalkeeper we were troubling but our own: a clumsy back heel by Gary Ferguson had Kenny Traynor sprinting across the penalty area to clear the ball with both shins before Kevin Nolan could pounce on it; and Xavier Pepe headed a parabolic West Ham corner that hit his own post and then almost rebounded off Ayrton Taylor's head into the back of the net. When George McCartney lost West Ham's ball, Nolan, as tenacious as a fox-terrier, won it back; and he kept on dropping deep, robbing Schuermans and Iñárritu, and sending long balls to Downing on the left. Nolan then combined with Mark Noble and lofted the ball straight up to Cole and Haider, both of whom had good attempts saved by Kenny Traynor. The rest of the time we were chasing our own tails and we could easily have been three goals down within twenty minutes.

Cole looked like a man much younger than his years; it was hard to believe that the player troubling our back four so relentlessly had started his career at Chelsea in 2001. With every minute that passed he seemed to grow in fitness and confidence, running at our defence with increasing purpose. But West Ham's second goal was an absolute howler. Raphael Spiegel, the Hammers goalkeeper, rolled the ball out to Leo Chambers, who punted it up the pitch in the hope that Cole would run on to it; the ball fell just short of the penalty box in front of Kenny Traynor, who was so far off his line he might have been hiking back to Edinburgh. The ball bounced and probably Traynor expected it to rise to his chest; unfortunately for him and for us the ball kept on rising off the hard ground and when Kenny finally realised it was going to sail over his head like a balloon and started to scuttle back in pursuit it was too late. By the time Kenny caught the ball it was across the line; he already looked like a fool and his hurried retrieval of the ball and quick return to the right side of his goal line only made him look even more ridiculous. Leo Chambers had scored West Ham's second from at least seventy yards.

'Does that stupid Scots cunt think nobody noticed it was a fucking goal, or what?' said Simon.

I groaned and buried my head in the collar of my coat in the hope that I might not hear the laughter of the West Ham fans or the curses of our own.

'Kenny did everything but try to hide the ball up his fucking jersey,' said Simon. 'He must think he's Paul bloody Daniels.'

'Jesus Christ.' I was beginning to detect the sour taste of disaster at the back of my mouth.

Cursing his own stupidity, Traynor booted the ball up the pitch in irritation, and it curled away into the stands.

'He wasn't so much off his line as out of his fucking mind,' said Simon.

I jumped off my seat and walked to the edge of my technical area, intending to shout something at Traynor; but by the time I got there I realised the futility of doing so. I knew he was feeling like a cunt and my endorsement of an opinion now shared by sixty thousand people would hardly have helped the young Scotsman's confidence. But nor did the referee, who proceeded to give him a yellow card for kicking the ball away; probably he was feeling guilty about the yellow card he'd given to Bruno Haider and was looking for an excuse to even the score. Referees are like that sometimes.

'What the fuck?' I yelled. 'How is that a yellow card, you mad fucking idiot? Goalies are supposed to kick the ball away, you stupid cunt.'

The fourth official marched towards me, arms held wide, as if expecting me to run onto the pitch like some twat of a fan and collar the referee. And seeing this 'incident', the referee, Peter 'Paedo' Donnelly, came running towards us at a lick. A lay-preacher and former army sergeant, and easily the country's highest profile referee, Donnelly had been the recent winner of an online poll for the Premier League's worst referee – in the previous season he'd had the highest average number of yellow cards per game, 5.14. I should have minded my mouth, but I didn't.

'How is that a fucking card?' I yelled again. 'It can't be for time-wasting. Look, the West Ham players are still off the pitch down there celebrating. The boy was just irritated with himself and put a bit more welly into the kick up the pitch than was normal. The wind caught it, probably. And if the yellow wasn't for that then where's the dissent? The cunt knows it's a fucking goal. He's not completely stupid.'

'If you don't mind your language, I shall cite you for dissent,' said Donnelly, 'and then send you to sit in the stands.

Under the special circumstances in which this match is being played I'm being lenient with you, Mr Manson. Next time it'll be different. Okay?'

I turned away angrily and sat down.

'I hate that fucking man,' said Simon. 'Thinks he's still in the fucking army, so he does.'

'Bastard.'

'From now on you'd better watch your language, boss. He's got your card marked. Nothing he likes better than to make an example of people who use profanity, which is what he calls swearing. Thinks it's the curse of the modern game. Or at least that's what he told Alan Brazil on TalkSPORT the other week. The cunt.'

I wasn't too worried; not yet. We gave Raphael Spiegel a scare when Ayrton Taylor hit the post from fifteen yards; and Jimmy Ribbans ran through onto a clever chip from Iñárritu, but with only Spiegel to beat he was adjudged offside, when the replay clearly showed this was not the case. Besides, League Cup games are often high-scoring fixtures – who could forget Arsenal's 6–3 victory over Liverpool in the 2006/2007 quarter finals? – and I figured we could easily overturn a two-goal deficit.

At least I did until just before half time when West Ham scored their third. After a dubious foul and another yellow card, this time given against Iñárritu for a trip on Leo Chambers, Cole rifled a free kick towards a mass of orange bodies around the penalty spot. The ball ricocheted off Ken Okri's knee straight in front of the foot of Kevin Nolan, who flicked the ball up and then volleyed it over the heads of our so-called defensive wall. Bruno Haider ran onto it and scored with an almost suicidal diving header that was faintly reminiscent of a kamikaze pilot at Pearl Harbor. Kenny Traynor got a hand to the header and was unlucky only to tip the ball into the top corner of his net. Three-nil.

'It's not his night,' observed Simon.

'It's not anyone's fucking night, so far,' I said, with my hand in front of my mouth. 'Least of all Zarco's.'

'The man must be turning in his grave.'

It didn't seem worth mentioning that Zarco wasn't yet in his grave; that he was probably still on a cold slab just a couple of miles north of where we were now, at the East Ham Mortuary; but I wouldn't have been surprised if he'd sat up on the slab and shouted a couple of choice swear words in Portuguese: *caralho* or *cona*. I'd often heard Zarco use words like that.

I sat back in my seat, laid my hands on my head and stared up at the black ceiling that was the night sky. Light snow was starting to fall and in the powerful floodlights that ran around the entire circumference of the Silvertown Dock stadium it looked like the myriad pieces of a betting slip torn up and thrown into the air by an angry god who'd made a heavy bet on us winning this game. But not as heavy as my own.

'That was the most piss-poor forty minutes I've ever seen us play,' said Simon. 'We were disjointed, uninspired, ragged, lazy; not to mention unlucky. And that's just our fucking back four. The rest look like they were wishing William Webb Ellis was playing for us; that he would pick up the fucking ball and run off with it and never be seen again. I tell you something, boss, when the whistle blows for half time it'll seem more like a fucking armistice. As for that cunt of a referee I think he must think he's playing bridge, the number of fucking cards he's shown.'

I didn't answer; the linesman's flag had gone up and we

had a corner. But it was poorly taken by Jimmy Ribbans. The ball could have been made of concrete and swinging on the end of a crane, such was the apparent reluctance of any of our forwards to head it, and Spiegel gathered it safely in his hands as nonchalantly as if he'd been jumping for a nice shiny apple on a tree.

'What are you going to say in the dressing room?' asked Simon. 'What *can* you say to turn it around when you're 3–0 down at half time?'

'Liverpool did,' I said. 'Against AC Milan in 2005.' I shrugged. 'Besides, I think you just told me what to do, Simon. To turn it around. And I don't think I'm going to say anything at all.'

And then the referee blew for half time. I might have breathed a sigh of relief but for the fact that there were still forty-five minutes to come and our players were walking in with bowed heads to whistles and jeers like they had spent the first half collaborating with the Nazis. The West Ham supporters in the far corner of the dock started to sing 'Bubbles' again, and this time you could hear every stupid word, like you were in the Bobby Moore Stand at Upton Park.

CHAPTER 46

I followed the team into the dressing room. A strong smell of liniment, Deep Heat and even deeper shame greeted my flaring nostrils. Through the adjoining wall we could hear the sound of the other team loudly congratulating itself on an excellent first half. I wanted to punch my way through the breeze-blocks and point these players out to my own.

'Look,' I wanted to tell them, 'the Hammers think this game is in the bag. And who could blame them for thinking that after the way you lot have been playing? Not me. The ladies' team could give West Ham a better game than you've done up until now. I'm embarrassed to be the manager of such a worthless bunch of no-hopers. That song they're singing is about you, the way they've sucked you in tonight and blown you out of their fucking arses like so many shitty bubbles.'

Instead I pushed my hands into my trouser pockets and looked at the ceiling as if searching for some inspiration. But none was there. And really, what was there to say? I'd already said everything that could be said before the game; to say anything else now would only look like I'd wasted my breath the first time. Besides, I'd have probably started to swear and chew the carpet like Hitler and that wasn't going to help anyone; not tonight. They say actions speak louder than words and short of throwing boots and punches and kicking backsides I decided there was really only one thing I could do.

The lads were all looking expectantly at me now, waiting for the full Al Pacino, the *Any Given Sunday*, inch-by-inch, 'I don't know what to say' speech that was going to work a miracle in their thick heads and turn the match around. I was all through with motivation. But I could, perhaps, offer a moment of epiphany, one simple symbolic gesture that would allow a leap of understanding where another thousand words would not.

I walked up to Zarco's picture and lifted it away from the wall. I stared at the face for a moment, caught the expression in the eyes, and nodded; then I twisted the picture around on its cord and placed it back against the wall, face first, so that the Portuguese would not have to look at the players who, so far, had disgraced his memory. At least that's what I wanted them all to think. Then I picked up my iPad and left the dressing room.

For a moment I stood outside in the corridor with all the noise of the stadium in my ears, wondering where to go. There were dozens of eyes on me now: policemen, officials, security men, ball-boys, television technicians and stewards. I had to get away from them, too, and as soon as possible.

I remembered I still had the key to the drug-testing station; I went in there and locked the door behind me.

I used the lavatory and drank some water. Then I sat down at the table with the black cloth on it and stared crossly at my iPhone and my iPad. As usual the iPhone wasn't picking up any texts, or receiving calls, for which I was grateful; but there was a good WiFi signal in there which meant there were some emails on my iPad, including one from Louise Considine expressing concern for my humour and letting me know that it would be perfectly fine by her if I couldn't face having dinner with her after the match. I realised I'd almost forgotten about lovely Louise sitting upstairs in the director's box and immediately I emailed her back to say that after the match I was very much looking forward to her company one way or the other: to celebrate with or, more likely, to help me drown my sorrows.

Ignoring an email from Viktor suggesting that it was time we considered some substitutions, I sighed, opened another bottle of water and wished it could have been whisky. Brian Clough once said that players lose you games, not tactics, and while I could obviously have picked a different team I didn't honestly think I should have done. There's a lot of bollocks talked in pubs and television studios about tactics, and nearly always by people who haven't coached and couldn't manage their own Ocado order. As far as I'm concerned tactics are what fucking generals use to get a lot of decent men under their command killed in as short a period of time as possible. I knew I'd made the right decisions because whatever people say, making them in football is a lot fucking easier than making them in life; that's why so many people go into football in the first place.

Not that any of it really mattered, as my doubts about Viktor Sokolnikov now seemed so compelling that I could see no real alternative to offering him my resignation immediately after the match was over. Because that's what you do when you think you've been played for a fool by a crook. I couldn't prove anything, of course; but perhaps, after the match, I might privately share a few of my suspicions with Louise. Given the likely result of the match my resigning would probably suit not just Viktor but the supporters, too. You see, it wasn't only the players who had been jeered at the end of the first half. I could still hear someone shouting, 'You should be ashamed of yourself, Manson,' when I'd walked off the pitch at half time.

This didn't bother me very much; when the world has fallen in on your head once before, it means you know where the tin hats are when it seems about to happen again. A few tossers handing out abuse from the stands is how you know you're doing a good job, because if everyone agrees with you then it's obvious that it's a job that absolutely anyone could do.

It was Zarco I felt sorry for. I'd honestly believed his players would have wanted to honour his memory with a famous victory. It wasn't that West Ham were so good; it was just that ours looked like a testimonial side – a few VIPs and guest players invited to kick a ball around to raise a bit of cash for one of yesterday's stars.

I was also sorry for the friends and relations of Zarco – the ones for whom he always arranged complimentary tickets to City matches. It can't have been very nice for them to see such a poor excuse of a football match. I knew they were here because Maurice had sent me a list of their names before the game; many of them were regulars at Silvertown Dock and had also been at the ground on Saturday for the match during which Zarco had been killed. His brothers, Anibal and Ermenegildo, his uncle, Jacinto and his sister, Branca; his best friend Dominique Racine, who had been managing PSG until he got sacked for – it was generally reported – failing to get the best out of Bekim Develi; and retired players like Paul Becker and Tano Andretti, who had been with Zarco at La Braga. Two tweets from Andretti about Zarco had been universally quoted in all of the newspapers, not least because it was a little unusual that an Italian footballer should have chosen to commemorate his Portuguese friend with four lines from Percy Shelley's poem, *Adonais*:

Peace, peace! he is not dead, he doth not sleep
He hath awakened from the dream of life

And:

'Tis we, who lost in stormy visions, keep
With phantoms an unprofitable strife.

On that particular night, against a rampant West Ham side that looked like it was going to score at least another three goals in the second half, I certainly felt it was an unprofitable strife in which we were now engaged.

I glanced at my watch. There were five minutes to go before the second half started. I unlocked the door and went back outside to the dugout where the mood of the crowd was a strange mixture of dejection and delight: our own supporters, quiet and subdued and fearing the worst; and the West Ham fans, who were sensing a great victory and daring – perhaps – to dream of their biggest win since beating Bury 10–0 in 1983.

It seemed my career in top-flight football management was over before it had begun because everyone would assume I'd just not been up to it. I could hardly help that; perhaps I'd get another chance to manage a smaller club, a club where the owner was not the type to have his manager thrown out of a window and then make a joke about it afterwards.

Another email pinged onto my iPad: a list of names that Viktor thought should be on the field instead of the 'kids and half-wits' that were already walking back out of the tunnel. I ignored it.

Besides, there was another list of names in my head as I took my place alongside Simon Page in the dugout. (It was hard to imagine Viktor giving the blunt Yorkshireman my job when I resigned.)

'What the fuck happened to you?' he asked. 'One manager disappearing at this club is unfortunate but two looks like fucking negligence. In case you didn't realise it, boss, the ceiling is coming down on our heads. We're getting done here. Maybe you should have wrung a couple of necks and kicked some fucking arses. I know which arses I would have kicked. That Scots twat in goal, for a start. He should never have come that far off his line. Not for a fifty–fifty ball like that.'

'We can still win this,' I said.

'Did you not think you should have told them that?'

'I did. But I did it my way. Just like Frank Sinatra.'

'I recall the regrets and the times when he bit off more than he could chew right enough, but I don't remember him staring down the barrel of a three-goal deficit.'

'Simon? Shut the fuck up.'

'Yes, boss.'

The players took their places in the centre circle; it was always my favourite moment of the game, when I had the sense that anything could happen. But for a few seconds I wasn't paying much attention; I'd found the list of names that Maurice had sent me and was reading it again on my iPad.

All of the names on Zarco's list of comps I was familiar with – bar one.

CHAPTER 47

Somehow the crowd at Silvertown Dock had managed to lift its spirits. Hope springs eternal in the breast of any football fan. That's the wonderful thing about football; it's about so much more than just football. That's what people who don't go to football can never understand. If it wasn't like this then no one would go. So when the Hammers fans started up with 'Over Land and Sea', our fans dug deep into their reserves of optimism and quickly drowned them out with a spirited rendition of 'Sitting in Silvertown Dock', to the tune of Otis Redding's '(Sittin' On) The Dock of the Bay'. It was one of those transcendent moments when you feel part of a much larger soul and realise that at the end of the day football is the only game that has ever really mattered. That will ever matter.

England has given the world a lot, but football is its greatest gift of all.

I don't know much about schizophrenia. I once saw a film called *A Beautiful Mind* about a Nobel-Prize-winning econo- mist called John Nash, who was a schizo. For half of his life he seems to have been a genius; for the other half he was barking mad. I'm not sure I'd want to make too much of a comparison between the beautiful game and *A Beautiful Mind*, but as soon as the second half began at Silvertown Dock it was clear to me that our team of 'kids and half-wits' was displaying a very different personality to the one they had exhibited during the first half. I won't say that the team was bordering on genius, because that's a word that gets overused in football, but, like Nash, they seemed to be greatly gifted and frankly, extraordinary.

By contrast, West Ham's players looked like they were playing with lead in their football boots and they did not have another shot at goal until the ninetieth minute, when Kenny Traynor saved a thunderbolt from Bruno Haider with what looked more like an audition for the role of the Roman god Mercury, such was the distance he covered and the speed with which he did it.

The tenor of the new half was set immediately when Ayrton Taylor scored within twelve seconds of the game restarting, finding the back of the net with a rocketing Roy of the Rovers volley that punished a miskicked clearance by Spiegel. The crowd at the dock went wild. 3–1.

'Fucking hell,' said Simon after we'd finished celebrating. 'Now that's what I call a fucking goal. That might just be the fastest goal in Premier League history.'

'Nope. That was Ledley King, Tottenham against Bradford in 2000. Ten seconds. Besides, this isn't a Premier League game.'

'You know what I mean. Top three, then.'

'Might be.'

'If Taylor can do it twice more I'll lick the ball clean after the match. And his balls as well, if he asks me nicely.'

'I'll remind you that you said that, you big daft Yorkshireman.'

But it was Zénobe Schuermans who scored our second after fifty-eight minutes, and it was only when I'd watched

370

the replay several times that I understood exactly what he'd done. It was the kind of something-out-of-nothing goal that you might have seen painted onto a vertical sheet of glass by Picasso in a single, simple uninterrupted line with a very fine brush. Much later on, Sky Sports showed Zénobe's goal in slow motion, accompanied by Glenn Gould playing the first of Bach's Goldberg Variations, which only seemed to underline the perfectly sublime and almost draftsman-like quality of what was happening in the picture. (Today, it's a goal that even professional players never get tired of watching in an attempt to deconstruct what makes a perfect footballer.) Xavier Pepe drives a long, low pass along the ground to Schuermans, who has his back to the goal. With his right foot, the young Belgian controls and flicks the ball around Chambers in one elegant pirouette, collects the ball on the other side of the defender at the same time as he blocks him with his arm and hip, and coolly opens his body to deliver a clinical finish with the toe of his left foot straight underneath Spiegel and into the far corner of the net.

There was nothing flashy about the goal, or the way Zénobe celebrated afterwards; you would have said it was a mature player's goal but for the fact that the Belgian was just sixteen years old. He collected the ball from the back of the net and jogged quickly back to the centre spot, high-fived Jimmy Ribbans and Ayrton Taylor, and looked for all the world as if he just wanted to get on with the game as quickly as possible with the least amount of fuss. 3–2 to West Ham.

'I don't care if we win or draw now,' I told Simon. 'I've just witnessed one of the best goals I've ever seen in my life from a player in a team of which I'm the manager.'

'I couldn't agree more. Jesus Christ, I'm supposed to try and coach that lad on Thursday. I reckon he could teach us both a fucking thing or two, eh?'

'That boy could play for another fifteen years and he'll never score a better goal than that.' I grinned as I saw a few West Ham heads fall. 'Look at them. That's their game plan finished. They know now they're just hanging to the lead by some well-chewed fingernails.'

As the match restarted Sam Allardyce, West Ham's manager, was shouting at his men – no one can shout as loud as Big Sam – to keep possession. Now that they'd lost control of the tempo of the game it was surely good advice; staying deep and passing the ball among themselves, forcing us to come and chase it, was the best way of keeping hold of their one-goal advantage. Unfortunately they hadn't taken account of the speed of our left-winger. A simple back pass from a careless defender to Spiegel was pounced on by Jimmy Ribbans, forcing Spiegel to the ground and, on the hard, slippy surface of the dock, he came scything towards the winger like a jack-knifing articulated lorry, collecting the player's legs and only then the ball in the process.

The referee did not hesitate and pointed to the penalty spot.

Ayrton Taylor's penalty was a master class in how to take one: a long, fast run-up with litres of venom in the strike, like Mike Tyson punching an opponent, as if he actually hoped that the ball might strike Spiegel hard in the face and drive the bone of his nose up into his brain. The kind of penalty that makes a goalkeeper want to get out of the way of the ball. 3–3. There were just five minutes of normal time left.

I jumped out of my seat, fisted the air and walked to the edge of my technical area, applauding furiously. 'That's the way to take a fucking penalty,' I yelled. 'Well done, Ayrton.

Fucking brilliant. Now let's show these cunts what we're made of.'

The fourth official turned to stare at me. 'You've been warned about swearing before,' he said and waved Paedo Donnelly towards us.

'What?' I said. 'You're joking.'

Donnelly listened to the fourth official for a moment and then walked over to my technical area.

'You were told before about swearing at players,' said the referee.

'It was my own player,' I said. 'Besides, I wasn't swearing at him. I was congratulating him.'

'Tonight of all nights I'd have thought that you might moderate your language,' said Paedo. 'Out of respect for Zarco's memory.'

'I'm not going to take any lectures from you about Zarco's memory. Nobody has more respect for his memory than I have. So don't even think about sending me off.'

'I've had enough of this,' said Paedo. 'I deem your behaviour inappropriate, Mr Manson. And I'm sending you out of your technical area. Go. Now.' He pointed to the stands behind me and then wrote my name on his yellow card. Then he turned and walked back to the penalty spot to restart the match.

I turned to the fourth official. 'You know something? He's a cunt and so are you.'

Meanwhile the crowd started to jeer and then to chant, 'Pae-do, Pae-do, Pae-do, Pae-do.'

One of the stewards pointed to an empty seat behind our players' bench and feeling rather aggrieved, I sat down next to our technical staff. But this seat wasn't far enough away to suit the fourth official and, to my amazement, he followed me and ordered me out of this seat, too. Much to my irritation I was obliged to get up a second time and to sit down alongside the real fans.

'Did it hurt when you pulled that card out of your arse?' one fan shouted after Paedo.

'Great game,' said another, shaking my hand. 'Well done, mate.'

'Fucking marvellous,' said another.

'Don't worry. That's just Paedo being a Paedo.'

I glanced at my watch. Normal time was now over. I looked anxiously at the fourth official to see how much added time there would be. If I'd not been looking at him I suppose I would have seen our fourth goal. And until I watched the replay on the big screen at the river side I had no idea who scored. West Ham had one last strike at goal by Bruno Haider saved brilliantly by Kenny Traynor, who cleared his lines with a huge kick and sent Soltani Boumediene sprinting for their goal. If West Ham hadn't been lying so deep the Arab lad would have been offside; as it was he checked his run just before the penalty box, looked as if he was going to shoot, which sent the hapless keeper to one side, and then tapped the ball gently straight into the net. 4–3. The crowd was in ecstasy and I found myself being hugged by nearly everyone around me.

'You're a fucking genius, Manson,' said one fan. 'What a team you picked.'

I nodded. For a young team lacking experience, it was hard to imagine that a team composed entirely of all our first-choice players could have done any better. Our midfield looked every bit as good as Arsenal's; perhaps even better. I had every reason to feel pleased.

Meanwhile the fourth official lifted his electronic board to reveal that we would play four minutes of extra time.

But this was the moment I had been dreading. In memory of João Zarco the crowd began to sing another favourite City anthem – 'Auf Wiedersehen Sweetheart', as sung by Vera Lynn, which seemed especially appropriate on that particular night. No fans are as sentimental as football fans, which is another reason I love it – because I'm a sentimental bastard myself.

Of course it's one thing promising as the song says, not to let the teardrops start; it's quite another to deliver on that when sixty thousand fans start singing a song like this one. Which is how I missed the fifth goal as well. I was crying my eyes out when the crowd around me jumped up as one; and again I had to wait for the replay on the big screen to see the goal.

Having scored a superb goal himself, Zénobe now had a wonderful assist, running the length of the pitch, drawing two defenders onto himself and, leaving them both for dead, hitting a fantastic cross to the opposite side of the penalty box to find Iñárritu arriving like Bond's Aston Martin at the end of *Casino Royale*. To say the Mexican boy struck the ball hard on the volley hardly describes what happened; he belted it – so hard that the ball turned in the air like a living thing, as if it was actually trying to avoid the keeper's hands.

5–3 and West Ham's rout was complete. The match restarted with the crowd chanting for six.

A minute later the referee blew full time and the dock erupted. It felt like the proudest moment of my life. As a fitting tribute to João Zarco it could not have been bettered.

And this feeling was only enhanced by the realisation that I had almost certainly guessed the identity of Zarco's murderer.

CHAPTER 48

'Whatever happened to dinner?' asked Louise Considine as we drove swiftly away from the dock in my Range Rover. The fans were still celebrating loudly and would be for the next few hours. There would be some sore heads at work tomorrow, I thought.

'I'm afraid there's not going to be any time for dinner,' I said. 'We've got something much more important to do right now.'

'Like what? I'm hungry. What could be more important than feeding me?'

'You'll see.'

'You really don't mess around, do you?' she said.

'How do you mean?'

'Well, let's see now; we're driving west,' she said. 'It's a bit too late to go to a restaurant in the West End. And since I'm supposed to be a detective I would surmise that we're going back to your flat in Chelsea. Where I imagine you're planning not to feed me but to take me to bed.'

I didn't answer. It was a nice idea and for a moment I let my imagination run free with it. She was a nice girl; bright, funny, and very pretty, and whenever I was with her I found it hard to believe she was in the police. And even harder to believe how much I liked her in spite of that. Taking Louise Considine to bed was a very attractive idea, and one that would probably keep me awake for the rest of the night. Especially now that she had led me to form the impression she was not averse to the idea.

'I suppose you're much too excited to eat after a match like that,' she added. 'I suppose you want to make the most of all that excitement. At your age I imagine you have to strike while the iron's hot.'

I grinned. 'The Viagra of football? Yes, there might be something in that, I suppose. I'm not sure my heart could stand too much of it. But I do feel pretty high after what happened tonight. And at my age that doesn't happen very often.'

'Don't get me wrong. I rather like the idea of you all sweaty and excited and keen to score.'

I laughed. 'Is that what you think?'

'Of course. I assumed that's why you rushed us away from the ground when everyone else who was there seemed keen to celebrate. But I'm glad. As a matter of fact I'm rather keen to score myself. And after a match like that, I'm up for anything. Even extra time.'

'How would that work?'

'I was thinking that you might want me to stay for breakfast.'

'You really do like my coffee, don't you?'

'Sure. Although I imagine the coffee's only the second best thing I can put in my mouth while I'm there.'

I laughed again; she really was a hell of a girl.

'How old are you, anyway?' she asked.

'Forty. That's not so old.'

'It is for me. I've never slept with anyone over thirty. However, I do have a question, first.'

'Fire away.'

'I was under the impression that you already had a girl-friend, Mr Manson.'

'I did have one. Sonja gave me the sack on Sunday night.'

'Did she give you a reason?'

'She said that when she finishes work on a Friday she wants a proper weekend.'

'Yes, I know what that's like myself. I mean, I've had boyfriends who didn't like the unsocial hours I keep.'

'She wanted someone to go shopping with after a week at work. Stuff like that. A Saturday and a Sunday with newspapers, which doesn't include football.'

'And now you want to bring on a substitute. Is that it?' Louise shrugged. 'Well, why not? I'm cool with that, I suppose. Just as long as this isn't a friends with benefits sort of thing.'

'You're hardly a friend,' I said. 'Besides, I already told you – I don't much like the police.'

She smiled a big smile. 'How's that working out?'

'For some reason I seem to be getting over it.'

'I'm delighted to hear it.'

'And now I feel I really do owe you an apology.'

'For what?'

'Because I may have misled you. I wasn't actually taking you to my flat in Chelsea at all.'

'Oh. I see.'

She sounded disappointed, which left me feeling pleased. I snatched up her hand and kissed it.

'No, you don't. Not yet. I'd like you to spend the night with me very much indeed, Louise. I can think of nothing nicer. And I sincerely hope you will. At the earliest opportunity. But the fact is, I've been investigating Zarco's death myself; and right now I'm taking you to meet the person who I think killed him. So that you can get the collar and the credit.'

Louise took her hand away and put it to her mouth. 'You're joking.'

'No, I'm not. I've thought about almost nothing else but Zarco's death since Saturday night and now I'm confident that I've found the culprit.'

She turned in the passenger seat and let out a gasp. 'Oh my God, you are serious, aren't you? Jesus, Scott. Are you sure you know what the fuck you're doing?'

I told her a small part of what I now knew; she didn't need to know about the bung and about the inside share deal; there was only part of the story she needed to know about now.

'That does sound fairly convincing,' she admitted. 'And now I'm sort of embarrassed.'

'Why?'

'You've done my job, that's why. How would you feel if I did your job?'

'Anyone can do my job. Being a football manager is just selecting the best eggs.'

'I don't understand.'

'Doesn't matter. Look, don't you want the collar? This will be a big feather in your cap, I'd have thought.'

'Well, yes. Of course. But—'

'I'd much prefer you to get the credit than the bitch you're working for. I'd rather not tell anyone than tell her.'

'Jane Byrne? Yes, she is a bit of a bitch, isn't she? But you know I really should inform her of what's happening. Otherwise she's going to have my guts.'

'Why don't you wait until we've confirmed my suspicions? You can tell her you didn't know what I was going to do until I'd done it. That you had no choice but to wait for me to make my play.'

She thought for a moment and then nodded. 'All right. You're the manager.'

'Besides, you owe me this after the way you handled telling me that it was Drenno's friend Mackie who raped Mrs Fehmiu.'

'That's true.' She winced. 'Shit.'

'What?'

'It looks like I'm working tonight after all.'

I grinned at her. 'Did you have other plans?'

'I did when I got into this car. Now they'll have to wait. It's disappointing.'

'That's how I feel about it, too.'

'Good. I'm glad.'

'But I have to see this all the way through. For Zarco's sake.'

'Don't worry. I understand all that. But you're going to have to make this up to me.'

'How?'

'I've been thinking about that.' She nodded. 'Yes. When this is all over, I'd like you to take me to your lovely flat and do whatever you like to me for twenty-four hours. I would say forty-eight hours, but I know you've got an away game against Everton on Saturday.'

'That's quite an invitation, Louise.'

'I'm glad you think so.'

'Anything?'

'Anything at all.'

'Christ,' I said. 'No one has ever said anything like that to me.'

I turned down a side street and stopped the car.

'What are you doing?' she asked. 'Why have you stopped?'

'I'm a bit old-fashioned,' I said. 'I can't think about doing anything until I've kissed you.'

'Neither can I,' she said and then let herself be kissed; she even allowed my hand up her skirt.

'Put your finger inside me,' she said after a while. 'Every time you touch your face I want you to know exactly what you missed having tonight.'

CHAPTER 49

I pulled up outside Toyah Zarco's big white house in Warwick Square and turned off the ignition. The car's engine pinged like a pinball machine and the trees in the communal gardens shifted uneasily in the breeze. The policeman still on duty outside Toyah's front door eyed us patiently. In his thick coat and protective vest his body looked too big for his legs; he might have made a good goalkeeper. The press had cleared off; somewhere else there was probably another widow in tears they wanted to film and harass with questions. A man walking his dog hauled the animal away from the tyres of my car before it could piss on them. The light from the full moon shone on a neat row of Boris bikes in front of the nearby church; it looked like a series of fitness machines in some weird, twenty-four-hour gym, as if the stained-glass window of Saint whatever-it-was might at any moment turn into a giant television set. But the church reminded me that I was going to Drenno's funeral on Friday and that I was dreading it.

'Do Drenno's family know what Mackie did?' I asked. 'And that Drenno helped cover it up?'

'No,' said Louise. 'Not yet.'

'Let's leave it that way, can we?' I asked. 'At least until after the funeral.'

She nodded.

'Thanks.'

'This feels weird,' she said.

'Why?'

'It feels weird that it's you who's going to try to get a confession and not me.'

'Relax. I already got a result tonight. I'm in the groove. Besides, I'm hoping I won't have to say very much at all. That copper standing behind us should give us all the leverage I'm looking for.'

'Just be careful. That's all I want to say. This isn't a game.'

'What, and you think football is? After a match like the one you just saw you should know better than that.'

'Maybe you're right. What do you want me to do?'

'You've got your ID?'

'Of course.'

'Just flash that copper your badge and put him under your command. I'm hoping you'll do the same when you come to my flat. I like dominant women.'

We got out of the car and walked up to the policeman. Frankly, he looked pleased to see us, like a dog that has been left for too long outside a supermarket.

'Evening, sir,' he said. 'Good result tonight. Mr Zarco would have been very proud.'

I'd forgotten the copper was a City fan. That was handy. 'Thanks, Constable,' I said. 'I think he would.'

'5–3. I just hope my Sky Plus was working.'

'Let me know if it doesn't and I'll send you a DVD.' I gave him my card; I was softening in my old age. I figured it was the effect that Louise Considine was having on me; she was living proof that not all coppers were bastards. Maybe there was still hope for me to become a decent, law-abiding member of society.

She showed him her ID. 'I'm Detective Inspector Considine,' she said, 'from Brent CID. What's your name?'

'Constable Harrison, ma'am. From Belgravia Police Station.'

'You wouldn't have thought they needed one in Belgravia,' I said.

'I need your help, Constable,' said Louise. 'Will you come with us, please?'

'Yes, ma'am,' he said, smartly. 'What's it all about?'

'I'd rather not say yet,' she replied.

I led the way down the street, to the opposite side of the square.

The mural of a house in front of number twelve rippled in the January wind as if a seismic event was about to take place in the quiet streets of Pimlico; and in a sense it was, at least for the inhabitants of the house next door. All of the lights were switched on. After the twenty grand I'd handed over they probably figured they didn't need to worry about the electricity bill. As I mounted the front steps I glanced through a chink in the curtains drawn in front of the big window and saw Mrs Van de Merwe and her daughter reading while, sitting on the sofa, was a man watching television. But it wasn't Mr Van de Merwe; it was another, younger, fitter man and he was watching the edited highlights of the match from Silvertown Dock on ITV. It's odd how different a match you've seen live looks when you see it on television.

I rang the ancient bell and we waited a while before the bolts were drawn and the door opened to reveal Mr Van de Merwe. As he caught sight of the policeman standing behind me his Adam's apple shifted under his collar like a small, sleepless man.

'Oh,' he said, in a tone of quiet resignation. 'You'd better come in.'

The three of us trooped into the hall. Constable Harrison closed the door behind us and immediately made the house seem small. There were several suitcases on the floor, as if the Van de Merwes were going somewhere – South Africa, probably – but if I was right, a passport to Pimlico was all they were going to need for the present.

We went into the sitting room, where the sight of Constable Harrison brought everyone to their feet. Mariella folded her arms and turned away immediately, while her mother stifled a short wail with the back of her hand, and sat down again; she took out a dainty embroidered handkerchief and started to cry.

'This is Detective Inspector Considine, from Brent CID.,' I explained. 'And Constable Harrison. Detective Inspector Considine has been investigating the death of João Zarco at Silvertown Dock on Saturday.'

I didn't call it murder; I figured we had more chance of securing a full confession now if I tried to play down the gravity of what had happened.

'Which I think you know about, Mr Cruikshank.' I was speaking to the man who had been watching the television. He was about thirty-five years old, six feet tall, stocky, with light brown hair and green eyes, and he was wearing jeans and a thick blue woollen pullover that looked as if it had been knitted by his mother-in-law.

'It is Mr Cruikshank, isn't it?'

'Yes,' he said dully. He sighed and then closed his eyes for several seconds. 'It was an accident,' he added. 'Please believe me when I say that I didn't mean it to happen.'

'I think you'd better tell us exactly what did happen,' I said.

385

He nodded. 'Yes, I think I had,' he said.

'Do you mind if we sit down?' I asked.

'No, please, go ahead.'

He pointed at the vacant sofa on which Louise, Constable Harrison and I now arranged ourselves, and then turned off the television.

'Would you like something to drink?' he asked.

We shook our heads.

'Do you mind if I do?' he said. 'I think I need one.'

'Go ahead,' I said.

He helped himself to a large whisky from a bottle of Laphroaig, emptied the glass and poured himself another.

'Dutch courage,' he said, sitting down in front of us.

'It's a pity you didn't have some of that on Saturday,' I said.

'Yes, isn't it? By the way, how did you—?'

'You were on Mr Zarco's guest list of complimentary tickets, Mr Cruikshank,' I said. 'On its own, of course, that wouldn't have been evidence that you killed him. But the piece of ceiling moulding you gave him when you met was still in his pocket when his body was recovered.'

I glanced up at the ceiling, and then from my coat pocket took out a photograph of the chunk of ceiling moulding photographed by someone at the East Ham Mortuary.

'It matches the piece missing from this ceiling. The piece that you gave him when you were complaining about his builders next door. It was them who caused the damage, wasn't it?'

Cruikshank nodded. 'You've no idea the distress this building work has caused my wife's parents,' he said. 'Day in, day out. They're old. They've a right to the quiet enjoyment of their retirement.'

Mr Van de Merwe went and sat beside his wife on another sofa, and together they gave every impression of two old people who were trying to enjoy their retirement, quietly.

'I can understand that,' I said.

'Can you?' said Mariella, bitterly. 'I doubt that very much. This whole sorry saga has driven us bloody mad, I don't mind telling you.'

'Please, Mariella,' said her husband. 'Let me handle this. By myself. The way I should have handled it before.'

'So, Zarco gave you tickets,' I said. 'For Saturday's match and tonight's match, too. As a sign of good faith, perhaps. A little token to help continue the dialogue you'd already had in the hope of resolving your dispute.'

'Something like that,' said Cruikshank.

'As if,' snorted Mariella. 'Trying to fob us off with some tickets, more like.'

'That's not fair,' said her husband.

'Isn't it?'

'Please, Mariella. You're not helping. I liked him, Mr Manson. Well, most of the time, I did. He knew I was a City fan – have been for a while, actually – and, well, as you say, he thought that if we kept on talking we could sort out our differences. Hence the tickets. And perhaps we would have sorted something out, I don't know. Anyway, he told me to come along to one of the hospitality suites on Saturday, before the match, so that we could talk. Number 123. It belonged to some Qatari businessmen who weren't using it, he said. He also said that he was going to make an improved offer – for my parents-in-law to get away from the square until the building work was complete. So I went along. And we talked. We were in the kitchen, having a coffee. At first it was all very amicable. Then I mentioned that this house was going to need redecorating after his builders had finished. As you can see for yourselves, the place is covered with dust, because of the vibrations from the constant drilling. I gave him a piece of ceiling moulding that had fallen on my mother-in-law's head last week as evidence of that. I mentioned a price – an estimate we'd had from a painter and decorator. Twenty thousand pounds. This was on top of the ten he'd already offered us. That was when he accused me of trying to cheat him. He said that he thought we were talking about a sum to enable Marius and Ingrid – that's Mr and Mrs Van de Merwe – to get away on holiday. And now here I was asking for three times as much to include redecorating as well.

'Anyway, I'm afraid things got a bit heated. He swore at me in Portuguese. Well, I can speak a bit of Portuguese – I used to work in Brazil. He called me a *cadela*. And a *cona*. I won't translate that but I think you can imagine the sort of thing it means. Anyway I got angry and so I shoved him. Just shoved him, that's all. I didn't even hit him. He fell against the window and the whole window just pivoted open behind him for no good reason that I could see, and he went straight out, head first. I mean the window just bloody opened as he fell against it. I tried to grab him – I think I got hold of his tie – and maybe he grabbed me, I'm not sure. As his tie slipped out of my hand I lost my footing and then he was gone.

'I heard an almighty clang as he hit something on his way down, but when I looked out of the window I couldn't even see him. But it had to be near enough sixty or seventy feet to the ground. And it was immediately obvious that he couldn't have survived a fall like that. At the time that's what I told myself, anyway. Because I panicked and ran away. I got home and thought about it and I was on the point of calling the police to explain what had happened when it said on the news that he'd been murdered. And then I lost my nerve to say anything. But for that I think I would have handed myself in. Really I would. I'm not a murderer, Mr Manson. As I said before, I liked the man. I'm so, so sorry.'

'I understand that, Mr Cruikshank.'

'What's going to happen to me?' he asked Louise.

'That's not for me to say, sir,' she said.

'But what I find a little harder to understand,' I said, 'is why you broke into Silvertown Dock and dug a grave for Zarco in the centre of my pitch and left his photograph in it. That really wasn't very nice at all; and hardly an accident. You want me to tell you how I know about that as well? Unfortunately you left some tools behind, Mr Cruikshank. One of them had the initials LCC on the handle. For a while I thought that meant London County Council, the forerunner of the Greater London Council. But that all seems a long time ago, even for a spade. Then I saw the name of Mr Zarco's builders on the mural next door: the Lambton Construction Company. I was actually speaking to one of the workmen the other day and he told me they'd had some tools stolen. That was you as well, wasn't it?'

Cruikshank nodded. 'It was meant to be a sort of poetic justice, if you like,' he said. 'I just wanted him to know what it was like to suffer the kind of disruption we'd suffered here: to have someone turn your whole life upside down. Frankly I was amazed when you managed to repair the pitch as quickly as you did.'

'Was that your idea?' I asked. 'Digging a hole in the pitch? Or was it your wife's?'

I looked at the woman with folded arms who was now

staring so angrily at the curtains her eyes might have set them on fire. For the first time since meeting her I had a clear sense of the hatred that lay within this woman.

'How about it, Mrs Cruikshank? You helped him, didn't you? I can't think of any other reason your husband would have bothered nicking two spades from next door. For all I know you may have meant the blame to fall on some of those poor Romanian guys.'

She said nothing.

'I mean, don't get me wrong, Mr Cruikshank,' I said. 'I think it's very noble of you to try to shoulder the whole blame for all of this. You have my sympathy; I did something rather similar myself once. But it doesn't do any good, you know. Speaking for myself now I think it just made things worse.'

'I'm afraid I don't know what you're talking about, Mr Manson,' he said.

'Yes you do. You see, according to the turnstile computers at Silvertown Dock, the two tickets Zarco gave you for Saturday's match were both used. Somehow I don't see Mr Van de Merwe walking all the way to the match. Not with that leg of his. Or somehow Mrs Van de Merwe. Which means you were there, too, weren't you, Mariella? You were in suite 123 with Zarco and your husband. To help with the negotiations.'

At this point in the proceedings her silence was eloquent enough.

'Yes, I thought so. You know, I'll bet it was you who had the presence of mind to close the window and put the three coffee cups in the dishwasher. A woman's touch? Or was it just to make sure it looked like neither of you were ever there?'

The woman turned from the curtains and looked at me with distaste. She wasn't bad-looking at all, I thought; fit-looking, too. As if she went to the gym a lot. The thin cotton singlet she was wearing afforded me a good impression of what her upper body looked like: strong shoulders, powerful biceps and well-defined nipples. But it wasn't until the moment when she leaned across the sofa to pick up her cardigan and put it on that I guessed what must have really happened in suite 123 at Silvertown Dock.

'You think you're pretty smart, don't you?' she sneered. 'But you can't actually prove any of this.'

'Can't I?'

'You're flying by the seat of your pants, Mr Manson.'

'In fact,' I continued, 'I don't think it was you who pushed João Zarco out of the window at all, Mr Cruikshank.'

'As if we haven't endured enough already with all this fucking building work next door. What gives you the right to come here and ruin our lives like this?'

'I think it was your wife who pushed Zarco out of the window, Mr Cruikshank. Wasn't it, Mrs Cruikshank? Probably when Zarco called you a bitch.'

'John? Don't say another word. Not without a lawyer present. Do you hear?'

'That's what *cadela* means, isn't it? You see, I speak a little bit of Portuguese, too. And while I can easily see why he would have called you a cunt, Mr Cruikshank, I really can't see that he would have called you a bitch as well. Not when Mariella here was in the room.'

'Get out.'

'I haven't known you very long but it's my impression that it's not you who's got the temper; it's your wife here. It was you who pushed Zarco out of the window, wasn't it,

Mrs Cruikshank? It was your husband who grabbed him, I reckon, and tried to prevent his fall; but it was you who pushed him in the first place.'

'Get out of this house, do you hear me?'

'Of course, I can't prove any of that. Then again, I don't have to. I'll leave it to the forensics team to match that little scratch on your neck to the tiny amount of skin and blood they found underneath Zarco's fingernails. But you know something? I wouldn't be at all surprised if you really meant to push him out of the window, Mariella. This, after all, is a much better explanation of why you didn't try to help him after he fell. Because you hoped he was dead and that all of this dreadful inconvenience you've experienced because of a little bit of building work would just go away forever. Isn't that it?'

I've never heard a banshee and to be honest I wouldn't know what one looked like, but I rather imagine that Mariella Cruikshank gave a pretty good imitation of one as, screaming something in Afrikaans, she threw herself across the room with hands that were reaching for my neck.

It was fortunate for me that I wasn't standing in front of an open window.

CHAPTER 50

'What *will* happen to them?' I asked Louise.

My rapprochement with the police force was progressing very nicely indeed. It was the following evening and Louise had not long come from the police station in Greenwich; we were lying in bed in my flat at Manresa Road and I had just spent an energetic hour making love to her. I had enormous regard for the police and the job they did, especially when the police looked like Louise Considine, who was now naked in my bed with her thighs still wrapped around my waist and my cock shrinking slowly inside her.

'To the Cruikshanks?'

'Yes.'

'That all depends on the Crown Prosecution Service,' she said. 'But speaking as someone who studied law, I think manslaughter might be a lot easier to prove than murder. The scratch on Mariella Cruikshank's neck and the fibres from her sweater we found underneath Zarco's nails are certainly enough to prove that she pushed him, but not enough to prove she actually meant him to fall to his death. So far she's been a hard nut to crack. Doesn't give away much under questioning. I'm not sure she even knows herself if she meant to kill him or not. Frankly she's an even bigger bitch than Jane Byrne.'

'I can almost believe that. Did Jane give you any grief for what happened?'

'Some.'

'Sorry.'

'Don't be. It's nothing I can't handle.'

I nodded glumly. 'It's the old couple I feel really sorry for. I mean, if the Cruikshanks go to prison it will be pretty tough on Mr and Mrs Van de Merwe.'

Louise shrugged as if she didn't care one way or the other.

'Don't you think so?' I asked.

'I wouldn't feel too sorry for them either,' she said. 'They left for South Africa this morning.'

'You're joking.'

'First class. It seems they think their daughter and her husband can cope with all of what's going to happen quite well on their own. The prospect of twenty-five-degree temperatures in January was just too tempting, I suppose.'

'Except that it's now February.'

'Is it?'

'Believe me, I should know. Today is February the first. The January window just closed and Viktor can't buy any more players. Which is probably just as well since I'm not so sure about the one we just bought.'

Louise groaned a little as I slipped out of her; then she rolled on top of me and kissed me on the forehead.

'Anyway,' she continued, 'it will be months before the Cruikshanks come to trial, by which time the Van de Merwes will be back home. The building work and the football season will probably be over.'

'I guess.'

'And you'll have been confirmed as the new City manager.'

'That already happened,' I told her. 'I spoke to Viktor Sokolnikov after I left you last night and told him about the Cruikshanks. I'm signing a new contract on Friday. So he was as good as his word.'

'Did you tell him that for a while you were convinced it was him who had killed Zarco?'

'Er, no. But I did ask him to explain exactly what he meant by that remark he made, to the effect that all objections to the arrival of Bekim Develi had been thrown out of the window. He said that he was referring to the Home Office. Apparently they had originally objected to him because Develi had planned to open a nightclub as well, which is against the rules for what they call a Tier 2 sports migrant. Anyway, he's given up that idea and he's just going to play football. Which is how it should be. Football comes first. Football always comes first. Without football, life would be meaningless.'

'That's not exactly Aristotle, Scott.'

'Actually, you're wrong there. It is.'

Louise frowned.

'Aristotle really did think that football contained the meaning of life.'

'Bollocks.'

'No, he did. Listen. This is what he says in his book, *Nicomachean Ethics*.' I paused for a moment to remember the quote exactly.

'This is going to be a joke, isn't it?'

'On the contrary. I think he knew exactly what he was saying, and as usual he was right. Aristotle says this: "Every skill and every inquiry, and similarly, every action and choice of action, is thought to have some good as its object. This is why the good has rightly been defined as the object of all endeavour. Everything is done with a goal, and that goal is good."' I shrugged. 'Well, don't you see? A goal changes everything.'

Now that's a philosophical truth.

PHILIP KERR

A SCOTT MANSON THRILLER

PREVIEW

HAND
OF GOD

July 2014

Never mind the Special One; according to the sports press I'm the Lucky One.

After the death of João Zarco (unlucky) I was lucky to land the job as the caretaker manager of London City, and even luckier to keep it at the end of the 2013–14 season. City were judged lucky to have finished fourth in the BPL; we were also judged to have been lucky to reach the Capital One Cup Final and the FA Cup Semi-final, both of which we lost.

Personally, I thought we were unlucky not to win something, but *The Times* thought different:

'Considering all that has happened at Silvertown Dock in the last six months – a charismatic manager murdered, a talented goalkeeper's career cut tragically short, an ongoing HMRC investigation into the so-called 4F scandal (free fuel for footballers) – City were surely very fortunate to achieve as much as they did. Much of the club's good fortune can be attributed to the hard work and tenacity of their manager, Scott Manson, whose fulsome and eloquent eulogy for his predecessor quickly went viral on the internet and prompted the *Spectator* magazine to compare him to none other than Mark Antony. If José Mourinho is the Special One, then Scott Manson is certainly the Clever One; he may also be the Lucky One.'

I've never thought of myself as being lucky, least of all when I was doing eighteen months in Wandsworth nick for a crime I didn't commit.

And I had only one superstition when I was a professional

footballer: I used to kick the ball as hard as I could whenever I took a penalty.

As a general rule I don't know if today's generation of players are any more credulous than my lot were, but if their tweets and Facebook posts from the World Cup in Brazil are anything to go by, the lads who are playing the game today are as devoted to the idea of luck as a witch doctors' convention in Las Vegas. Since few of them ever go to church, mosque or shul, perhaps it's not that surprising that they should have so many superstitions; indeed, superstition may be the only religion that these often ignorant souls can cope with. As a manager I've done my best to gently discourage superstitions in my players, but it's a battle you can't ever hope to win. Whether it's a meticulous and always inconvenient pre-match ritual, a propitious shirt number, a lucky beard, a pair of charmed socks, or a providential T-shirt with an image of the Duke of Edinburgh – I kid you not – superstitions in football are still as much a part of the modern game as in-play betting, compression shorts and Kinesio tape.

While a lot of football is about belief, there's a limit; and some leaps of faith extend far beyond a simple knock on wood and enter the realms of the deluded and the plain crazy. Sometimes it seems to me that the only really grounded people in football are the poor bastards watching it; unfortunately I think the poor bastards watching the game are starting to feel much the same way.

Take Iñárritu, our extravagantly gifted young midfielder, who's currently playing for Mexico in Group A: according to what he's been tweeting to his one hundred thousand followers it's God who tells him how to score goals; but when all else fails he buys some fucking marigolds and a few sugar lumps, and lights a candle in front of a little skeleton doll

3

wearing a woman's green dress. Oh yes, I can see how that might work.

Then there's Ayrton Taylor, who's currently with the England squad in Belo Horizonte; apparently the real reason he broke a metatarsal bone in the match against Uruguay was that he forgot to pack his lucky silver bulldog and didn't pray to Saint Luigi Scrosoppi – the patron saint of footballers – with his Nike Hypervenoms in his hands like he normally does. Really, it had very little to do with the dirty bastard who blatantly stamped on Taylor's foot.

Bekim Develi, our Russian midfielder, also in Brazil, says on Facebook that he has a lucky pen that travels with him everywhere; interviewed by Jim White for the *Daily Telegraph*, he also talked about his recently born baby boy, Peter, and confessed that he had forbidden his girlfriend, Alex, to show Peter to any strangers for forty days because they were 'waiting for the infant's soul to arrive' and were anxious for him not to take on another's soul or energy during that crucial time.

If all of this wasn't quite ludicrous enough, one of City's Africans, the Ghanaian John Ayensu, told a Brazilian radio reporter that he could only play well if he wore a piece of lucky leopard fur in his underpants, an unwise admission that drew a flurry of complaints from the conservation-minded WWF and animal rights activists.

In the same interview Ayensu announced his intention to leave City in the summer, which was unwelcome news to me back home in London. As was what happened to our German striker, Christoph Bündchen, who was Instagrammed in a gay sauna and bar in the Brazilian city of Fortaleza. Christoph is still officially in the closet and said he'd gone to the Dragon Health Club by mistake, but Twitter says different, of course. With the newspapers – especially the fucking *Guardian*

4

– desperate for at least one player to come out as gay while he's still playing professional football (wisely, I think, Thomas Hitzlsperger waited until his career was over), the pressure on poor Christoph already looks unbearable.

Meanwhile, one of London City's two Spanish players in Brazil, Juan Luis Dominguin, just emailed me a photograph of Xavier Pepe, our number one centre back, having dinner at a restaurant in Rio with some of the sheikhs who own Manchester City, following Spain's game against Chile. Given the fact that these people are richer than God – and certainly richer than our own proprietor, Viktor Sokolnikov – this is also cause for some concern. With so much money in the game today players' heads are easily turned; with the right number on a contract, there's not one of them that can't be made to look like Linda Blair in *The Exorcist*.

Like I said, I'm not a superstitious man, but when, back in January, I saw those pictures in the papers of a lightning bolt striking the hand of the famous statue of Christ the Redeemer that stands over Rio de Janeiro, I ought to have known we were in for a few disasters in Brazil. Soon after that lightning bolt, of course, there were riots in the streets of São Paulo as demonstrations against the country's spending on the World Cup got violently out of hand; cars were set on fire, shops vandalised, bank windows smashed and several people shot. I can't say I blame the Brazilians. Spending fourteen billion dollars hosting the World Cup (as estimated by Bloomberg) when there's no basic sanitation in Rio de Janeiro is just unbelievable. But like my predecessor, João Zarco, I was never a fan of the World Cup, and not just because of the bribery and corruption and the secret politics and Sepp bloody Blatter – not to mention the hand of God in '86. I can't help feeling that the little man who was named the player of the tournament in Argentina's World Cup was a cheat, and the fact that he was even nominated says everything about FIFA's showcase tournament.

As far as I can see about the only reason to *like* the World Cup is because the United States is so bad at football and because it's about the one time when you'll ever see Ghana or Portugal beat the crap out of the USA at *something*. Otherwise the plain fact of the matter is that I hate everything about the World Cup.

I hate it because the actual football played is nearly always shit, because the referees are always crap and the songs are even worse, because of the fucking mascots (Fuleco the Armadillo, the official mascot of the 2014 FIFA World Cup, is a portmanteau of the words *futebol* and *ecologia* – fuck me!), because of all the expert divers from Argentina and Paraguay and, yes, you, Brazil, because of all the England 'we can do it this time' hype, and because of all the cunts who know nothing about football who suddenly have a drivelling opinion about the game that you have to listen to. I especially hate the way politicians climb on the team coach and start waving a scarf for England when they're talking their usual bullshit.

But mainly, like most Premier League managers, I hate the World Cup because of the sheer bloody inconvenience of it all.

Almost as soon as the domestic season was over on 17 May, and after less than a fortnight's holiday, those of our players who had been picked for international duties joined their respective squads in Brazil. With the first World Cup match played on 12 June, FIFA's money-spinning competition gives no time at all for players to recover from the stresses and strains of a full Premier League season and affords plenty of opportunities for them to pick up some serious injuries.

Ayrton Taylor looked as though he was out of the game for two months and seemed certain to miss City's first match of the new season against Everton on 16 August; worse than that, he was likely to miss City's Group B play-offs against Olympiacos in Athens the following week. Which – with our other striker now the subject of intense speculation as to the nature of his sexuality – is just what we don't need.

It's at times like these I wish I had a few more Scots and Swedes in the team as, of course, neither Scotland nor Sweden qualified for the World Cup in 2014.

And I can't decide what's worse: worrying about the 'light adductor strain' that stopped Bekim Develi playing for Russia in their Group H match against South Korea; or worrying that the Russian manager Fabio Capello was playing him against Belgium before he'd given Develi a chance to properly recover. You see what I mean? You worry when they don't play and you worry when they do.

If all that wasn't bad enough I have a proprietor with pockets as deep as Johannesburg's TauTona goldmine who's currently in Rio looking to 'strengthen our squad' and buy someone we really don't need who's not nearly as good as all the TalkBollocks pundits and callers insist he is. Every night Viktor Sokolnikov Skypes me and asks my opinion of some Bosnian cunt I've never heard of, or the latest African *wünderkind* who the BBC has identified as the new Pelé, so it must be true.

The *wünderkind* is Prometheus Adenuga and he plays for Nigeria. I just watched a *MOTD* montage of the lad's goals and skills with Robbie Williams belting out 'Let Me Entertain You' in the background, which only goes to prove what I've always suspected: the BBC just doesn't get football. Football isn't about entertainment. You want some entertainment, go and see Liza Minnelli fall off a fucking stage, but football is something else. Look, if you're trying your damnedest to win a game you can't really give a fuck if the crowd are being entertained while you do it; football is too serious for that. It's only interesting if it matters. Just watch an England friendly and tell me I'm wrong. And now I come to think of it, this is why American sports are no good; because they've been sugared by the US television networks to make them more appealing to viewers. This is bullshit. Sport is only entertaining when it matters; and, honestly, it only matters when it's all that fucking matters.

Not that there's anything very honest about the way football is played in Nigeria. Prometheus is just eighteen years old, but given that country's reputation for age-cheating, he might be several years older. Last year, and the year before that, he was a member of the Nigerian side that won the FIFA U-17 World Cup. Nigeria has won the competition four times in a row, but only by fielding many players who are much older than seventeen. According to a large number of bloggers on some of Nigeria's most popular websites, Prometheus is actually twenty-three years old. The age disparities of some African players in the Premier League are even older. According to these same sources, Aaron Abimbole, who now plays for Newcastle United, is seven years older than the age of twenty-eight that appears on his passport; while Ken Okri, who played for us until he was sold to Leeds at the end of June, might even be in his forties. All of which certainly explains why some of these African players don't have any longevity. Or stamina. And why they get sold so often. No one wants to be holding those particular parcels when the fucking music stops.

8

That's just one reason why I won't ever become the England manager; the FA doesn't want anyone – even someone like me, who's half black – who's going to say that African football is run by a bunch of lying, cheating bastards.

But it isn't the true age of Prometheus, who plays for AS Monaco, which is currently occupying the journalists grubbing around the floor for stories in Brazil – it's the pet hyena he was keeping in his apartment back home in Monte Carlo. According to the *Daily Mail* it bit through the bathroom plumbing, flooding the whole building and causing tens of thousands of euros' worth of damage. A pet hyena makes Mario Balotelli's camouflaged Bentley Continental and Thierry Henry's forty-foot-high fish tank look sensible by comparison.

Sometimes I think that there's plenty of room for another Andrew Wainstein to start a game called Fantasy Football Madness in which participants assemble an imaginary team of real-life footballers and score points based on how expensive those players' homes and cars are, and how often they get themselves into the tabloids, with extra points awarded for extravagant WAGs, crazy pets, lavish Cinderella-style weddings, stupid names for babies, wrongly spelt tattoos, daft hairstyles and off-menu shags.

I bought Fergie's book when it came out, of course, and smiled when I read his low opinion of David Beckham. Fergie says he kicked the famous boot in Beckham's direction when his number seven refused to remove a beanie hat he was wearing at the club's Carrington training ground because he didn't want to reveal his new hairstyle to the press until the day of the match. I must say I have a lot of sympathy with Fergie's point of view. Players should always try to remember that everything depends on the fans that help to pay their wages; they need to bear in mind what life is like for the people on the terrace a bit more often than they do. I've already banned City players from arriving at our Hangman's Wood training ground in helicopters, and I'm doing my best to do the same with cars that cost more than the price of an average house. At the time of writing, this is £242,000. That may not sound like much of a restriction until you consider the top-of-the-range Lamborghini Veneno costs a staggering £2.4 million. That's almost chump change for players making fifteen million quid a year. I got the idea of a price ceiling for players' cars the last time I looked in our car park and saw two Aston Martin One-77s and a Pagani Zonda Roadster, which cost more than a million quid each.

Don't get me wrong, football is a business and players are in that business to make money and to enjoy their wealth. I've no problem with paying players three hundred grand a week. Most of them work damn hard for it and besides, the top money doesn't last that long and it's only a few who ever make it. I'm just sorry I didn't get paid that kind of loot when I was a player myself. But because a football club is a business, it behoves the people in that business to be mindful of public relations. After all, look what's happened to bankers, who are today almost universally derided as greedy pariahs. Perception is all and I've no wish to see supporters storming the fucking barricades in protest against the disparity in wealth that exists between them and professional footballers. To this end I've invited a speaker from the London Centre for Ethical Business Cultures to come and talk to our players about what he calls 'the wisdom of inconspicuous consumption'. Which is just another way of saying don't buy a Lamborghini Veneno. I do all this because protecting the lads in my team from unwanted publicity is an increasingly important way of ensuring you get the best

10

out of them on the football pitch, which is all I really want. I love my players like they were my own family. Really, I do. This is certainly how I talk to them, although a lot of the time I just listen. That's what most of them need: someone who will comprehend what they're trying to say, which, I'll admit, isn't always easy. Of course, changing how players handle their wealth and fame won't be easy either. I think that encouraging any young man to act more responsibly is probably as difficult as eradicating player superstitions. But something needs to change, and soon, otherwise the game is in danger of losing touch with ordinary folk, if it hasn't done so already.

You've heard of total football; well, perhaps this is total management. A lot of the time you have to stop talking to players about football and talk to them about other things instead; and sometimes it all comes down to persuading average men how to behave like gifted ones. In this job I have learned to be a psychologist, a life counsellor, a comedian, a shoulder to cry on, a priest, a friend, a father and, sometimes, a detective.

Follow@theScottManson on Twitter

A letter from the publisher

We hope you enjoyed this book. We are an independent publisher dedicated to discovering brilliant books, new authors and great storytelling. Please join us at www.headofzeus.com and become part of our community of book-lovers.

We will keep you up to date with our latest books, author blogs, special previews, tempting offers, chances to win signed editions and much more.

If you have any questions, feedback or just want to say hi, please drop us a line on hello@headofzeus.com

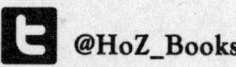 @HoZ_Books

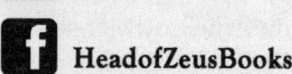 HeadofZeusBooks

www.headofzeus.com

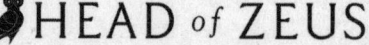 HEAD *of* ZEUS

The story starts here